A HOLLYWOOD CONSCIENCE

A Hollywood Conscience

Ned Cresswell

Millivres Books International
Brighton

First Published by Millivres Books (Publishers)
33 Bristol Gardens, Brighton BN2 5JR, East Sussex, England

Copyright (C) Ned Cresswell
The moral rights of the author have been asserted

A CIP catalogue record for this book is available from the British Library

ISBN 1 873741 19 7

Typeset by Hailsham Typesetting Services, 4-5 Wentworth House, George Street, Hailsham, East Sussex BN27 1AD

Printed and bound by Biddles Ltd., Walnut Tree House, Woodbridge Park, Guildford, Surrey GU1 1DA

Distributed in the United Kingdom and Western Europe by Turnaround Distribution Co-Op Ltd., 27 Horsell Road, London N5 1XL

Distributed in the United States of America by InBook, 140 Commerce Street, East Haven, Connecticut 06512, USA

Distributed in Australia by Stilone Pty Ltd, PO Box 155, Broadway, NSW 2007, Australia.

Grateful thanks and love to Nigel Quiney and Sarah Standing. They know.

Thanks also to Matilda Quiney, John Jesse, Gary Carver, Ben Goold, Martin Lovelock, Sally Tagholm, Ven Hart, Rae Coates, Andre Delanchy.

"There is no great, dark man..."
QUENTIN CRISP

"Alone you are, alone you will always be..."
FEDERICO GARCIA LORCA

"Attention home pornographers. Fancy earning a few bob? Well, if you own a camcorder and are prepared to indulge in a spot of carnality in front of it, read on. Yes, folks, naturalism has wended its way into the pornography industry. Today's connoisseurs are tired of perfectly developed actors/actresses with imperfectly developed scripts. The call now is for a bit of realistic rough, the girl or grand-dad next door look. In America, amateur movies have captured a chunk of the $325,000,000 porn market - one adult video shop says a third of its tapes are home-made. Mickey Blank of San Diego's Home Grown Video says that since appearing on TV he has been beseiged with calls and cassettes from would-be porn stars. `The only thing that these tapes have which the others don't is sincerity,' he adds sincerely."

THE GUARDIAN Thursday March 7th 1991

"... Friendship, it's such a rare commodity. People come together for a purpose - it lasts as long as some interest binds them, or motives. But just friendship by itself, people coming together without any purpose, that is an achievement. I value it. That's one thing I feel for, you know? We are so close at some point in our lives, and then we lose everything. It's just like a spray, a spray of water - it'll just disappear. That is a thing which puzzles me."

R K NARAYAN

Prologue

It was Saturday when Andy's letter to Brik arrived. It was clearly stamped with a Hollywood postmark.

By this time, several weeks after the thunder of the applause in the Peter MacMurdo Memorial Hall had faded to an echo, most people in Scottland, Ohio, had forgotten Andy Horowitz. I don't think anyone, other than Mrs MacSween, my landlady, had known Andy was a talent agent. I'd made him promise to be low key and, for once, he kept his promise. And in return, he made a promise. Andy left Scottland for the coast with his promise ringing in my ears, the promise that he would personally ensure that Brik Peters became a star.

Foolishly, I set little store by it. Andy's most-used words were: "I promise . . ." and the words had many times rung hollow. Having had intimate experience of his broken promises over the years, I fancied that I'd learned to discount the less fulfillable ones and making my best student a star was one of his promises I could easily discount.

Andy's promises were like a water torture, each drop splashing like a tear on the pillow at night, so wet and real and hopeful, full of the promise of remorse and yet by morning so dry as to never have been. Although it had been almost three years since I'd terminated my life with him in LA, every so often, there it'd be again. That drip . . . drip . . . drip, wearing away at my resolve, seeping up from the depths beneath the prairie itself to torture me. The 'phone would ring and there he'd be again. Usually calling from the airport - ". . . just for the weekend, Jeremy", ". . . I really *needed* to see you, Jeremy", "*Have* to *talk*, y'know". And how Andy Horowitz could talk. It was his stock in trade. And by the law of averages, the more he talked, the more he promised.

So why did I keep seeing him? Good question. There's only one answer – I always imagined that the, hitherto, only love of my life might have changed.

The last time Andy showed up in my life, it had been for Scottland High's graduation play. At the end of his visit, during which we had had no rows or arguments, I fondly thought I had been vindicated. I thought the leopard had changed its spots. He seemed genuinely impressed with what teacher, as he now referred to me, had pulled off. I had worked hard. Perhaps too hard. *Rosencrantz and Guildenstern* was a difficult play for a graduating high school class. But it had been the right year, perhaps the only year it would ever happen, the only year there'd be the necessary cast to enable the drama teacher to be so ambitious. With my missionary zeal, I took advantage of this one chance for the burgers of Scottland to ever be tempted to taste the promise of real theater. Scottland, Ohio, was not exactly a fecund nursery of talent and usually not the kind of place where *Rosencrantz and Guildenstern* could be quickened for long enough to be given even the chance to die. The likelihood of another Berwick Peters turning up, let alone another Ryder McKigh was remote. Both boys had taken their bows and, visibly ten feet taller, had then taken their places the following day in the graduation line.

What am I talking about? There was no likelihood at all! School was finally out forever and for good. Scottland would see no more proms, no more graduations or school plays. Scottland High had become too small and was to be integrated with the school in neighbouring, and expanding, Doddsville.

So, 'bye 'bye Brik and 'bye 'bye Ry. It was the last year for a lot of people. And 'bye 'bye Andy, who had also promised to be in touch soon.

Since his departure, I'd heard nothing.

I watched the little town settle into summer vacation, a ruffled old barnyard mother hen arranging its feathered skirts onto a dusty nest as other, less broody birds, pecked lazily at the well-trodden dirt, clucking and cawing in the dull heat. There was some scurrying about in the cool hours of early morning but by mid-day, whether in town on Main Street or in the outlying areas, little moved around dreams . . . But, 'fess up, girl, it was only ever the faintest chance.

For Mitzi, the slingshot elastic had always been too weak, the pull of the horizon too strong. The elastic would snap and the horizon would die. The bus had never come back. I wish I could have been around to tell her it never would. Mitzi tucked the paper under her arm and turned to walk back to the farm. She didn't notice the letter for Brik. I wish I'd been with her. I'd have found it. I would have *smelled* it; I'd have known it was there even it was wrapped like a corn dolly smelling of wheatfields and dust, invisible like a harvest mouse's nest. But I wasn't there and Mitzi Peters wasn't looking for "that nice Mr Horowitz's letter". It remained in temporary concealment, slipped between the advertisements and the sports section.

ONE

The Peters and the McKighs, through the male line of course, had been neighbours through four generations. Though their farms merely adjoined, their lives had fearlessly over-lapped, at church, in the supermarket, at picnics, fairs and hayrides. Three generations of children had been through school together, through four wars, through countless dances and romances together, ceremonies of adolescence celebrated on sunday school picnics, at proms and drive-ins. Somehow, there'd always been a male Peters or McKigh who survived the tribulations of growing up to wed, not one of their own thus far, but another, local girl to prime the pump that fuelled the motor that ran the tractor, the harvester, the pick-up and the car that took the next generation to the drive-in.

Except, in this story, Berwick Peters and his sister Janna, begotten by Don and Mitzi, together with Ryder McKigh, only child born to Gordon and Dory, were already the next generation. And, the last.

As though to add insult to the terminally injured class of 1992, the last driveable drive-in movie theater, in Doddsville, had closed too, though they'd redeveloped the site as a cineplex. But it wasn't the same. Cineplexes are almost too serious for teenage movie-going. Better to rent movies while the parents aren't home. Rent and neck.

That's just what the kids did. That's what they were reduced to. So was I, in Scotland, Ohio. I rented too, though not always the best films and certainly not for the best reasons. I had no one to neck with.

Without asking for it and ignorant what the merge had meant, the kids' had joined with mine to become the video generation. And something died.

I felt that all Scotland was dying that summer as the children of that fourth generation prepared to leave. The farms were no longer prosperous. The corporatizers had seen to that and they waited yet, perching on the fenceposts at the perimeters of the plains acreages like crows, waiting. Always hungry. No longer would the sons work with the fathers, no longer would the daughters of Scottlanders marry into their own and soon the crows would have to wait no longer.

Donald Peters was to be the last small farmer, though he didn't yet know it. Gordon McKigh had already gone, brought, so it was said not only by credit and stress and Dory to a premature plot in the graveyard but by a war that everyone had tried so hard and so quickly to forget.

Vietnam.

The crows had seemed to sense the newly dug mound of tired earth over Gordon McKigh and, each cawing like poor relations at the reading of the will, had flown in with such a swirling and flapping and beating of wings that would have sent even van Gogh screaming from the canvas. Dory's land became Ryder's mess of pottage. She'd sold up and was moving in the fall into town. To a duplex. New. No land. No risk. No future either, but no risk.

Brik and Janna were going their separate ways. Brik, facing a somewhat stodgy future insisted on by Don was honour and duty bound to major in engineering at Illinois State - Janna was headed further east, to Smith College where she'd gained a scholarship in literature. Ryder, without the benefit of the prescence of such a wise father and armed with the little money that Dory had settled on him after the sale, was going to New York, to try his luck. Needless to say, Dory didn't approve. There was too much risk, although, in her private moments, she would have had to concede that there were few alternatives.

But there were still two months of vacation before the parting of the ways was due. The class of '92 and their acolytes had decided to make it their last summer, together.

The day that Brik's letter came found them all at the swimming hole. The Forbes boys, still a year of youth to go, and the MacMurdo girls, rich girls who weren't bound by time, who had all the time they needed in the world that their grand-daddy's money had bought.

And so it was at the swimming hole that they spent the

heat of that Saturday, three girls and four boys and they were waiting for me. Brik had asked Janna to invite me to their picnic. She said it was the only way they could say thankyou to me for what I'd done for them.

I was late. I fear they spent two hours waiting lunch for me. So when, finally, I arrived, it was three girls, four boys and, God couldn't you have made the age gap less, me. Jeremy Page, their thirty-two year old teacher.

But on that day, as on all days since he'd given up faking romantic interest in Betsy Strong, Brik was left the odd man out until I arrived. Brik was finding himself odd man out more and more frequently.

If I finish threading up the loom with the last strands of weft, my half-finished tapestry trams like this, something like an impressionist "Dejeuner sur l'Herbe", something after Manet. Ryder and Janna can be made out in the bottom left hand corner setting their cans in the cool of the stream's shallows, the Forbes boys and the MacMurdo girls, Brian and Lucy and Jim and Madeleine respectively, were already necking as, so I presume, they had fallen to as soon as the boys' pickup and the girls' Ford had parked. Anyway, they can be seen sort of in the middle of the picture, each couple off-centre.

But where in this tableau vivant does that leave my odd man out?

If you picture the stream flowing away directly from my viewpoint, Brik had walked a little way down the bank, a long stem of grass poking from his mouth. He was standing, looking back at the others and wondering if I'd show that day like I'd said, for he had something to ask me, something he'd had on his mind for an achingly long time.

So there is Brik. He stands in the middle of the canvas, the central motif around which the others depict merely complementary decoration, mere putti prettying the slopes of his Olympus. Why is Brik in the middle, do I hear you wondering? What, do you conjecture, was it that was so significant about Brik Peters that placing him anywhere else but the centre of the picture would have been impossible to accept? Well, forgive me. I'm only human and to say any different would be damnable. The gods would never forgive me. It was simply that Brik Peters was and is, as Andy Horowitz my erstwhile ex had pronounced on seeing him in Rosencrantz's tights, "drop dead gorgeous". Six feet two, long, thick, straight dark hair burnished somehow as though with henna, the physique of a natural athlete improved on by a tasteful development of the muscles through weights, tanned normally dark skin, judiciously and silkily hirsute in all the right places. Drop dead gorgeous. And, may I add, I choose in my telling to report Andy's indubitably venal comment as referring to Brik's mind and personality as well as his body although Brik's mind was the last thing that would ever have interested Andy.

Me? Oh, don't pay any attention to me, yet. I'm writing this and I choose to remain outside the picture. Mine is merely the divinely guided hand whose fingers wield the bodkin that stitches in the colours in the conveniently numbered and previously colour-coded patches. That's the irony. In a lifetime hellbent on my own designs, why is it that I felt that day that my best work was not mine at all but the incomplete creation of someone else which I had merely been bequeathed.

If the tableau seems a little static at the moment, it's all to the good. And, remember, I honestly had nothing to do with putting Brik in the centre. If he thought it had been my fault, he would never have forgiven me.

I can't but confess I'm pleased he does end up in the centre. I confess to being prejudiced, shamelessly prejudiced though it bugs the hell out of me because I should know better; I shouldn't hold out such hopes. Daily, and I'm talking at least a thousand days to date since I first met Brik in the classroom, I've denied my hopes. Until that day at the swimming hole, it had been ethically impossible for me to do otherwise.

Though I can still dream, can't I? I can still dream?

Of course I dream . . . though I'm now only too well aware what the reality currently is, so long after that day at the swimming hole; I'm bugged because I know I have to wait, to wait for him to come to me. Maybe he will, maybe not. If I make any move, I know it will be the wrong one and I will have blown the chance of heaven in this life. I just know I'd fluff it.

But I have to permit myself to keep the hope and the only way I can is to deny myself. I know only too well that it'll probably never happen. But to live without the hope? That would be no life. Not any life I could live.

I wouldn't pretend to know what it is that makes us love and I would disbelieve anyone who said they did. Not `fall in love', mind you. I'm talking the grown-up stuff here; the stuff that a man feels for a man or a woman and vice versa and all combinations thereof. I'm talking the stuff that lives on when all passion is spent or denied or is non-existent; the stuff that never judges or criticises through selfish frustration; the stuff that never atrophies with habit or palls and wilts with intrusive familiarity. Just that quiet stuff, that gentle, secure yet awesome bond that makes you want to laugh the same minute the tears are flooding down your face, that strange combined feeling of wonder at the beauty of a thing knowing all the while that beauty is so fragile and delicate that even attempting the memory of it would be to destroy it. That stuff that I can only call holy.

Have you ever looked at a rose, full and deepest red in its zenith of perfection and while taking such pleasure in the appreciation have derived equal fulfillment in the certain, unalterable knowledge that soon it will wither, dry up, rot and vanish? If you haven't, never mind, although you'll never know true beauty. Maybe I'm deluding myself, perhaps I am arrogant as Andy says but that's what I felt that day looking at Brik in the middle of the canvas I wish I'd been the one to design at the swimming hole. I really believe I knew true beauty.

I did show that Saturday. And I was late for a good reason. I was writing UCLA accepting the job. I wrote with some regret and not a little unease.

Three years ago, wild horses couldn't have dragged me back to LA. Little did I know that by Sunday, wild horses couldn't have kept me away.

TWO

"Hey, Brik. Brik! He's here!"

Janna called out to her brother as my Jeep crunched over the rough track ending at the willows of the swimming hole. The neckers, the face suckers as those less mature might have called them, barely broke for air as I switched off the motor. Brik was nowhere to be seen although at Janna's call, a dark quiff of hair emerged from the horizon of wheat beyond the oasis of willows and scrub. He didn't get up at first. He was, as the Americans with their apologetic euphemisms say, "au naturel".

"Hi, Mr Page," said Ryder, still creaming his shoulders with sun screen. "What kept you?"

"The future," I replied.

"That's pretty cosmic for a hot Saturday, Mr Page," Janna observed. "Hey! Brik! Come on over here!"

I threw down my rug and towel next to theirs, sat down and started taking off my boots.

"Not my future, Janna. And please, guys, we're all grown ups now. It's Jeremy, please."

I didn't see Brik running from the field and crossing the fallen tree over the stream behind me. I didn't hear him until he was standing behind me, a little out of breath.

"Hey, Mr Page! You made it!"

I turned round. The sun had found a gap in the foliage and I had to shade my eyes.

"Sure, I made it. Good to see you Brik."

"Okay . . . Lunch everyone." This was Janna. Born to bring order to chaos. She began opening baskets, bags and coolers.

"Oh, great," said one of the Forbes boys. "I'm starved."

"Can't see why," Ryder observed wryly, "you've had your mouth full of Lucy for two hours."

"Ry!" warned Lucy. "Really. We have company."

"Please, guys. How many times must I tell you. I'm not your teacher any more. We're all in this thing together now."

Brik settled onto the rug beside me.

"What thing?"

"I think Mr . . . Sorry . . . Jeremy! I think Jeremy meant this life thing?" Janna looked up in the midst of arranging chicken legs on a paper platter, one eyebrow cocked.

"Something like that," I replied.

"Life's a crock," said Brian Forbes, assertive and dismissive at once.

"Life's a gas, man, whaddya mean?" urged Ryder. "Life's just great."

"You haven't gotta go for another year to a new school where you don't know anyone," Jim Forbes parried. "You're not the one who's being left behind by all your friends with nothing but assholes for miles."

"Thank *you*, you big creep!" pouted Lucy MacMurdo. "Just watch who you're calling asshole round here!"

"Ah, cherie, cherie!" Jim mocked and took another suck at Lucy's face. "Pas du tout. Pas du tout. Vous n'etes pas un asshole."

"Une, jerk. Une asshole. That's right isn't it Mr . . ., I mean, Jeremy? I *am* female."

"Unmistakably," I replied.

"New York, New York!" hammed Ryder. "Oh for New York."

"Don't rub it in," said Brik. "And don't talk too soon. New York might not be that great."

"At least it won't be here," Ryder replied. "At least there might be a little *real* action, away from all you country bozos."

"Airhead!"

"Oh, yeah!"

"Who's calling who the bozo, bozo?" were some of the cat-called replies.

"Now come on, Ry." Janna's picnic buffet was ready. "Let's have a little discipline here. Brik, would you pass round the chicken? There's potato salad here and corn bread and pickles in that snaptop box. Take a plate everyone and help yourselves. Ry, will you get the beers?"

We ate lunch, drank the beers and afterwards, Brik and

Ryder played frisbee. The neckers went off for a walk and I lay propped up on one arm as Janna cleared away.

"So," she concluded in that matter of fact tone, just like a mother. It was a portent to the teasing out of hitherto withheld information. "I'm glad you could come, Jeremy. We wanted so much you should spend the day with us."

"Thanks, I'm pleased you asked me." A dying frisbee landed right in my lap. Brik ran over, panting.

"Heeey! Hope it didn't spoil your marital prospects, Jeremy!" He winked at me.

I handed him back his frisbee, but it was a discus. I was the mentor and Brik, the ephebe. I was the Grecian elder and he the bronzed athlete, the laurelled youth diving into a marble pool as I lounged, exquisite with the superiority of my years, content to merely watch.

"No, they're intact," I smiled and he ran off.

"They'll miss each other," Janna observed as the two boys continued their game. "I sometimes ask myself whether we'll ever be together again." She laughed, as though banishing the doubt although her question hung in the air. "It's not as though our lives are mapped out for us like our parents'. Not any more."

"Yes," I said. "It is kinda sad. I wish I could tell you it would be otherwise, Janna. All I know is that even the best times have to end sometime."

"Ummm." Her reply was at best non-commital as her eyes narrowed, looking, as I was, at the boys at play. "I guess nothing stays the same forever."

"Are you sure it's just putting away childhood things," I wondered aloud to her, "or is it something more specific?"

"If being sentimental is childish, then I guess you're right."

"I was meaning *someone* specific, actually." She glanced at me, scanning my question before replying.

"How did you know?" she smiled.

"Put it down to great old age," I replied.

"Nonsense, Jeremy," she kidded. "Tell me. I thought I was real expert at hiding things."

"You are," I assured her. "But there are some things that

aren't meant to be, however obvious and logical they seem."

"I've known Ryder a long time. Perhaps I know him too well."

"But you've never even come close?"

She laughed again. Not a little girl giggle, not coyly. She had always struck me as being more serious than the boys, always just slightly serious as though hers was an old head despite the youthful shoulders.

"Oh, we've been close alright. *Very* close in fact."

"So what went wrong?" I enquired.

"My dad," she replied flatly. "He caught us one night out in the yard. In Brik's truck." Her eyes filled with tears. "I couldn't understand . . . I'd never seen him as angry as he was . . . Like he was crazy, shouting and screaming and dragging me out of my seat and hauling me across the yard. Yet . . . he didn't say a word to Ry. Just left him there."

"Very unsentimental," I said. "I am sorry, Janna."

"And he wouldn't even discuss it," she went on. "He made me promise never to tell mom, never to speak about it or mention it again. Just made me promise that I would never let Ry near me again." She paused and wiped the back of her hand across her eyes. "Perhaps it *was* sentiment," she sniffed and grabbed a napkin and dabbed at her nose.

"Did Brik know?"

Janna shook her head.

"Don't think so. At least, if he did, he never let on."

"You were pretty serious about him, right?"

"Guess I was," she murmured. "And apart from that, I would have loved for the two families to be together. Daddy was so close to Ry's dad and mom with Dory, too. Like you said," she added, "it seemed so logical."

"And what about Ryder? Did he know how you felt?"

"I don't know. He's very hard to get close to. He always tries to make out he's so independent."

"Tries?"

"Right. A lot of it has to be an act."

"So how did he react? After the scene in your yard?"

"That was real strange too. We none of us saw him much, except at school. He was so quiet and . . . kinda sulky. But then Gordon was dying . . . Wasn't two weeks after and he was dead."

"He must have been pretty cut up," I observed. "He couldn't act that, surely?"

"That's what I would have thought," she replied. "But he made like it was nothing. The funeral was no sooner over than he was round calling for Brik and they went out to the movies."

"People cope with things in different ways," I said, trying to soothe. "Perhaps that was Ryder's way."

"There's a lot more to Ryder than meets the eye," she said, her composure quickly returning. "He'd kill me if he knew I was telling you this but . . . I'm not sure how well he'll cope without Brik. He needs . . . oh . . .," she faltered. "What do I know?" She began to tidy away more of the picnic.

"Go on," I said. "If you want to talk, that is."

"I was going to say he needs the competition. I don't think he can hack it by himself."

"I wouldn't say their friendship has ever struck me as competitive."

"Brik's isn't," she replied, smiling again in that Giaconda way, hinting at a mystery which she couldn't fully communicate. "I'm amazed you haven't noticed it. Especially with the play an' all."

"I thought they were both tremendous," I countered.

"Oh they were. Don't get me wrong. They were almost too good. But did you never know why?"

"Talent?" I offered. "I know talent when I see it. That's one thing I do recognise and it makes me so sad that neither might take it any further."

"Oh they will. At least Ryder will. Somehow."

"Tell me."

"Ryder needs it. He needs to be more than good. He has to be the best."

"And Brik doesn't?"

Janna shook her head.

"He's quite happy just being Brik. Whatever he does. Ry has hunger. He has a drive. And he needs Brik to fuel it. Maybe he'll find someone else, though it'd be pretty tough for anyone new to accept Ry was using them like some yardstick. Maybe it'll be a girl." She winced. "And I so wanted it to be me." I felt for her hand and squeezed it. "I don't think Brik even notices it. He has no real ambition. And I don't mean that badly. He's just a very comfortable guy . . . With most things."

"Most things? What are the things he's not comfortable with?"

"Now there I do plead the fifth amendment," she laughed. "And anyway, you probably know more about that side of Brik than I do."

"I do?"

She was silent for a moment, almost embarassed, her hands for something to do scrabbled with the fasteners of the cooler. I waited. Hers was an old head and I could sense the questions she wanted to ask. She was so close, too close, and like a true wimp, I wasn't about to volunteer what she wanted to hear. I could feel my heart beating faster. If she did ask, it would be the first time I'd come out to anyone. I heard that familiar voice ignored, at peril of soul and salary, by so many thousands of teachers: `It's gonna happen . . . One day . . . Someone's gonna find out'.

"He thinks a helluva lot of you, Jeremy," she concluded, without looking at me. "But I trust you. You won't let him down." She stood up quickly, cutting off any reply I could have made. "Ryder!" she called. "You wanna swim now?"

Turning to answer her, Ryder missed the frisbee which sailed into the creek.

"That's my best goddam frisbee, McKigh!" Brik called. "Go get it back, butterfingers."

"Race you, farmboy!" Ryder rejoined.

I noticed it then. Now Janna had initiated me, I noticed it. Ryder made no move after throwing out his challenge but waited for Brik to respond. Which he did. He whipped off his trainers and his jeans almost in one motion and ran naked towards the bank of the creek. Ryder anticipated almost to the second. They jumped off the bank and hit the water together, splashing towards the frisbee that was already filled with water and sinking sideways in the murky shallows. Janna too went naked into the water.

Why did I feel uncomfortable? I don't know.

Embarrassment? Whatever. I got up and stood on the bank, watching. I'd never thought myself a prude and had never suspected that any prurience I might have suffered was a significant character defect. But I was mesmerised, as though watching a screen. It was unreal, as though I was a camera and the boys in the creek were actors in a Lawrentian script.

Though it was Ryder who got to the frisbee first, it was an easy task for Brik to wrest the prize away. Brik was that much taller, that much stronger and again I saw what Janna had inferred. Ryder really struggled to get the frisbee, Brik was almost gentle in his resistance, naturally making allowances for Ryder's impotence and obviously prepared to ultimately allow Ryder to win the round. Janna defused the moment, perhaps as she had always done as she swam up behind the thrashing pair and heaved herself up onto Ryder's shoulders and ducked him. Turning his attention to Janna, Ryder forsook what he could have so easily won as though he knew possession of the frisbee would constitute only a phyrric victory. In her turn, Janna was duly ducked, not once but at least three or four times and life regained its equilibrium. Brik laughed and tossed his thick mane of hair backwards sending a stream of shining droplets high into the air. Clutching his frisbee, he turned from them and waded out of the creek and walked dripping up the bank towards me.

I was standing, barefoot, at the top of the slippery slope. He saw me and stopped. God, was I staring? I suppose I must have been. His wide smile slipped as he stood so still and very gradually he repositioned the frisbee to cover that part of him I had made him aware of. My throat was dry and my sense of guilt at realising I was peeking made me feel I was the naked one. I was the one who should have

17

been embarassed.

"It's okay," I heard myself saying. "We all have one."

"It's just . . . kids stuff. Y'know?" he mumbled.

I stood aside from the top of the well-worn path and walked back to the rugs. I sat down and on purpose didn't look at Brik as he hurried over to where his jeans and trainers lay just where he'd thrown them. I was no more composed when he arrived, dressed and lay down in the sun opposite me.

"I haven't been skinny dipping for years," I remarked. "Can't remember the last time."

"Hope we didn't shock you."

"No," I laughed. "No. Shocked I wasn't."

"Nuther one of Ry's dares. Least, that's how it started. Been doing it every summer since."

"I thought so," I replied. I dared to smile. "You have no tan line." I could see even under his tan, Brik had reddened. It wasn't the blush of embarassment. More the blush of being discovered. "Now tell me you're just a nature boy."

"Guess you're right."

The yips and yells from the swimming hole seeped over the bank. The face suckers had reappeared and had joined in the battle. Brik jumped up and ran to the bank and hurled the frisbee into the water.

"Go get it, suckers!" Whoops and sounds of frantic splashing ensued. Brik turned and beckoned.

"Who? Me?"

"Yeah. Wanna show you something." He started to walk away before waiting for me to get up and follow him. "We have to cross the log down there. Careful of your balance."

"Catch me if I fall?"

"Sure. But you won't fall."

Brik was soon across the fallen willow and waited for me on the other side.

"So what's this all about?"

"Aw. You'll think it's dumb but it's kinda special to me."

"There's nothing out there but corn," I remarked as we headed through the scrub bushes towards the golden acres.

"It's wheat, not corn. Grows real tall this time of the year."

"You mean we're gonna walk through it? Isn't that a little anti-social, trampling it down?"

"They got enough. Anyway, I've made a path. Make one each summer. Start it early."

A few yards in from the edge of the wheat, the path through the stalks led to a circular wheat-free space, the undergrass and weeds being long since flattened and browned by the sun. Seen from above, it would have looked like a cutaway cross-section of a burrow, like a mole's or a prairie dog's.

"Here?" I asked.

"This is the end of the line," Brik grinned in reply. He sat down. "Join me?"

I smiled and shook my head. I felt awkward being alone with him. He stretched out on his stomach and kicked off his trainers. His body was darker than the colour of the corn, his eyes bluer than the sky, his teeth whiter than the clouds. I sat with my knees pulled up, hugging them.

Down there on the prairie floor, the wheat was taller than we were. We had effectively vanished.

"Only place where the wheat don't grow, the only place in O-Hi-O."

"I'm sure there must be others," I said.

"None that I'd feel comfortable in."

The sounds of laughter from the swimming hole had subsided. Apart from the call of some corncrakes and the buzz of insects, it was perfectly still, perfectly quiet.

"So this is where you do your sun-worshipping," I offered. "It's very . . . private."

"I love the sun," he murmured. "The feel of it. It's like liquid, running all over you, getting in every pore like it possesses you."

"Ryder has a tan line."

"Uh huh."

"It's very European of you. I didn't think Americans went in for the all over look."

"Then that's their problem. I don't have it."

"And don't mind me."

"Excuse me?" he said, turning towards me.

"I meant if you wanna . . . y'know? Commune or whatever you call it?"

Brik laughed.

"No way. I've had enough sun this summer. Get to this point in the year and you know it'll pretty well have faded away in a month. Anyway, they'll be harvesting in a week."

"True."

"Learned all my lines here, Jeremy. These stalks know every word, probably backwards."

"I hope they go to make a very cultivated loaf," I quipped. He didn't react. I glanced across and he had his eyes closed. His chest rose and fell as he breathed.

"What's it like, Jeremy?" Brik asked his question without opening his eyes.

"Excuse me?"

"Being . . ." He stopped and raised himself first onto one elbow and then stood up. I saw him looking around as though checking his secret was still safe. He squatted down again and began pulling blades of dried grass from the ground. "You've been around, Jeremy. I mean, you lived in LA, didn't you?"

"For my sins, yes."

Brik swept back the hank of hair which now fell unruly over his eyes and looked at me.

"What sins?" he said slowly.

Twice in one day. This must have been some kind of record. I felt myself retreating into teacherliness, although what protection that quirk of conceit afforded me, I had no idea.

"Come on, Brik," I murmured. "Shouldn't we be getting back?" I started to get up but he pulled me down. We faced each other kneeling in the dead grass.

"You said we were in this together," he said. It sounded like an accusation. I drew breath and sank back onto my haunches. I think I even folded my arms. Magisterial enough?

"Brik . . ." I began but faltered, tripped by the first hurdle of intimacy. Honesty. "Look," I started again, "is this some sort of `If I show you mine will you show me your's' because if it is, it isn't a game I . . ."

"You've seen mine," he interrupted instantly. He grinned, a rogue's grin. No, a wrestler's grin, sensing in that split second a weakening, knowing that the upper hand was there, for the grasping.

"Well I'm not showing you mine, Brik."

"I don't want to see your's. I'm not Ryder . . . Is it true that all actors are faggots?" he added, the words spurting out like blood from a mortal wound.

"That's a really dumb question, Brik. Whoever gave you that idea?"

"Ryder."

"And who gave him that idea?"

"I dunno. Guys. Girls too."

"You mean jocks?"

"Perhaps."

"But you're a jock too, Brik. You're on all the teams. What do you say? You've even been an actor."

His eyes let go of me for a moment and he visibly relaxed.

"Shit," he breathed. "This is *not* going well, Berwick."

"I'm not so sure," I replied. My advantage.

"Look, man . . . Jeremy. What have you got to lose? You'll be outta here in two weeks. Gone. Scotland, adieu. Hasta la vista."

"So will you."

"I know. So I know I've got two weeks."

"Is that some sort of a problem?"

Suddenly he jumped up and stretching his arms out wide into the sky he closed his eyes and roared. He trumpeted a yell of such depth and power to the sun I thought he'd harm himself. The veins on his neck bulged, his face grew redder than the poppies in the wheat. His stomach jerked into a washboard of moulded corrugations. Exhausted, he slowly pulled his arms down and sank back to his knees.

"The problem, *Mister* Page, is that I have two weeks, two

weeks, Mister Page, *sir*," he panted, "to have you teach me something you never could in class. I need you to tell me all you can about . . . being gay!"

THREE

It was Don Peters who found the letter.

That afternoon he'd been in the yard changing the oil in the tractor. He slid from under the sump of the motor, the very picture of James Dean at the end of *Giant*, face spattered with oil and dirt.

Curled up on one of the couches in her designer living room, Mitzi was watching a game show from Hollywood. Jeopardy or something. The television was usually elegantly disguised in its cabinet, crowned by the voluptuous concoction of silk flowers. Mitzi maintained her living room in pristine perfection. If she could have had it placed it under a glass dome, it would not have been less of a showpiece, always available for the admiration of honoured and important company.

But she rarely had company.

Don managed to open the screen door with his wrists."I need a rag, Mitz!" he yelled to her through the back door. He had oil on his boots and he knew Mitzi would erupt if he trod it in.

"I'm watching television. Whaddya wan' a rag for?"

"Just get me the goddam rag for Christ' sake!"

"I got better use for rags than waste 'em on that tractor. Take the advertisements from the paper!"

"Then where's the goddam . . ."

The paper was on the chair inside the swing door. Don ripped off the string binder, smudging the paper with oily thumb and finger prints. As he pulled the ads section the letter fell out. Don bent to pick it, assuming it was junk mail, another insert telling you how to get rich quick. As he was about to discard it, he turned it over and instead saw it was for Brik.

"Did ya see the letter for Brik, Mitzi?" he called, competing with a whoop of joy from the Jeopardy studio audience.

"Whaddya say?"

"Aw, save your breath," he muttered to himself and

threw the letter back on the chair and returned to the sump. The swing door flapped shut.

Mitzi came through from the living room.

"It's the only time I get to myself in the whole day and . . ." There was no husband in the kitchen and so she stopped herself. She went to the door and he was across the yard, back under the tractor. The newspaper, untidied, lay where it had fallen and she bent to pick it up, straightening it out and refolding it neatly. About to put it back on the chair it was then she saw the letter.

"I thought he said something about a letter," she murmured aloud. She picked it up. Who'd Brik get a letter from? Unlike a husband, Mitzi, being a wife, went straight for the postmark, like a bat to a jugular. Puzzled, her mind went to work. Who the heck'd Brik met from Hollywood who'd send a typed letter? A friend on vacation would've sent a postcard or if it was a letter on hotel stationary, it would have been hand written and there was no hotel name on the envelope. She held it up to the light but could see nothing. Her instinct was to open it. Her own mother would've opened it. How was it they did it in the movies? With steam? But how would she glue it down again? If she did open it, she could say she did it by mistake, like she thought the letter was for her, or Don. And perhaps she had a right to open it, more a responsibility. She was his mother, that gave her some rights, surely?

The thrall of Jeopardy paled and Mitzi went through to the sitting room and switched the show off. She set the letter in the middle of her magazine table and sat on the edge of the couch, just looking at it. Who *was* it from Hollywood that could possibly be writing to her Brik?

It was six before the kids got back that afternoon.

Janna arrived first. She'd already separated the trash from the picnic. Cans and foil into one sack. Paper was a problem. It sure needed to get recycled but what was a sensitive conscience to do with eight used sets of napkins and platters? Janna was very green. She'd been green for three weeks now. Seriously green.

"Still savin' the world?" her father called from the tractor. "Waste as much gas takin' that trash to the recyclin' as you'll save by leavin' it be."

"So you keep telling me," she called goodnaturedly. "Hope you saved that engine oil like I told you! World might be needing that too before long."

Don strolled over to his favourite child, wiping his hands on the last piece of the ads section of the paper.

"Got a kiss for your old dad?"

She grinned and picked up the cooler.

"Nope."

"So," he joked, "just like I always predicted. Shows what education can do when a sassy young madam turns her back on her poor working daddy."

"Listen, you poor working man, you . . . If I could find a piece of your face that wasn't covered in oil, I'd kiss it with pleasure." He tried to put his arm round her and she yelled and skipped away and ahead, laughing. "Daddy! You're disgusting!"

She let him catch her in the end then they strolled together across the yard.

"Where's Brik, honey?"

"He'll be along. He dropped Ryder off. Dory's probably feeding them milk and cookies."

"Little old for milk and cookies aren't they?"

"Not to Dory, dad. Where's mom? She's usually on the porch these summer evenings."

"Aaah," he said wisely.

They stopped, just outside the back steps.

"What is it with aah?"

"Your mom's got herself into quite a state this afternoon, *as* you will see."

"She hasn't . . ."

"Oh, no. Not one martini has slipped past Miss Mitzi's lips."

"Then what, daddy?" Janna was worried.

"Letter came," he replied. "For Brik."

"So? Probably from college."

Don shook his head and indicated that they go inside.

"Last I heard your brother was going to Illinois State not Hollywood High. But then no one tells me anything round here anymore."

Mitzi was still sitting on the couch. She had exchanged the letter as the focus of her attention for the recently framed graduation photograph of Brik, mortared and gowned, smiling with those perfect tombstone teeth full into the camera like he could just climb straight out of the picture. She was holding it in her hand.

Janna came in behind her. Not even the television, not even the plastic draped table lights had been switched on. It was as if Mitzi was floating in a bubble, way, way off.

"Mom?" It was a moment before Mitzi reacted. Janna went round and sat down next to her, taking up her mothers hands. "Mom? What is it?"

The whole family were used to their mother by now. She only fell off the wagon occasionally these days but when she fell, she fell. Though it was only ever for one day and only ever martinis. Brik said she thought martinis were glamourous and that's why she did it. The family had always acknowledged mom's occasional slips but instead of confronting them, their condition had been disguised in good humour and turned into part of their family folklore. `Has mom been misbehaving?' Tonight, however, was patently not an occasion when Miss Mitzi had been misbehaving.

"Oh . . . It's you. Hi, sweetie." Mitzi put down Brik's photograph and leant her cheek to her daughter. "I'm fine, really. Just . . . Well, I been thinking, that's all."

"About what, mom?"

Mitzi sighed and looked around her designer living room. She got up from the couch and as she did her mood changed; her whole presence changed as though she were plucking herself back from a void and replacing herself like a child might replace a toy soldier into the gap in the ranks.

"Nothing that someone who isn't a mother would ever understand," she replied briskly. "My, that cannot be the time! Ten-after and I haven't even thought about dinner."

Janna was left on the couch, mystified as to her mother's

swift mood change. Mitzi hurried out to the kitchen. Don was already at the table, a cold beer in one hand. Janna followed in.

"Something about a letter, mom?"

Mitzi was pulling ingredients from the refrigerator, bending and peering deep into its recesses for what she wanted.

"Yeah. Brik has a letter." She sounded flat, quite unconcerned, as though the letter was the last thing on her mind. Don winked at Janna and gestured. Slow down.

Brik's pick-up skidded to a halt outside by the barn. Mitzi parted the multi-coloured blind at her kitchen window and watched him briefly as he ran across the yard with the rugs and the wet towels.

"Y'see, Janna," Mitzi said, allowing the blinds to snap back to straight, "until you're a mother yourself, you'll never understand." Brik came through the door at that moment.

"Hi, mom. Hi, dad." He went straight through to the washing machine and dumped the towels on the floor beside it. He came back and started to fold up the tartan blankets before he realised that there *was* a silence and it clicked that everyone was looking at him. "So?" No answer. The hiatus was deafening. "It's not magic I'm doing here. I'm folding blankets. See . . . Top to bottom, then to the middle . . ."

"There's a letter for you, Brik," Janna said quietly.

"And there's potatoes to be peeled, salad to be washed and the table set!" Mitzi barked, sharply. "Just like everyday . . . Someone has to do it . . . So, just for once, it's *not* gonna be me!"

Now it was the others who looked strangely at Mitzi. She'd snapped, like a twig underfoot. With no warning, she burst into tears and ran from the kitchen.

"Was it something I said?" Brik asked aloud.

Don sighed and clapped his son on the back.

"I'll go after her. If I don't, I don't know what misbehaving Miss Mitzi'll be up to." Don turned at the kitchen door. "Wish me luck. And Brik, just read the goddam letter and put your mom out of her misery!"

"Well go on!" Janna urged. "Like the man said, read it." She picked the envelope and the newspaper up from the chair at the door and handed them to Brik.

They sat together at the kitchen table as he opened it.

"Beats me," he pronouced, slitting the potato knife along the fold. He removed the single folded sheet.

"So?" chivvied Janna.

"So . . . I can tell you who it's from. Andrew C Horowitz. Andy. 'Member him? Jeremy's friend from California."

"The guy who was at the play?"

"Uh huh . . ." Brik read the letter slowly. Then frowned. Janna could hardly contain herself.

"For God's sake Brik . . . What *is* it?"

"Lemme read this again," he smirked. "I gotta read this right . . ." And he read it again. Janna knew when he'd got to the end and snatched it from his hand.

"Hey, give me that!"

They jumped up from the table as Janna led the dance round the kitchen reading the letter aloud as she ducked and dipped and dived, trying to escape.

"`Dear Mr Peters . . .' No! Brik! I'll scream . . . `This confirms my telephone conversation with you that I have arranged a meeting with the producers of a new series planned to shoot in the fall for which they have specified previously unknown talent . . .' Let go, Brik! . . ."

Brik managed to snatch the letter away.

"It's mine!"

"Then read it to me."

". . . Where is it . . .? Okay . . . `unknown talent. I was so very impressed with your performance that I feel certain that I am presenting a very serious opportunity. It would be sad to see talent such as yours not utilised to its fullest potential. Please confirm soonest. I have already spoken to your drama coach who as you know is a very dear friend of mine. Look forward to seeing you in LA . . . Andy'. That's Andrew C Horowitz, Vice President, Buckman Miller."

"Brik!" Janna laughed. "I know you! You made all that up."

Brik sank down onto a chair as the realisation sank in. He handed Janna the letter.

"Read it yourself," he said, almost under his breath. As Janna read, his thoughts tumbled out. "What telephone conversation? And what about Jeremy? He didn't say a word this afternoon . . . And mom? And dad? What will they . . .? I won't tell 'em."

Janna was no less shocked than her brother.

"You gotta tell them, Brik." She paused. "And *what* are you gonna tell them? Are you gonna go or not?"

"Dad'd go crazy. You know what he thinks about acting."

"Mom'll go crazy," balanced Janna. "You know what *she* thinks about acting."

"It's civil war, sis."

"Yeah," breathed Janna.

Brik refolded the letter and put it back in its envelope.

"Better let 'em read it themselves," he said as he went out the door. "Mom first."

"Brik! Where are you going?"

"Gonna see Ry," he called over his shoulder. "Then our *Mister* Page. He got me into this."

Janna was left, holding a very big baby. As she went through to her parents' bedroom, she could not but help hearing Bette growling: `Fasten your seat belts . . .'

※ ※ ※ ※

The telephone was ringing as I parked the Jeep and ran into the apartment.

"Yeah. Jeremy Page . . ."

"Hi. It's me. Isn't it great? And where the fuck have you been for three days?"

"Andy! What are you talking about?"

"The interview. Didn't you get my letter? I mailed it three days ago with a copy of wonderboy's . . ."

"I haven't looked in my mail today, Andy. Can you start from the beginning?"

As he talked I pulled a cold beer from the refrigerator.

He got to the crux just as I snapped the tab.

"Son of a bitch!" I swore.

"What's that . . .? Hey, Jeremy . . . Jeremy, are you there?"

I've forgotten since with whom I was more angry, the beer can or the schmuck on the line. I do remember hurling the beer can across the kitchen.

"You have done *whaaaat*?"

I yelled like Brik had yelled that afternoon. Anger, frustration, surprise . . . If we'd been face to face, I swear I'd have strangled the idiot. It took that much rage to even dent Andrew C Horowitz's overblown self-confidence.

"But what have I done, baby? Didn't Andy do right? Don't tell me he's fucked up again?"

He was started to bleat, that poor little boy act that everyone except me seemed to fall for.

"Cancel it," I barked. "Just scrap it. Call Brik now and tell him it's all a big mistake. Tell him anything."

"And rob your homeboy of the only chance he's ever likely to have? Jeremy! Come on. Think how disappointed he'll be."

"You read it wrong, Andy. Brik's going to College. His plans are set. You have no idea what you're doing here."

"Have you? Have *you*, Jeremy, *Mister Teacher, Mister* know-it-fucking-all? Lemme tell you something . . . No, lemme tell you *two* things. First of all I did this for *you*, man. Just bear that in mind before you go mouthing off. And second, what right have *you* got to go pushing your shit onto a nineteen-year-old kid? Okay, so you have your prejudices. Just because it didn't work out for you in LA, just because you and your highminded tightass British superiority fucked you up in LA doesn't mean that someone else, someone *American* won't take their chance and *make* something of it!"

I couldn't answer him. Not in those terms. Andy gave very clever 'phone. It was useless playing his game. He was the master.

"Is that what you really think of me?"

"As it happens, yes."

There was silence for a moment.

"Heck, Jeremy, what do I know? Maybe it *was* that you weren't cut out for it. Maybe you are best with Rosenprick and Goldenpants or whoever . . . Hello. Hello! Don't hang up on me, Jeremy!"

"I haven't," I muttered. "I won't. I'm not *that* petulent."

"Listen, he'll be great. I just know it. He's a natural. You know it too. I saw it in your eyes."

"Saw what, Andy?"

"Can't say I blame you, man. He suuure is cute."

"It's not like that. And I won't talk about it. You wouldn't understand."

"Have you seen him?"

"Yes. Today. We went swimming."

"Alone?"

"Alone with half the kids in the county, okay?"

"Don't worry, coach. I'll take good care of him."

"You won't have to. I will though."

"Excuse me?"

"I said, `I will'. I'm coming back."

"Here? To LA!"

"Yes. I start in the fall. UCLA. Creative writing. I accepted today. Dean Stuart likes my work."

"Jeez! That one fucking novel's been real sweet to you, honey. Is it still optioned?"

"No."

"Oh. Would you like if I took it . . ."

"No, I would *not* like. Leave it alone, Andy."

"Just offering. Hey! This is great. I'll start getting your room ready. I've got just the greatest new videos. And the new pool boy is to die for."

"There's no need. I've accepted Dean Stuart's invitation to stay with him. He wants me to try and write again."

"Oh, Dorothy, Dorothy . . . Pleeeze take the towel off your typewriter."

"Fuck off."

"Don't you still love me just a little bit, then?"

"Certainly not."

"So you love me a lot."

"Goodbye, Andy."

31

"I still love you, Jeremy. I will see you, won't I? Moment you get in?"

"I won't rule it out. But I won't promise. Don't cancel your life."

"And you'll talk to Brik for me? I tell you, Jeremy, I've built this guy up to so much my ass isn't touching the line, it's spread right across it. I'm dead in this town if your kid fucks up."

"Don't tempt me."

"I mean it."

"Okay. I'll talk to Brik."

"Call me, hey?"

"'Bye Andy."

* * * *

Dory McKigh was a great anticipator. As long as she could avoid it, not for her would ever be the predicament of being caught out, at anything. Even on the day the chariot swung low for her, she would be first on line, bags packed and ready, everything neatly labelled and accounted for which had to be left behind. This obsessive nature kept her a busy woman, in mind and body, unable to believe that anyone else was as well-equipped as her to deal with life, determined that all identifiable disasters could be avoided. For a long time, for years before Gordon had finally died, Dory had had to do things by herself.

Sandwiched amongst her frustrations and her fretting was her son. She was convinced that without her, Ryder could easily prove to be a great disappointment. Her current frustration was that Ryder was equally determined to be without her. The only power she figured she had over Ryder now her husband had passed, was money. Ryder hadn't even been consulted on the sale of the farm. Or the house, which she could have kept. Gordon McKigh had left no will and so Ryder had been bequeathed only a dependence on what Dory perceived as sufficient to arm his future but sparing enough that he not be able to waste ammunition. Dory saw no virtue in excess. Too much temptation could easily commute Ryder's fragile virtue to limitless vice.

Yet Dory doted on her only son though her attentiveness was meted out only on what she perceived his needs to be. Ever thankful to have borne her son, Dory hadn't noticed that he was now a man.

Consequently, Ryder felt himself to be on an unfairly short leash and didn't have a lot to say to her. He had learned, lately, that to humour her was more convenient than to brook her `And now I'm just a poor widow' rebukes.

Anticipating the removal to her brand-new duplex, Dory had packed most of the McKigh house in crates, boxes and grocery bags. Not for Dory was the waste of money on purpose-packaging provided by the moving company. Against these overwhelming odds, Ryder had managed to keep most of his room intact although it wasn't entirely sacrosanct. Dory's invasive whims to talk at her son whenever she thought she would, often brought her through his bedroom door at the most inopportune moments. When alone in his room, Ryder had therefore taken to lying under his quilt.

When he heard the sound of Brik's pick-up and the familiar bip bip of the horn, he swore. He had been somewhat preoccupied. Scotland had been just about big enough to accommodate Ryder although it had been short a year, short on inspiration to feed his fantasy. Exploring had been fun and from the age of twelve, Ryder had been seriously exploring. He had fostered and ultimately acquired the reputation of a wolf, a young rebel with an eye for the ladies. For a while, it had suited him until he got bored. Ryder bored easily. Rather sooner than later, he'd tired of being adoring and being adored was what his women seemed to like. What they never understood when they were left high and dry was that their young Lothario was the one who needed the adoration. He'd tried changing tack, lounging broodily against the juke box in the diner, taking nonchalant belts at his beer in the club in Doddsville and waiting for them to come to him. For a time it had worked as he discovered that girls could be just as predatory as boys. However, none of them had seemed to be able to do for him what he could do more easily for himself. A girl's hands, Ryder had concluded, just weren't the same . . . and as yet he hadn't met the girl who had figured out that her mouth could be used for more than kissing.

And so, perhaps more so than the ingenuous Brik, Ryder had found himself, through necessity, expertly inventing the skeins of fantasy which temporarily satisfied him.

As he heard the front door slam, he teetered on the brink, a rather painful and dubious ecstasy, calculating whether he did or didn't have time, toying with whether to or whether not to. He decided against and managed to stop himself. He sat up and grabbed the battered copy of `New York on $10 a Day' Dory had found at a church bazaar for fifty cents. When Brik came in he pretended he was reading.

"Hi, man," said Brik.

"Hi."

"Are you sick or something?"

"No," said Ryder, sounding bored. "Just killing time."

"You were jerking off!"

"I was *not*!"

"Were."

"Go eat shit, farmboy!"

"Prove it, McKigh," yipped Brik as he yanked the quilt off of the prone Ryder to reveal the killer of time with his pants down. "There!"

Ryder tossed the book aside and leapt off the bed.

"Gimme my quilt, asshole. Just 'cos you do it all the time, doesn't mean the rest of us do!"

In the struggle for the sheet, they fell to the floor, grappling as they had done for many years in a series of mock brawls. There was never any contest except when Brik let Ryder off the hook.

"Take that back," Brik laughed.

"I will not. You do it so much you can't make with a chick."

"Who says I can't?"
"Betsy Strong says so."
They rolled over and over on the floor.
"What would she know?"
"She told me. Couldn't get it up for Betsy, hey, farmboy?"
"She did not say that."
"Wanna bet?"
Brik finally straddled his friend and kneeled across him, pinning his hands to the floor and grinning at him. Ryder grinned back though Brik, dear innocent Brik, couldn't see the malice behind the smile.
"Fuck Betsy," said Brik between clenched teeth.
Ryder continued to grin, feigning defeat but tensing himself to take his advantage.
"I have, Brik," Ryder said slowly. "It was *great*!"
Taken by surprise, Brik let slip his grip on Ryder's arms and after a short struggle, it was Ryder's turn to straddle his prone sparring partner.
"You're lying, Ry. I know when you're lying!"
"Wanna bet?" replied Ryder, teasing and toying with the victor turned victim.
"I can easily find out, Ry."
"Oh, sure . . . You're just gonna walk right up to Betsy and *ask* her?" Ryder simpered, still smirking.
Brik was no longer interested in wrestling. His mind tumbled with memories of his teenage, the growing up he thought he shared so inextricably with Ryder. He looked up at his best friend and sensed for the first time the unbridgeable rift which had sprung open between them. The time had long, long passed when Ryder would ever dare him again in the virility stakes, never again could they horse around, measuring sizes, peeing distances, shooting distances. It all meant something completely different now, something puzzling, something so perplexing to Brik that he couldn't equate the pleasure he found in Ry's friendship with that other feeling, that need to physically overpower Ryder and do the . . . the F thing. And all of it without any sense of heart . . . That was what was the weirdest. Though

he wanted to, there was no chemistry in it for Brik, no magic that would somehow have made his thoughts pure, his desires clean. Ryder had long since conveniently forgotten what they had used to do together. It was as if the programme of their growing up had been wiped clean before being ejected, so carelessly it seemed, from the drive, and the disc mutilated. It was another Ryder who claimed current victory. Another Ryder who had secrets just as Brik had secrets. Brik couldn't figure if they were the same kind of secrets and he couldn't figure out if he told Ry what was on *his* mind, like he wanted to, like he knew he somehow *should* do, could he assume now that Ryder could be trusted? Would Ry be for him what he felt he would always be for Ry? Brik realised that it was somehow important to know whether or not Ryder *had* fucked Betsy not because it was important to him if Ryder *had* fucked her but because he needed to know if Ryder was telling the truth.

"So, Brik, prick, do I get my quilt back?"

Brik nodded and shelved the real issue. He felt he must not communicate his unease but also found himself transgressing the first law of intimacy - honesty; it was not the first time, but it was the first time he realised why he was doing it and he was sorry.

"Crawl back under your goddam quilt," Brik grinned, scrambling up from the floor and grabbing the darts from Ryder's desk. Thud, thud, thud. The three darts plupped into the board on the back of the door.

"I was just kidding about Betsy, man."

Brik returned to the throwing line and took aim. Plup, plup, plup . . .

"It's your life, Ry. I'm not here to judge you."

"Got you pretty mad, though," Ryder laughed. Brik retrieved the darts and pondered how unconcerned Ryder sounded. Perhaps Ry *was* lying about what Betsy had said?

"So," Ryder went on, spreading the quilt back over the bed, "have you had dinner yet?"

"No."

"So whaddya wanna do . . . go to the diner?"

"No."

Ryder picked up a pair of barbels from the floor and started pumping.

"Well, let's drive into Doddsville, man. Shit I wish I hadn't sold my damn car. Say, you wanna buy my weights?"

Brik sat on the edge of the bed and toyed with the flights of the darts.

"No."

"So what the fuck are you doing here spoiling my day?"

Brik didn't reply but lay back on the bed, hurling the darts with an easy action at the dartboard.

"Remember that guy Andy, Ry? You know. Jeremy's friend. At the play?"

"That faggot!" Ryder said with a sneer as he looked at his bicep stressing.

"How do you know he's a faggot?" snapped Brik.

"Oh, please. Farmboy! I know a faggot when I see one. Just like our dear *Mister* Page. Coupla cocksuckers, man."

Brik blushed and got up off the bed so's Ryder couldn't see his face. He grabbed the bar of the weights and hoisted them to disguise the blush.

"He wrote me today."

Ryder interrupted his exertions.

"He what?"

"He wrote me. From his company."

"He's after your ass, man."

"He said he was after my talent."

"Always thought you kept your talent in your asshole," Ryder rejoined.

"Did you know he was an agent?" Brik asked, pushing the bar to chest height. Ryder set down the barbels.

"Real estate? Or CIA, perhaps? `Faggot's the name from the Cee-I-Ay, Don't mind me I jus' walk this way!" Ryder rapped.

"Quit it, Ry. It's agent like in teevee. Movies. That stuff."

"No kidding?"

Ryder's prejudices seemed to evaporate no sooner than they had condensed.

Brik allowed the bar to lie on his chest before setting it down.

"Sit down, Ry." The boys sat on the edge of the bed. Ryder had changed gear and was into 'impressed' mode.

"So the guy contacted you! That's neat, man. Jeez, he could have been talent scouting! Wow, I wish I'd known. Why didn't he tell us? We could have been fuckin' teevee stars, man? Maybe movies? Hey! Perry! Move over, dickhead!"

"He wants me to go to Hollywood for some meeting," Brik announced, as low key as he could make it.

Ryder's jaw dropped open.

"Excuse me?"

"You heard. Some teevee thing in the fall. Reckons I'd have a chance."

"But . . ." Ryder at that point in his life, in a clinch, lacked all guile. Although he would learn quickly to correct this trait, just now he said exactly what his first thought was. "But what about me, man?" he blurted. "I mean . . . We're a team, dammit. You and me together. Didn't he say anything about me?"

Brik shook his head.

"Negative."

"Shit."

There was silence between them as each digested the data exchanged.

"You reckon I shouldn't go," Brik asked rhetorically.

"Didn't say that," Ryder replied. "Go. If that's what you want." He got up. "Shit. S'better than goin' to college."

"But I *wanna* go to college."

Ryder got up and went to the door.

"Then you need to see a shrink," he said as he went out of the room. "You wanna coke, Brik? I mean . . . Let's celebrate," he added with flat sarcasm.

"I wanna . . .," Brik started to say.

"Christ! You wannabees," Ry interrupted.

"I wanna have you along too, Ry."

For a moment Brik thought Ryder was about to make some smartass comment but he didn't answer. He turned his back on Brik and went off to the kitchen. Brik heard Dory offering cookies too.

"No, Ma. No cookies. Not only are cookies for little baby boys but cookies make little baby boys into *fat* little baby boys!" he heard Ryder say scornfully.

Brik felt abandoned as he sat on the edge of Ry's bed, his head in his hands. He sighed and leant back against the wall. Ry came back and tossed him a can.

"Man, I jus' figured something," Ryder announced in entirely different mood as he started to pace the room. "Hey. And thanks for the invitation." He sucked on the coke can. "Now, you *and* me. Now that is something to *talk* about. Let us consider this thing . . . I mean, New York is New York but . . . it's not LA, is it? In New York it could take a guy forever to make it. LA's different. I mean . . . LA's where it happens, right?"

"I guess. Course, I can always come back. It might not work out."

Ryder was getting into this. His pacing became faster, almost manic as he unfolded his particular logic, kneading at the news, adding his yeast to Brik's flour, deftly mixing the ingredients to produce a cake whose slices would be enough for two birthdays, not just one.

"Man! There you go again! You can't think like that. Y'have to be positive, man. Y'have to tell y'self that this thing *will* work out because we'll *make* it work out and that everything's gonna be just *great*! See?"

"Are you telling me you *want* to come with me, Ry?"

Ry pretended to choke on his coke.

"Do I hear doubts again? Are you crazy? D'ya think I'd let my best buddy go into the arena unarmed and alone? We're a *team*, Brik. It's you and me. Against them all! All the faggot agents and all the faggot producers in the world couldn't split us up, man!"

Ryder extended his hand. The grand gesture; Ryder knew he'd swung the vote just how Brik wanted it and he knew it was a vote he couldn't afford to lose.

They shook hands. The faggot issue was forgotten, overruled by the arcane laws of friendship.

"Thanks, Ry."

"You owe me," said Ryder, smiling. "All for one . . ."

"And one for all," added Brik.

* * * *

Brik's gloomy prediction about an outbreak of domestic hostilities proved correct.

By the following morning, the usually settled, if resigned, atmosphere in the Peters' home had finally polarised but it wasn't a happy conclusion. The climate indoors had successively witnessed eruption, cyclone, tidal wave, hurricane, twister, fog, mist, ice, gale and storm and every other analogous phenomenon that human emotions can perpetrate. A lot of hot air was the prevailing, causal condition.

Though I'd been seriously contemplating a speedy exit from the parish that very morning before all sense of my carefully constructed cover was blown for good, a 'phone call from a desperate Janna had both summoned me as arbitrator and aroused my conscience at least into acknowledging that what had happened had been at my instigation, however unwitting. I suppose that I'd been hoping a call would have come from Brik, rather a different call maybe but . . . I kicked my two suitcases back beneath my bed and reminded myself that Brik had no reason to want to contact me. It had been me who'd let him down the previous day in an hour of need which was, surely, of much greater importance to him than that which I assumed currently threatened.

Briefly, Janna had explained - Don and Mitzi weren't speaking. In fact, no one was speaking. Her parents had slept apart, not that strange and not unheard of when Mitzi had gotten really upset with all of them. But it wasn't unheard of for Mitzi to do many strange things. What was unheard of was Mitzi staying up all night, martini-less, sitting on the porch and staring blankly into the night.

Both Janna and Brik had been grounded and Don remained adamant that neither of his children was ever going anywhere for whatever reason. By morning, Mitzi had sided roundly with Brik and was so much on his side that she'd announced that as Don obviously no longer respected her, wanted her or needed her, she was going to accompany Brik as chaperone. Janna wasn't talking to anyone, especially her mother, as Mitzi had concluded her plans by telling Janna she would have to stay behind and look after her father.

"You're our only hope, Jeremy," she'd pleaded.

So, cursing the mephistophelian Andy Horowitz but knowing that I was the one they probably saw as the horned one with the cloven feet, I reluctantly drove out to Indian Road on Sunday morning.

Someone driving only a short distance ahead of me had kicked up the dust. On the pretext of driving his mother to church and then feigning an upset stomach, Ryder had borrowed Dory's car.

He was leaning against the side of the old Plymouth with his arms folded as I parked beside him next to the barn.

"Hi, coach."

"Morning, Ryder. Are you here as a second or a spectator?"

"Hey," he said, holding out his palms and shrugging away any prurient intent, "I'm just glad you're the referee and not me."

"Thanks for the vote of confidence," I replied and glanced uneasily over to the house. I hitched up my chinos and rolled down my shirtsleeves. "I take it you know why I'm here?"

"I know why they asked you but I can't figure why the hell you came."

Though I had had much to do with Ryder in school, our newly opened dialogue as equals was leaving me at a disadvantage. What he thought of me, I knew not and cared less but I sensed an antipathy which I hadn't felt as his teacher. I still felt like his teacher and I wished dearly he was still my pupil. I was discovering an insolence about Ryder, an attitude of unspoken defiance, an ever-present undercurrent of challenge. I felt threatened, insidiously, by the young man whose smile would have seemed to belie my gut reaction. Ryder was always smiling. I had begun to compare him to Brik. I knew it was unfair, as I had no reason except inclination to make an example of Brik. But even on such arbitrary scales, I found Ryder more than wanting and, as the months ahead were to pass, increasingly wanting.

We talked for a moment before I went inside. Nothing significant. He lounged rather than leant against his driver's door, folding and unfolding his arms to make gestures, bringing guileless emphasis to his remarks. His legs crossed and uncrossed synchronically, almost in rhythm, as he spoke and worked his hands, like his whole aura was being orchestrated to project exactly what he wanted his audience, me, to believe. I fought what had become the inevitable, odious comparison. Even the way they wore their clothes . . . Brik's clung. You seemed to know what you were getting with Brik. His was an uncomplicated statement of the fact of him. Ryder's clothes, worn as they were on a much rangier, leaner physique sort of . . . hung, hinting rather than communicating, alluding to rather than revealing the character of the man beneath.

"So, I'm for Brik, man. It's great. Go get 'em, coach!" and he punched the air with a victory fist.

As I walked across the dusty yard to the house, I had a feeling I was about doing Ryder's business; it certainly wasn't mine. Or Brik's.

I went to the front door and immediately knew that this was no informal, howdy-neighbour call. The whole family was ready and waiting in Mitzi's designer living room, for the first time in its creation fulfilling its promise. Even the plastic covers were off the lampshades. Janna closed the front door.

The whole family rose. Only Don seemed discomfitted. Janna offered me coffee and went off to the kitchen. Brik came over immediately and shook hands.

"No point introducing you," he grinned awkwardly.

"You know mom and dad, Jeremy."

"Of course."

"Brik! Where are your manners? Jeremy, indeed. Good morning, Mr Page."

"Oh," I laughed. "That. I have asked them to call me Jeremy, Mrs Peters. I wish you'd do the same. Mister makes me sound like an old man."

"Then it's Mitzi and Don," she said, gushing. But I could see she was nervous. She was best-dressed and her hair had been painstakingly backcombed into that compromise that a lot of sixties girls turning mid-forty affected. "Good morning . . . Jeremy. Don, you remember Jeremy, don't you?"

Don extended a hand and mumbled his "Good morning". He sat down again immediately. He had not compromised. Don Peters was a handsome man, smaller than Brik and leaner and though his hair was gray at the temples and there was salt in the pepper, it was still magnificently luxuriant, swept into a fonz without, it seemed, the need for grease. Don Peters blared biker, not beatle.

"Here you are, Jeremy. You don't take cream, do you?" I nodded. "Sugar?" I shook my head.

"Thanks, Janna."

"Please, sit down . . . Jeremy."

"Let's all sit down," echoed Janna, glaring at her father. We took seats, the couch and chairs around Mitzi's magazine table.

"It's still so warm, don't you find, Jeremy? 'Course we can't complain. But a little rain wouldn't harm. Perhaps when the . . ."

"Mom!" Brik laughed, trying to lighten the atmosphere. "It's okay. We all know why we're here."

"Do we?" snapped Don. "Can't see it myself. Dragging strangers into family business. Ain't necessary, far's I can see."

"We'd've solved nothing going on they way we were," Janna offered.

"What's to solve?" Don interrupted. He was an angry

man, his position and word being thus questioned. I sensed a potential walk-out.

"Well I for one would welcome Mr Page's . . . I'm sorry, Jeremy . . . Jeremy's opinion," Mitzi crooned like a hot knife through jello.

I smiled at her. I was sitting on the couch next to her and she had laid her hand on my arm, reassuring both herself and me, I imagined, that I was in their trust.

I paused and set my mug down on the table before feeling composed enough to say anything, I felt even more awkward because I hadn't the faintest idea what I was going to say. I only knew that Don must not storm out.

"From what Janna has told me on the 'phone," I began, trying to hold Don's eyes however much he was trying not to look at me, "Andy Horowitz has set a cat amongst the pigeons here and I must have you believe from the off that it was nothing to do with me. I would have wished he could have spoken to me first but he didn't. However, I have spoken to him now and all I can tell you is that he really believed he was, how can I put it . . . playing Santa Claus. However, he is not a teacher, he has only ever lived in cities, he lives and breathes his work and he would be sincerely very upset to know that his efforts had caused so much harm. He is very upset," I added. I paused half-expecting to gag on my defence of the indefensible, yet hoping that I was injecting sufficient reason and pathos in my explanation to reach Don Peters. "In a way," I went on, interposing a deliberate sigh in the break, "I wish I could undo what has been done but I can't . . ."

"Oh, don't . . . *Please*, Mr Page. You can't!" Mitzi pleaded, this time grabbing my arm with both hands.

"Why the hell not?" Don spat. "Just have him tell his fancy friend the deal's off!"

"Dad," Janna soothed. "Please. You promised you wouldn't yell. Jeremy's only trying to help. You sound like you're attacking him."

Don appeared to be about to erupt again but merely muttered. "Okay . . . Okay."

I glanced over at Brik. His face betrayed no particular

emotion and I couldn't catch his eye. He looked steadfastly at the carpet.

"Don," I ventured, "I do understand how you feel, believe me. Being a parent isn't unlike being a teacher, you know. You watch the kids as they grow, you think you know what they're good at, you encourage what's best in them and you want the best of them because it's in them that the best of you lives on. We're all of us only human . . . When things go wrong, when they screw up in some way, when they don't do what you want them to do, you feel angry, powerless, like they're being ungrateful or spiteful or just . . . well, plain dumb."

"So let's hear it," he urged, his anger still simmering, "what do *you* think should happen?"

"I can't say," I said quietly. "And it would be wrong of me to say, wrong for everyone though mostly wrong for me. I am only his teacher."

"That's pussyfooting in my book," said Don, glowering."

I suppose it is, but," I countered, "don't you think it's up to Brik to say what should happen? It's his life, not ours. Not yours, not your wife's and certainly not mine."

"He *has* to go," Mitzi wailed. "He just has to. Anyone in their right mind can see that!" She pulled a tissue from a box beside her and dabbed her nose.

"Do you?" Don barked at Brik. "Do you *have* to go?"

All eyes turned to Brik. He leant forward in his chair and still looking at the floor said quietly, "I guess not."

Mitzi began to sob.

"Brik?" Janna asked with a frown of concern.

"You heard me," he muttered.

"Sense at last!" exclaimed Don and brought his fists down on the arms of his chair. He got up. "Sorry to have wasted your time, Mr Page. My son seems to have solved the problem just like you said."

"No!" screamed Mitzi. "You don't mean it Brik. Tell him you don't mean it!" She all but leapt from her seat and threw herself at the chair Brik sat in, draping herself over it, clasping Brik to her.

"What do you expect me to do, mom?," he flashed, struggling out of her embrace. "It's tearing us apart."

"Not me, it's not," Mitzi rebuked. "You have to do this for yourself, Brik. I'd never forgive myself if you gave in to him. Stand up to him. Tell him, you'll go."

"If he goes," Don threatened, "there'll be no coming back. I warn you. As long as he lives under my roof he does as I say. If he goes, he goes. He gets nothing more outta me."

"That's blackmail, daddy," Janna reasoned.

"Call it what you like, young lady. I worked my butt off for years to get enough together to get you kids off to a decent start. I done without for years to help you get something more outta life than what I did. Something secure, something that'll take you places. I'm damned if I'm gonna see all my hard work tossed away on some damn fool chase after . . . after rainbows." He was breathing heavily, almost panting out his anger. "And that's what it is . . . rainbows. Nothing at the end of rainbows but nothing."

"But Brick has talent, daddy. Real talent. Doesn't he, Jeremy, he must have."

"Of course he has talent," Mitzi chimed in, as though anyone would be a fool not to agree. "*He* wouldn't see it," she accused, pointing at her husband. "*He* didn't even come to see either of . . . dammit, it was our son in the play!" She fell again to weeping.

"You know damn well why I didn't come," Don bridled, "damn well. I was fixin' the goddam pump on the goddam well so we wouldn't need another one for another year. I was saving us money, Mitzi, money that'll get Brik an education, a proper education."

My presence had been completely forgotten. The battle lines had been drawn and the fight was not about Brik anymore, or Janna or me or the letter, it was about Don and Mitzi and years of her pent-up anger; her years of making-do and his life of compliance and truce.

"Well I'm glad I heard that little word us," Mitzi spat at him. "First time I seem to have been included in this and it's about time 'cos I'm your equal half in this, Don. Brik's not just *yours* - he's *ours*. You hear me on this?"

"Ain't nothin' to hear, dammit!" Don barked.

"Is that so?" Mitzi came out from her corner and edged round her precious magazine table to confront her husband. "Well hear this, Don Peters, 'cos you got it coming and you've had it coming for more years than I care to count. You seem to think that it's all been down to you. Well, you're wrong. As much as *you* think you've gone without, so have I! I've sacrificed too, maybe more than you can ever know, you only bein' a man and I figure you ain't got nothing to say about this 'cos if you have, I swear I will deevorce you then half of what's *yours* will be *mine* and I will make sure my kids have what they need so they *never* have to live our life. D'you hear me? *Deevorce*!"

Janna began to cry and Brik rushed from the room. I sat down next to Janna and . . . well, I put my arm round her. She brushed me off and followed Brik out and along the corridor to their rooms. The door to the living room slammed shut.

"You're crazy! You're insane, woman!" He looked over his shoulder as he whispered his defiance.

"Am I? *Am* I!" she retorted in that same, almost silent snarl. Don had got up and grabbed both her hands. I wasn't sure who'd hit me first if I'd tried to intervene. "I got reason for deevorcin' you, Don and I have had for years. You know it and I know it!"

"Known what?" he spat back. "All I know is that I had to do what I did, Mitzi. You know I had to . . . An' I thought we had a deal!"

"Well now I'm calling the deal off, buster."

He seemed to reel slightly, as though she'd slapped his face. Slowly he let go her wrists.

"But you agreed. You said it was okay. As long as it was never mentioned again and you know as well as I do, Mitzi, we ain't *never* mentioned it. What the hell are you doing to us? You're crazy, Mitzi. You don't know how crazy you are."

"I'll get as crazy as I have to," she hissed, "if it means

that Brik won't lose out. My Brik! *Our* son!" She grabbed her husband's hand and started to drag him to the window. She tore aside the blind behind the no cut, no sew drapes and pointed. "See him? *Look* at him, dammit! If he can have the chance to live his own life, do as he wants, then so can *our* Brik!"

She waited for a moment before letting the blind drop back. She held his eyes all the while, daring him to contradict her. She let go his hand and knew she'd won when he sank down on the rocker beneath the window. I then witnessed that extraordinary ability she had to switch her mood, literally switch, like she was turning on a light. The viper vanished. Light returned, sweetness honeyed out of the smile she turned upon me. It was pure Tennessee.

"I do apologise, Jeremy," she said lightly. "I sure do hate family squabbles and I pray you can forgive us." She was sensible, polite and articulate as though all the emotional exertion had been sloughed off leaving only a gossamer skin that the breeze was blowing quickly out of sight.

I shrugged.

"I think I should forget this morning," I suggested.

"I think that would be wise, Jeremy," she concurred. "My husband and I would sure appreciate it. And you have helped us. Believe me, you have helped. I reckon we can just work things out ourselves now."

"What about . . .?" I indicated the direction Brik and Janna had taken.

"Well, of course . . .," she announced reasonably, "they must never know. I feel I know you so well now, I don't even have to ask for your word on that, do I?"

"Er . . . No. No," I mumbled.

"I do wish my husband could see how talented Brik is," she continued, straightening up the seat pillows in her beautiful, designer living room. "I've always known it, of course. He gets it from my side of the family, I do believe. Course, I have always *loved* the movies . . . There's not a thing I couldn't tell you about any of the big stars . . . She seemed entranced as her mind sifted her roladex of images. Who was she seeing? McQueen, Redford, Newman . . .

Were they her generation of dreams? "You see, Jeremy," she concluded, "I *do* believe in rainbows. If I didn't, I think I'd surely have died many years ago." She picked up my mug, wiped the glass table top with the skirt of her dress, and left the room as calmly as the swish of an intermission curtain.

Don Peters remained in the rocker, his head hanging forward, his hands clasped as he leant on his knees. There was no more reason for me to remain. I got up to go. My move seemed to stir him and he looked up. His eyes were black, empty like a slaughterhouse cow at the head of the line.

"She thinks she knows so much," he said.

"And she doesn't?"

"She doesn't know Brik," he replied. "I'm only trying to protect him, y'see. 'Cos I know. I know. I been out there an' I've met . . . people."

"What do you know?"

He drew breath and I felt he was about to speak. But he didn't.

"Forget it," he said, pulling himself up out of the chair. "Brik coulda made a good engineer."

"He still might," I smiled. "He might have to."

"Goodbye, Mister Page." He extended his hand. I shook it. "You seem like a good enough guy," he added. "Understand you're headed for LA yourself."

"So it seems," I said. He walked over to the front door and opened it.

"Do me one favour, hey," he asked.

"If I can."

"Keep an eye on my boy."

He didn't let me reply. The door closed too quickly.

Ryder was sitting in the Plymouth with the radio on when I reached my Jeep. He didn't hear me until he saw me climb into my seat. He jumped out of the car, pulling off his Raybans.

"Brik ready yet?" he asked.

"Ask him," I replied.

"We're gonna see a Bronco some guy's got in town,"

Ryder announced. "Shit! Wish I hadn't sold my Mustang. Now that would have been cool on the coast."

"Can't you buy it back?" I asked fishing out my keys.

"Need something more reliable, something like this," he said, running his boot carelessly along the chrome strips of my running board. "Won't have Brik's dad in LA. He was just the best at fixing that car. Loved it like it was his own." Ryder grinned. "But you know how it is . . . Gotta face the grim realities, hey, coach?"

"You bet," I smiled as I turned the motor over. "Good luck, Ryder."

"Yeah. Thanks," he said. In my rearview, I watched him watching as I drove away. He never stopped smiling.

I drove the long way back to town, my conscience floundering between the hard place and the rock that had just been turned over to reveal the wriggling, worming implications it had concealed for so many years.

"Shit!" I exclaimed, frightening myself as I braked hard at the MacMurdo Street light I had failed to notice. As I pulled up in front of my apartment, I understood just how Don Peters must have felt catching Ryder and Janna in the pickup. I found myself praying that Janna was indeed the sensible girl I held her to be. Mine had suddenly become an even more unconscionable position in Scotland. I felt I should tell someone. All my rational instincts told me that keeping this secret would do no one any good. I tried to turn my back on the rock and settled for the hard place.

FOUR

I saw Brik once before I left Scottland.

Two days before the lease on my apartment expired, I was nearly packed. The books were the problem. Crates and crates of words. The moving company was dealing with them. I left re-boxing the word processor until the last moment. I used it every day although every day I hoped I'd start using it again for the right reason. Until that time, journal entries were all it stored although since the Sunday morning out at Indian Road, I'd written nothing. Something was blocking me even there as though I was afraid to commit the situation to disc for fear of being forced to speculate and expand on what had emerged.

✽ ✽ ✽ ✽

My apartment was the upper floor of an Edwardian house off and off again of Main Street. It was actually called MacMurdo Street like everything in Scottland of any public significance was called MacMurdo something. I preferred my nomenclature. It was a map reference to where I was in my life, Main Street, Midtown, Midwest, USA. Anonymity itself. No one, least of all me, would have thought to look for me there which is exactly how I wanted it to be at the begining. I'd rather had enough of myself. Moving to Scottland and going back to teaching had been the least challenging route I could have chosen. It was other people I was after, not myself. I wanted other people's lives, realities I knew I was somehow by-passing in my self-absorbed obsession. Of course, until those last months I found nothing in Scottland except, and perhaps you've guessed, myself. It had all come together, it, them and me but in such a way that, and I have to confess now, in order to tell you about it, Scottland isn't the real name. You won't find it on any map so don't bother looking.

But back to my apartment; the house reminded me of where Mindy lives, in *Mork and Mindy*, the one with the chateau style turret at one corner. Kinda safe and permanent and weatherproof, a bastion against the forces of doubt and censure and criticism which I suppose was what I wanted. Then.

My landlady, Mrs MacSween, was the focus of my life in Scotland. She'd given up teaching school when she'd married but now she was a widow, Doctor MacSween having died several years ago. For a while, Doc MacSween's replacement had kept the surgery where it was until he too married, at the same time a new medical centre was built by, you guessed right, the MacMurdos.

As far as I'd let her, Mrs MacSween mothered me. She baked me little gifts; when I was sick, she'd wipe my brow and bring me soup. I insisted . . . She insisted. Not that she was lonely. In fact, it was through her I realised it was I who was lonely, but she was the cause for my loneliness being so vividly peopled with the characters who now filled my journal entries, more often than not, characters whom I would never meet but who had lived and died their way under Mrs MacSween's scrupulous gaze. As she was almost ninety and hail and spry with a memory as sharp as a photostat, her gaze had raked practically the whole century.

It was Mrs MacSween who had first told me about the Peters and the McKighs when I came home at nights enthusing about Brik and Ryder's talent. But it was me who finally put two and two together that morning out at Indian Road.

She had of course come to see the play. Laughing, she'd agreed to be my date and after the performance, I'd walked her home.

"Dear, dear Jeremy," she mused as we crossed Main Street at the one and only light. She patted my arm which was linked through hers.

"Is that as in `Oh, dear'? I feel I am about to hear wise words of advice."

"There's too much inside you for you to stay here," she announced.

"That's very kind," I demurred. "But remember, I can't

stay anyway. No job."

"No. Not just that. It's time for you to be moving on anyway."

"I'm not looking forward to it."

"S'right that folks move on. S'wrong to take backward steps an' stay still. That's what you're doing, jus' standin' still."

We turned into our street.

"I don't know. There's something to be said for standing still. Look around you . . . Scotland hasn't done so bad standing still."

"There's a lot of bad been done round here. Lotta folks have been in too much of a hurry to stand still. Been a lot who should have moved on and stayed moved on."

"I'm glad they didn't," I chuckled. "I wouldn't have had the cast I had tonight."

"There's two like you," she said, as though I had vindicated her. "I do hope those boys don't come scamperin' back just like their poppas did."

"You mean Berwick and Ryder?"

"Uh huh."

"You mean after Vietnam?"

"Should've left the farms to the old folks and moved on," she defined. "Saved a lot of misery. Those boys brought it back with them as surely as a curse."

"What on earth are you saying?"

She stopped outside her house and looked up at it as though she were in a gallery, observing a huge, mysterious canvas.

"Can't say exactly," she said, squinting. "Goodness, I left a light on. D'you think my mind's goin', Jeremy?" she laughed.

She leant on my arm as we climbed the steps to the porch. She sat down on the cane chair and fanned herself with the single-sheet programme she'd saved. I sat next to her and together, quiet, we reviewed the street.

"War's a terrible thing," she announced quietly.

"Did Mr MacSween go?"

"Wasn't thinkin' about him," she said firmly. "And not

that war. I was thinkin' more about Gordon and Don."

At that time, these were names that hadn't figured in her tales of the town.

"Who?"

"McKigh and Peters," she clarified, as though I ought to have known. "Those boys' daddies."

"Ah! That war."

"They were about the same age." She sighed and then chuckled. "I can still see 'em now, swashbucklin' down MacMurdo Street in their new uniforms. Like hounds on a leash, those two boys."

"Surely not to go to Nam?"

"Hell no. They didn't give zip for where they were going. All they cared was that they were *going*."

"At least they came back."

"Not entirely," she muttered. "One-and-a-half of 'em did."

"Who was the half?"

"Gordon."

"Ryder's dad? He's not long dead, is he?"

"God rest his poor tortured soul."

"And you're saying they shouldn't have come back?" I paused. "It was their home, surely? And perhaps they had wives or girlfriends. Were they married then?"

"Questions, questions," she exclaimed, teasing me. "If I wasn't so sure you were going to do something with all us folks, I should box your ears and tell you not to be so curious, my boy." She chuckled. "That's what killed the cat."

"They have nine lives, though," I added. "To compensate."

She laughed again and waved goodnight to her neighbours who called their acknowledgement as they passed by outside on the street.

"MacSween always said it was a miracle he survived," she mused. "Terrible injuries. For a man, that is."

"It's always the psychological scars that are most difficult to heal," I opined.

"They're not the sort I'm talking about," she said. "And

that's enough . . . my tongue'll get me into more trouble than I can handle."

"You can't do this to me," I joked. "What am I going to tell my diary?"

"That ain't no diary," she grumbled. "Diaries are books. What you clicky clack away on upstairs is a contraption."

She leant forward and started to pull herself up. I went to help her but she waved me away.

"Nope! I can do it . . ." And she did. "Day I can't get up from my own chair is the day I never get up again. You can give me your arm now, though."

I opened the door. She never locked it and refused all my suggestion that she should. I left her at the foot of the stairs and pecked her goodnight.

"Won't you finish telling me about Gordon?"

"Make it up," she called as she went through into her kitchen. "S'what folks round here have been doin' for years!"

I didn't think of that particular part of the evening again for weeks.

❈ ❈ ❈ ❈

I was expecting him. Not an appointment, as such. Not at a particular time on a particular day. I just knew Brik would come.

It had been a hot night. I woke up covered only by the sheet. All the windows were open. I heard a rumble of motors from MacMurdo Street which I could see from my turret window where I always sat and drank my coffee, sitting on the banquette. I pulled on my shorts and went to look. It sounded like a military column, something like what I imagined the passing of tanks and transports to sound. It was a column of combines, huge harvesting machines. I knew they'd been working on the other side of town and they were now moving to cut the prairie to the south. They were followed by the grain trucks, a parade of mechanised hardwear which epitomised the changing nature of Scottland.

The last of them passed by and I was just about to turn from the window and shower when I saw the yellow Bronco pull up outside. Brik looked out and up to my window. I felt like the Lady of Shallot. He waved and pointed up. I nodded and beckoned and leant out of the window. I couldn't see Ryder. Was Brik alone?

"Sure! Come on up. Door's open. Just call to Mrs MacSween that it's you, okay?"

I left the window and hurriedly pulled a robe over my shoulders and ran my hands through what remained of a once glorious thatch. I couldn't help myself as I thought at once of literature's `gen'lemen callers'. I heard Andy Horowitz' mocking laughter cackling across the ether.

My apartment was in no way self-contained. It's very open arrangement was one of the deciding factors in my taking it. I would be unable to be private and therefore immune to compromise by whatever temptation might have befallen me. I heard Brik chatting to Mrs MacSween at the foot of the stairs.

"Well, I'm very pleased for you. Take care of yourself, Brik. Don't forget us when you're famous!"

"Oh, I won't, ma'am. Count on that."

I heard his footsteps on the stairs. I'd never heard anyone call him Berwick. The Americans cannot pronounce it. Well, they can but it comes out `Burr-wick'. I figured it was how he must have first pronounced his own name, as a toddling infant. `Berrick' to `Brik'. It had stuck.

"Morning, coach. Did ya like the wheels?"

"You mean the Jeep?"

"Bronco, actually."

I stood aside and indicated he come in.

"Yours or Ryder's?"

"Ry's, I guess. But we're sharing the driving."

"Right. D'you want coffee? Or juice? You can have a beer but it's a bit too early for me."

He shook his head and waved his hand.

"No. Thanks. Just came by to say . . . well, thanks, I

suppose."

We went and sat down on the banquette by the window. I closed the door.

"So, when are you leaving?"

"Tomorrow."

"Me too."

"No fooling? How about a convoy."

"I don't think so," I replied. "I'm having stopovers."

"Oh." He sounded disappointed.

"So when's the big day?"

"Andy . . . Mr Horowitz, I mean . . . He's picking us up from the hotel early Wednesday."

It was already Thursday. They had five days to cross as many states.

"Us?" I enquired, cocking an eyebrow.

"Yeah. Ry's gonna be my driver."

"And who's picking up the hotel tab? And for how long?"

"Guess Andy will."

"And when will you know?"

"Pretty soon, he reckons. Coupla days. Maybe a test or something first."

"And how are your folks now?"

"Like dogs in a ring. We're holdin' them, though."

"And when you're gone."

"They'll work it out. They always have. Mom's threatening to come out but I can handle her. Not that I wouldn't want her to but . . . well, not 'til things work out."

"Or not."

"Then I'll come back and go to college," he said.

"Sure," I said.

"You can almost smell the wheatdust from here," he said, twisting his body so he hung his head through the window. He turned back to the room, flashed a big smile at me and got up. He walked around the room as he talked, touching the crates, running his fingers over the dead keyboard, picking up objects as his eye lighted on them - my watch, a Rolex, a present from my grandfather on my twenty-first birthday, I explained; my filofax, a hangover from the days when I had appointments, I said by way of excuse; my overnight bag - `Hey, what a neat bag!' - a present from Andy for a long-forgotten anniversary, although I said I got it on Christmas; my photograph of my parents, dead, I said - he apologised.

"Everything else is packed," I offered as he replaced the photoframe with a sweet reverence. "I assume you were looking for clues?"

He laughed.

"That obvious, huh?"

Like the wimp that I was, I saw that by procrastination, I had been given a second chance, one to redeem myself. I now had no excuse not to open the door I'd slammed so heartlessly the previous Saturday.

"So what can I tell you, Brik?"

"The truth," he said, pulling a chair from under the table. He turned it and sat on it backwards. "Shoot. Are you?"

I nodded. What a cop out.

"Okay," he concluded, as though we were now talking on an equal footing, all pre-conditions about talks about talks, as the diplomats say, set aside.

"What do you want to know?"

"Everything."

I cleared my throat and pulled the robe a little closer round me.

"How much do you know already?"

"You mean, have I done it?"

"Seems like the place to start. You are sure, aren't you? How do you feel about girls for instance? You can do it, you know, and then . . . stop."

"Well, I have done it . . . sorta. And as far as girls go, sure . . . I like 'em but not . . . enough. Not for sex, y'know?"

"Did you have any feelings for who you did it with?"

He laughed.

"You mean, `Was it love?'". He laughed. "Hell no, man."

"Just a casual thing . . . was it?"

He shook his head.

"Every week or so. Over in Doddsville. I can't tell you. I

58

promised. It was part of the deal."

"Deal?" I pursued.

"Yeah," he said with no trace of embarassment. "This guy . . . well, he saw me one day. In the bus station. I was waiting for mom to come pick me up. Musta been about October . . . maybe November. This guy, he says, `Can I buy you a drink?' and I says, `Sure'. So, he bought me a coke and we sat and talked. He says, `You ever been photographed?' and I says, `No'. Then he says he'd pay me ten dollars for him to take some pictures and I says, `Sure.'"

"Oh, God," I groaned. "What a shit."

"No way, man," Brik insisted. "He's okay. I liked him real well. I got all the money saved." He chuckled. "Had to. Couldn't spend it. They'd wanna know."

"Your parents?" He nodded. "And this guy, did he . . . what did . . . Hell, *did* he?"

"No. He was cool. Told him I'd meet him the next day. I got a ride into Doddsville and he was waiting for me, like he'd said. He drove me back to . . . well, never mind where and, y'know, we got inside and I just . . . Heck. I just did it. Dunno why but I just took off all my clothes. Thought that was what he'd meant and it didn't mean nothing to me. I think he was real surprised 'cos he says, `Could you put some of 'em back on?'"

I blinked. I wondered whether I should be hearing this. I wondered whether I wanted to hear. I took an instant dislike to `the guy', immediately categorised him a cradle snatcher, child molester, pervert, sicko and also felt very, very jealous which in turn made me feel utterly ashamed and guilty, as dirty as the dirty old man from Doddsville whom I had so quickly censured. I also felt I wanted to know who the guy was.

"And this happened every week . . . ?"

"Uh uh. But most weeks. Each time was different and it turned me on. I couldn't help it." He laughed and covered his face momentarily with his hands. "More'n Betsy Strong had ever done, that's for sure. Anyway . . . I s'pose it's kinda freaky, looking back on it but sometimes he made me put on real weird clothes . . . like Greek or Roman. Then his uniform. He'd been in the navy."

I snorted in disbelief.

"No, really," Brik protested. "He had. I saw his medals. He'd done a hell of a lot actually. He'd been a fireman, a policeman. Had a great collection of police stuff."

"Don't tell me," I droned, ". . . now he works in construction."

"Excuse me?"

I reminded myself I was talking to an innocent and so didn't confuse the issue with the kind of bitching Brik obviously didn't follow. I cringed as I rolled the hands of his clock forwards to a year from now, perhaps less, when he'd know exactly what I'd meant. I think I found that the scariest - how predicatable life was. I wondered if I was wise or just old and whether my cynical prophesy stood even a rat-in-a-trap's chance of being thwarted.

"So this was just a professional thing?" I resumed. "He only wanted photographs?"

"For a time . . . 'Til I . . . well, what the heck. Didn't do any harm."

"If you're saying what I think you're saying, I hope you were careful."

"You think I'm stupid? I know what's goin' down, Jeremy. Sure I was careful . . . Are you?"

"Celibate people don't have to be careful," I replied.

"Does that mean you *never* do it?" I shook my head and instantly regretted it. "Jeez," he whistled. "That must be pretty rough. Do a lotta guys don't do it?"

"As an educated guess, I'd say, `No'."

"Oh," he said. "You ever been in love, Jeremy?" he asked after a moment's reflection. He got up from his chair and came across the room. What I wanted was what I didn't want as he sat next to me and put an arm round the back of the window seat, his finger tips just an inch from my shoulder. My skin felt prickly like his hand was discharging a current of laser light burning its way through the terry cloth.

"I don't know," I replied, swallowing saliva which

seemed to be drenching my mouth. "I suppose."

"What's it like? I mean, does it ever happen."

"Sure it happens. I know guys . . ." I hesitated.

"Go on . . . please."

"I know plenty . . . well, a few certainly, who've been together for years."

"Do they still make out?"

"You mean like your mom and dad?"

"I guess."

"I expect so."

"Doesn't it kinda wear off, though?"

"I think being friends helps," I suggested. "These guys . . . they're all of them each other's best friends. Like you and . . ." I stopped. I could have chewed my tongue right off.

". . . and Ry," he said, finishing my sentence. "We don't . . . not anymore."

"Is Ryder . . .?"

Brik shook his head.

"That was just foolin' around. Kids' stuff."

"Oh," I said. My mind filled with memories of the same kids' stuff of my own school days except, looking back, what had been kids stuff to the majority of us had left two I could be certain of and one I still hadn't confirmed heavyhearted for at least a year after we'd gone our separate ways. It seemed to me to be those who'd gotten emotional about kids stuff, those for whom the experience had been more than just a schoolboy crush, who'd turned out to be queer. Was it easier, the way it'd happened to me? Was Brik's the better way, thrown in at the deep end with no feelings attached? "So . . ."

"Yeah," he said, rather small. "So . . ." He grinned and though I didn't want to, I shrugged. Before either of us spoke again, we seemed . . . Or did we? Did I *really* feel he wanted something else or did I kid myself? . . . We seemed to communicate; hopes and dreams and whims and fancies and needs and desires and fears and regrets, I felt we threw all of these out in front of us, like we were standing on opposite rims of a vast canyon, trying to fill it with enough substance to be able to walk out, each from the safety of the edge, and meet in the middle without falling. I feel we did meet but not enough . . . or maybe it was enough, enough to know we could dare . . . if we'd dared.

"Will I see you?" he said softly, hoarsely. "Can I call you?"

I wanted to say that I'd promised his dad. I wanted to say that I had the family seal of approval, that it would be alright if we saw each other - a lot. I believed it. I really believed that was what Don Peters had meant . . . `Look after the boy', that's what he'd asked me.

"Sure, Brik."

I got up and tore a leaf from the filofax and looked up Dean Stuart's number and address. I scribbled it down and handed him the note.

"By the way," I added, "I can be very stubborn. And bossy. And mule-headed. And very pushy. I warn you."

He looked at the LA address I'd written down and folded the note carefully and put it in his jeans. The next time he saw that address, he'd be sitting on the kerb, outside it, waiting for me to get home.

He grinned.

"Thanks, coach," he said and got up. We didn't shake hands. He hugged me. He didn't say anything more but turned and left. I think he was crying.

FIVE

When I arrived in America, one of the first things I bought was a framed poster initially published, I think, as the front cover of the New Yorker or, perhaps, New York Magazine. In cryptically simple terms it portrays The United States as a map, New York in cartoon rising mightily in the foreground and Los Angeles, similarly portrayed, simmering in the distance; the rest, the middle bit is compressed by clever perspective into a featureless paperscape conveying no impression of the vast distances and differences `the gap' contains.

In America, it's not only step by step, it's in or out, you are or you aren't. If you have an itch, you scratch it. If the itch goes away, you have no need to scratch. On the other hand, if it keeps on itching, you keep on scratching. In America, life has become an unending process of itching and scratching. There are so many choices, so many itches and a lot of people are such bad scratchers.

Amongst the fallen brave on this battlefield of choice, I was merely one of the walking wounded. Attempting to remove myself from the ranks had far from rendered me immune and, trouble was, I was still no nearer to reaching my particular itch to even start scratching it.

※ ※ ※ ※

Andrew Horowitz parked his red Mercedes under the carport which separated his house from his neighbour's on the leafy, tree-lined east side of Dicks Street, West Hollywood. Several other houses on Dicks, Keith, Norma and the other streets of Boystown re-embraced their occupants. Car doors slammed, security alarms were de-activated, front doors closed against the slings and arrows of outrageous fortune yet closing in around their leafy enclave. The sunny early afternoon re-assumed its outward tranquillity. Another funeral was over.

Andy's house was larger than most in that area between Sunset and Santa Monica which had once resounded, any time of day or night, to the fevered scratching of a statistically significant American itch. But I digress. Andy's house boasted a pool. It took up most of the backyard leaving just enough room for a tiny sundeck with four loungers and a table big enough to carry his 'phone.

In my old room where Andy now kept his clothes and fitness machines, he changed his clothes, leaving the Armani suit crumpled where it fell. He pulled on shorts and with his 'phone went outside with a diet Seven-Up to wash away the sins of the day. He swam a few lengths of his pool and showered off the chlorine reflecting how it was that funerals, even after so many, made the hours before dusk go so slowly. He checked the water-proof Rolex and called his mother in Florida. He always called her on Shabat.

"Yeah, that's right, mom. He's coming home."

Dora Horowitz was pleased. That her son was like he was . . . what could she say? That her son was lonely, that she could talk about.

"I know, ma, I know . . . Of course we should be together but he had to have that space, ma . . . You know what writers are like."

No, Andy. Your mom has never known what writers are like. As far as she is concerned, if people are together they are together and together they should be. That Andy is how he is she can cope with if she knows he is being looked after and she assumes that I had fulfilled that role, her role, and thought there'd been no one else since. That she didn't understand about those people isn't entirely her fault. If Andy had fed her the truth rather than the half-truths he regurgitated, even the blinkered Dora would have understood better. Maybe she could have told him something about commitment, sacrifice, giving and taking. Then maybe, he and I could have talked about it like I've always said we should talk about it. Andy has never given her, himself or me the chance but I had remained the convenient excuse both he and Dora needed to go on being mother and son and further eke out their debt-burdened relationship. I had to be thought to still be around.

"Sure I'll have him call you . . . Probably Tuesday . . . Okay, ma. Love you . . ."

Andy clicked off the 'phone and his lie evaporated in the hot sun.

* * * *

On the other side of Sunset, where the canyons get steeper heading to the summits of the backdrop of hills behind Bel Air, another few feet were being added to the miles of celluloid tinsel which was the meat, drink and decor of the town. Filming had temporarily stopped. All that had been fit to cut and print had been achieved and it wasn't a lot. And it wasn't film. Not being shot for the big screen, it was videotape.

The slightly built and slightly dumb Mexican boy had been shot arriving at the gate of the mansion with a pizza. The gates had been filmed opening and the last the camera had seen was the young man, acting: `Gee, what's going on here?', pushing open the unlatched front door and going inside. The director's next shot was story-boarded from the pool out back, a shot panning from the muscular blond poolside sunbather, rousing himself from slumber and looking at his watch, frowning with annoyance, to the appearance of the delivery boy at the sliding patio doors a few feet away.

But the star was late and the buzz on set was *why* Trick Rambler was so late. Not that the buzz had far to reverberate - it was a very small crew at work, not even second or third unit size. No Winnebagos or location caterers or wranglers or stand-ins or doubles. In this movie, the actors did their own cunning stunts.

Doctor Morrell snipped sugically at his roses, confining his dead-heading to the beds by the gate on Stone Canyon Road. He had absented himself from the set rather than suffer the tirade of rhetorical curses Tommy Cattini was bringing down on the head of the star of this afternoon shoot. He heard the squeal of tires as a car stopped suddenly having passed the entrance to his secluded and paid for Bel Air retreat. He heard the car, in reverse, align itself to his driveway and footsteps hurrying over to the video entry button.

Outside, Trick jumped as Doctor Morrell appeared as if a special effect, materialising from behind the brick pillar.

"Shit! What the . . . Oh, it's you, Doc. Jesus, ya shouldn't do that to a guy!"

Kenneth Morrell opened the gate manually and Trick drove his car through.

"You're late, Trick."

"I know . . . I know," the star grumbled. "Is he mad at me?" He affected a little-boy whine, a crass juxtaposition of flesh and the fantastic. Kenneth Morrell laughed. Trick shook his still-wet mane of shoulder-length streaked blond hair. "I overslept, Doc. Honest."

"You're working too many nights, Trick. Anyone I know?"

"Uh uh. Outta towner." Trick inhaled deeply and stretched back in his seat. "Doc, you gotta give me somethin'. I need whatever ya got to get me through today."

"Cup of coffee?" the bland Doctor suggested, his offer laden with saccharine sarcasm.

"Look at me, Doc. Coffee wouldn' wake it up let alone get it up."

"I wouldn't make a habit of being so frank," Morrell observed sardonically. "Doesn't help your reputation which, some tittle-tattling little birds have told me, is starting to slip."

Trick frowned.

"Aw, come on, Doc. Fix me somethin' from your little black bag and I'll see y'alright. Can't we do our usual deal?" Trick parted his lips and snarled his famous smile, the irresistible fantasy-fuelling smile that had taken him and his splendidly accoutred body to star status in his particular area of the business of the town.

As well as his on-screen performances, Kenneth Morrell

had sampled the availability of Trick's off-screen delights several times already on the basis of sex for drugs and the temptation to do it one more time hadn't yet paled. Just the thought that he could have for a few cents what others paid hundreds of dollars for was enough to whet his venal appetite and plug any holes in his vaulting vanity.

"Okay. Drive me up to the house," he said and got in beside Trick, squeezing one of the star's denim-soaked thighs and relishing the power. "But not today, Trick. Let's make it another time. Pay me when you're feeling rested."

When Trick appeared at the window overlooking the pool, the first part of Doctor Morrell's prescription was already numbing his nostrils and he was ready to take on the action, any action. The other, last ditch remedy was in the tube he stuffed in the side pocket of his bag.

By five o'clock when it ought to have been a wrap, nerves were more than frayed. Paquito, the young Mexican, rolled off the poolside dining table.

"Sheet, man, don' *do* thees to me!"

It was Paquito's first appearance and he was more than anxious to please.

"Sorry, man," Trick apologised, wiping his sweating forehead with a towel, "Hey Clem, lemme have five?"

Paquito hurried to the mirror. With his fingers he fluffed up his dark curls and ran his tongue over his irregular teeth. He wanted to get them fixed and this afternoon's work was, he had figured, a sure-fire way of getting the money to do it. It would put him in a different league. He'd been in Los Angeles three months and the river still felt none too dry on his back.

The director hurried over and put his arm round the boy's shoulder, whispering encouraging words to buoy up his flagging confidence. There was nothing Clem could do for Trick's condition that Trick couldn't accomplish for himself and Clem reminded himself that it had been the same on the last shoot and it had come right in the end. The Mexican kid was a different matter, being a novice and, besides, Paquito was Clem's protege. There was nothing Trick could do for Clem.

Tommy Cattini fingered the heavy gold chain at his throat. He usually stayed in the background but then things usually went better than this and it was only the third scene in the movie. He looked at the Patek Philippe flashing at his wrist and number crunched, wondering whether to abandon the whole movie before concluding that he couldn't afford to. He flipped open his filofax and made a note to tell the editor to go through all the material on Trick and find matching sections they could use if if the star failed to deliver.

"Fuckin' coke-head," he swore under his breath. Someone tapped him on the shoulder. Tommy turned and raised his eyebrows. "I could fuckin' kill that jerk! *Kill* him!!"

"Now Tommy, dear, as your Doctor I have to help you with these stress levels. Most unhealthy. How about a scotch?"

"Gemme outta here, Ken," Tommy hissed. "And can't you give him somethin'?"

Kenneth Morrell ushered his patient away from the set and into the den.

"You have to face it, Tommy. Trick's losing it. Best dump him as soon as you can. If you don't, it'll end up costing. There's plenty more where he comes from and they're just itching to go."

SIX

I drove into LA on Route 10 through San Bernadino from my last stopover at Grand Canyon. I hate Las Vegas although I've never been and so I hadn't even contemplated overnighting there, the only real halfway point. One day, when Andy's taught me what superior, tightass and highminded are in terms that I can understand to correct these virulently anti-social qualities he says I have, I will take my superiority and my tight ass and my high mind to Vegas to make sure that I really do hate it.

At the end of the ten hour drive, having vainly looked for hitchhikers who weren't deranged psychotics or vacationing psychopaths, I pulled my Jeep into Eldon Stuart's driveway and switched off the engine. It was midevening, it was warm, the street lights shimmered behind the jacaranda leaves. The door was open and there was a light in the hall.

Hilgard bisects the gently sloping campus of UCLA and is very respectable. In terms of greater Los Angeles and certainly in comparison with neighbouring Bel Air and Beverly Hills, the homes are comfortable without being pretentious, commodiously landscaped without being tortured and, what is most appealing, quiet without being isolated. One has a sense of things happening but on a very gentle, cerebral level. Of course, in terms of the university community, the houses on Hilgard are extremely desirable and I'm sure sought after by those academics and their wives who choose to run in that particular race. Eldon Stuart was not one of that breed.

Even before it had not been overtly acknowledgeable, Eldon Stuart had not merely been `a bachelor'; everyone who knew him knew him to be exactly what he was. That he was also friend and intimate of the California literati of course did him no harm; he knew Christopher and Don and went to parties at Hockney's; when visitors of literary or more general cultural distinction arrived in LA from England, France, Spain, Germany or Italy, it was to Eldon

Stuart whom they first presented their introductions.

In their turn, these great and good congregated at Eldon's Hilgard home on the occasions of his often impromptu soirees and met all the neighbours and campus colleagues and their wives - especially the wives - who would probably have judged Eldon less acceptable had they not spent an evening basking in the reflected glory of such eminent company.

Now respectably in his early sixties, in no one's terms other than mine own, Eldon Stuart was eminently admirable, nay heroic.

I'd met him, like many other transatlantic virgins, when I'd first come to America, recommended with an advance copy of my novel dispatched by a friend on the Times Literary Supplement. There'd been no complications in our first meeting - anything sexual would have been a Martha and Martha and so he had no ulterior reason for liking me. But he had not only liked me, he'd been kind to me, even seeing to it that I got my all-important green card. There was also no competition between us - Eldon was a superb literary critic whilst I was merely a writer. Perhaps that's what we each found in the other, what we couldn't do or didn't do or aspire to do ourselves. Anyway, he became my soul's father, the vindication I'd always sought yet thought I'd never find. I suppose that now I merely wanted to emulate his example. But then, and there it goes again, we all have our itch.

He was small, like a bird, with bright eyes and still wonderful hair. He appeared in the doorway, dressed in understated jogging pants and polo shirt, the telephone in his ear and beckoned to me smartly, a broad smile on his face. I took my overnight bag and my housegift and heaved myself, aching, from the confines of the Jeep.

When I got to the door, he'd replaced the telephone and held out his arms. We hugged. He unwrapped the antique Navajo quilt I'd picked up in Flagstaff and cooed ecstatically.

"Dear boy. Dear, *dear* boy!" He touched my cheek in gratitude. "Come through, come through. I shall put it out immediately." He draped it over one of the three cream linen couches in the living room.

"I'm glad you like it."

"Oh I do. But you shouldn't. It must have cost an arm and a leg!"

I held out my arms and bent my knees.

"Nope," I joked. "Look, all present and correct."

"Well, it's lovely. Just delightful. Now . . . a drink? Or would you like to go to your room first?"

I sank into one of his enveloping wing chairs and mimed drink. He bustled over to his drinks table and mixed us martinis. I closed my eyes as the ice rattled comfortably in the shaker and he twittered on about my generosity.

"Here you are, Jeremy." He took a seat across the pine, sawn-down coffee table. "Welcome. Welcome back to Los Angeles."

"Thankyou, Eldon. I think it's good to be back."

"You think? You don't have any regrets, do you?"

I realised how ungrateful I must have sounded.

"Not about the job, no. Certainly not. I'm looking forward to it. I hope I won't be a disappointment to you."

"I'm not worried about the job, dear boy. Ha!" He whistled through his teeth. "You're a born communicator and a very good teacher. You care. That's quite enough. No, what will disappoint me is if you don't start work again. Your own work. That would be a waste."

"I shall let you be my deadline, Eldon. That's bound to keep me up to the mark."

He pushed over a bowl of chips.

"I had them put your boxes in your room. I take it the ones marked `fragile' are your word processor."

"Oh, they're here already?"

"This morning. Two very accommodating young gentlemen struggled in under the burden."

"Accommodating?"

He laughed and toasted me with his martini.

"Oh and by the way, Andy called for you? Do I take it that he is still a significant other?"

I chuckled, wondering what priority on Andy's call list I

had made that day."

"Significant, yes. Other, yes. Significant other . . . definitely not. What time did he call as a matter of interest?"

"It was a message. Quite early, though. I went out to the gym at seven-thirty so he must have called sometime before nine when I got back." Oh, I thought . . . I should have been honoured. One of the first calls of a busy agent's day.

"So what have you been up to, Jeremy. Out there." Eldon waved eastwards, airily. "Have you written anything or has your drama work taken over completely? How was life in the heartland?"

I grinned at him and shook my head. He re-filled our glasses.

"It was . . ." I was about to say interesting. I was about to say what I thought he wanted to hear. "It was lonely, Eldon. Very, very lonely," was what I finally admitted to.

"It can be lonely anywhere," he observed.

"But how is it possible to miss something you don't want?"

"Aaah," he chuckled. "Dogs can survive on brown rice."

"That's very Confucian."

"Yes, I rather like it. It's one of those images you have to think about a bit but it comes, in the end. You see, however much the dog fills its belly with rice, he always dreams of meat. And talking of meat, I hope you're hungry. Eugenia has left us a delicious casserole." He got up and hurried through into the kitchen. I heard him opening the oven and clattering plates. I heard glasses chinking and cutlery being arranged. Other thoughts crowded in as I remembered that big kitchen room, some evenings of heavy, heated discussion, others of quiet, erudite conversation. The living room was a haven of peace, comfort, continuity and stability. I remembered my own home, my parent's home in Sussex, where I'd felt so secure, safe and positioned, like a link in a solid chain, as important as the links on either side and the the ones next to them and . . .

I looked around this room, its walls hung with paintings

and drawings of friends, from friends; at the needlepoint cushions from friends, by friends; at the pots and artefacts collected all over the world but mostly presents from friends; the photographs in their frames, smiling groups with Eldon somewhere in the middle and always with someone's arm round him, always being kissed by someone, always with someone.

That's what I hadn't brought back with me from the heartland. I'd found nothing there to walk away from; I'd left nothing behind.

"Dinner's ready, dear boy."

"Coming," I called and got up. The martinis were strong and I felt a little light-headed as well as very, very tired. "I did have one rather interesting encounter, though," I announced as I went into the kitchen.

✻ ✻ ✻ ✻

Brik and Ryder had arrived earlier the same afternoon. Cool as they'd tried to be about coming out to LA, they were fazed by the maze of freeways. Neither wanted to be the first to admit that they were lost but it was some two hours after hitting Glendale when they finally pulled up outside the Century Wilshire Hotel, 90223 Wilshire Boulevard.

As LA hotels go, the Century Wilshire is okay. It was close to to Andy's offices at Buckman Miller further east on Wilshire and so it was convenient and Andy was playing his hunch about Brik with a very tight fist. He wouldn't have booked any other of the agency clients in there but then other agency clients would be paying for themselves.

However, to Brik, the hotel was just fine. Better than fine. After they'd registered and been shown their room, Brik brought in the bags - no porter at that time of the afternoon - and Ryder parked the Jeep belowground.

Both boys showered. As Ryder took his, Brik called Andy and was put on hold.

Ryder came out of the shower, a towel round his waist.

"Who're you calling?"

"Andy. He said to soon as we got in."
"Oh. Right."

Ryder went to the window and drew back both the curtains and the nets behind them. The room had a view of the pool and there was a little balcony outside the french windows. Several guests were sunning themselves around the pool's limited confines. As Ryder appeared in the window, they seemed to sense a change in the horizon and looked up. Ryder withdrew quickly and came and sat on the edge of the bed opposite Brik. Brik watched him combing his wet hair. Ryder had been fine the whole trip, full of plans and schemes, dreaming big dreams out loud but he had gone strangely quiet as they'd been driving in to the city.

Brik had been holding some five minutes. "I'm sorry, Mr Peters," came the voice of Lindy Green, the Buckman Miller telephonist. "Mr Horowitz will call you right back." Brik replaced the receiver. Ryder's somewhat disinterested behaviour made Brik embarrassed about the excitement he felt. He had tried to generate enthusiasm by gee-whizzing about the hotel, the beds, the size of the room, the kitchenette. Ryder had come back with merely "It's okay, man". Ryder had decided to be decidedly unimpressed by anything.

"What's the shower like?" said Brik as he stripped off his clothes and laid them over the back of the chair by the window. From his jeans pocket, he removed the letter from Andy Horowitz and the now scrunched up sheet of Jeremy's filofax with the telephone number and address. He stood in front of the window trying to iron out the creases in both pieces of paper.

"Better watch it, man. There's people round that pool."
"So?"
"So they'll see you, dammit," snapped Ryder.

"Oh," Brik said, acquiescing. He refolded the papers and left them on the table and moved away from the window, into the bathroom.

"This ain't some swimming hole in the sticks, Brik," Ryder called as the shower jet whooshed into life. "You gotta be careful."

Brik didn't reply; perhaps he didn't hear. He certainly didn't hear Ryder's muttered addendum . . . "Now you're gonna be a fuckin' star." Ryder got up and pulled the cord that drew the nets. As he passed the table he picked up the addresses Brik had left there. He glanced at them for a moment and then very deliberately tore up the creased filofax sheet into small pieces and carefully disposed of them between the yellow pages of the LA telephone directory.

The telephone rang. The ring was soft. Ryder waited, knowing it was for Brik, waiting if Brik would hear it. There was no reaction from the bathroom. Ryder lay back on the bed and lifted the receiver.

"Hello."

"Brik?"

"No. This is Ryder McKigh." Ryder knew full well who it was but played it grand. Distant. He sounded cool, he thought. Authoritative.

"Hi, Ryder. This is Andy. Is Brik there?"

The noise of the shower from the bathroom continued.

"Er . . . No. He's . . . He's just stepped out. Can I help?"

"Yeah. Just say that I called, say welcome to LA and tell him I'll be round to pick him up to go see Gerri Muntz at nine sharp tomorrow, okay."

"Sure," said Ryder, obligingly, performing with a matter-of-fact diffidence any director would have been pleased with. "Is that Muntz with a tee zee, Andy?"

"That's our lady."

"And that was nine in the morning, yeah?"

"You got it."

"Should I take that address and number? Just in case."

"Good thinking, Ryder. It's 8924 Sunset, corner of Robertson and Sunset. Gerri Muntz Associates." Andy waited for a moment, assuming Ryder was writing all this down. "Got it?"

"Sure. I'll tell Brik."

"So, how are you enjoying LA, Ryder?"

"Oh, we love it. 'Course, I've been here several times

before," Ryder lied. "So it's no big deal for me."

"Oh, right," came Andy's reply. "Well, I gotta get on. See you tomorrow, probably."

"Probably," said Ryder. "'Bye now."

"'Bye 'bye."

Ryder replaced the receiver and grinned. Probably? Definitely.

He rearranged the pillow against the headboard of the bed and lay back, his arms folded behind his neck. The shower stopped in the bathroom and he heard Brik swish back the plastic curtain. He appeared, drying himself, towelling his hair

."That feels great," he said, standing in the doorway. Ryder didn't reply. "You okay, Ry?"

"Sure," Ryder replied curtly without looking. "Why shouldn't I be?"

"No reason."

"Andy called."

"He did? What did he say, man?"

"He said he'd pick us up tomorrow at nine. See someone called Gerri something. Didn't catch the last name. Some casting director."

"Oh, yeah. He told me about her. He said she was the person I had to make a real good impression on."

"We will," said Ryder slowly. "Don't you worry. She sure as hell ain't gonna forget us."

✱ ✱ ✱ ✱

I made my excuses to Eldon after we'd done the dishes and he showed me to my room. It was not unfamiliar to me. I had stayed there for a month after moving out of Andy's house, whilst I was waiting for the reply from Scotland about the job that would take me out of the ugly arena I'd been so vainly fighting in. Then, almost three years ago, the last call I would have dreamed of making would have been to Andy. Tonight, remembering our last conversation, I wanted to call. If time was a fish, I was reeling it in that first night in LA, rewinding the line connecting me to the past. But now I felt the tide was with running with me, that the fish didn't have the advantage of the ebb. My pole wasn't bending and straining; the action on the reel was smooth and easy.

"Hi, Andy. It's me."

"Hey! At last! When d'ya get in?"

"Couple of hours ago."

"Good trip?"

"Wonderful. Went to the Canyon. Grand, by the way, not Laurel."

Andy giggled.

"Honey, I get vertigo even on Laurel. You coming over?"

"Not tonight. Just checking in."

"Still guarding that precious virginity?"

"For a while. I kinda like it. Are the boys here?"

"Sure. I'm taking Brik to see Gerri Muntz tomorrow. Say, what's this with the other guy. Ryder?"

"Oh, Ryder. I think you'll find they come as a package."

"You mean?"

"No, I don't mean. Go easy on them, Andy."

"Right, coach. So, when will I see you?"

"Is tomorrow soon enough?"

"Er . . . Tomorow's not good for me right now, Jeremy. Could we make it Thursday? Dinner? Lemme take you to Citrus."

"Or you could come over here. Eldon wouldn't mind."

"Er . . . Let's go out."

"Why?"

"Eldon makes me nervous."

"He likes you."

"He makes me nervous. Always did. So come over here about seven? If I'm not back, you know where the key is."

"Okay. 'Night, Andy."

"Night. Oh, mom sends her love. I just finished talking to her. She's longing to hear from you."

"Thanks. See you."

SEVEN

The following morning, before Brik had stirred, Ryder was awake and up. He was the first into the coffee shop to eat the continental breakfast the hotel provided. The attendant in the coffee room was foreign, not Mexican, not oriental; some race Ryder hadn't seen before. The man seemed to speak little English, at least no English that Ryder could understand. He downed his second cup of coffee and the muffins and then checked with the desk clerk the street reference Andy had told him the day before.

He rode the elevator down to the parking lot beneath the hotel and started his Bronco. He drove out into Wilshire traffic and followed the boulevard to Beverly Hills, turning left onto Santa Monica and left again onto Robertson leading to the building housing the casting director's company.

Having made sure he knew exactly where it was, he then drove back to the hotel.

Brik was awake, watching television, when Ryder returned to the room with coffee and muffins.

"Where the fuck have you been, Ry?"

"Just gettin' my boy here some breakfast. Shouldn't you be getting up? Gotta make a good impression, remember?"

"Yeah. Did you eat breakfast already?"

"Not hungry. Had some coffee, though. Now move your ass, Brik." Brik threw back the bedclothes and emerged naked for his baptism. "Shit, don't you *ever* wear clothes, Brik? If I see your dick one more time this week, I'll throw up, man."

"Your're just jealous, McKigh." Brik glanced down at his early morning detumescence. "Git down, boy. Your ole Uncle Ry's acting all riled up today." Brik dashed for the bathroom as two pillows flew across the room in his direction.

"What're you gonna wear?" Ryder called.

"Whaddya think I should wear?"

"What y'always wear," Ryder replied. "Shirt and jeans.

Go like the part reads, man."

As Brik showered, Ryder sipped his coffee. What he'd figured was that if somehow, he didn't get to go along with Brik and Andy, he would offer to collect Brik afterwards. He figured if he went along while Brik was being seen and waited in the office, he could elicit more information about the rest of the casting. It wasn't Brik who was the problem; in fact Brik would insist Ryder came along. It was Andy Horowitz. Andy was the unknown quantity that morning and Ryder was taking no chances.

The 'phone rang. This time Brik heard it. The bathroom door was wide open.

"The 'phone, Ry."

"I hear it."

"Will you get it? I'm right in the middle of shaving."

"Sure." Ryder picked up the 'phone. "Hello."

"Brik?"

"No. It's Ryder. Is that you, Andy?"

"Yeah. Listen, I'm running late at my breakfast meeting. Can Brik get himself to Gerri's office. I'll meet him there?"

"I'm not sure," said Ryder, uncertainly. "I guess I could drive him in my car. He doesn't have one of his own. I guess I could cancel my appointment."

"That'd be real kind, Ryder. I'd be very grateful."

"My pleasure," Ryder replied. "What I was doing can wait, I guess. After all, anything to help a friend. It's a big day for Brik."

"Great. I'll see you there nine-thirty, okay?"

"Okay. See you."

Ryder was just replacing the receiver when Brik came through, wiping shaving foam off his ears. He was wearing his shorts.

"Who was it?"

"Andy. He's running late. I'm gonna drive you to Gerri Muntz's."

"Oh. Great. Did you take the address? Do you know where it is?"

"I'll find it. Move it, Brik."

Forty minutes later they parked in a side street at the top

of Robertson, on a meter.

"Guess I'll just hang around down here and wait for you," said Ryder, inflecting just enough pathos to put his point across.

"I'm not going in there alone," Brik said. "You gotta come with me, Ry. Please. Don't die on me. Not now. I need you, man."

"Okay," Ryder agreed, with sufficient reluctance. He removed the keys from the ignition. "Got any quarters?"

"I think so. But why?"

"The meter, dummy. This is a city, Brik. It's not a hick town. Here you have to pay to park."

"Shit," said Brik and handed Ryder his change.

Five minutes later, the boys rode the elevator up to the fourth floor and presented themselves at the reception.

The telephonist looked up, quite pleasantly but with no special deference. Two good-looking boys were mere stock in trade and they weren't thin on the ground in her part of town.

"Hi," she said briskly. No smile, but no offence meant.

"Hi," said Brik. "We have to meet Mr Hororwitz here. Andy Horowitz. The agent?"

"Yeah," drawled the pencil thin black girl, her red nails hooked like talons round the telephone. "I wasn't expecting him but if he is coming, he's not here yet."

"My friend has to see Miss Muntz," Ryder chimed in. "At nine-thirty."

"Okay," replied the receptionist, "let's see." She ran the talons on her other hand down a list. "You Brik Peters?" she rapped out to Ryder.

"No."

"So you're Brik Peters?" she directed to Brik.

"Uh huh."

"Good. Okay. Ms Muntz has been a little delayed. Take a seat and wait, please." She indicated a couple of couches rectangled round a white melamine table and the boys sat down.

No sooner had they done so but the opaque glass doors swung open and Andy Horowitz came in with a woman.

They were chatting, Andy's enthusiasm being more gushing than his companion's.

"Morning, Gloria," said the woman, a shortish, plainish, thirtyish dark haired woman with round, owl glasses, black blouse, culottes and boots, an enormous newsboy-type satchel slung over her shoulder. "You remember Mr Horowitz, don't you?"

Andy was unctuous with the receptionist. Useful people, receptionists. Gerri Muntz collected her mail and her calls and rifled through them.

"Of course. Nice to *see* you again, Gloria." It was then Andy noticed Brik and Ryder. "Ah! There you are, Brik." Brik rose to his feet, feeling nervous, gawky and awkward. The low table cut into his knees as he tried to edge round as quickly as possible. "Gerri, I want you to meet Brik Peters."

Gerri Muntz turned round, smiled and held out her hand. Brik stumbled over Ryder's feet and out into the hallway, not knowing whose hand to shake first. He got to Gerri's first. Then Andy's.

"Nice to meet you, Brik," she said. "Andy has told me a lot about you. I do so admire agents who travel. Too few do it these days."

"I think it makes a better agent, Gerri," Andy opined. "I travel a lot."

"So, where is it you've come from again, Brik?"

"Scotland, ma'am. Scotland, Ohio."

"Sounds a long way away," she smiled. "It was your graduation play, wasn't it?"

"Yes, ma'am," Brik grinned. "Rosencrantz and Guildenstern Are Dead." He paused. "By Tom Stoppard. He's British."

"I do believe I have heard of him," she said and winked at Andy. "But, I believe, not British by birth. Anyway, very commendable," she commented. "You must have had a very adventurous teacher."

"Oh, we did. Ryder and I will always be grateful to Mr Page."

"Ryder?" she murmured. "Who's Ryder?"

"This is Ryder." Brik turned and indicated Ryder who lounged, as nonchalently as he possibly could, in the corner of the couch. "My best friend."

"And," Andy quipped quickly, "as you can see, Gerri, they're far from dead. Hello again, Ryder."

It was Ryder's turn to get up. He did so easily, without Brik's clumsiness.

"Hi," he said, smiling.

"Gerri Muntz," said the casting director, holding out her hand. "Pleased to meet you. By the way, which was which?"

"Excuse me?" said Brik.

"In the play. Who played what part?"

"Brik was Rosencrantz," Ryder replied. "I was Guildenstern."

"So which one am I seeing this morning?" Ms Muntz asked, half turning to Andy but her eyes firmly on the two young men in front of her.

"Er . . . it . . . er . . . was Brik, Gerri," Andy piped up. With no reply, Gerri Muntz turned sharply on her booted heel and made for an office on the far side of the hallway. Three pairs of eyes watched her every step. She turned at her door. "So why don't I see *both* of them, *Mister* Horowitz," she announced. Brik and Ryder looked at each other, then Andy, then back to `our lady'. "Come on, guys. I'm a busy, busy girl." She disappeared into her office.

Andy put a firm hand in the smalls of two backs and fairly propelled Brik and Ryder in the right direction.

"She likes you," he whispered, hissing into the space between their ears. "I have a good feeling here. Just go for it, guys. Don't let me down."

Inside the office, Gerri indicated two chairs in front of her desk. No one knew where to sit.

"Andy, if you don't mind, I'd like to hear the guys alone. And before you say it, I know it's their first appointment. Don't look so worried. I won't eat them."

"Sure, Gerri. I'll be right outside. When you're finished. If you need me."

Gerri indicated the two chairs and the boys sat down as

she closed the door on Andy.

She sat down behind the desk and flipped open a yellow legal jotter and flushed through a script. She handed Brik four sheets of paper, part of a script.

"Now, Brik. Here are your sides." She paused and glanced across at him. "Brik," she mused. "That's a punchy little name. Perhaps a little too punchy. Got another one?"

"It's short," Brik explained quickly. "For Berwick."

"Berrick," she repeated, scribbling down the name on her pad which was exactly how his name was spelled from then on. "Much better. Brik's a little . . . how shall I put this . . . raunchy." Brik coughed. "Now you . . . Ryder?" Ryder nodded. "What's your surname?"

"McKigh," Ryder pronounced. "I'm Ryder McKigh."

"Now that I like," Gerri affirmed. "Just as it is. Here, take my script," she went on. "I want the both of you to read. Berrick, you read Danny. And Ryder, you take Tony. But before you do, can you remember anything from Rosencrantz? How are your memories? I want to see first what it was that Andy saw that took him so far out on a limb.

✲ ✲ ✲ ✲

Ron Windel drove into the parking lot at the airport, took a ticket from the dispenser and parked. He always found it remarkable how Cleveland's airport had grown since he was a child.

He took his bag from the trunk and central-locked the BMW with the remote. He walked towards the courtesy bus stop, dragging the wheeled suitcase and clutching his briefcase with its precious contents in the other hand. His heart quickened with his pace as he saw the bus pulling round the lot and he began to run.

His annual visit to Kenneth Morrell in Los Angeles had been a long time coming that summer and he looked forward with greater anticipation than ever to the reunion. Kenneth always had something brand new and very exciting to show him although, this year, Ron had decided to take with him something which he knew would equally excite Kenneth. Something which only he had had, something which Kenneth now would never have.

Ron clambered aboard the bus. He was no longer as svelte or as well-proportioned as he had been at med school. Kenneth had been on at him for the past two years to do something about himself but he'd ducked the issue as soon as he returned to the monotony of life in Doddsville. He'd started drinking again and he'd never been able to refuse good food which was his only constant comfort. He was, he knew, definitely out of shape. But right now, he wasn't worrying too much. He had something that vindicated his lack of condition. Ron Windel had money, money that would be only too acceptable by the new and urgent young men whose availabilities had been collected for him by dear Kenneth, young men who would gladly make his stay in LA both pleasurable and memorable - American Express, sir? That will do nicely.

And memorable his two week vacations each summer had to be for they were the only weeks in his year Ron Windel got to properly lose himself in his fantasies. Not that Kenneth's contacts came cheap but then what else, Ron justified, did he work so damned hard for? For what else did he so dutifully fulfill his parents wishes and assuage that ingrained Jewish guilt? His small country practice and his life in Doddsville, Ohio, was penitentiary to Ron; his trips to stay with Kenneth were his only real parole.

Since Brik Peters had left for California, no longer to be as available as he would have been in Illinois just across the state line, Ron Windel was determined to make the most of this summer's vacation. There was no knowing when another Brik Peters would show up in Doddsville. Like never. Right?

EIGHT

"How long have you guys been in town?"

Gloria's question was tinged with incredulity. Brik and Ryder were waiting outside Gerri Muntz's office after their appointment, high on their performance with which Gerri, for Gerri, had demonstrated sincere appreciation.

"We got in yesterday," Brik replied. "From Ohio."

"O-Hi-O," Gloria repeated, monosyllabically as though she had heard Brik say `Betelgeuse'. Ryder was busy scribbling details down with pen and paper he'd gotten from Gloria's desk.

"That's correct, ma'am," Brik grinned. "It's maybe not much to you but it's home to us." Gloria ignored what she could have taken for a rebuke.

"And your *agent* is taking you to *lunch*?". Gloria couldn't believe she had heard Andy Horowitz right. Wasn't it the frosting on the cake? Wasn't that an accolade awarded only to the cream of the crop? She still hadn't quite overcome her amazement at seeing an agent arrive with his clients at what was only a pre-preliminary meeting. Who *were* these guys?

"Anything wrong with that?" Ryder said, looking up. He'd been writing down every name, company and location Gerri Muntz had mentioned in her briefing as to where they were due and what they would have to do at their film test the following day.

"Nuthin' at all," Gloria replied. "It's just that . . ."

"What?" Ryder demanded.

"Well, lemme tell you, I know guys who've been in and out of this office a hundred times. They may change their names but I gotta good memory for faces. I bin seein' them for years. These guys have hardly ever *seen* their agent, 'cept once, when they signed on." Her telephone rang and the scarlet talons clattered over the buttons on her micro-switchboard.

"I feel kinda weird," Brik whispered aside. "What's so strange about lunch? I thought everyone in this town had lunch. D'ya reckon it's code for something we don't know about?"

Ryder rolled his eyes.

"Lunch is lunch is lunch, Brik." He sighed. "She's just lettin' us know she's impressed, that's all."

"Like we're privileged or something? Gee, Ry."

"No. Like Andy Horowitz thinks he's on a roll. She liked us, Brik. Didn't you get that?"

Gloria ended her call. Another buzzer sounded and she answered Gerri's invitation to step inside the office.

"Kinda like being at the doc's," Brik suggested. "Or waiting outside the principal's office. Is that what you mean?"

"A roll, Brik," Ryder jibed impatiently. "Think like a *bank* roll. Andy thinks he can make money on us." He paused. "And you know what that means?"

"That he's gonna make a lotta money?"

"That *we're* gonna make a lotta money too."

"Oh," said Brik. "But that's good, isn't it?"

"Sure the fuck is, buddy."

Gloria returned with Gerri's script and she photostated four pages. These she handed to Ryder. She passed them over, cheekily, lasciviously, bending sufficiently low to allow him to see the promise of her prominent femininity.

"You're Ryder, right?" Her bright pink tongue darted over her heavily reddened lips.

"Yeah."

"These are your sides. Same as his."

Gloria nodded her head towards Brik. "You have to learn 'em for the test tomorrow."

"Thanks," said Ryder. Gloria lowered herself, the movement constricted by the tightness of her leather miniskirt. She managed to end up perching on the edge of the table, next to Ryder, her skirt now impossibly high on her thighs.

"Are you gay?" she said, sounding like a black Mae West.

"Wouldn't think a pretty girl like you needed to get off on faggots," Ryder opined, almost with a snarl.

"I don't," she replied. "Just askin'."

"So I'm tellin'," Ryder countered and out came that bright pink tongue again.

"Wanna know somethin'?" she offered with a conspiratorial wink.

"Tell me," Ryder replied with a gratifying leer. "If it's worth knowing."

"You're in this thing with a chance, guys. A big chance. Good luck to you."

"Thanks," said Ryder. "Anything else?" He leant back on the couch, stretching his legs out in front of him beneath her seat, spreading his legs slightly in the process. His eyes never left the girl's yet they contrived at the same time to take in every inch of her body, giving her the full attention her attitude required.

Like a tall black rocket straining to leave the ground, Gloria got up, reluctantly abandoning the launch pad, leaving behind her a cloud of Giorgio and the promise of giant leaps for mankind.

"Perhaps," she murmured.

"Hey! Like what? Don't leave me this way!" Ryder drawled.

"Like leaving me your number, Mr Ryder. You never know when something might come up for you."

Brik blinked. He stared wide-eyed at this blatant interreaction. Ryder tore off a corner of paper, scribbled down a number and handed it and her pen back to Gloria. She glanced at it, folded the scrap of paper and tucked it into her blouse.

"The name's McKigh," Ryder prompted. "And by the way, that's an impressive filing system," he grinned.

"It's the best," Gloria replied, turning on her high heel as she heard Gerri's office door open. "Important things tend to get overlooked in the office roladex."

Gerri and Andy came out of the office and shook hands. Ryder and Brik took their cue and got up, hovering.

"See you tomorrow, guys," Gerri called and waved. "Gloria, bring my script in would you and then get me Lou Hales at Burbank."

✽ ✽ ✽ ✽

Andy hustled the pair out of the office and into the elevator.

"Okay, guys," he said, smiling widely as the doors glissed shut. "I *think* it's time to talk a little business."

They followed him across Sunset to Hamburger Hamlet. After they'd been seated and given menus, he started in.

"Okay . . . It's like this," he began. "Hey, Brik! Put down the goddam menu, hey?"

Ryder frowned.

"Sorry, Andy," Brik apologised. "Sorry."

"Right. Now, tomorrow you drive over to Universal, right? You know how to get to the Valley?"

"We'll find out," assured Ryder.

"Right. You give your names to the gate and they'll call up Lou. That's Lou Hales, right? He'll either send someone down to collect you or the gate marshall will direct you to the Telemax office. Lou has to meet you before they do the test and so has Dick Molina too . . ." Andy paused. "You with me so far?"

"Er . . .," Brik faltered.

"Sure," Ryder asserted. "Lou Hales is the . . ."

". . . producer," Andy interrupted. "Lou *is* Telemax as far as you're concerned. He has partners but Lou's the guy *you* guys need to know about. Dick Molina is the director. He did most of `Washington Heights' and wrote most of it too. 'Member that show?"

"I liked it okay," said Brik a little dismissively. "Got a little ragged though."

"So don't tell *him* that," said Ryder urgently. "As far as he's concerned, it was a rave from start to finish, okay?"

"You *cried* when it came off, right?" Andy added and clapped his hands. "Good boy, Ryder. You're learning."

"So what about this test?" Brik asked.

"Just do what you did today with Gerri. She just *loved* you, by the way. Told me she'd never seen such great interaction."

"And what do we wear," Ryder continued, "or do they

give us clothes? I think what we got on today is just right."

"Absolutely," Andy agreed. "Perfect."

"Will you be there?" asked Brik.

"Uh uh. You're on your own from now on. I can't do anything else for you . . . until *after* you get the roles, right?" Andy beamed. "Then we'll start cooking." The waitress appeared.

"Okay . . . Are we ready to order?" she intoned, pen poised over pad.

"Coffee for me . . . and maybe a salad," said Andy. "Guys?"

"Can I have one of those?" said Brik, pointing to a neighbouring bruncher's platter of burger and fries.

"Sure. Dressing on your salad?"

"Thanks," said Brik.

"I meant what *kind* of dressing . . . Thousand Island, Ranch, French or Blue Cheese," recited the waitress with a sigh.

"Oh . . . er, French?"

"You don't like French, Brik. It has garlic. Make it Thousand Island and I'll have the same," said Ryder, taking over. "And two coffees . . . Please."

"No. I'll take a Coke," Brik corrected. "Please."

The waitress hurried off, her sensible shoes squealing as they grudged their way back to the kitchen. Andy pulled an envelope from his pocket. He removed the papers it contained and with his pen changed a few of the words on each of the two pages. The boys looked on, Ryder craning over the table. Upside down, it seemed as though one sheet was a copy of the other.

"What's that?" he asked as he saw Andy writing his name beneath Brik's and adding another line of dots for an extra signature.

"It's just a temporary agreement," Andy murmured, concentrating on attending to the crossed t's and dotted i's. "'Til I can get the proper contracts drawn up."

"You mean we have the job?" Brik gushed.

"Not so fast, Brik," Andy grinned. "That's outta my hands. All I can do is give you the *chance* to get the job."

Ryder was doing some rapid thinking. Brik's excitement gave him the leeway he needed.

"Oh, I see," Brik replied. "You must think I'm pretty dumb."

"Not at all," Andy replied. "It's good that you ask questions."

"So the contracts you're talking about here are with you, Andy. Right?"

"With my company," Andy corrected. "Your signature gives me - us - the authority to negotiate on your behalf, see?"

Ryder leant back. He picked up his fork and toyed with it. He moved sufficiently to allow the waitress to set down the coffees and the coke. He watched Andy explaining all the above to Brik. He watched Brik happily accepting all that Andy was saying and as he watched, something held Ryder back, some niggling, wriggling doubt prevented him from joining in what should have been a delirious brunch. He heard what Andy was saying but not in the same way Brik was hearing.

"And," Andy continued, "we have to be sure we're acting on your authority because my company is laying out money for you. Hotels, this brunch - that sort of stuff." He laughed. "They're very strict with me. It's not all expense account. Those days are *way* past. We have to be able to legally reclaim this from your paychecks."

Think. Think, Ryder urged himself. Think, McKigh.

"Can I read it over first?" Brik asked. He lightened his request with a laugh. "Like they say in the movies, always check the fine print, hey?"

"Sure," said Andy encouragingly. His salad arrived. "I'll have the finished contracts ready for you tonight. Have Jeremy look 'em over if you like but I do need your signatures now, on this. Right . . . there." He pointed and doing so, brushed his fingers against Brik's hand. Andy looked up for a reaction, left his finger dangling but Brik was too involved, too excited to either notice or pursue. {See?"

Ryder saw.

"How much does your company take?" Brik enquired. His tone was so friendly and open that Andy was unfazed and he started explaining the percentage, the whole proceedure of how the production company paid the agency who then paid the client.

"Sounds fine to me, Andy."

As Brik spoke, Ryder arrived at the conclusion of his scrabbled consideration. He remembered his father; he didn't often think about Gordon but sitting at that table, one memory of Gordon materialised through the ether. It had been after church one Sunday. Ryder was ten, maybe twelve.

He'd asked his father why they always put so much money in the collection plate.

`For the church', Gordon had said.

`Why, dad?'

`It's our duty, Ry. It's up to us to keep the church going. Pays the preacher for one thing.'

Ryder didn't especially like church, didn't enjoy sitting still, unable to ask questions or answer the rhetorical exhortations launched over the heads of the congregation by Pastor George. "And *how* will you know the Lord," the Pastor would roar. How indeed, Ryder always wanted to answer. Ryder disliked being smartened up and cleaned up by Dory, could see no attraction or advantage in the unkempt Pastor George and definitely couldn't understand why his father gave him money to put in the collection plate when both Gordon and Dory were endlessly discussing how little money they had.

`But what does Pastor George *do*, dad? He only works Sundays. You work all week.' Gordon had smirked then laughed out loud, winking at Dory the far side of the bench seat.

`No answer to that, is there, honey?' he said.

Dory turned on Ryder.

`Pastor George is the man who gives us the chance to be with God,' she explained, rather peremptorily. `Can't put a price on that, Ryder. It's beyond price.'

`But who *is* God,' Ryder had demanded, `I ain't never

seen him. What does he do for us? We need the money more'n him, surely, mommy?'

`Ryder!' Dory scolded, `I'll hear no more of this. You mind your tongue when you talk against the Lord that way. Mind it or he'll make it fall off!'

But Ryder noticed that his tongue hadn't fallen off. It didn't even feel loose. Gordon opted for silence as they continued the drive back home.

`Daddy?' Ryder pressed on, dangerously close to the line, `have you ever seen God?' There'd been a sharp intake of breath from Dory. Gordon hadn't answered for quite a while, long enough for Ryder to begin to urge his question again.

`No, son. Can't rightly say I have. But there's some things you just do. Like when your Uncle Don and I joined the army. You sign your name on the dotted line for your country and off you go to fight. Not that you ever see your country, or even the President. You just do like you're told.'

`Like little boys do like *they're* told,' Dory added, `and that includes you. No more questions, Ry. Do like you're told.'

Think like you're told, do like you're told. The memory of this lowgrade theology lesson faded from Ryder's mind although its message was branded into his program of reactions. Then, sandwiched between his parents on the front seat of the old Chevvy, he'd been taught the best moment to quit, one of the first of many childhood occasions when the child learns to keep its own counsel, to save it for a better day. Think what you like, ran the lesson. Just know when to keep your mouth shut and when to open it and holler.

Now, years later, sitting eating brunch in Hamburger Hamlet, two thousand miles from home and church and light years away from childhood, Ryder knew he'd grown up. He knew he didn't have to sign on the dotted line until he knew exactly *why* and for *whom* he was signing. No one was there to make him sign and he knew why, as yet, he didn't feel in the least inclined or obliged to sign.

As with girls, Ryder needed to be wooed, even seduced

and, as yet, he felt distinctly taken for granted.

"Ryder," said Brik, passing over the now signed covering letter. "Your turn. Right here, see? Just below mine."

Andy pushed away his hardly touched salad, scrunched his napkin and picked up his filofax. He pushed his chair back.

"Stay round the hotel today, guys. You need to get on top of those sides, anyhow. I'll bring your contracts by later." Ryder, holding the pen, scanned the agreement almost desultorily. "Don't wanna rush you, Ryder but I *do* have a meeting."

Ryder put down the pen and looked at Andy, smiling all the while.

"There's no rush, Andy," he replied, quietly, pushing the letter across the table, through a dribble of dressing spilled on the polished wood. The letter soaked up the oil, soiling it, rendering it almost contemptible.

"Ry . . .?" Brik frowned.

"Is there some kind of a problem?" Andy asked, rather firmly. His eyes were suddenly cold, all the yahoo bonhomie had flown the coop.

"No problem at all."

"So? Why aren't you signing?"

"Because you haven't asked me if I want to sign with your company? I'm not Brik, Andy. I'm me. Ryder. Ryder McKigh."

"Aw, come on, Ry!" said Brik, impatient and more than embarrassed. "Andy's bust his ass for us here."

"Correction . . . Partner," observed Ryder. "He's bust his ass for *you*. Me? I just came along for the ride, remember? I'm just the sidekick. I'm Tonto, man. You're the Lone Ranger in this show. I was just doing you guys a favour. All the way down the line. All for one, remember?" Ryder sipped the last of his coffee. "One for all?"

Andy put down his filofax, drew his chair back into the table. He folded his arms and leant forward resting them on the table.

"Okay . . .," he began, the formal courtesy etching his

words. "Okay, Ryder. I take your point. Look, I would really like to have you sign with our company. I believe you *could*, note could, have some kind of a future. You've started off well but you've only *just* started." He paused. "But let me make one thing clear. *If* you get this part and *if* the pilot is made and *if* the networks take it up, Telemax will *not* be interested in you negotiating on your own behalf. It's like in a court. You *have* to be represented."

"Why?" Ryder asked gently, his frown of affected ignorance masking his impertinence.

"It's just the way things get done in this town," Andy explained, as patiently as he could muster. "Look guys," he said, sensing as surely as his instinct told him that the moment had come to apply the pressure. "I don't *have* to do this for you. We can just pull out. Simple. Anytime we want."

"No one's talking about pulling out, Andy," Ryder offered, almost generously and acting offended.

"If you don't like the deal, I can cancel this whole damn thing," Andy ultimated with icy reasonableness.

"Hey!" cried Brik in alarm. Ryder quickly put out his hand onto Brik's arm.

"Look, Andy," Ryder countered, "I *do* like it. Brik likes it but don't tell us that you'll cancel this thing because you won't. You can't. Gerri Muntz really digs us, man. I *know*. You *can't* cancel `this whole thing'. If you did, you'd look pretty damn foolish. Excuse me. I mean no offence."

Ryder finished. Andy kissed his teeth. The waitress brought the check.

"So, where do we go, Ryder?"

"We go on, Andy. I'll sign with you. For this deal, okay?" Ryder paused. "Then we'll see. If it's a turkey, whaddya lose? If it's a success, then persuade me . . . Persuade me to stay with you."

Andy sighed.

"Brik?" he asked. "Are you still cool?"

"Me? I'm fine, Andy," Brik replied briskly. "I'm great."

Andy gathered his filofax once more and got up.

"Right. I'll have the papers drawn up and I'll see you

guys later, right?" He reached for the check. Ryder's hand got to it a split second before.

"That'll be *my* pleasure, Andy," he smiled.

"Oh . . . Right." Andy was rarely wrong-footed. "Thanks, Ryder." He spoke slowly. Something . . . He met Ryder's smile. Jesus, he thought to himself, this guy is something else . . . He returned Ryder's smile with an equally beguiling one of his own. Yes, he thought, I can do business with this guy. "Perhaps you guys'd like to come to the house one day?" he heard himself saying. "Whaddya doing Saturday?" The boys looked at each other and shrugged agreement. "Great. But I'll see you tonight, about six, okay?" They nodded. "See ya later."

Brik stood up as Andy left. Ryder counted out bills and change and left them on the check plate. This was his church now and he knew only too well why he was contributing.

"Gee, Ry. You *sure* you know what you're doing?"

"I sure do, buddy. I sure the fuck do." He pushed back his chair and winked at Brik. "Come on, we're outta here. I'm expecting a call."

NINE

Gerri Muntz stood patiently next to Lou Hales and Dick Molina. They had all now taken stock after the initial interview with Berrick and Ryder. All had been pleased with the word-perfect reading the boys had delivered, Gerri especially and now she basked quietly in the vindication of her professional recommendation of which Lou and Dick had been initially so sceptical. Casting directors have feelings too.

Clem Barber re-positioned his camera and the lighting team re-set the minimum rig. Dick had already blocked the boys' moves. Brik was lying full length on his stomach on the long couch in the Telemax bungalow which was standing in today in lieu of the ultimate set. Ryder stood behind the couch as Clem pulled focus, running through the various moves Dick'd rehearsed with the boys for light and sound.

They were making like the office bungalow was the living room of `Tony's' home. `Tony' was Ryder's character's name . `Danny', Brik's character, is `Tony's' best friend. `Tony' and `Danny' are two high school friends but from opposite sides of the tracks. `Tony's' family has money and he is set to go on to college, `Danny's' has none, is large and Mexican, the father being sick and needs `Danny's' income just as soon as he can start work after graduation. The pilot script had been written to develop into another Freshman, Frat House, Happy, Happy Days with a social point. The four page scene the boys had read showed `Tony' smarting after his parents have announced their impending divorce and `Danny' persuading his best friend that if he thinks positive, life can be okay.

Dick had had no need to call for quiet on the set. The crew went about their business silently and efficiently. Clem murmured requests and the actors went through their moves noiselessly on the deep pile carpet.

"I like 'em," Lou muttered under his breath to no one in particular. Thinking aloud. Gerri, her ear ever attentive, heard and smiled to herself. "The magazines'll eat 'em up."

"Let's wait for the moment of truth," counselled Dick who had assumed that Lou's remark had been meant for him. "They might look shit on tape."

"I like 'em," Lou repeated emphatically. He gave himself further silent encouragement by wondering if the boys could sing, working out who he could guide them towards for recording spin-offs from which Telemax could earn and, reminding himself that as debutantes, he could get the boys cheap. Top quality at bargain prices. That pleased Lou Hales most of all. Buckman Miller wasn't an agency to really reckon with. Andy Horowitz wasn't an agent whose calls had ever been Lou's first priority to return. Lou loved that feeling of power, that certain knowledge that it would be *him* calling the shots. That was the particular buzz *he* derived from the whirligig of the entertainment carousel.

"Okay, Dick. We're ready here," Clem Barber called from the camera. Dick Molina strode over and stood beside Clem. "They're gonna look good," Clem ventriloquised to his boss as the lighting and sound crew withdrew to join the other Telemax secretaries and assistants who had all gathered to watch, drawn magnetically by news of good news. In Hollywood, all news was good news except when it was bad. Clem stood back and allowed his director to look through the viewer.

"Mmmmm." Dick couldn't help but agree, but he was a cautious man. "Okay, guys," he called. "In your own time. I'll call `action' and then take it whenever you're ready."

A thick, velvet hush enveloped the darkened bungalow.

"Action."

TONY　How could they do this to me, man? Now of all times.
DANNY　So when's a good time to face the truth? Tell me that.
TONY　Not right before I go to college, dammit.
DANNY　You're being unfair. (Pause) And you wanna know something?

DANNY COMES ROUND FROM THE BACK OF THE COUCH AND SITS NEXT TO TONY ON THE COUCH.

TONY   You're gonna tell me anyway.
DANNY   Someone has to. Not only for your own good, for everyone's. I like your dad, Tony. And your mom. But they're unhapy. It's killing them. It's much better they split.

TONY ROLLS UPRIGHT AND SITS ON THE EDGE OF THE COUCH.

TONY   That's okay for you to say. Your folks'd never dump on you like this. (Pause) God! I HATE 'em.
DANNY   No you don't. (Pause) You're just a little scared and there's nothing to be scared about. They still love you even though they don't love each other.
TONY   If this is love, buddy, lemme tell you . . . Leave me out of it. I don't need it. Let 'em go to hell. Both of them. I don't need it and I DON'T need them. I don't need any of you!

DANNY MAKES AS IF TO PUT HIS ARM ROUND TONY'S SHOULDER BUT ULTIMATELY REFRAINS AND GETS UP.

DANNY   Oh, you do, Tony. Believe me. Do us all a favour, hey? You're supposed to be the clever one. The one with all the brains. Let's see you use 'em . . .

DANNY LEAVES AND TONY IS LEFT ALONE. HE REALISES DANNY HAS GONE AND TURNS AND PUNCHES THE COUCH PILLOWS ANGRILY THEN CRIES.

"Cut," Dick called.

Immediately, a ripple of spontaneous applause broke out as crew, production team and cast alike turned, as one, to Dick. Brik returned to the couch and stood. Ryder rose to join him.

"Do we go again, boss?" Clem barked, defusing any excess of euphoria. The boys looked expectantly as Dick swivelled his chin, his 'thinking' mode.

"Why waste good tape?" Molina grinned and clapped Clem on the shoulder. "That's it folks. Thank you *very* much."

A buzz of conversation broke out as Dick went over to

congratulate Brik and Ryder. "That was okay, boys. You did good. Just what I was looking for. The script will be better, I can promise you that but I've only been on the project a coupla weeks. It needs me, believe me." He winked. "You wanna take a break now? Go for a stroll. You might spot some famous faces if you go to the commissary."

"Can we *move it along here*!" Lou shouted over the noise. "I want my office back pronto. You," he barked at a tardy secretary, "get back to work, dammit! Clem, lemme have that tape fast, right?" The bungalow was quickly repaired. Lou Hales led Dick away. "Nice work, guys!" he called over to Brik and Ryder. "Stick around. We need to talk."

"Sure," Brik called back. "We ain't going anyplace."

Ryder smiled and waved. He nudged Brik.

"Come on, man. Let's take a walk."

No sooner had they got outside into the late morning, late summer LA sunshine, than their excitement erupted, unrestrained any longer by `cool' deportment. Brik let out a whoop of pure, pent-up joy and Ryder yelled `Yeah!' and punched the air. Then they hugged each other and danced round and round.

"We're on our way, Brik old buddy!"

"You reckon? Gee, that felt great, didn't it? What a *buzz*, man!"

"The best," Ryder panted as they disentangled. "Oh, dear Lord, the best!" He sank back against the fender of the yellow Bronco, pulled up alongside Lou's Rolls on one side and Dick Molina's Porsche on the other.

Brik felt as high as the hills, felt the top of his head somewhere level with Mulholland Drive where it snaked invisibly along the ridge of the Hollywood heights. He too was adrenalised, his veins pumping with boundless, throbbing energy. He started doing push-ups against the fender.

"Some (up) rush (down) hey (up) Ry? (down)." Brik pushed himself up with a bounce and let another whoop of excitement. "When d'ya think they'll tell us?"

"Now, man. Today. I *feel* it," said Ryder, leaning back

against the hood, tilting his face upwards, to drink in the sun.

Gerri Muntz and Clem Barber came out of the Telemax bungalow. Brik and Ryder came to attention, like two naughty schoolboys caught truanting by teacher.

"Would you look at that?" Gerri said to Clem. She smiled, nodding in the boys' direction. "It's days like this when I feel I've done something worthwhile."

"But do they know what you've gotten them into, sister?" Clem remarked flatly, his somewhat high-pitched voice hissing like a spray can, besmirching with dog latin graffiti Gerri's noble, lofty sentiment. Whatever. It brought her back to earth. She was forced to acknowledge that the monuments to *her* particular art and craft seldom remained pristine for long. She wasn't yet in the Stalmaster league.

"Who cares," she snapped, stung by the cameraman's cynicism. "I'm not their mother and, thank God, I'm *not* your sister." Gerri was aware of Clem's `other' work and her feminist sensitivities bristled. "Anyway, do *you* care? I would have thought you'd not exactly recoil in horror at the prospect of some fresh meat on the rack."

"Oh. Tooshay," Clem camped. "And *where* did I hear you found them?"

Even without knowing what she knew about him, Gerri had disliked Clem Barber on first meeting. That he was good at his work, there was no doubt. Dick Molina used him a lot and she'd done replacement casting on 'Washington Heights'. As soon as they'd been introduced she knew there was something unsavoury about his very aura, something which slavered like a hungry, cringing dog. Gerri didn't usually dislike anyone but this drawling, drooling queen, however good his professional reputation might have been, offended her. She abdicated further confrontation and just walked away from him, his original question still ringing in her ears.

"A little place east of Sodom, dear," was her parting riposte. "And way off your map."

Clem sniggered. He could afford to get under her skin. Other people got under his so why shouldn't he get under hers? Big fleas have little fleas upon their backs to bite 'em, and little fleas have lesser fleas and so . . . ad infinitum.

"Andy'll be in touch, guys," Gerri called out through her open window as she started her engine and reversed out. The boys waved.

I am as horny as hell, Ryder reflected as he watched the casting director drive away and wondered what she might be like in the sack. After all, he'd already got a date with the secretary, why not the boss?

"Hi Mr Barber," Brik said as Clem walked towards the Bronco.

"Better make that Clem," replied the cameraman.

Ryder re-focused his attention on the possibility of immediate advantage and grinned as he lounged against his car.

"So what did it look like, Clem?" he asked, embellishing his attitude with that special, roguish, lop-sided grin.

"Pretty good," Clem replied, taking in Ryder's pose with a quick up and down. Then it was Brik's turn for appraisal and here Clem found what he had been looking for, what Brik's nervousness and his own attention to his work had hitherto clouded. "From my point of view, at least," he said to Brik.

Brik felt his stomach knot. It wasn't a cramp, nothing serious. Just a surge of rather pleasurable anticipation. He was well aware of the sign. It was a signal. He knew he was being observed. He knew Clem Barber was not only reading his face but that he was x-raying his body. He too grinned, but his smile was boyish, not roguish, real, not performed, joyous, not veiled. Brik too leant back on the high black fender; slowly, he crossed one leg over another, adjusting the contours of his jeans and noted the directional change in Clem's frame of vision.

"Have they seen a lotta guys for our parts?" Ryder pushed on.

"Some," said Clem. "But they've all been actors."

Ryder threw out his hands.

"So what does that make us?"

"You're fresh," Clem replied. "Sorta natural. You'll get to

know what I mean when . . . I mean, *if* this thing goes ahead. So far, the casting's all pros, kids who were already acting in diapers."

"And us just a coupla country boys," Brik shrugged in jest. "Green as winter wheat."

"Are you?" Clem remarked suggestively. "You look about as green as baled hay to me, kid. Are you sure you guys haven't done anything like this before?"

"Only in school," Brik answered. "Acting class. That's all."

"But you look . . . I don't know," Clem whined, "kinda familiar."

"You must be thinking of someone else," Ryder countered. "We only just got here."

"Yeah," said Clem. "Probably. But I got a real good memory and I just wouldn't forget a . . . faces like your's," he added, looking directly at Brik. "Berrick, isn't it?"

"So they say," Brik grinned. "But my friends call me Brik."

"Right," Clem drawled, his adenoidal whine extruding deeper implication from the word. "So, see you guys around, hey?"

"Sure," Brik replied. Clem moved away and walked over to his car. "Hey, nice meeting you, Clem!"

"Likewise!" Ryder added. He waited until Clem had got into his Mercedes sports before spitting out, "Faggot!"

"Ry! Ssshhh," Brik cautioned.

"Well he is so."

"Everyone's a faggot to you, Ry." Brik protested dismissively.

"Not everyone," Ryder retorted. "Thank God there's a few good old boys left," he concluded. "Right, my man?"

TEN

Conversation between Kenneth Morrel and Ron Windel on the drive into Bel Air from the airport had been quite as usual. Business, Aids, traffic, the weather, Kenneth's name-dropping.

Kenneth turned the Bentley to face the gates and pressed the button on the remote box he withdrew from the compartment between the deep leather seats. The gates swung open.

It was a moment Ron had long anticipated. He derived an almost atavistic thrill from the sight of his oldest friend's home, reeking as it did of money and status; the right home in the right place. The ultimate in the American dream, a far cry from Doddsville. Kenneth had surely been lucky in meeting Sherman although it seemed to Ron that Sherman Franck, despite his keystone importance in the arch of Kenneth's life, had been quickly forgotten. Sherman had only been dead two years.

The millionaire and the medic; a couple for the sixties. But now it was the nineties and life ran on. Ron had been there with Kenneth that summer on the beach in St Thomas when the meeting had been forged. Then he and Kenneth were just two freshly graduated med students with their eyes on the future.

Funny, Ron remarked to himself as he did every year. The gates swung silently closed behind the purring Bentley. Funny how things turn out, he thought to himself. Twenty years ago, on that beach, sunning themselves, Ron had had his eyes closed whilst Kenneth's were always open. Ron had thought that they were so alike. Like two chrysalises, pupating the same moth. But from Ron's had emerged a rather retiring creature who shied away from the flames; from Kenneth's came a fearless predator who not only looked for flames but found them and extinguished them, devouring them beneath the smothering folds of his dark wings. To the young Kenneth Morrell, Sherman Franck, the millionaire carpet queen, was an irresistible flame. Funny,

Ron reflected as the car climbed the winding drive up to the house, how easy it was for some.

"The gates really make it, Kenny," Ron complimented his host. "Sherman'd've approved."

"No he wouldn't," Kenneth snapped back. "He'd have screamed at the idea, fainted at the budget and died when he got the bill."

The car came to a stop in front of the house and a white-coated Salvadorean hurried out of the double front doors, down the steps and opened Kenneth's door.

"It was a constant battle," Kenneth said, unfastening his seat belt. "I had more trouble over twenty years getting that man to spend money than you'll never know."

"Well," said Ron, wondering which control opened his door, "it looks like your troubles are over, dear." Being high off the road, he had less than his customary difficulty in exiting the car with the required degree of elegance befitting his surroundings.

"Damn right," Kenneth replied. "Get Mr Windel's bags, Julio," he commanded the impassive Salvadorean manservant loftily. "Then bring us some coffee if you would. In the study."

Julio opened the trunk.

"Er . . . no. Not that one," said Ron, his fat hand snatching at his briefcase. "Just the valise."

"Yessir," mumbled the manservant and waited, deferentially, until the master and his houseguest had entered the house. "Yessir, fuckin' yessir," he then swore, his distaste unfettered.

"So what's so precious in the bag, Ronnie?" Kenneth threw out as they crossed the cool, dark hallway and into the study. "And by the way, dear, as your personal physician, I'm warning you now that you're not leaving at the end of this vacation without *promising* me faithfully that you'll do something about yourself. You've gotten dangerously overweight again, dear. Look at you! You're dripping."

"It's the heat, Kenny. You know how the heat gets to me."

"It'll be the fuckin' mortician that gets to you first, Ron, believe me." Kenneth slumped into the depths of one of the pair of tartan upholstered antique wing chairs. French doors were open onto a verandah-ed terrace outside, bougainvillea and passion flower trailing from the edges of the roof, brilliant purple and orange. The study itself was the epitome of Californian opulence, anglicised in ambience, library shelves running round the walls, persian rugs on the floor and the whole tastefully appointed with imported mahogany furniture.

Ron took off his jacket and loosened his tie. He unhooked his suspenders from his well-rounded, Rubenesque shoulders. He sank into the chair opposite Kenneth and patted his briefcase.

"Do I have something for you in here, dear?"

"Do you?"

"Uh huh," Ron replied, gleefully, running his fingers over the pigskin suede nap. "Something that only comes along once in a long, long while."

"You'll be struck off one day," Kenneth teased. "I've heard what small-town gossip can do. I should know. I live in one."

"Doddsville isn't so small anymore. Lotta Cleveland companies have moved in. We're almost a city. Anyway, I'm careful. Only outta town boys from the small ads."

"Except," Kenneth observed, "as I am obviously meant to infer, your latest subject."

"This was one was worth it, Kenny. Believe me."

Kenneth couldn't resist baiting his over-keyed country cousin. He knew full well that as friends they had lost anything they may once have shared. Kenneth now rather pitied his med school contemporary and usually, two days after Ron arrived in California, Kenneth found himself wondering why he perpetuated the annual institution. The only reason, he concluded, was that Ron unwittingly provided perspective although a little of that artifice went a long way in Kenneth's current circumstances.

"So, you'd better show me," Kenneth replied, still determined not to be impressed. Julio appeared with coffee. "Set the tray down there, Julio. I'll pour. That'll be all. Tell Dolores to set lunch by the pool."

"Yessir."

Julio withdrew, silently closing the study door behind him.

As Kenneth poured the coffee in Wedgewood cups, Ron snapped open the catches on the briefcase and withdrew three large manilla envelopes. Reserving two on his fat lap, he handed one to Kenneth as he took the proffered cup of coffee.

"I take it that you still take cream and sugar, dear?" Kenneth sighed.

"Please."

"Then help yourself. Your death is not going to be on my conscience using my sugar."

Kenneth opened the envelope as Ron spooned sugar and poured cream into his cup. He sat back and watched as Kenneth began idly flipping through the first few photographs.

Kenneth's mask of affected idleness instantly dropped.

His pace of rifling through the ten-by-eights of Brik Peters slowed and after the first dozen, even the world-weary, hackneyed Doctor Morrell could not fail to be impressed.

Ron smirked as he sipped his coffee, now confident that at least on one occasion in their competitive, emulatory relationship, he, Ron, had acquitted himself `cum laudae'. For Ron Windel, it was a moment of great reward.

"So whaddya think?" Ron cast out rhetorically. "Dear?"

"I am . . ." Kenneth paused, feeling his loins incorrigibly stirred. "I have to congratulate you, Doctor. Quite a specimen."

"It's the way they grow 'em out on the prairies. Magnificent genes, don't you think?"

Kenneth finished the first batch and Ron was there ready with the second. Kenneth removed two photos from the first batch and set them on one side. They were from the Highway Patrol collection.

"So what does this agricultural phenomenon do?"

"He's going to college. At least, he was."

"I meant, dear heart, have you `known' him as they say in the Bible?"

Ron almost squealed with delight. For Kenneth to demonstrate such a curiosity meant that Kenneth was envious. Imagine, Ron had wished as he sat on the plane, imagine Kenny being jealous. Of *me*!

As Ron graphically admitted that indeed he had had such `knowledge', he fairly trembled with joy; he fairly crowed as he recalled and recounted the weekend afternoons when, after the photographic preamble, his subject had become his master, when the gentle high school jock had turned disciplined coach; when he, Ronaldius, the humble slave had prostrated himself, abased himself, grovelled on his knees at the feet of Brikio, the glorious, victorious young patrician hero, towering so nobly above him, the sunbeams kissing the golden skin of the warrior god as the light inched through the rents in the curtains of the ten dollar motel bedroom.

"And where did you meet him, pray?"

"At the bus station."

"Oh. Puhleeese!"

"No, truly. He was waiting for his mom to come pick him up."

"Who now brings you apple pie in a little rush basket covered in red gingham," Kenneth quipped, unable to resist.

"Kenneth! I'm serious!"

Kenneth fanned himself with one of the photos.

"Well . . . good for you, dear. So when's the wedding?"

"I told you. He's going to college. Rather he *was* going to college."

"Is? Was?"

"He got this call . . . It's all garbled really. Y'see, he was in a graduation play and his teacher had a friend who's a movie agent here in LA. The agent was visiting, saw the play and got the kid an audition. He's here now. Somewhere."

"And you mean to tell me you don't know *where*?"

Ron shrugged, helplessly.

"As I said. We're hardly engaged. It was a very professional relationship."

"So he *is* a whore?" Ron shook his head, definitely.

"No way. Not at all," he protested.

"But you paid him?"

"Sure I paid him. Only a few dollars."

"How many dollars?"

"Twenny. Sometimes thirty."

"You certainly don't believe in sparing the rod, do you?" Kenneth whistled.

"Look, he's just a real nice kid. He seemed to get off on it all just as much as I did."

"Oh, puhleeese! He got off on your money."

"What do I care?" Ron snipped. "But you're wrong. I wish you could have met him. I always said you should come visit."

"Would you mind if I had some of these," Kenneth asked, ignoring the veiled rebuke. "My private collection, you know."

"Be my guest," Ron replied magnanimously. "They're all yours. I brought them for you as a housegift."

"How thoughtful, dear," Kenneth murmured. He set aside the final envelope and sipped at his coffee. "I shall treasure them." He looked at his watch. "By the way," he added, "we're being joined for lunch."

"Oh? By whom? Anyone I know?"

"No. I don't think you've met Tommy."

"But is he cute?" Ron letched, sensing that Tommy might be the first in what was the long line of playmates Kenneth had usually procured to fill his vacation schedule.

"Tommy Cattini is not cute," Kenneth replied. "Except perhaps to Mr and Mrs Cattini in Jersey City whose loins he sprang from. No, Tommy is my new business partner."

"Business? I thought you'd sold Sherman's business."

"Oh, I did, dear." The sensitive Doctor faked a shudder of horror. "Mass market carpeting was *never* my bag, *as* you will recall."

"So?"

"Tommy is a movie producer. And distributor."

"Would I have seen any of his movies?"

"There is that possibility, yes."

"How exciting! What are his credits?"

"Does *anyone* remember the credits on porno movies, Ronnie?" Kenneth replied lazily, dropping this shock pearl adroitly into the conversation.

"Porno?" said Ron, wide-eyed and now bolt upright in his chair.

"Sure. Why not?" Kenneth threw away carelessly. "Makes more than medicine, honey."

Ron whistled.

"And you were telling *me* I could get struck off!"

"And if I was," Kenneth said languidly, "who'd care? Certainly not my investment broker. The only reason I stay with the practice is that most of my patients are my friends - at least people I know socially. Why should they object when they get little pharmaceutical cocktails from me as well as their videos hot and fresh off the copying machines? Anyway, I'd resign before they could fire me."

"Don't you care anything about medicine now?"

"Nope," Kenneth said flatly.

"But Sherman was so proud of you."

"Sherman was a sick old man," Kenneth retorted, quickened to annoyance. "I was his insurance. Simple as that. And I *don't* want to talk about it," Kenneth vetoed.

Ron knew when to quit. He lightened up immediately although a rather worrying seed had been sown in his mind.

"They'd never believe this in Doddsville," he chuckled and reserved consideration of the other matter until he could ponder it alone.

"We're not in Doddsville," Kenneth sparked back with acid distaste. "Anyway," he went on, lightening up himself, "Tommy has a little movie for us to see. *And*, dear heart," Kenneth went on, lowering his voice and injecting a proportionatal secrecy into his tone, "*if* you're free Tuesday evening and *if* you're a very good boy, you could have a personal audience with the star."

"Who is?" Ron hardly dared to ask. He felt his mouth drying. He felt that visceral stab of nerves deep beneath the folds of flesh that now overlaid his lap; he moistened his lips and leant even further forward in his chair.

"Oh . . . just Trick Rambler," said Kenneth quickly. "More coffee, dear?"

※ ※ ※ ※

Ron had excused himself to his room after lunch when Kenneth announced that he had some business with Tommy.

"Jesus!" Tommy whistled as he handed Kenneth the check in the privacy of the study. In his other hand, he was holding one of the photos of Brik. "And you're *sure* we don't know where this guy is?"

"Sorry, Tommy," Kenneth replied as he locked the Innuendo Productions dividend check in his desk drawer. "And such a natural, wouldn't you say?"

"Jesus," Tommy repeated and fell silent for a moment in admiration. "Hey!" he said suddenly, "I know some cops. I could have them put out an APB on our boy!"

"For what reason, dear?" Kenneth enquired. "Even your bent cops would have to give a good reason to their superiors." He sighed. "No, Tommy, I'm afraid that there are some things in life you get and some that get away . . ."

"Mind if I take one?" asked Tommy, running his chubby, be-ringed finger lewdly down the contours of Brik Peters' inner thigh.

"Be my guest." Kenneth picked up the cassette on the desk. "I take it Trick made it after all?"

"Oh, yeah. But you're right, Ken. He's gettin' in too deep. I heard from some of the guys he's in to `the man' for more than he's earnin'."

"Oh for the days of the contract stars," Kenneth commented wearily. "So. Any other ideas?" Kenneth asked.

"Sure! Like this wonder!" Tommy enthused, tapping the photo he held. "Don't we even have a name?"

"No."

"Shame. Still, magazines'd snap these up. I know I could sell 'em, if your friend Ron would give me the rights. I could get him two, three hundred?"

"Small beer, Tommy," Kenneth said curtly. "And don't ever mention you've even had that thought in front of Ron." Kenneth smiled, like a hawk, if it knew how, would smile as it hovered high above a helpless jackrabbit. "He still displays worrying symptoms of integrity."

"Poor guy," mocked Tommy. "Is it dangerous, Doc?"

"Nothing I can't cure. Let me work on my *oldest* and *dearest* friend for a while. There are more ways than one, Tommy dear, of skinning a cat..."

ELEVEN

The telephonist from Buckman Miller called at six to ask me if I would meet Andy at Citrus, instead of at his home as we had arranged.

I was disappointed not to have had a call from Brik by the time I left Eldon's around seven that Thursday, leaving half-an-hour to get to Citrus and my ice-breaking dinner-date with Andy. I consoled myself at least with the prospect that I would have news of him from the horse's mouth, over dinner. My logic told me horse's ass but I drove with as open a mind as possible.

Words of truth or words of crap? That ever-present alternative seemed to aptly sum up my relationship with Andy Horowitz. But there were many other alternatives - logic versus emotion, reason versus sentiment, addiction versus need. Always the `versus'. Though my relationship with Andy wasn't a declared war, it bore an inevitable potential for conflict. I was determined not to be late. He was the one who had always been late in our shared past and tardiness was a piece of ordnance on either side that the battlefield would be more survivable without.

As I drove along Wilshire and made my way through to Melrose, it was a balmy evening. I hadn't had the cover on my Jeep all summer and I was reminded of the very first night I arrived in LA I'd hired a convertible, very extravagant and bought a Beach Boys tape amongst others from Tower Records on Sunset. I drove the Boulevards and Avenues that first night, the Wilson boys' harmonies on the stereo locking me irrevocably into the Californian dream.

Seven years later, I played the same tape, somewhat crackly, but it fitted the same bill. I felt rather silly. Like I was going on a date, the hope of bright new mornings ahead. I reminded myself that I'd woken on the bright new mornings and discovered that the sun didn't always shine all day long in California.

On Melrose, I was held up for some reason in a line of traffic. I saw a police car's beacon light flashing white and blue ahead.

Please, *please* let me not be late for him! Perhaps there'd been an accident. Or a shooting, not an unheard of occurence. Maybe there was death or injury; non-redeemable human life was possibly ebbing away on the sidewalk just ahead and all I could ask God was not to make me late. Was this the California conscience I'd acquired? If it is, please, *please*, my kindly English God, if you're there, forgive me?

Had I been meeting anyone but Andy, I might, just might, have been on line for an indulgence. But for Andy Horowitz? No chance.

The line of traffic eased past what was only an arrest. Two policeman had a Black splayed out against the side of a decrepit Chrysler Baron. I heard one of the cops snarl an order, the last words of which were `black bastard'. One heard such things in open-topped cars. But they were only words. At least they weren't beating up on the poor guy. Relieved, my mind warped back to Andy as I drove on.

I suppose I must have fallen into a classic trap with him when we first met. Fresh off the London plane, I'd fallen for what was only the third Los Angeleno I'd spoken to. Undoubtedly there'd been mutual attraction; unforgettable, on my part, even now. Physically, we were a perfect yin yang, an exquisite fit; those early days were the works, together we made a smooth and effortless machine, its camshaft rising and falling in exact synchronisation with the belts of fuel, air and electricity delivered by the engineering. He was tall, dark and very handsome to my tallish, fair and okay in certain lights. He was Gable, action, at 'em and ardent, to my Kelly, cool, cultured and capricious. He was LA. I was London. We each sought and saw in each other what we most wanted to find because of what we each felt we lacked and without which were incomplete. Together, for a while, we had made a whole.

We went through that and we came out the other side; the cowboy, chafed by culture, wore the acquaintance uneasily. The cloth was the best but the coat never fitted despite the many, vain alterations. The ice queen, kissed by fire, had melted mis-shapen, irregular. There were awkward bumps where there had once been only perfect contours.

Looking back, I know I *could* have changed. It wouldn't have been that difficult, given that I couldn't change him. But I hadn't changed and Andy hadn't even understood why he should even try. So we called each other names, spiteful maybe but nevertheless therapeutic. I've forgotten what cruelty I'd employed in dreaming up the epithets I hurled at him. Mercenary was probably in there somewhere; egotistical came close behind. Superior, tight-assed and high-minded were the qualities I was bequeathed. Oh, and `English'. Somehow `English' was always used in conjunction with either and or all of the above; like black - `you bastard' is not great but it's okay. But try `you black bastard'. Not nice at all. `You bastard' I could live with. `You tight-assed English bastard' veered to the racist. I suppose we did beat on each other although I never called him Jewish - maybe I should have countered race with race. Maybe that would have given him the excuse to hit me and for me to have hit him back. Then, perhaps . . . Maybe . . .

Maybe, maybe. Maybe we *could* have then made up, having cleared up that necessary spillage of disappointment, anger and reproof which was by then leaking obviously from the cracked seal between our hitherto hermetic yin and yang, a leak we proved incapable of plugging.

It was valet parking at Citrus. In the restaurant, the sliding windows had been opened and the hot breath of night-time LA, an indescribable smell but embracing hot steel and viscous tar, permeated the cooled interior of the minimalist white restaurant.

The maitre d' led me to Andy's table. To be ideologically sound and incredibly perfectly politically correct, as the role was occupied by a female, I suppose maitre becomes maitresse d' and the lady concerned certainly conveyed the impression that she was mistress of all whom she surveyed entering her domain. She power-dressed too, stopping short of dominatrix but definitely a fearsome chatelaine.

Anyway, my arrival was obviously not a surprise.

"Oh! *You're* Andy's friend!" she beamed as though the intimacies of me and Andy were common knowledge in this neck of the woods. "He's waiting for you, Jeremy."

My Englishness quivered as I followed her through the packed restaurant. I'd forgotten the instant familiarity of the casualness of LA, having become used once again to the deference of the provinces.

And there he was.

"Hi!" he said as I arrived at the table. He got up, got out and enveloped me in a big hug. For all to see. "Sit down ... And have you noticed?" He grinned, that wide, generous mouth parting to show off that expensive and enviable miracle of Beverly Hills orthodontic achievement.

"What?" I smiled, looking around me. "It's nice. Nice place. Is that it?"

"No, dingaling! I'm on time!"

He could be so damn smart and so bloody charming. I laughed. At moments like this, he could be so very lovable.

"I hope I am. I haven't even looked at my watch," I lied. The wine waiter appeared and we ordered something. Wine, I think.

"It's so damn good to see you, hon," he said.

"Yes," I said. And it was. It was a little bit of something I'd returned to. Not exactly needlepoint cushions and family photographs but it was something.

"You look great. That tan suits you."

"That's what driving through five states gives you," I replied.

"Well, it's great that you're finally back."

I felt coy as I murmured "Likewise". I knew how much he was trying. He was wearing the shirt I'd sent him last Christmas, even the watch I'd bought him when my novel's option money came through. He'd actually remembered and, I had to confess, if he hadn't, I would have forgotten I'd ever given him these things.

I'd even forgotten what his body was like, really like. In my mind, what memory I retained was now unreal, distorted by fantasy and by my attempts to block out the past. I could feel his eagerness and it made me shy, almost to the point of recoil. Our knees touched under the table and I felt embarrassed, like we weren't somehow allowed such corporal contact.

We ordered our food and then we toasted ourselves.

"And while we're at it, let's raise a toast to your protegeés," he added. "To Berrick and Ryder."

Though I instinctively raised my glass, my mood collapsed, like an incorrectly-balanced souffle removed unpropitiously from the oven. Not his fault. He wasn't to know that he had broached the only subject other than himself which I nurtured. The person I sat opposite disappeared as the doppelganger materialised. Andy Horowitz, the man, was suddenly commuted into Andy Horowitz, the agent. I thought he'd displayed an excessive pleasure in seeing me again but I could say nothing, least of all because for those few moments on first sitting opposite him, I'd forgotten Brik altogether and I felt cheap, as though I'd betrayed myself for a sentimental convenience.

"Do I take it that your ass is now *off* the line?" I ventured. I felt even sillier than I had on the way to the restaurant; but this wasn't `a date', was it? I was his `dinner meeting', at the other end of Andy's day from his `breakfast meeting'. For all I knew, there was probably a `nightcap meeting' to come, perhaps not `inked' but probably `pencilled' in his fucking filofax. You're a fool, Page, I reminded myself. You're old enough to know better.

I slapped myself resentfully, reproaching myself for having allowed myself to drift into a situation in which, I suppose, I'd vaguely thought that meeting Andy again on home turf would resolve my own life; in which I would have been led, gratefully, back to that completeness, that whole I felt such need of. Dammit. Was it *so* much to expect, that someone else might voluntarily take the reins and whip my life in the semblance of a positive direction?

Andy finished recounting the incidents of the last two days, incidents which were already being mythologised into a good story.

"Ryder was never backward coming forward," I replied on hearing about Ryder's `grit'. That I thought him a pushy little bastard, arrogant and insensitive, was not a definition Andy could have taken on board. It would have cast him in a very poor light and detracted from his story.

"They went overboard about you, hon," Andy went on. "Every chance they got. And you know something else?"

"What?"

"Gerri Muntz knew you! Not that she's *met* you but she *read* your book." He spoke as though it was incredible that anyone in his exalted pantheon of contacts should admit to such a bizarre practice as reading.

"I wonder if she bought a copy or merely borrowed it," I wondered aloud. "Either way, tell her she's my friend for life."

"You could still do it, you know, Jem," Andy urged seriously.

"The only thing I seem to be able to do at the moment with any certainty and confidence is nothing," I replied.

"You need energising, hon. You need someone like me to put a little zip into you."

"Personally I prefer buttons, dear."

He laughed.

"That's hardly my department," he said. "Is it?"

"No," I said, smearing grin onto the grief sandwich that passed as my face. "I suppose it isn't."

"Don't you think it's great we've got all that behind us?" Andy asked, quite sincerely. "Sex and . . . y'know, that stuff. It really got in our way, don't you think?"

"I rather thought it was supposed to," I replied but he didn't hear me.

"We sorta forgot what it was really all about. Being friends. And we *are* friends, aren't we? I know I am. I mean . . . we could really get on with our lives, now."

"We have been," I said. "Haven't we?"

"I mean together," he said. "You need pushing. I need to push. I could do that for you, if you'd let me. But not from afar."

"I don't need pushing," I said, predictably over-reacting.

I bit my tongue and sighed, "Andy, I need to *want* to again. To want to do something. Anything."

"So move back to the house, Jem."

"No," I said quickly. "I mean, no thankyou, Andy. It's very kind of you but I'm quite happy at Eldon's. I'm going to take things slowly and one at a time."

"Oh," he murmured. "But I'd give you all the space you needed, all the time you wanted to be by yourself."

I know, I thought. And it would be *your* gift and I could never forget it. I felt a complete heel. The very thing I'd thought I'd wanted had been offered me on a plate with my after dinner chocolate mint and all I could do was leave it lying there and eat the mint. I suppose, to add the impossible to the unobtainable, it would have to be the *right* hand to lead me, a hand I wanted rather than one I needed.

"Tell me, are you lonely, Andy?"

"Me!" he exclaimed. "Jesus, I wish I was. I run my ass ragged round this town all day, everyday. I can hardly find the time to get laid."

"I think I'm lonely," I said.

"But you're a writer," he observed with all the confidence of a connoisseur of the genre.

"Only when I'm alone," I said. "Not when I'm lonely. It's like I'm paralysed."

"You need to get laid," he sprang, as though it were a tedious and unnecessary panacea to trot out.

"You're absolutely right, Andy."

"So, I'll arrange it."

"I'm sure you could, love. And a bloody joyless jack-off it would be." I sipped the last of my wine. I could feel the `meeting' drawing to an end. "I have one problem. I still have my hang-up."

"Ah," he concluded. "That."

"Yes. Silly, isn't it."

There was nothing more to say.

"So, whaddya doing on the weekend?"

"Don't know," I shrugged. "Any suggestions?"

"You wanna come over Saturday night?"

"Sure."

"Brik'll be there."

"Oh," I said, "I've just remembered. I can't Saturday. How about Sunday?"

TWELVE

On hearing Brik's good news, Mitzi wanted to come out to the Coast immediately. Brik managed to dissuade her, explaining how much there was to do and how they'd never see each other while the pilot was filming. Brik was trying to bring the call to an end when Ryder came back from grocery shopping at Westward Ho.

"Is that your mom?" Ryder mouthed at Brik. Brik nodded and put his hand over the mouthpiece.

"You wanna speak with her?"

Ryder shook his head and took the two bags of groceries into the kitchen.

"Tell her to say hi to your dad," he called loudly from across the room.

"Did y'hear that, mom? Ry says hi," Brik repeated down the 'phone. "To dad . . . No, mom, of course to you too . . . Dad's where? . . . Oh. Does that mean we're talking or not talking . . . I see . . . Yeah. I hope so too, mom . . . 'Bye. Love you."

Brik put down the receiver. Ryder came out of the kitchen of the junior suite with a beer.

"So how's it back home? Has your dad come round now it's certain?"

"It's better. Not great but it's better. Haven't you spoken to Dory yet, Ry?"

Ryder shook his head.

"It'll keep. Anyway, your mom'll tell her all she needs to know. Janna okay?"

"Yeah. She sends her love." Brik lay back on the bed. "Y'know something, I wish we didn't have to wait so long to get started on this thing."

"Heck, it's only a week, Brik. An' like Andy says, we'll be pretty busy next week with wardrobe and stuff. The time'll soon go."

"It'd be great to get some money, too," Brik ruminated. "How's your's holding out?"

"Okay," Ryder replied. "As soon as that bank gets onto my mom, I'll have my allowance sent through . . . Brik?"

"Yeah?"

"Do me a favour . . . a *big* favour?"

Brik sat up.

"Okay . . . What is it?" he asked warily.

"I gotta date."

"I know. With Gloreeaaah!" Brik kidded. "So where you guys goin'?"

"Er . . . we're not. I don't think it's going to be a movies and pop corn kinda date. I got the strongest vibe she wanted to stay in."

"I see . . . I get it," Brik grinned. "So you want me outta here, right?"

"I'd do the same for you, Brik . . . Honest."

"Okay, okay. I'll hold you to that." He paused. "Just two things. For how long and do I get to use the car?"

"'Til as late as you can make it and yes." Ryder fished in his jeans pocket and tossed Brik the keys to the Bronco.

Brik caught the keys and got up off the bed. He scooped up his money from the table and went into the bathroom. He came out a scond or two later and tossed a package in a brown bag to Ryder. Ryder dropped whatever it was and bent to pick it up.

"Rubbers, man," Brik laughed. "And if you want my advice, wear two up."

"Thankyou, Doctor Ruth!" Ryder called as Brik dodged the high-top that flew across the room and got to the door.

"So where're you goin'?"

"I'll go see Jeremy," Brik replied. "But I'll take a drive first. Up to the Hollywood sign. Catch ya later."

Brik fairly ran down the corridor to reception. He had been longing for a moment like this, when he could be free for a while. Though they had been neighbours all their lives, living cheek by jowl in such close proximity to Ryder necessitated a break especially with so many new bases to touch.

Brik drove out into the traffic and headed north in the mid-afternoon heat. It felt so . . . so damn good. He glanced at himself, shaded by his Raybans, in the driving mirror. He looked good, too. He knew it. At every light, the occupants of the neighbouring car would look over - he knew what they were thinking, asking each other . . . "Is that anybody?" He watched the hurried exchanges of conversation, the rapid scan of TV-tuned memory banks to confirm or reject the possibility. Some would wave, mostly women, in case they *might* have been waving at `somebody'. Off-duty stars in the Los Angeles firmament were known for dressing down. Plain white T-shirt, jeans and boots topped with the ubiquitous Raybans often spelled `somebody'. One of the Sheen boys perhaps? Or Tom Cruise? Nah! Too tall for Cruise.

Brik tried to keep sight of the Hollywood sign and headed in its general direction through Hollywood along Sunset to Western where he made a left. At the junction with Los Feliz he decided for some reason to turn off and drove down that tree-lined boulevard with its two and three storeyed apartment buildings. He lost sight of the white painted letters of the Hollywood sign and so had to guage their position and therefore his route.

At the light before Commonwealth, a youngman in an open-topped Suzuki pulled abreast and looked over. This time, Brik looked and tilted his Raybans. He raised himself up slightly in his seat, seemingly so innocently as though adjusting his comfort within the tautness of his jeans. The youngman did likewise, grinned and licked his lips. The Suzuki pulled away first, flashed a right turn and moved into Brik's lane. Brik jabbed his flasher and stayed in lane on the Suzuki's tail.

They convoyed for some time until the road started winding up through scrubby trees. The Suzuki pulled over at one of the few permitted parking places. Brik slowed the Bronco to a crawl and the youngman jumped out and stood, legs apart, thumbs hooked into the loops of his Levis.

Brik watched him in the driving mirror but didn't stop. He saw the youngman throw up his hands and then turn and walk away into the scrub. Brik drove on uphill and finally came to the forecourt of the Griffith Park observatory. He got out and looked up at the impassive concrete building and then walked to the parapet with the view over downtown LA.

"Excuse me, ma'am," he asked the woman of a couple standing close by looking out at the skyline overlaid by the dark gray ceiling indicating the smog level. "What is this place?"

"This is the observatory," she replied. "This is Griffith Park. Are you on vacation too? We're from Texas . . . Say, do I know you? Weren't you on *Dallas* for a time?" The woman would have gone on if Brik hadn't curtailed the conversation with a curt, "No, ma'am but thanks for the information. Have a good time."

One of Ron Windel's stories came back to him. Ron had mentioned Griffith Park one day as one of the places in LA to visit. Ron hadn't said too much more; he'd always been wary of telling Brik too much but Brik sensed that he had stumbled across something he'd long wanted to find, a human game park where the hunters and the hunted were one and the same.

He strode away to an unoccupied stretch of parapet and looked out. It seemed such a huge place, as big as the whole of Scott county, back home but sown with buildings and people and life, not just wheat. The hill sloped away sharply from the observatory, beneath which there were trees and scrubby bushes. The sun had sunk in the sky behind him and Brik took off his shades as he saw flashes of movement amongst the trees. Occasionally, figures would emerge from the obscurity the park provided and Brik noticed that all were single men.

It came again, that familiar churn of his guts.

Driving back down the hill, there seemed nowhere to park until just ahead, a van pulled out and Brik took the space. He took the keys from the ignition and got out. From this small indented parking space, a path led off to the left and Brik strolled to the opening in the trees and took stock. He started walking.

Not a hundred yards along the path, an older man stood to one side, playing with himself, his hand stroking a well-worn patch on the crotch of his jeans. The man leered but

Brik walked on, pretending not even to notice. He risked a backward glance but the man hadn't followed. A youngblack in running shorts panted past, dripping sweat, the hood on his black running top pulled tight round his face, masking his mouth like a ninja disguise. Brik turned but the man ran on.

He rounded a corner in the path where another path veered off to the right. Brik stopped, deciding which one to take when suddenly there was a crashing through the undergrowth and two young whites dashed out, their arms and faces scratched by the sharp, dry branches into which they stumbled. From both paths, running, two more men appeared and brushed rudely past. Then a third.

"Hey, what's going on?" Brik asked. The third man, a tall and exceptionally fine youngman with a mane of streaked blond hair, wearing a singlet almost moulded to his fine pectorals, black cycling shorts hugging his powerful thighs and Reebok high tops, grabbed Brik's arm roughly and pulled him along, back in the direction Brik had walked.

"Cops, man," Trick panted. "You gotta car?"

"Sure," Brik replied as Trick let go his arm. Brik followed as the path narrowed, dipping in Trick's wake to avoid the prickly twigs which overhung their escape.

They reached the road and Brik ran to the Bronco and jumped in. Trick wrenched open the passenger door and Brik fumbled with the key in the ignition.

"Let's *go*, man," Trick urged. "Go, go, *go*!"

Brik started the engine and pulled the car out of the space. He made as if to turn back down the hill.

"No," yelled Trick. "Up, man. Drive up to the top!"

"Okay!" Brik threw the car in gear and rubber burned as the Bronco took off up the hill.

"Not so fast," Trick ordered. "Make like we was tourists. If they stop us, lemme do the talking, right?"

"Sure," Brik replied. He was confused and not a little scared. The onrush of panicked men back in the woods had left him frightened.

"I was just walking back there," Brik struggled to

explain.

"Yeah, yeah . . . That's what they all say, man. Doesn't do much good. They still take you in and book you for somethin'. An' I for one, can live without it. Doesn't do my business *any* good."

They reached the top and Brik parked.

"This okay?"

"Let's hope."

"Did you see the cops?"

"No, but that doesn't mean they weren't there. Doesn't happen often but when it does they round everyone up and head 'em downtown." Trick opened his window. "Gotta towel, man?"

"Sorry," Brik said. "Why do they do it and what were you all doing down there?"

Trick glanced across, a frown and a sort of gimlet-eyed suspicion on his face.

"Oh shit. You're not one, are you?"

"One what?"

"You're a cop, aren't you?"

"No!" Brik protested. "Honest. I don't even know how I got here."

"So you on vacation or what?" Trick interrogated, still not convinced.

"No. Well, not exactly. It might turn out to be a vacation." Brik, versed by Ron Windel in the basic arts of dissemination, pulled together presence of mind sufficient not to blurt out his story to a complete stranger however attractive.

"Well, you must be pretty new in town," Trick said. "You're lucky I grabbed you back there or you'dda had a short vacation."

"Yeah, thanks," Brik replied, still unsure as to the exact rationale surrounding his first encounter with this particular trial besetting what was to be his new lifestyle. "D'you reckon it's safe to leave now?"

"You in some kinda hurry?" Trick asked. He had begun to relax. "But then perhaps you're meetin' your mom and dad at Disneyworld?"

"No, man. My folks are back home in Ohio. I'm here with my friend."

"Oh," Trick parried. "Married so young?"

"No . . . no," Brik faltered. "We're just . . . we're friends. From way back." He felt awkward, being bounced into talking so openly and to a peer who was obviously vastly more experienced and `out' in the big, bad world he had hungered to know so much about from Jeremy Page. "He has a date back at the hotel. I'm just out giving them some space, y'know."

"I think just out is pretty damn near the mark," Trick observed. "How old are you?"

"Nineteen."

"Ever been kissed?"

"Excuse me," Brik said, feeling himself blushing from his very feet and all parts upwards.

"Hey, relax," Trick grinned, enjoying the game but feeling suddenly protective to this innocent. "Only kidding. You *are* new in town, aren't you?" Brik nodded. "Want someone to show you the ropes? Show you around?"

"Sure." He allowed himself a smile. "If that wouldn't be too much trouble. And I owe you, man. Saving my hide, back there. I guess I'm pretty green."

"You're pretty," Trick aknowledged. "Forget the rest. It'll change colour soon enough." Trick leant back in his seat and stretched his tall frame as far as he could. Brik couldn't help glancing across and admiring the perfection of Trick's physique, the easy allure with which he displayed his hardening software. Brik grinned. Trick cocked his head to one side and smiled quizzically at the young outta towner. "You really don't know who I am, do you?"

Brik shook his head.

"Sorry. Should I? Are you somebody?"

Trick laughed.

"Am I somebody?" He laughed again, convulsed by some source of mirth unknown to Brik in his innocence.

"You're laughing at me," Brik said, feeling sleighted.

Trick's amusement subsided. He put out his hand and

rested it on Brik's thigh before kneading the firm musculature. Brik was so nervous he couldn't prevent his legs from shaking. Trick turned in his seat and sought his younger companion's eyes.

"Sorry, man. It's not you. I was laughing at myself. It was suddenly so weird, y'know."

"No," Brik replied. "I really *need* to know . . . Tell me."

❋ ❋ ❋ ❋

And so Trick told and Brik got his first proper lesson, the one that he never learned at the knee of his fallen idol back home in the house on MacMurdo Street. Trick spilled every bean he'd managed to collect as the two youngmen sat side by side in the Bronco for over an hour, recounting the story of how he'd gotten into making movies, gotten into big-bucks tricking, gotten into some of the best homes in Beverly Hills and Bel Air, gotten into personal appearances at clubs, bars and discos, gotten into being a star, gotten into . . .

❋ ❋ ❋ ❋

". . . and could I do with some blow, man," Trick concluded at the end of his story.

"Is that . . ." Brik hesitated. "Is that . . . y'know."

"You mean is that goin' down on some guy?"

"Yeah."

"No, man! I'm talking about a real high." He put a finger against one nostril and sniffed significantly. Brik's face was blank, incomprehending. "Coke, man. You wanna do some with me while we fool around?" Trick looked at the clock on the Bronco's dash. "And we gotta move before they close the park. Can you take me to my car? It's down on Commonwealth. Then you can follow me home."

"Where do you live?" Brik asked, as he turned over the motor. He reversed out. Brik bent forward and fished his car key out of his sock.

"West Hollywood. Know where that is?"

"No," said Brik as he drove away down the hill. He kept

checking his mirrors and ahead, expecting to see round each bend and curve a row of black and whites, lights flashing, road-blocking their exit from the park. "Would you mind if I said something . . ." He was about to say Ry, instinctively adressing himself as to his inseparable friend and realised that although he and Trick had been talking for so long, neither knew the other's name.

"Go ahead," said Trick.

"I don't know your name. I'm Berwick Peters. You can call me Brik if you like."

"I like . . . Brik," Trick grinned. He held out his hand. "Name's Rambler. Trick Rambler." Better late, they shook hands. "Now what did you wan' ask me?"

"I don't do drugs," Brik managed to say. He felt a little foolish but it was a powerful spectre.

"That's cool," Trick replied. "Nor do I." He sniffed and brought one magnificent bronzed knee up on the dash. "Little coke's no problem. Makes life a touch sweeter, that's all."

❋ ❋ ❋ ❋

I found Brik sitting on the kerb beside the parked Bronco when Eldon and I got back from a pre-semester faculty meeting. Arriving unannounced, Brik had decided to wait. He heard the telephone ring a couple of times inside the house. He didn't guess it was Ryder.

"Something tells me that child is not the replacement poolboy and he certainly isn't a graduate student and definitely not waiting for me," Eldon remarked drily as I pulled into the driveway. Brik got up slowly and waved before walking up to the car. "So do I deduce he's one of yours?"

How my heart leapt to see that amazing grin! He *had* turned up, after all.

"You are about to meet Brik," I said jumping out of the Jeep as Brik hurried up. We pumped hands, not knowing whether to hug or not.

"Suffer the little children . . .," Eldon murmured under his breath.

"Hi, Jeremy."

"Hi, you," I smiled, relieved and happy to see him in the flesh. Eldon came over.

"Brik, I'd like you to meet Dean Stuart. Eldon this is Brik Peters I've told you so much about."

"I believe congratulations are in order," Eldon said. "I understand you're on your way, Brik."

"So they tell me, sir," Brik grinned.

"Eldon, please," the dean quietly corrected. "Come inside, boys. I'm sure you have a lot to talk about. Go through to the yard, Jeremy, dear. I'll make us some tea."

We went inside and I dumped my files in my room before leading Brik out to the cool, stone-paved patio under the shade thrown by the ever-green magnolia grandiflora. The sweet scent of the regally-sized blooms hung in the air as we pulled up chairs round the oak table.

"He's great," Brik observed.

"He's the best," I confirmed. "So what have you been doing? Andy's told me the news and I'm so very pleased for you, Brik." I glanced at Eldon through the kitchen window. He saw me and winked, gesturing that we were being left alone.

"Is it alright to talk?" Brik said, lowering his voice. "I need to talk to you, Jeremy."

"I think Eldon's being diplomatic," I smiled. "And even if he was here, you could talk all you wanted. He's a very wise man." He nodded. "How're you finding LA? Or is it still a little overwhelming."

"Have you ever been to Griffith Park?" he asked and before I could answer, he recounted the history of his afternoon's experience.

"But no one's called Trick," I said as he finished telling me about the mirror and the razorblade and the twenty dollar bill. I merely assumed that, afterwards, they'd fooled around. I wasn't told.

"No, it's true," Brik affirmed. "He showed me one of his movies. I saw his name."

"Oh," I said, now fully aware that Brik's afternoon had culminated in a ritual initiation which would have been the proud and privileged boast of any Boystown virgin. "I see." I wasn't sure whether to be relieved that he had declined the coke or worried that he'd taken a grave sexual risk. I had to know. "You didn't . . . ?"

He reached over and patted me on my knee, like an uncle. It was another of life's richer ironies, the turn of the young to re-assure the old.

"I told you, Jeremy . . . back at Mrs MacSween's. I *know* what's going down out there and, no, we did not exchange bodily fluids. Okay?"

"I told you I was pushy," I acknowledged.

"Don't stop," he said. "So far, I like it." He took my hand, almost protectively, in his. I caught his eye but I wasn't sure what I was supposed to read there and I flunked finding out.

"How's Ryder?" I asked, attempting to steer away from risking a silence which might say too much.

"He's getting laid. That's why I'm here. He needed the room. Two's company, y'know."

"Who's the lucky girl?"

"The casting director's secretary."

"Yes," I said. "Three would be a crowd on top of that kind of insurance policy."

Eldon appeared with two mugs of tea on a tray with a saucer of lemon slices.

"Do you take sugar in tea, Brik?" he asked. "If you do. I'll get some."

From the curious look with which Brik looked into the mug, I could tell that tea wasn't often drunk in the household at the end of Indian Road.

"Er . . . no. No sugar, thank you, sir."

"Eldon!" said Eldon, wagging a finger as he went back into the house. "I shall be lying down, Jeremy. I have a horrendous dinner to go to tonight."

Brik sipped cautiously at the tea. I think he liked it.

"But it's Ry I wanted your advice about," Brik continued, clearing his throat. "Trick wants to show me around on Saturday and I can't tell Ryder not to come."

"Why not?" I parried. "He told you to get lost while he

was getting laid. Ryder can't go on writing the rules for ever."

Brik shook his head.

"No. It's crazy. I have to face it, Jeremy. Ry's gonna find out sooner or later . . . About me. It's not something I could do alone . . . Telling him. He hates faggots."

"And of course he has such a depth of experience," I sniped. "If he's your friend, Brik, he'll understand. Why is it such a big deal for him? If you ask me, Brik - and as you've asked, I'll tell you - I suspect that Ry thinks you are gay and because he only thinks, he doesn't know how to react. He probably feels awkward."

"But what if he . . .?" The question trailed away and Brik took a sip at his tea. "I mean, he's like my brother, Jeremy."

Suddenly I was trapped irrevocably in that chasm between the rock and the hard place, which if I were not careful would slide together like two unstoppable geological plates, a seismological phenomenon which rendered me utterly impotent.

"Then in that case he should understand," I said, remembering Don Peters and the inference I was undoubtedly meant to have drawn from our first and last conversation about the son whom he had entrusted to my loco parentis. "Make a big deal of it, Brik and so will Ryder."

He sighed, lost in his rumination.

"Yeah," he said. "Gee, it's tough."

"No one ever gets a rose garden," I replied. "Only the jungle." Time to lighten up. "How d'you like Eldon's tea. Earl Grey. It's an English favourite."

"It's okay," he demurred. "Whaddya call it . . . an acquired taste?"

"Isn't everything?" I replied. "The trick, if you'll pardon the pun, is to be sure you only acquire the right ones."

He grinned.

"You coming to Andy's tomorrow?" he asked. "He said you were."

"No," I said quickly. "I can't, I'm afraid. I have some faculty thing . . . Semester'll be starting and I have to get on top of things, y'know. But how about Sunday?"

※ ※ ※ ※

After Brik had gone, summoned by a call from Ryder, I returned and sat in the yard, in the gloamin' - an old fashioned word for an old fashioned world where an old fashioned girl found her mind in a whirl . . .

Cold tea; no sympathy.

No Brik.The lights came on suddenly in the yard and flooded out my gloomy hideaway.

"Oh, dear," said Eldon as he came out, spruced and shiny from the shower, dressed to go to his dinner.

"Hello," I said, looking up with the worst of phoney smiles. "You look very . . . dapper?"

"Thankyou." He pursed his mouth as he looked at me, quizzically. "You, dear boy, on the other hand, look like shit."

"I . . ." There was no point in bleating. Anyway, Eldon immediately held up his hand to stop me.

"I'm going to be rather strict with you, Jeremy," he began, quite gently but very firmly. "I shall be out for perhaps three hours and I am going to set you a little task."

"Name it," I said, grateful to have something practical to occupy my empty evening. I imagined doing some filing for him or clearing out a closet.

"You are going to your room and you are going to turn on your word processor. You are then going to sit down and stare at that screen until you write something. Anything. Even a word. A one-word title would be quite sufficient and you will then write beneath that word: "By Jeremy Page". Beneath that you will add: "Copyright 1994". That will remind you that you are starting a new piece of work."

I groaned.

"But . . ."

"Sssh." He silenced me immediately. "As you were about to say you have nothing to write about, I am giving you the one word title of the project. `Parallel'. It was a very good novel, Jeremy and it will make a very good film script. That's what you're here for."

"But I don't want to write a film . . ." He cut me short.

"Try . . . Just try." The encouragement sounded more like admonishment. "Try it first for me . . . Start it for me and then you'll see."

"See what?"

"That you'll be finishing it for yourself."

He patted me on the shoulder and left.

THIRTEEN

Though an hour late, Trick was true to his word and showed up at the Century Wilshire on Saturday around one in the afternoon. Whether Trick would have shown up if Brik hadn't told him, after the steam had condensed after their arduous performance the previous afternoon, the real reason he and Ryder were in LA, I don't know.

And Brik had not taken the plunge out of his closet. I understand he had semi-primed Ryder as to the nature of his new acquaintance. That Trick was a model was what Brik had decided that Ryder would be prepared to accept.

From my standpoint, I cannot even imagine what it must have been like meeting Trick Rambler with no foreknowledge of him whatsoever. Trick, though I had not recognised his name when Brik told me of their meeting, was indelibly familiar to me. His video persona, arriving as it did in plain brown wrappers from the Innuendo mailing address to which I occasionally quoted my Visa number, had helped me though many solitary moments over the past couple of years in Scotland.

Ryder, on the other hand, shook hands with Trick as I would have shaken hands with any of Eldon's acquaintances, as peers, as fellow human beings endowed with no other mystique or magical quality than a desire to be sociable.

As they drove out of the Century's underground garage in Ryder's car that afternoon, to the uninitiated casual passer-by the three occupants of the Bronco looked for all the world like what, I suppose, they really were - three very dishy California hunks out for a little window shopping.

* * * *

Brik sat spread sideways on the back seat of the Bronco, watching the world go by and listening to Trick telling them about The Beverly Hills Hotel, the Chateau Marmont,

Mann's Chinese Theater, the Hollywood Bowl, The Memorial Cemetery. It was a very professional introductory tour.

Ryder was full of questions.

"How long have you lived here, Trick?"

"Left at the next light," Trick navigated. "That's it . . . Ease over now. Me? I'm born and bred. Not in LA but just outside."

"And how did you get into modelling?" Ryder laughed. "I mean, that's a real dumb question I know."

Brik coughed and gently pressed his hand against Trick's shoulder. Brik had also primed Trick on the delicacy of the situation he faced with Ryder.

"No. Not dumb. Someone came up to me in a bar. That's where it started. It's all luck. Right place, right time. That sorta stuff. Park there, Ryder. Gonna take you to lunch at this little place on Melrose. D'ya like pasta? Everyone's into pasta in this town. Pasta or sushi."

"I'm starved," Brik commented. Trick surreptitiously reached his hand through the seats and squeezed Brik's knee.

The boys locked the car and walked down the quiet side street and into the full panoply of high LA street cred earnestly performing the Saturday afternoon paseo along the happening avenue.

At first, the waiter at La Tavola wanted to put them inside, almost at the back.

"It'd be kinda nice to sit outside," Trick ultimated, having elicited no response from the chubby little Italian teenager. "Those people are almost done," he added pointing towards the street.

"They're not done yet, we don't take reservations Saturday afternoons and we ain't got room for waitin'," the waiter itemised curtly.

Ryder and Brik had turned to leave. They almost missed the magic show.

The maitre d' at La Tavola must have been in the john. Anyway, he wasn't on the floor. On returning to his station, he stopped almost in his tracks as his gaze fell upon the fabled features of Mr Rambler whose shades had been pushed back onto his head, catching that fabled mane of hair like in a macho alice band, creating a halo of blonded waves around an already hallowed head.

"Just one moment Mr . . . Mr Rambler," he oozed, swallowing his excitement in a bid to retain his cool.

"'Rico, what's the problem here?"

"This guy wanted to sit outside and there ain't no table," rejoined the thwarted waiter. "Who'm I s'posed to be? God?"

Trick turned on his best smile. No, you jerk, he thought to himself, you're not; but I am.

"I'm sorry, Mr Rambler. If you and your party would follow me." The maitre d' fairly glided through the crowded restaurant and presented himself to the two women who had finished their dessert and coffee and were chatting. "I'm sorry," he announced, "there's been a terrible mistake. This table was reserved. You should never have been put here."

"But we're here now," replied the younger woman, equally challengingly. They looked like visiting mother treating daughter in residence.

"I have to ask you to leave. There'll be no charge."

"I should think not!" smarted the daughter defiantly."

I've never been so insulted in my life!" added her mother, gathering her day's purchases in her hands and fluttering up from her seat. "Come, dear. It's an insult, d'you hear?"

"Puhleeese!" the maitre d' declared in mock Bette Davis, quickly clearing the table top and allowing himself to stand just that bit too close as Trick brushed past to take his seat, "the insult was that God gave her that *ugly* daughter!"

"Hey, that's good!" Trick complimented. "D'you do anyone else?"

"Only in private," the maitre d' came back, glibly. "It's a pleasure serving you, Mr Rambler. Here are your menus. Take your time, gen'lmen."

"Jesus!" Ryder whistled as he unfolded the laminated menu. "What was that all about? Do you *know* that guy?"

136

"Never seen him before in my life," Trick admitted. "The tortellini is *very* good, guys. D'you want beer or wine?"

"Maybe wine," said Brik. "How about you, Ry?"

"Yeah. A little wine'd be good. And I'll take that totellini, Trick."

"Same here," Brik replied.

Trick hailed the maitre d' back who took their orders. The truculent Rico brought a bottle of wine with their icewater.

"So what kinda modelling do you do?" Ryder asked as they raised their glasses.

"Anything, really." Trick felt Brik's knee pressing against his beneath the table. "And I've made a few movies," Trick added, almost throwing the admission away. Before Ryder could come back with "Movies!", Brik excused himself to go to the john. Being absent for the next few minutes was the only way he felt he could cope. He thought that, perhaps, when he returned, the writing he'd seen coming would finally be on the wall. That he might not have to shake the can and spray the letters himself would be a bonus.

As Brik headed off to the john, Ryder heard his name being called.

"Well, small world, Ryder?" Gloria said. She and her companion, a primped little wardrobe queen from ABC, stopped at the table.

"Hi, Gloria!" Ryder replied. He didn't bother to get up. That he had met someone he knew caressed his ego. "How goes it?"

She wriggled in her all-black lycra and leather outfit and ran that clever pink tongue across her lips . . .

"Haven't had breakfast, yet." She winked and Ryder grinned. God, this was good.

"Oh," Ryder said, "like you to meet my friend Trick. Trick this is Gloria."

"We met already," Gloria smiled. "But in another life."

"Are you Trick Rambler?" asked the companion, betraying unmistakable signals of incredulity.

"Sure," Trick replied and stuck out his hand. The boy

went to take it as though he were selecting a particularly bruisable cucumber from a supermarket selection. His eyes ricochetted back and forth between Trick's face and the outstretched hand. "Well, go on. It won't bite!" The hand that had coaxed so much pleasure out of so many for so many was duly shaken.

"Glad you made it, Trick," Gloria said. "An' Trick's much better than . . . what was it you called yourself then?"

"Was it Taylor?" Trick grinned. "I dunno. Shelton, maybe?"

"Forget it," said Gloria. "I prefer Trick." She turned to Ryder. "So, when shall we three meet again?"

"Three?" Ryder repeated.

"Or four or five," Gloria said, winking at Trick. "It'd be fun, hey William?" she added, throwing the remark over her shoulder to her walker. Poor William was so overcome, he could do nothing but gulp and swallow like a trapped sardine being savoured by a circling shark. "Call me," Gloria instructed as she started to sashay on her way. "Soon, Mr McKigh. Have a good day, guys."

Ryder grinned and sipped at his wine.

Brik returned as it came Trick's turn to ask a question.

"She says she knows me but I can't remember her. Where does she work?"

"Gerri Muntz's," said Ryder. "Jesus, but does she come on strong, man? And when she comes . . . Whew!"

Brik sat down.

"Was that Gloria?"

"Sure was. So, Trick. What about these movies? You must have gotten to a lotta people? Seems everyone knows who you are?"

Brik saw immediately that his turmoil was unresolved, that his ploy had back-fired.

"Man, I make skin flicks. Porno, y'know?"

"You do what?" Ryder repeated.

"Porno, man. Screw movies, fuck films."

"No," Ryder said, shaking his head. "No." He laughed, disbelieving. "Do you?"

"Sure," grinned Trick. "Don't I, Brik?"

"Er . . . oh, yeah," Brik nodded, as masculine as he could, attempting to shrug away such a basic revelation in as worldly a way as he could muster. "Trick showed me one. Yesterday."

"Jesus," Ryder whistled. "Could I see one?"

"Whaddya think, Brik?" Trick asked. "D'ya reckon he's ready for it."

"Sure I'm ready, man," Ryder enthused. "I mean, let's go!"

"But you're just killing time, right Trick?" Brik interrupted. "I mean you wanna be an actor, don't you? Legit."

"Doesn't everybody in this town?" said Trick. "I tried. Man, how I tried but it doesn't come easy. Hey," he added, "maybe you guys could be my mascots. You sure seem lucky to me. Look at you. Here less'n a week an' you're already cookin'."

"We gotta break," Ryder said carelessly. "D'you have an agent and stuff?"

Trick chuckled.

"Oh, I've had lots of agents, one way an' another." He glanced over at Brik who felt himself reddening. "But . . . Y'know how it is, they only end up screwing you."

"Do I know," Ryder agreed emphatically, presuming an entirely different meaning to Trick's remark. "Some are okay, though. Ours is pretty good, wouldn't you say, Brik?"

"Andy? He's great. You should meet him, Trick. We're going round to his house, later. You should come." As he spoke, Brik felt Ryder's boot find his shin under the table. He winced.

"I'm sure Trick has better things to do tonight," Ryder diverted. "If I was him, I know I would. That right, Trick?"

Their food arrived.

"No. I have nothing on, tonight. I'd love to come. That okay, Brik? Hey . . . this is great, guys. Y'know, like that movie . . . What was it? The Musketeers?"

Ryder glared at Brik behind the waiter's back who was setting down the plates. Brik looked away. He remembered what Jeremy had said about writing the rules.

"Sure, Trick. Andy won't mind."

Ryder, mercurially, fell silent as he ate lunch, listening to Trick talk and watching Brik lapping up every word spoken with an easy ear. There was an eagerness in Brik's responses to Trick's conversation which irritated Ryder, an eagerness which Brik had never displayed when he, Ryder, had something to impart. Had Janna been with them, she would have noticed and immediately compensated by attracting Ryder's attention, giving him attention.

Ryder felt his skin prickle. He shifted in his seat which was suddenly uncomfortable. He was aware of himself sitting at the table next to that teeming sidewalk as an individual, apart from the others, a separate entity. Suddenly, everything he had taken for granted seemed a very long way away and nothing was sure. He couldn't understand why Brik was making it worse. Let Trick make his own luck, Ryder thought.

The close-knitted world they had left in Ohio had fashioned for all of them, Brik, Janna and Ryder, a warm, snug comfortable sweater, passed round one to the other whenever it was needed. They'd never needed to wear it at the same time and the situation of who needed it most had never arisen. But that all-important sweater hadn't been packed. It had been left behind for it was no longer a shareable garment; in fact, no longer even wearable. Back home, over the years, any holes had been quickly patched and didn't notice. Out here, even if they'd thought to bring it with them, the sweater would have been too warm and the darns would have showed up embarassingly under the arc lights, the lovingly applied patches telling all the world that he or she who wore the sweater was sick, in need, weak and vulnerable.

Now that he and Brik were on their own, Ryder concluded, they would have to buy their own clothes.

✽ ✽ ✽ ✽

Clem Barber turned his red Mercedes into the parking lot in back of the Innuendo building on Pico, corner of

Cloverfield. He crossed the lot and buzzed at the entryphone on the rear door. There was no front entrance; the door onto Pico was only for show. Only the mailman used its mailbox. No one ever walked in off the street and the window was heavily curtained. Stuck between a security company and a funeral parlour, the building attracted little attention.

Inside, the banks of copying machines whirred almost inaudibly, creating only at atmosphere of noise, like the `sshhh' in the cabin of a jetliner. The tape copiers were all men, un-prepossessing. They checked and re-checked, walking up and down and back and forth between the machines as their counterparts had done the world over since Arkwright invented the Spinning Jenny. They loaded and unloaded the magazines with as little concern over the contents as a rating in the bowels of a battleship's gun turret would feed fresh shells into the breach.

Clem was as unconcerned about this side of Tommy Cattini's business as the tape copiers and the mail order people on the first and second floor appeared to be about his. This side of the movie business wasn't one where oscars were handed out and no one sought or expected praise for their art and subtle craft.

Just gimme the money, man.

Clem climbed the stairs to Tommy's office on the second floor. The door was open but Clem rapped on the frame.

"Yeah?" Tommy barked from within. Clem put his head round the door. "Oh. Clem. Hi. Come on in."

Clem entered the small and cluttered office. The walls were one vast pinboard of schedules, photos, calendars, 'phone numbers; cuttings and clippings fluttered carelessly like flakes of skin peeling from a bad case of psoriasis as the electric fan, like a radar scanner, moved the stale and smoky air first to left, then to right, then back to left.

"Jesus, Tom," Clem said, fanning his hand in front of his face. "It's unhealthy in here. Don't you ever open a window?"

Tommy was counting money, the eternal cigar stuck into the side of his mouth as much a comfort as ever was a baby's dummy and purported not to hear. He waved Clem to sit and Clem sat opposite his clandestine producer.

"Four-eighty, ninety, five hundred," Tommy finished and wrapped the wad in a rubber band. "Here's your wages, Clem." he leant back in his executive chair and flicked the wad, almost with a distaste, as if it were untouchable, across the desk to Clem. "Whaddya doin' next weekend?"

"Difficult," said Clem, eyeing the money yet leaving it for the moment where it lay. "I start work Monday. Pilot."

"How long?"

"No idea. Coupla weeks if we're lucky. Why the hurry?"

"Fuckin' Trick, that's the hurry. I need to get as much on him as I can before the schmuck disappears up his own asshole."

Clem nodded.

"I can't promise, Tommy. My gas money is all very well but it wouldn't satisfy my savings and loan." Clem leant forward and picked up the wad of notes, fanning through it disinterestedly. He was just about to get up and go when he saw the photograph on the cluttered desktop. He was seeing it upside down. "Mind if I take a look, Tom?"

"Be my guest," Tommy demonstrated as he relit his cigar. "May it do you more good than it's doing me."

Clem took the photo and immediately knew its subject. Brik Peters. The patrol officer's peaked cap and the open shirt didn't disguise the youngman whom Clem would be shooting in the course of the next two weeks. Unmistakable.

"Amateurs," was all Clem said and tossed the ten by eight back onto Clem's desk. "The lighting sucks."

"Screw that. It's the kid that counts." Tommy sighed. "I could make him a fuckin' star. Did you ever see such a smile," he leered.

"Certainly not since I got up today," Clem replied.

The 'phone rang and Tommy started a conversation. Clem sat and watched his sometime employer as he greased and charmed his way up another rung of the ladder of his trade. The call seemed to involve a deal on a consignment of blank tape - prices were being quoted in grosses and Clem watched as Tommy chipped and scraped and sliced a cent off here, a cent off there. Clem looked at the five hundred in his hand. The balance of his fee for the last shoot. He wanted more. He needed more. But was this the right time to try?

As Tommy wrapped up his deal, Clem glanced at the photo of Brik and wondered if . . . How grateful would Tommy be? How much grateful? On the other hand, he calculated, if the pilot took off, if a series was successful and he worked on right through the first season, then the second and . . . Not only would the mortgage company be happy, he could indulge his other, costly, peccadillos in ever increasing variety. The jailbait that Clem Barber favoured were astute and hard-bargaining little businessmen. No. On balance. He decided not to. Fulltime salary on Dick Molina's show was better . . . for the time being.

As Tommy put down the 'phone, Clem got up to go.

"So," concluded Tommy. "Call me, hey? Lemme know."

"Sure, Tommy. See ya."

Tommy didn't even bother to reply.

FOURTEEN

"Are you sure you won't come around later?" Andy pleaded with me on the 'phone. "Your meeting can't go on all night, Jem."

"Case of wait and see. I have to get used to all this academic stuff all over." I was lying. I was sitting in front of my little green screen and what had over-ridden my initial reluctance to be in the same room as Andy and Brik at the same time was that on the program's page number indicator box, the `5' digit was displaying. "I'll take a rain check," I replied as I pressed `enter' and the digit changed to `6'. "But if I come, I come. How about that?"

"If you would, I promise I'd be very grateful," he said, *most* sincerely. "I have no ulterior motives if that's what's worrying you. It's just that Ryder and I are a little sticky as yet."

"You're on your own with that one," I replied. "Just don't go at the problem with a meat cleaver."

"Your little lambs will be very safe with me. Don't worry."

"And there speaks a kosher butcher," I quipped. "I do worry. And speaking of kosher butchers, how's your mother?"

"That is beneath you, dear. She speaks very highly of you."

"Have you talked to her today?"

"Just about to. She'll ask me why she hasn't heard from you."

"Give her my number."

There was a pause as Andy marshalled his front.

"Perhaps when you come over you'd call her up tomorrow? Give the poor old thing something to look forward to. Tomorrow is still on, isn't it?"

"Sure. Why not," I replied, having not heard from Brik as to whether he and I would be getting together.

"Great," Andy said.

"Andy..." I began. "No... it's okay. Forget it."

"Hey come on," he chided, "don't do that. You always do that. Tell..."

"I'm writing," I muttered.

"You're what! Okay... I heard. What are you writing?"

"A script."

"'Parallel'?"

"Uh huh. Page five. Six now."

"You haven't got a fucking faculty meeting at all, have you?" he scolded gently. "I know you, Jem."

"Zounds!" I giggled. "Foiled again!"

"Then I'm not offended," he said encouragingly. "At friggin' last, man! It's been a long time coming. When'll it be ready?"

"Typical," I joked. "Now you're my agent."

"I've always been your agent. I wanna be your partner."

I heard his doorbell chime in the background.

"There's your doorbell, Andy. Goodbye."

I hung up, imagining his face at the other end. He so wanted to be a producer.

✳ ✳ ✳ ✳

The boys had gone by the hotel after their afternoon's wanderings only for them to check their messages and for Trick to collect his car. Brik and Ryder followed him back to West Hollywood. Though Ryder was pressing for Trick to show him one of his movies, Brik insisted that they shouldn't be late at Andy's. They waited in the Bronco outside Trick's apartment whilst Trick ran inside.

"Imagine screwing all those chicks," Ryder whistled. "An' gettin' paid for it. Hey, we shouldda told him to bring one along to Andy's." He halted. "'Cept I forgot. He's a faggot. He'd hardly be into seeing a straight movie."

"I... I think Trick's pretty cool, man. About that kinda thing. The one I saw was a threeway," Brik dared to say.

"Oh, man. Two chicks at the same time. Wow!" Ryder gushed, rubbing his crotch. "Makes me hornier'n shit."

"It was... It w...," Brik stammered, forcing himself to

explain to Ryder where Trick was coming from. The words were there but they were stuck.

"Not . . . two guys and a chick!" Ryder said, wide-eyed. Brik looked away as Trick came out of the apartment building and ran to the car. "Wow!"

"Just picking up some candy," Trick said as he got in back of the car. He jabbed a finger into Brik's shoulder. "Turn around and then take a left," Trick guided. Dicks is about four blocks."

Andy was wearing shorts, singlet and deck shoes when he answered the door.

"Come in, guys . . . Glad you could . . ."

Then he saw Trick, bringing up the rear.

"Hi," Ryder said, entering first. He handed over a litre of wine they'd picked up. Andy took it almost remotely and Ryder bristled as he felt that now-familiar electric frisson that the un-invited guest was generating.

"Andy!" said Brik grasping the agent's hand and pumping it. "You don't mind that my friend Trick's with us, do you? He's been so great to us today, showing us round town and all."

"Hi, Brik," Andy grinned although he looked straight into the eyes of Trick Rambler. "Not at all. Absolutely, not at all." He extended his hand. "Trick. It's my pleasure."

"Hi," Trick drawled, only half at ease. Though aware that Andy was aware, Trick toned down his aura in the face of a prospective opportunity. Actors having to put out to get ahead was one thing; porno people peddling their wares too obviously would not bring about the desired results. He'd been in this situation before, several times and blown it on each occasion. No, Trick had figured. Let Andy Schmandy come to him. He'd be there, but he wanted the agent to make the running. "You have a beautiful home, Andy," he said rather gruffly and with no hint of intimacy.

"Thanks." Andy closed the door and blinked to himself as he stood for a moment with his back to his guests before steeling himself for what now looked as though it could be a very interesting evening. "Shall we go out to the pool?"

His priority reflection as he ushered his guests out back was that Jeremy, on balance, would not show up. He decided to see how the evening progressed before making an insurance call. Jeremy would not be amused if he did show up.

"D'ya think he's cool?" Trick whispered to Ryder when they were left alone. Brik had gone back inside with Andy to bring cold beers. As he spoke he inhaled sharply on a joint.

"Excuse me?"

"I brought a little coke with me," Trick confided. "You have no objection, do you? Brik seems not so sure."

"Me? Hell, no, man. Don't know about Andy, though."

"I think he's cool. This is Boystown, y'know not Green Gables. You wanna toke?"

Though Ryder didn't yet know he was in Boystown, he took the joint and inhaled. He was no stranger to dope although Brik had only ever tried it once, to his knowledge. Trick fished in the pocket of his T-shirt and handed Ryder a whole spliff.

"Thanks." Ryder said. "I owe you, Trick."

Andy and Brik returned and passed round the cans. Andy set two big bowls of cornchips and popcorn on the table.

"Sorry, Andy. Started this without you. You wanna toke," Trick offered.

"Sure," Andy said. The first drag confirmed the joint was of the purest, ninety-percent hash, a far cry from gentle grass. "Shit, that's good stuff!" He handed the joint to Brik who took a draw and then passed it back. As they talked, the first two joints were quickly consumed, two more lying ready on the poolside table.

"So, Trick's been showing you the town?" Andy said, relaxing onto one of the full length pool beds. "How was it?"

"Great," Ryder replied. "There's a lot to see. It's so goddam big. I can't wait to get to know it better."

"You will," Andy said. "But not for a while. You guys're gonna have your work cut out on this pilot. They shoot like every minute they have. You won't know what day it is by the time you're done."

"Suits me," Ryder said.

"How's the deal coming, Andy?" Brik asked. He passed on the newly lit third joint and lay down on the spare pool bed. He felt very light headed and beads of perspiration were breaking out on his forehead.

"I never talk business on the weekend," Andy lied, laughing. "But it's great . . . I'll be right back to you as soon as we're there."

"There was a message tonight from some chick called Laura," Ryder mentioned. "Laura from Telemax? It was too late to call her."

"She does the publicity," Andy explained. "Get to know her."

"I figured," Ryder replied.

Andy and Ryder chattered on. Trick looked over to where Brik lay with his hands folded behind his head, looking up at what was a clear night sky. The lights beneath the surface of the limpid pool suffused the yard with a satin glow. Brik suppressed the smile he sent Trick in return and wondered when he would be able to see Trick alone again.

Brik sensed his thoughts, swirling, as first one formed, then another, like cells, only to split and breed, spreading over the screen of his mind in random patterns of association. He thought of Trick and then immediately thought of Ron Windel. The two images fought each other, jostling in comparison, almost competing. There was pleasure in both, elements of equal satisfaction although having now been with Trick, Brik now knew how satisfying could be the intimacy of a peer. Then memories of Ryder appeared, memories of them wrestling in the snow, struggling in the water as they splashed through their past summer vacations . . . Exploring how far they could take the fascination they had with the urgent demands of their changing bodies.

All of these images were the structure of Brik's chord of fantasy and yet no single note had yet sounded out above the others to resolve that deeper need he felt for fulfilment.

He didn't hear the end of Ryder's staccato conversation with Andy.

"When we get some bread, Brik," Ryder concluded after hearing what Andy had to say about publicity, "we're gonna have to have some photos done . . . Hey, Brik!"

Brik was asleep.

"He's wiped out, man," Trick observed. "Let him sleep. You gotta mirror, Andy?"

Trick removed the thin, snap-top plastic bag from his pocket inside which was a blade.

"Oh, that kinda mirror," Andy said. "Sure, in the bathroom."

"May I?" Trick asked.

"Be my guest," Andy grinned. "It's over the washbasin. Trick went inside. "This doesn't shock you, does it?" Andy murmured, addressing Ryder but with his eyes seeking other constellations overhead.

"What?"

"Trick cutting coke."

"Nah! I'm cool."

"Of course you are, Ryder. I forgot. You've been to LA before, haven't you?" Andy chuckled and then found whatever it was that was making him laugh hilarious and howled with mirth.

Neither was Ryder by now so sensitised and, contagiously, Andy's laughing got to him and he too began to giggle though he didn't know why he was laughing.

Trick returned and squatted beside the pool and trailed his hand in the water.

"So what are you up to these days, Trick?" Andy called over.

"Aaah . . . y'know. Just hanging out. Not a whole bunch going on right now, is there?"

"Some," Andy replied. "There's a lot of mid-season replacement right now. Been up for much?"

"Some," Trick lied. "So *you're* busy?"

"Pretty much," Andy said, drifting into a state where he was hearing himself talking and wondering whose words he heard. He was overcome with a more powerful urge which he neither cared nor deemed fit to verbalise. Ryder's prescence melted away into an area of peripheral awareness until he heard Trick say:

"Wanna swim, Ryder? Water's great. By the way, it's all lined up in there, Andy, when you're ready."

"Thanks, Trick," Andy said and pulled himself up on the bed. "You swimming, Ryder?" Andy said, knowing that he was putting the youngman on the spot.

"D'you have a costume?" Ryder asked.

"Sure, if you feel the need. But my neighbours have seen it all before."

"You bet," Trick grinned. "Come on, Ryder, I dare you."

Trick stood up and peeled off his T-shirt and pulled off his boots. Deftly practised, he maintained perfect balance whilst executing a move which would have had others falling and tripping over their socks. As cool as if he were the champion horseshoe thrower of the south west, he threw first one and then the other boot to land perfectly at Andy's feet. Andy picked them up and felt them warm, smelled them musty and dark before putting them gently and neatly on one side.

Ryder got up but only after he'd removed his boots and socks. He began to peel off his T-shirt. Beneath what felt like a second skin of euphoria, he was nervous.

"Hey, Brik," he called, walking over to where Brik lay, the beatific half-smile of a sleeping angel on his face. "You gonna swim with us?" Brik stirred but didn't wake. "Hey, Brik!" Ryder said urgently.

"Leave him," Trick murmured as he flipped the buttons on his Levis. Andy watched, not believing. Trick was by no means the first youngman who'd undressed by this pool but the deshabille had never before been achieved with such professional cunning and such promise. Andy was so excited by what he watched that he felt almost sinister, threatening the stability of the boundaries of his already wide experience.

Trick shucked his Levis and tossed them to Andy. He stood entirely still, like one of the statues round the pool atop Hearst Castle and looked challengingly at Ryder, grinning.

Ryder, ultimately acquitted himself well. His T-shirt and then his Levis came off and he walked over to the pool, not looking at Trick or Andy, acting all the way to the water's edge, knowing he was being observed in what was the performance of his short career.

"Okay," said Trick. "After three . . . One, two . . ."

But three never came. Ryder was in, like Flynn, gathering his knees up to his chest to make the biggest splash. Ryder was in first.

"Okay, man. Ten lengths, yeah?"

Trick joined him and together they swam a few lengths of the pool. Andy gathered up towels and flung them in a heap at his feet as he stood by the pool cheering on the two contestants in what had become a race. Ryder won and hauled himself out at the farside of the pool. Trick stayed in, panting heavily and sweeping back his long hair, wringing it out behind his head with both hands.

Andy watched as Ryder walked round for a towel and had at least one of two unasked questions answered. So, he thought, that's what Ryder looks like. He too couldn't help comparing Ryder to Brick, or rather what he thought Brik was like. Ryder was almost everything that Brik was but there was less; less height, weight, hair . . . less a lot of things. Great proportions but not breathtaking. Andy also knew now that whatever thoughts he had entertained about Ryder were groundless; Ryder was not a prospective playmate but Ryder *was* something else.

It wasn't his body that Andy found so fascinating about Ryder McKigh. It was the whole thing; the attitude, the aura, the vibrations of a fully vital, aware being. It went deeper. Andy knew he was in the prescence of a stalking, hungry, prowling animal, a wild, atavistic beast whose very nearness provoked visceral stirrings both of fear and a thrilling anticipation. Although he'd been hanging fire before finally acknowledging his thoughts, as the cumulative result of dealing with the sparky and questioning pugnaciousness of his latest client, what Andy saw walking towards him round the poolside that night was, quite simply, a star. He handed Ryder a towel.

"You wanna line, Ryder?"

"Sure," Ryder replied. The water had cleared his head. The performance had sharpened his wits. He felt safe. They weren't going to get to him. He felt in charge, in command again.

"Trick," Andy called. "You coming?"

"Go ahead," Trick replied. "I'll join you in a while. Go ahead."

Andy waited as Ryder dried off and dressed and then went ahead to the bathroom. On a six-inch-square mirror, six lines of coke were neatly laid out. Andy had all the equipment and took the short, thin metal tube and closing one nostril with his forefinger scooped up the first line in one. He handed the tube to Ryder who bent low over the mirror. Seeing how Andy had done it, he followed the shining example. He decided he wasn't going to copy Andy exactly. He'd already worked out a move, one that would establish him as different, already a master of the game. He only took half of one line in his right nostril. He then changed hands and snorted the remaining half into his left. He laid the tube down beside the mirror and twitched his nostrils, like he'd seen them do in the movies . . .

"I don't do this very often," Andy found himself saying. "And never during the week. Times have changed. No one says they do it anymore in this town. They do, but they don't . . . get me?"

"Uh huh," Ryder replied. "Hey, thanks, Andy."

"You want the other one?" Andy asked, indicating the third line.

"No," said Ryder. "Not right now. Brik might want some. You never know."

"I think I'll wait for Trick," said Andy.

"Yeah," Ryder said, looking at himself in the mirror and smoothing back his hair. "I'll see if Brik's okay."

Trick was finishing scrunch-drying his hair when Ryder returned to the pool. Brik was still fast asleep. Instead of his jeans, Trick was wearing the same black lycra cycle shorts he had been wearing the day before which he carried in his jeans pocket. As his body carried no spare fat whatsoever, the shorts looked to Ryder to have been sprayed on, a second skin, reifying everything there was to be imagined about the private parts of the body beneath.

"How was it?" Trick grinned and ran his fingers through his hair.

"Grrrr!" Ryder growled. "Certainly makes you sing, Trick!"

"Yeah. Doesn't it? Think I'll go and have me a line."

Alone, Ryder sat back in a chair and drank another beer. He had the munchies and as he drank, he finished off the bowl of corn ships, staring up at the stars.

Neither Andy nor Trick had returned and so Ryder decided to wake Brik. He moved over and sat down on the pool bed and shook his friend.

"Ummm," Brik muttered sleepily. "What . . . What time is it?"

"Time to get up, old buddy."

"What happened?" Brik said, raising himself on his elbows and then pulling himself up to sitting position.

"The usual," Ryder said. "You and the weed don't live too well together do you?"

"What did I do?" said Brik, unaware of anything since he had fallen asleep.

"You missed the dancing girls."

"The what?"

"Skip it. We went in the pool. Trick and me."

"Where is everybody?"

"Inside. Trick brought some coke."

"Oh," said Brik. "So what's happening?"

"I think we should go." said Ryder.

"Why?"

"No reason. You coming?"

"Okay. Let me have ten minutes in the pool and we'll go, yeah?" Brik stripped quickly and eased himself over the side of the pool into the water. "Hey, Ry . . . Remember where we were a week ago?" Brik backstroked the length of the small pool. "D'ya believe it?"

"Pinch me!" Ryder called. He felt the need to take a pee and went back inside the house. The kitchen was empty and he opened a couple of doors to check for a john but the doors were only closets. He went through to Andy's living room; there was no one there and he couldn't hear voices. He went on, through to the bathroom where he could see the lights were on.

They hadn't closed the door.

What Ryder saw winded him; seeing Andy on his knees greedily devouring Trick hit him full in the chest harder than a Tyson punch, deeper than a javelin hurled from close range. Andy's hands kneaded Trick's taught abdomen and bronzed pelvis as he greedily consumed Trick, emitting a string of primitive grunts and primal growls, slavering and dribbling like a ravenous carnivore tearing apart the carcass of a fresh kill . . .

As Ryder appeared in the doorway, Trick turned slowly away from his reflection in the huge oval mirror above the washbasin. His eyes were half-closed and his face betrayed no emotion; he looked at Ryder as a disembodied spirit would peer over a graveyard wall, as a hopeless prisoner would look up through the bars at the passing of a warder, as a homeless junkie, squatting on the steps in front of a deserted building, looks up at a curious passer-by.

"Hey . . . Ryder . . .," Trick said, very slowly, almost inaudibly. "Wan'another line, man?" That Ryder's expression betrayed shock, hurt, anger, amazement was not anything Trick was in a state to pick up on.

Andy allowed his concentration on enjoying Trick to the full to lapse only for the time it took to look up and grin at Ryder and to say: "Just snacking, Ryder."

Ryder exploded.

"Shit! You . . . you're . . . sick!" He lashed out with his booted foot and kicked the bathroom door. He kicked out again, cracking the wooden panel.

His actions brought swift reactions. Trick withdrew and backed off against the wall, standing awkwardly, his shorts peeled down like black banana skins somewhere round his knees. Andy whipped round and stood up.

"Hey! Quit that! What the fuck're you doing?"

"What am I doing!" Ryder yelled. "What have I got to do with it?"

"You've wrecked my damn door, Ryder, that's what!"

"You fuckin'. . . sleaze!" Ryder retorted. "You're sick . . . both of you, y'know that? Sick! Why dincha tell me you were a whore, Trick. You're nothing more than a damn *whore*!"

Ryder turned from the room. Andy was after him and grabbed his shoulder as they reached the living room.

"That's enough, Ryder . . . Enough!"

Ryder was breathing deeply, his fists clenched at his sides, dangerously close to getting out of control. Brik, wrapped in a towel, appeared in the doorway from the kitchen.

"What the hell's going on with you guys!" he exclaimed in alarm. He had heard the raised voices from outside.

"Tell him!" Ryder screamed at Andy. "Go on. Tell him what you and the *whore* were doing back there!"

"What I do in my own house, Ryder is my own business," Andy replied grimly. "And be very careful about who you're calling whore."

"So what is he, a fuckin' angel?" Ryder spat. "And you were praying, hey?"

"We're all whores in this town," said Andy letting go of Ryder's shirt. Ryder walked straight towards the front door. "Where are you going?"

"Ry?" Brik called. "What's wrong?"

"I'm leaving," Ryder announced, panting. "I suggest you leave too."

"But . . .?" Brik looked back and forth between Andy and Ryder. Trick appeared behind Andy, excused himself and went out of the room.

"If you're coming, Brik, get your clothes and meet me outside," Ryder ordered. "Or stay with these faggots!"

"Faggots?" Andy laughed. "Whores? Come on, Ryder, wise up, dammit. Do yourself some good. That's all Trick wanted to do. I knew it, he knew it. Where's the harm?

What's so terrible? There isn't one rule for you and one for us."

"Meaning?" Ryder threw out, his hand on the door latch.

"Was what Gerri Muntz's secretary did to you the other day any different?" Andy said angrily. "Aw, go to hell, Ryder." Andy dismissed him with a wave of a hand and turned away. "Do what you like. Makes no difference to me. But you're blowing it."

"How did you know?" Ryder asked, wrong-footed.

"About you and Gloria?" Andy threw over his shoulder. "Gerri told me."

"Gerri!" Ryder exclaimed. "How'd she know, for Chrissake?"

"Gloria told her. Girls do talk, Ryder. In *great* detail, may I add. And some of them can't help telling their friends."

"Ryder," Brik soothed. "Sit down. Let's talk this through."

"No," Ryder replied quietly. His thoughts tumbled about; his eyes, swivelling between Brik, Andy and a focus far away, looked like the windows of twin washing machines, the wet, tangled laundry slopping about behind.

Andy sensed he was breaking through.

"You had a good time, Gloria had a good time. I was having a good time, Trick was having a good time. People remember good times, Ryder. They like good times. That's what it's all about. You have a good time and you remember and you think, yeah . . . That's how favours get done." Andy sat down on a couch. "But don't ever kid yourself. You know what I'm saying, Ryder. That's how you get things done. You're no plaster saint, nor am I and as far as whores go . . . Did I give Trick money?" Ryder was silent. "Did you give Gloria money?" Andy paused. "No. Well, then. You haven't met a whore yet, Ryder. You're too young, too green and too blind. You will meet them, though, in this town. They're everywhere. But you leave now and . . . well, just don't come crying to me."

Brik waited. Ryder was taking his time,

"Yeah . . ." Ryder said finally, rather sadly. It seemed to

Brik that he'd taken Andy's words on board. It seemed that he was sorry. "Brik?" he said, persuasively but with no tone of coercion.

"I don't know, Ry," Brik replied uncertainly.

"Okay," Ryder replied. "Whatever." He took two steps towards Andy. "Look," he began. "I'm not leaving, right . . . I'm just going home." Brik felt how difficult this was for his friend. He was lost, confused and alone.

"Lemme get my clothes," Brik said. "I'll come with you."

"No," Ryder said. "No. You stay. If you wanna stay, it's right you stay. It's my problem. Let me work it through. Andy, I'm not leaving, you understand me?"

"I understand, Ryder." He shrugged and smiled, rather touched by what he perceived as Ryder's climbdown. "No hard feelings?"

Ryder grinned.

"Sorry," he grinned, tapping his crotch. "Not on this boy."

Andy laughed.

"See you soon, hey? Don't worry about Brik. I'll drive him home. My stars have to get their beauty sleep."

"Ry? You sure you'll be okay? I mean, I'm with you, man. Just say the word."

"Thanks," Ryder replied, shaking his head. "Thanks but no thanks. I'm gonna take a drive. Catch ya later."

"Yeah," said Brik.

"Say good night to Trick," said Ryder as he opened the front door. "Tell him, sorry."

Outside, Ryder closed the door and waited for a moment on the step and breathed in deep the flower scented night air. The lights outside Andy's door were on and there were insects and moths, fluttering around the wrought iron brackets, clustering round the naked bulb.

"Goodbye, Brik," Ryder murmured before walking the short distance though the front yard to the street.

FIFTEEN

The deal that Andy wrung out of Telemax for Brik and Ryder was all he could get. Lou Hales got his bargain, as he knew he would. The boys didn't do badly, but it wasn't a lot more than scale and scale wasn't a lot. The options would hike it up some but Andy didn't have a lot of leverage.

But it was enough for Brik and Ryder to move out of the Century Wilshire. Lindy Green, the receptionist at Andy's office was more than her job title suggested, especially to the agency clients for whom she used her unique position to develop a brokerage, usually in real estate and apartments, placing those who had and who didn't need with those who hadn't and were desperate. One of the last season's soap names, Booth Calhoun, had gone back east where he'd come from, to do Broadway on a twelve-month contract and, give or take a turkey in which case the deal was nullified, Brik and Ryder got to move into Booth's house on South Bentley Drive which ran off Westwood Boulevard, south of Wilshire at two thousand a month. Small house, big bucks but, as Ryder said, "What the hell."

The two weeks shooting that the pilot show demanded was, as Andy had predicted, a busy time for Brik and Ryder. They had no time for anything more than buying frozen food on the way home, eating it and learning their lines for the following day and they saw no one, other than Trick.

He'd arrive at some point every evening, not at the same time but anywhere between seven and eleven. Often he'd sit and hear their lines as so many of their scenes were together. Other times he'd take the part of another actor or actress so either Brik or Ryder had something to play against other than themselves. He seemed genuinely interested, not only in Brik but as friendly and encouraging to Ryder. He was as supportive as his schedule allowed. He'd never announce his departure, only look at his watch and gather his keys and leave, running out of the house shouting 'Good luck'.

Two or three times during that period, while Ryder was in the shower, he and Brik would make love. In the kitchen, in the den, once even right outside the bathroom door as Ryder rapped his way through a currently charting song. It wasn't particularly satisfying to Brik, although the danger appealed but Trick's visits did provide a continuity of the momentum that had begun that first weekend they had met.

However much Brik may have thought that he still stood shoulder to shoulder with Ryder, Ryder was aware of the change in the climate of their friendship. Ryder was like radar, sensitive to a pin lying forgotten on the carpet, dropped from a newly opened shirt. He was as attuned as a barometer to the slightest change in the pressure of the emotional atmosphere surrounding him. He'd return from his shower and know that something wasn't right . . .

He had pretty much guessed about Brik, that his oldest and closest buddy was gay and he knew that if his guess was correct, it didn't much bother or concern him; in the short time of filming, Ryder had talked to everyone on the set; actors, crew, production staff. He'd made it his business to know everyone, to never pass someone by without saying 'Hi' and calling that person by their name. In talking to so many people, Ryder had discovered all sorts of attitudes, some vehement, some loose, but none polarised. All opinions were open, flexible and changeable depending on the direction of the wind. He learned that when you're on the up in Hollywood, everyone's with you but as soon as the breeze drops and you start to flag, you're alone on the Marie Celeste.

So he figured that applecarts weren't for upsetting, unless in the fracas you could get away with more apples than you were caught with. He also learned that physical beauty in either sex and of whatever persuasion was a quantity valued only marginally less than the constant number one. Money.

After the night at Andy's, Brik had expected Ryder to not only ask questions but to quiz him mercilessly. But

Ryder had said nothing. The incident was never mentioned again, at least, not until very much later. Because of that vacuum, Brik did not feel at all ill at ease being with Trick when Ryder was around. Trick was a very tactile man. He touched at every opportunity and it was that easy physicality which Ryder picked up, noting that difference between the way Brik acted with him and the way he was with Trick.

Brik knew he wasn't in love with Trick; no way. But he couldn't and didn't want to deny their mutual attraction. Their relationship was nothing like that with Ryder. He and Trick weren't racing each other round a course; it wasn't a competition where one would pull ahead only to be overtaken by the other and so on and so on until one just pipped the other to the post. It was a frolic, a gambol of two magnificent stallions, loose in a field, running, then leaping, then wheeling and turning rejoicing in the sheer freedom and sensuality of being together.

Behind his smile, Ryder logged all this. He didn't feel excluded as he had felt at first and what he felt was not an occasion for upsetting their particular applecart. He just knew that that they were different from him.

SIXTEEN

Why is it that bad news nearly always comes when it's least expected? And why is it, that however much the facts and figures which statistically pit the possible against the probable are explained, a negative outcome is always such a downer?

The television industry in Hollywood produced some two hundred pilot TV shows during the 1994 season for entry into the annual sweeps, as the network selection process was known.

An overview of the situation would show all the runners, jockeying and jostling like marathon entrants corralled behind the starting line, waiting for starter's orders. The white ones, the black ones, the mix-and-match, the make-and-mend, the disabled, the handicapped, the hopeless and the chanceless and each one sporting the sponsor's pennant and the hopes and dreams of endless training sessions and serious investment.

In a marathon as in any race, there can only be one winner at the finish line and that season there were thirteen possible winners in the TV sweeps. It wasn't the glory of winning that mattered, the prize money was colossal and there were no rules governing the number of entries. Telemax had its bets riding on three contenders of which Brik and Ryder's show was only one.

It lost.

The telephone lines crackled right across town as the judges' verdicts were handed out. The judges were the networks, ABC, NBC, CBS, FOX anonymous corporate acronyms, three little letters which always ended up spelling out G.O.D.

✳ ✳ ✳ ✳

Brik and Ryder had been down at the beach. Ryder was elated, having made dates with two girls who had approached the boys after a great deal of giggling and provocation from a neighbouring set of towels. What publicity the boys had done, always together as their `rags to riches' story, farmboys to movie stars, had been taken up by several teenage magazines and breakfast chat shows.

"I did it yesterday," Brik complained as Ryder pulled the Bronco up in the driveway. "She's your date, you clean up."

"All I'm asking is a little help, here," Ryder said as they swung their bags out of the rear door and hurried to the house. "I'll do the trash if you do the dishes . . . Deal?"

"Aw . . . okay," Brik flounced. "Jesus, Ryder, if you'd just clean up after you, we wouldn't have these conversations. D'you have your key?"

The telephone started to ring inside as Ryder fumbled through his keys.

"Come on, come on," Ryder urged himself. "Brik, we have to get an answermachine."

"When we're rich, we'll have a service," Brik replied. "I think that's kinda classy. Trick has a service."

Ryder finally inserted his key, opened the door and raced for the 'phone.

"Yeah . . . Hello." It was Lindy Green at Buckman Miller.

"Hi. Who's that?"

"It's Ry, Lindy."

"Oh, hello, Ryder. I have Andy for you. Hold on . . ."

Ryder tucked the 'phone into his shoulder and started clearing up beer cans and the leftover pizza that had staled and curled in the boxes since last night.

There was silence for a minute and a half before Andy came on the line. Ryder covered the mouthpiece and called to Brik.

"Are my other jeans still in the dryer?"

"I don't know! I do your dishes, Ryder, not your damn laundry!"

"Ryder?" Andy sounded upbeat.

"Yeah. Hi, Andy. What's up?" Ryder said.

"You want the good news or the bad." Ryder was caught off balance. The afternoon hadn't prepared him for bad news of any sort. Brik came in from the kitchen, drawn by the pregnancy of Ryder's silence.

"Shit. I don't know. The bad, I guess."

"Who is it, Ry?" Brik stage-whispered.

Ryder silenced him with an irritated wave of his hand.

"There's only one way to tell you guys this . . . Look, ABC didn't take the pilot." Andy paused. "Sorry, Ryder. Told you it was bad news. Is Brik there?"

"Yeah. He's here. It's Andy," Ryder said to Brik who was by now standing next to Ryder, straining at the earpiece. "ABC haven't taken our show."

"Oh," Brik said, deflated. The shock was a while coming. Like, 'You're gonna die' takes a moment to sink in.

"Lemme speak to Brik," Andy said. "Put him on."

Brik took the receiver.

"Hi, Andy."

"Sorry about this, Brik. It was the show they didn't like. They thought you were great, both of you. Don't be down. It's gonna be movie of the week pretty soon."

"Hey, that's great!" Brik inferred great things from this news.

"It's not that great," Andy qualified. "A lotta failed pilots get to be Movie of the Week but at least you'll be seen and you have some great work to show around."

"Do we get any more money for Movie of the Week, Andy?" Brik asked.

"Uh uh," Andy replied. "Only on a repeat and . . . well, don't count on it, Brik."

"Right. Well, I guess that's it?"

"Guess that's it . . . But put me back to Ryder, would you?"

"Sure." Brik handed the 'phone back to Ryder. "He wants you, Ry."

Ryder took the 'phone and Brik took his disappointment back to the kitchen. Doing the dishes suddenly became the most important thing to do in the world.

"Hi," Ryder said, laying back on the couch. "I'm back."

"Is Brik still with you?" Andy checked. His lowered voice made Ryder immediately lower his.

"He's around. He's out back. Why?"

"I said there was some good news. Gerri called me."
"Yeah."
"She has something for you. Starts in two days."
"Great!" Ryder exclaimed. "Does she want to see us." He looked up to see Brik standing in the kitchen doorway."

I said *you*, Ryder. *Just* you. Not Brik. He's too tall . . . too obvious for what they want. Estevez doesn't like the idea of physical competition."

"I see," said Ryder. Brik's face, registering enquiry, made Ryder turn away. "So, let's hear it for the short guys. Tell me more."

"The part is yours. The producer and the director saw your work on the pilot. Gerri had a copy from Lou. It's four weeks straight. You're on screen a lot of the time but *not* a lotta dialogue. It's not too different from the Tony character. I've had Gloria messenger the script over to you."

"What's the deal?" Ryder asked.

"Hey, slow down. I take it *we* have a deal too, Ryder?" Andy said, unable to disguise a certain amusement. "Remember?"

"Oh, that," Ryder chuckled. "I was just looking you over, Andy."

"Guess that's better than being overlooked," Andy replied.

"Damn right," Ryder laughed. "So. How much?"

"Four a week."

"Try for five," Ryder replied.

"Take it or leave it, Ryder. Gerri likes you but not that much."

"Four-five," Ryder said. He glanced up at Brik. "I have a family to feed. Tell Gerri I'll take her out to celebrate."

"Wouldn't do you any good, Ryder. Unless you're a closet dyke. I'll get back to you . . ."

"Thanks, Andy. 'Bye."

"'Bye."

Ryder replaced the 'phone.

"So what was all that about?" Brik asked.

"Sit down, ol' buddy," Ryder said and patted the couch.

Brik sat. Ryder stuck out his hand. Brik looked at it.

"Ryder! What is this?" he smiled.

"Take it," Ryder said.

"This is one of your screwy stunts, Ry, I know it."

"Absolutely not," Ryder replied, smiling broadly. Brik hesitantly shook Ryder's hand, tensing himself all the while for the punch. "There." But Ryder didn't let go.

"This might come as a shock, Brik but you *have* to know . . ."

"Know what? What's worse than bad news?"

"Gerri Muntz . . .," said Ryder conspiratorially, looking over his shoulder and peeking round the room as he spoke, ". . . is a dyke!" He whispered the last bit.

"Quit fooling, Ry!" Brik laughed. He tried to withdraw his hand. Ryder held on.

"Remember our deal, Brik?" Ryder said urgently. Brik was determined not to be fooled again.

"What deal? You're not making sense, Ryder . . .," Brik sparred in a sing song. "We're out of a job and you're making jokes."

"Our deal," Ryder went on. "All for one," he began and waited for Brik to complete their oath . . .

"And one for all . . . Yeah, yeah."

"Deal, right?" said Ryder.

"Sure!" Brik cried impatiently. "Get to it, Ry."

"I gotta part in a movie."

"But . . . that's great?" Brik exclaimed. "Isn't it," he added, unsure of how Ryder was expecting him to react.

"You're pleased?"

"Sure, I'm pleased, dummy. Whaddy'expect me to be?"

"I don' know," Ryder said, withdrawing his hand. "You sure you're not pissed?"

"Ryder! You're crazy! It's great. It's like you said, about guys waiting for years in New York for a break. You did the right thing coming out here. Like it was . . . I don' know, meant to be."

"But what about you?" Ryder asked.

Brik got up and started clearing what Ryder had cleared and then abandoned.

"It's been great, Ry . . . Bein' out here an' all," Brik said, crushing the beer cans in his left hand and piling them onto the pizza box. "But like I said back home, if it didn't work out I'd go to college, like I'm obviously meant to . . ."

"But you can't . . ." Ryder interrupted fiercely. "We had a deal. You jus' said so."

"Aw, come on, Ry . . . You can't hold me to that for ever. We were kids then."

"You can't leave," Ryder insisted.

"And I can't stay," Brik replied. "I have no more money, Ry." Brik took the trash out to the kitchen. Ryder followed.

"We'll make it," Ryder urged. "You'll see. We have to stick together, Brik!"

The doorbell rang; the ding-dong echoed through the house.

"There's your date," said Brik flatly. "And, don't worry. I'll leave you alone." Brik put out his hand, palm upwards; Ryder fished in his pocket and slapped the keys onto Brik's palm, covering it for a moment with his hand.

"You don't have to go, Brik. We're a team, remember?"

"Not in the sack, Ry," Brik replied sharply and brushed Ryder aside as he headed to the door.

※ ※ ※ ※

I found Brik sitting with Eldon in the kitchen when I got home.

"We have a visitor," Eldon said as I dumped my bag and jacket and joined them. "Tea's still hot if you'd like some, Jeremy? Brik and I have been shooting the breeze, as they used to say. Haven't we, Brik?"

"Yes," Brik said rather uneasily.

"Yes, tea. Thankyou, Eldon. So," I said as Brik got up and gave me a hug. I glanced at Eldon pouring my tea as I hugged Brik back. Not too much, but close enough so's he could feel my heart.

"Good to see you, coach," Brik muttered, close to my ear. He pulled back and grinned at me, holding me at arm's length by my shoulders. I sensed the rue behind his smile. I glanced again at Eldon who flashed one of those regretful smiles he must have used a thousand times before when handing back some grad student's term paper on a course they'd loused up on.

"Is everything okay at home?" was my first question, sensing that only a real disaster could effect the doom-laden atmosphere which hung over the table.

"No," Brik replied. "They're all fine. Spoke with Janna yesterday and she said be sure to send you her best."

"That's nice. So what's the problem?"

Brik spilled his sorrows and we listened, Eldon for the second time. I had no idea how long Brik had been with him.

Eldon was called away by the telephone which relieved me. I hadn't wanted to appear rude by asking to see Brik alone but I felt Brik was being restrained.

"So what do you want to do?" I asked in conclusion.

"I guess it's back to college. Maybe I should be Rosie the Riveter after all?"

"Who?" I queried, remarking at the same time upon a certain glib, camp throwaway which Brik had somehow assumed in the past two months.

"S'what Trick calls me. When I talk about winding up an engineer."

"Oh," I said. "I don't have that reference."

"Something about war work," Brik said. "When women did men's work. Fixin' rivets on ships and stuff." He shrugged and grinned.

Ah, I thought. Trick.

"But I take it that you don't want to go home . . . to college?"

"I notice *you* didn't go look for a job in Doddsville. Or Cleveland," Brik returned.

How I hated this part of his growing up. That incipient barbed wit which machine-gunned across gay bar rooms the whole world wide. `Jus' wasn't fittin', as Blanche may have said. There I go . . .

"Have you talked to Andy?"

"No," he sighed, shaking his head. "Not yet. I just have

this feeling."

"About what?"

"Can't say." He fell silent for a moment. "Guess I should go out and get a job."

"You have no money, do you?" I posed the question, knowing the answer.

"Guess I could borrow some from Ry," he observed wryly.

"Don't," I said. "How much do you want?"

"No," he said definitely. "It mustn't be like that. Not with us."

"But I have more than I need. You'll need a car, Brik. For starters. And your rent money. How much is it?"

"Thousand a month," he replied. "But I said no, Jeremy and I mean no." I heard Eldon return. He had overheard.

"I'm sorry to interrupt and I know it's none of my business," Eldon said returning to the table. "But you simply must, dear boy."

Brik was obviously uneasy. I sensed that pressurising him might be the wrong thing and I didn't want to frighten him away.

"I hate this," he said. "I should never have involved you, Jeremy."

"But I want to be involved," I insisted. "And think how I feel, Brik."

"How?" he asked, pouncing on my remark not with animosity but with concern.

"Well . . . I feel . . . Look, you're here in a way because of me. I'm part of this, Brik. So let me play my part. I know you can make it and I know you'll be okay but none of us will be okay without a little help. I promise I'll never mention the loan again. Ever."

"But money is such a . . ."

"Money is for buying things," Eldon interjected. "It only buys . . . things. In the end."

Brik glanced across at Eldon but he didn't smile. He just looked.

"Please," I begged.

"One way or the other," Eldon shrugged. "It might be

simplistic, Brik but you have absolutely no choice."

Brik toyed with the dregs at the bottom of his mug, swilling them round, tilting the mug back and forth as he thought.

"I figure . . ." He stopped for a moment. "I figure I owe you so much already that a little money isn't gonna do any harm."

"Good," I said. "At least that's settled. I have a free morning tomorrow. Let's go car shopping."

Brik put out his hand and took mine, not in a shake but in a hold. As he gently and firmly squeezed my fingers, I could have given him the world.

✳ ✳ ✳ ✳

Brik sat in the Bronco down South Bentley for over an hour before he saw the girl from the beach come out and drive away. He waited another five minutes before returning home.

"You must be psychic," Ryder laughed as Brik walked through the door. "She just left."

"Really?" said Brik. "Was it love?"

"Her family own supermarkets," Ryder replied. "Where ya been?"

"Jeremy's."

"How is he? Didya tell him about my movie?"

"He says to say `Great'."

"He doesn't like me," Ryder reflected, not vindictively, merely matter-of-fact.

"Sure he likes you, Ry."

"I *know* he doesn't." Ryder sniffed. "So I suppose Goody Two Shoes persuaded you to go back to college?"

"And if he did?"

Ryder kicked off his trainers and took up the lotus position in one of the single armchairs.

"I shan't let you go," Ryder announced. "I've been thinking it through."

"Ryder," Brik parried. "You have not. You've been screwing."

"So perhaps it wasn't the greatest," Ryder admitted, "but at least I got *us* all worked out."

"You have?"

"Sure. It's simple. I gotta job. You haven't. I'll be going to work everyday so why don't I pay you to be my driver. Then, when you get a job and I'm flat, I can do the same for you."

"But I have got a job," Brik announced and flopped down on the couch. He flipped on the teevee with the remote. "I just fixed it. One of the guys from the show put me on to it. 'Member Ronnie? The klutzy one with glasses? Him. It's nights, though. In a bar."

"Great," said Ryder. "Where?"

"Santa Monica," Brik said, waiting to see if Ryder would press for further details.

"So you're staying?" Ryder persisted.

"Yeah. 'Til Jeremy finishes his movie."

"Excuse me?" Ryder said. "Our coach is writing a movie?"

"Sure."

"Teachers don't write movies, man. Gimme a break," Ryder scorned.

"No!" Brik said angrily. "Give him a break."

"He wants to get in your pants, Brik. Can't you see that?"

"So what!" Brik exclaimed angrily. "Maybe I'll let him!" he shouted at Ryder. "What would you have to say about that?"

"They're your pants," Ryder shrugged. He could see Brik was seething with frustration. He said no more but sat and waited. Slowly, he began to smile, fixing on Brik's anger and teasing it away, digging deep into their ragbag of fights and pulling out a square of just the right colour and displaying it like a matador's cape, luring the angry bull into dropping just enough guard for him to feint in the required direction.

"You're an asshole, Ryder," Brik finally said. "Grrrr!" he roared, hitting his fist against his palm in mock reproof. Ryder laughed and whooped in triumph at yet another successful defusing of Brik's fury. "You are a total shit, you know that?"

"Likewise, partner!" Ryder grinned. "So will you be my driver? Least we get to pay the rent."

"I'll see," Brik said. "No promises. You never know what Andy will find for me."

"Now there's a guy you should let into your pants," Ryder said.

"So let him into your own pants!"

"Maybe I have," Ryder replied slowly, that mysterious grin once again leading Brik helplessly to an impossible conjecture. "Maybe I have . . ."

SEVENTEEN

It was neither Brik's nor Ryder's active fault that the bubble of innuendo was allowed to float around their lives unpopped. Not only did it seem convenient to have it hovering in the South Bentley Drive house but they batted it between them, back and forth, often for quite a time before their attention became distracted and the bubble was abandoned, left bobbing around on the ceiling like a balloon with its string dangling just out of ordinary reach; it was pretty, almost mesmeric, something to look at when there was nothing much else to talk about and nothing much else on TV.

Though Brik had lost his fear of Ryder finding out about him, he initiated and perpetuated the nightly charade of going to work. The balloon idea was a reminder to them both. Had they wanted, either could have stood on tiptoe and reached up, caught the string, pulled the balloon in and pricked it with the truth. But then, what would be left?

For a time, the innuendo revitalised their friendship, the mystery it supported, helping both Brik and Ryder to avoid the risk of familiarity sapping the strength of the bond between them.

For the majority of young men in LA in a similar situation to Brik and Ryder, the daily ritual of going to the gym was as important a part of the training as acting classes. In fact, the latter were virtually irrelevant, privately scorned, except by a small and tousled few. Trick had introduced both boys to his gym but Ryder had attended only two sessions before calling Dory and asking her to ship out his unsold weights. They arrived, packed in the crate with warm winter clothes and several foil-wrapped packages of home-baked cookies and home-made candy and preserves. Ryder decided to work out at home. It had been an overheard conversation in the locker room at the gym at the end of his second session which had un-nerved him and decided him on the in-house course of keeping his body beautiful. Trick may have been something of a star but, like the royal family, it did not put him above the range of the destructive power of evil gossip.

'So which one is the new Mrs Rambler?' remarked one deceptively be-muscled hunk to his friend in a pinched, nasal twang. 'Wouldn'cha jus' die to be a fly on the bedroom wall!' camped the friend.

It wasn't the sexual connotations that annoyed Ryder, it was the implication that he might be taken as anyone's mere appendage. But then, going to the gym wasn't simply going to the gym. There was more, much more; Ryder, his predilections being as they were, felt no clamouring need to be assimilated into that inner circle, knowledge of whose secrets were as advantageous to the participating bodies beautiful as any membership of a masonic lodge.

Ryder's tactic, lately discovered in Scotland, of letting his sex life come to him seemed to pay off best for him in LA. That way, he could get to choose, uncompromised by his own motivation; like, he could never be rejected. If what he permitted to approach him was something he didn't ultimately fancy, he could then make an excuse or just say no; he could gain further kudos from the situation by graciously acknowledging the compliment by his declining the invitation and inventing a wife and child or, at least, a girlfriend waiting for him at home. If he said yes, the game was played on his terms, on his turf by his rules. Ryder adored being adored but he could take only so much before it bored him and any mutual, shared tomorrow morning came only very infrequently for the girls he would have back to South Bentley Drive while Brik was out at work.

Brik, on the other hand, was finding life more complicated.

As far as the gym was concerned, Brik found the quivering, quizzical eye contact stimulating as he worked out next to Trick on the machines. Often, knots of sweating gymsters would gather round the pair as they worked their bodies into rivers of glistening perspiration. In the locker room, as Brik and Trick changed and showered, always together, the same men would gather, lazily towelling themselves as they quite blatantly watched the pair horsing around with the soap or the shampoo, as though an impromptu performance were about to take place and the onlookers would be privy celebrants in a religious ceremony extolling their own quest for physical masculine perfection. How their own status as cult acolytes would have been enhanced and vindicated by their witnessing the living example of their own two high priests. Although it never happened, there was, it was whispered, always the possibility that such witness just might one day be borne.

As Brik and Trick were never apart, Brik never encountered the situation where one of the other gymsters might make a pass; he was never allowed the chance to accept or rebuff the offer to go to breakfast afterward, or meet for a drink later or come round to the house after work. But it was not a matter for regret, Brik merely wondered what it would be like.

Trick knew what it was like and it was because he was always being pestered, always being approached that at first, he fostered his alliance with ". . . that new guy". Working out with Brik removed him from the immediate, casual arena of availability. Being with Brik raised a formal institution exuding its own protocol, which his adulants found difficult to breach.

No one is wholly responsible for their reputation; it takes the perceptions and ascriptions of others to make somebodies out of nobodies. As immutable as the instinct for hunting, was the instinct in the young LA male, of whatever persuasion, for challenge. Rising to and seeing through the challenge of a free session with Trick Rambler had lit up the horizons of only a handful of fellow gym-goers in the past and so the lure of the challenge to the remaining school was just as great. Despite their macho attitude, any one of the gilded butch of the Santa Monica Nautilus assault courses would be more than prepared, given the opportunity, to fall prey to the temptation to assuaging the reputedly unsatisfiable appetites of Trick Rambler using any means and under any circumstances Trick might care to name, the whole preferably achieved in public, so necessary would be corroboration of the story.

So Trick did nothing to lessen or dispel the talk about him and Brik being an `item'. The `are they or aren't they?' debate merely fuelled his unobtainability which, of course, made him still more desirable. And Trick knew that his desirability had to be maintained, now even more so, in direct proportion to the gradual decrease both in his libido and in his facility of being able to turn on to anyone. Trick had to earn his two hundred dollar fees; disappointing a client was a spectre which had been assuming an all too solid form of late.

So, for a while, coupled as he was in public with Brik, Trick's desirability soared, for the challenge now became a dual one, an insuperable one so it was rumoured, for no one yet had had the ultimate chutzpah to claim he had had them both.

As far as Ryder was concerned, Brik was doing a six-hour shift. He would leave the house at five-thirty and not return until past midnight. They were a long seven hours to kill. He would drive the streets or go to the beach, parking someplace where he could sit listening to tapes or the radio and watch the people passing. Rarely would he get out of the car. He didn't have money to go and drink in bars; occasionally he would go to movies. He tried reading but as he always parked where he could watch gays going about their life, his concentration was always broken whenever anyone passed the car. Sometimes he would catch someone's eye, often purposely exciting his observer only to find himself chickening out of an encounter as soon as the observer broke attitude, grinned and walked over to the car. This, interspersed with spending infrequent parts of an evening with Trick, went on for several days.

It was therefore Ryder's presence which assumed permanence in the house on South Bentley Drive. Brik was excluding himself through this self-imposed status as refugee and the feeling of rootlessness began to get to him. Nor was it that Brik was lazy; far from it. And neither was it that he couldn't get a job; he knew there were many jobs he could do and that he could get. That necessity would soon propel him to do so, he accepted, almost craved, for the burden of Jeremy's loan pressed heavily on his thoughts. But in order to take that step, to make that move, Brik realised that it would involve a step into nowhere, that it would involve the final estrangement from Ryder and that such a future, from his current standpoint, sported no safety net. What Brik realised he lacked, for the moment, was confidence. He could, if he closed his eyes, see it; there were times, self-blindfolded, when he fancied he had it in his grasp but it wasn't quite there yet . . .

One evening, curtailed by a 'phone call which Trick took in the bedroom and which Brik couldn't overhear, Brik left Trick's apartment when Trick announced he had to go out. Instead of driving away, headed for nowhere, Brik waited in his new but one-year-old black Volkswagen and watched Trick as he came out of the apartment carrying a black-and-white sportbag and get into his car.

Brik followed. Up to Sunset and left. Through Beverly Hills, past the Beverly Hills Hotel and on, towards the Freeway at Brentwood. Brik trailed at a safe distance and watched as Trick hung a right and drove into the Bel Air Estate.

Almost at the top of Stone Canyon Road, Brik watched as Trick disappeared round a corner. Brik slowed, not wanting to be seen and when he came around the corner saw the rear of Trick's car disappearing through the tall iron gates of an unseen property up to the left. The gates swung closed behind the car as Brik stopped the Volkswagen outside and sat for a moment, the motor idling, before driving right to the top of Stone Canyon, turning the car and heading back.

Brik parked for a few minutes opposite the gates and got out to see . . . But there was nothing to see. The property's flagged driveway with its floor-level lights wound first to the left and then disappeared out of sight. Brik returned to his car but had only been inside for a minute at most when the Bel Air patrol car cruised slowly by.

It scared him and he fumbled with the ignition as the patrol car came almost to a stop next to him as he finally got the motor started. He had the presence of mind to wave and smile at the two security officers. They frowned suspiciously but his car wasn't old, therefore not suspicious and Brik looked as though he could have been the scion of a Bel Air dynasty. So, when Brik moved off, although the patrol car followed him, as he accelerated the Volkswagen down the hill, Brik noticed the headlights recede in his mirror.

He drove back to Westwood down Hilgard, slowing outside Eldon Stuart's house, wanting to stop and talk to Jeremy. But there were no lights on and it was almost a safe time for Brik to return home. What Brik had hitherto been able to accept on face value about his new acquaintance was becoming impossible not to question. Brik, having asked the question, now needed the answer.

Brik knew that Trick knew a lot of people but other than himself and asking questions of Brik and Ryder about work at the studios, Trick never spoke about his society. To Brik, Trick Rambler's existence was as mysterious as that of quantum physics.

Though Brik was quite able to acknowledge that, this far, love did not seem to be on the menu at Trick's restaurant, he knew that there was something of more substance than mere appetizer. Brik found himself becoming genuinely fond of the porn star, relaxed in his company and although he easily acknowledged this closeness to his guide, he thought for a long time it was not being in the least reciprocated. Trick, called by the 'phone, would often break off in the middle of some loveplay and, as though flicking a switch, would discard the urgency of his attention to Brik and merely pick up his clothes, go take a shower, only to return dressed and coiffed to announce that he'd ". . . gotta go". As Brik anticipated the end of the honeymoon with his life in LA, he felt he didn't need mysteries. His decision to ask Trick where he'd gone that night was Brik's unwitting acknowledgement that he had discovered his elusive confidence.

※ ※ ※ ※

Lou Hales had come out of the pilot stakes a winner. Two out of his three shows had been taken up and he used this clout to have the network schedule Brik and Ryder's show almost immediately.

As it happened, the two stars of that show watched themselves together in `Opposite Horizons', as the show had been re-titled when it came on as Movie of the Week. Brik announced that he'd gotten the night off from his job and they watched the show not at the South Bentley house but at Trick's, the night after Trick had made his out-call to rendez-vous with Ron Windel at Kenneth's; it was their second meeting, so successful had been the first.

Ryder had made his excuses almost as soon as the credits had zipped unreadably up the screen and left, acknowledging the plaudits Trick had heaped generously on his performance. It was only a couple of days before he started work on the Estevez movie and he said he needed his sleep.

"They must be fuckin' crazy," Trick swore, returning to Brik after seeing Ryder out. "That is a good show." He sniffed, as though laying irrefutable emphasis on his critique. "Yeah," he asserted. "But probably too good," he added as conclusion. "You really are something, Big Boy." The appellation was a recent endearment.

"Thanks," Brik replied. "At least you've seen some of my work now." He smiled and shrugged. "Probably the last, the way things are going."

"Don't say that, man," Trick encouraged. "Betcha 'phone will be red hot tomorrow after folks see that. Hell, Big Boy, you really have got what it takes."

"So have ten thousand other guys in this town," Brik replied. "I'm not sure I want it, Trick."

"You wanna share this with me? To celebrate?"

Brik shook his head as Trick spooned a little coke out of a small vial into his nostrils. It reminded Brik of another puzzlement. He had never spent an evening with Trick when at least four of these 'cocktails' as Trick called them had not been consumed. He'd also noticed that it was only after a 'cocktail' that Trick could achieve a climax.

"I'm thinking of getting a job, a proper job and going to college."

"Sure you won't?" Trick repeated his offer, holding out vial and spoon.

"No thanks. That stuff must cost you a fortune, Trick," he observed quietly.

"So it's what I work for," Trick replied. "Havin' a good time, Big Boy."

"Where do you go? When you leave me?"

Trick often drifted for a while after snorting his coke and he seemed to be drifting as Brik spoke.

"Why d'ya wanna know?" he replied, almost inaudibly.

"I followed you last night," Brik said, tensing for what was an unpredictable reaction.

Trick laughed.

"I know," said Trick. "I knew you would sooner or later. You took your fuckin' time."

"You're not mad?"

"Why should I be? I'm not ashamed."

"But you never talk about it."

"What's there to talk about? It's just a job."

"You make out like you were a . . . I don' know. Like some teevee repair man," Brik said, his mind alighting on the first object association that hit his vision.

"So show me a teevee repair man who takes his work home with him," Trick retorted.

"But I'm interested. Really. I'd like to know," Brik pursued. "I think I have to know."

"And maybe I don' wanna tell you," Trick replied negatively.

"But why? You said you're not ashamed."

"Perhaps I'm tryin' to protect you, Big Boy. I like you."

"Protect me from what? I'm not some retard who doesn't know health risk from a hole in the ground."

"I'm not talkin' about that," Trick replied edgily.

"So what is it that you do, Trick? And *how* do you do it?" Brik urged. "Whadda they want, these guys you go to see? D'you ever bring them back here?"

Trick clapped his hand to his head and rolled over on the

couch. He groaned.

"Quit it," he said, burying his face in a pillow. "Don' spoil it for us, Brik. It's my *business*."

"And no room for questions, I take it."

"No room for questions and no room in it for you, Big Boy. You got other things to think about, like a future."

"Huh!" Brik exclaimed. "Like driving Ryder to location?"

"No!" Trick yelled, sitting upright. "Like your fuckin' career, man!"

"From where I'm sitting," Brik said, "my career came and went. If you weren't watching tonight, you'dda missed my *great* career!" He paused. "Haven't heard from Andy in a week."

"Fuck Andy," Trick mumbled.

"Oh, not you too," Brik huffed. "Anyway, I wouldn't."

"Why not? You never know," Trick advised.

"I'm not selling myself that cheap," Brik replied. "And I *do* know. It's too close to home."

"Well if you *had* been home tonight, he'd'a called," Trick argued. "Betcha there's a message for you when y'get back."

"We don't have a machine," Brik replied flatly. "Or a service. But you have, Trick."

"So I need one."

"So I *want* one," Brik replied. "And my own place and money to go to college and pay back Jeremy and I ain't about to get those things waitin' tables or pumpin' gas!"

Trick moved across the couch and put his arm round Brik's back. Slowly, he eased down beside Brik so that he was curled up in the crook of Brik's free arm. As he looked up at Brik, he ran his hand affectionately down the side of Brik's cheek. It was the most intimacy Trick had ever displayed. As Brik assimilated the new position, as he realised that Trick had dropped guard long enough to let him in, really in, Brik decided to take advantage and explore.

"Is this really what you want, Trick?"

"I don't know," Trick sighed and averted his eyes. His

fingers scratched at a loose thread in a rip on the knee of Brik's Levis. He inserted one finger gingerly between the fabric and Brik's revealed thigh and made little stroking movements. "I don't wanna lose you, Big Boy. I can't explain what I mean but I don't wanna lose you."

"You won't," Brik whispered gently. "But I don't wanna have secrets, Trick. I got enough of those with Ry and it don't work. I like you . . . I like you a lot. Who knows, perhaps that's what it's all about . . . Perhaps this is it and perhaps there's more. But I don't know. And I want to find out and so you gotta tell me."

Trick sighed. Curled in Brik's arm, against what he knew to be his better judgement, he recounted the events of the previous evening, the fruits of which had been just another payment to his ". . . man".

"It's all an act, Brik," Trick confessed at the end. "You're just playin' a part 'cept there ain't no script and no director to tell you where to move and when to speak. It's like one long, long audition and performance all in one. You're the publicity, the marquee, the box office, the hat check, the usherette, the projectionist, the popcorn and the weenies, the janitor who cleans up afterwards . . . You're the whole damn picture show, Brik." He stopped the relentless recitation as though he'd said too much. "An' sometimes it gets to be one heavy son-of-a-bitch," he said, his voice dead and abdicant.

"And how many shows a week?" Brik asked softly.

"As many as I can git," Trick replied, a far away feeling in his voice. "Fast as I can rewind the film."

He sniffed and slowly removed himself from Brik's closeness. He picked up the vial and the spoon and looked at it for a moment before unscrewing the gold cap and emptying a pile onto the back of his hand. Up it went. The vial was empty.

"And now I really gotta go out," he said numbly.

"If you didn't do that, you'd be a rich man," Brik observed supportively.

"An' if I didn't do that I wouldn't be able to get to be a rich man."

Trick slid from his seat to the floor and edged along so that he sat with his back against the couch between Brik's opened legs. He leant his head back so that it rested on Brik's crotch.

They sat like that for a long while that evening, Trick staring at the ceiling, Brik stroking Trick's hair, each trying to unravel the other's thoughts.

"Wouldn't it be great?" Trick murmured finally. "Wouldn't it?"

"It would be," Brik sighed. "But we both know it's not gonna happen."

Trick felt a lump forming in his throat. He felt the sting as tears bit like acid at the edge of his eyes. He shook, a tender convulsion which he tried to disguise with a cough. Brik just went on stroking his hair.

"Do me a favour?" Trick managed to say.

"Sure," said Brik. "If I can."

"Tell me you didn't mean that."

"Okay. I didn't mean it. There."

"Thanks," Trick murmured, squeezing Brik's ankle. "Do me another favour?"

"Sure."

"Stay with me tonight, Big Boy?" Brik smiled. He sat forward on the couch, keeping Trick's head gently between his thighs. He reached his hand out and took the 'phone off the hook. "Okay," Brik agreed tenderly.

They waited until the dial tone changed to that long, continuous, unbreakable "... eeeeeeemmmmmmmm".

❋ ❋ ❋ ❋

Tommy Cattini's wife and kids watched `Opposite Horizons' that night. Tommy was out.

Julio and Dolores Sevendez also watched the show. They rather enjoyed it. At least they could identify with the large and poor Mexican family the boy Danny came from.

Maybe it would have been better if Tommy hadn't been out and had watched the show. It would have certainly saved him five hundred bucks. And if Kenneth hadn't been fopping around in a tux at one of his partner's son's Barmitzvahs, it would have saved him five hundred bucks too. Actually, the ratio of share ownership in Innuendo Productions was 49/51, so, strictly speaking and because of the majority, Kenneth's saving would have been marginally more than Tommy's.

Whether the dollar equivalent of thirty pieces of silver had gone up some or down some in two thousand years is arguable. What is not arguable is the token significance, for mankind was still buying and selling each other in the shadow of the noose.

To be fair, though why bother? Clem Barber had had other things on his mind than Brik Peters since seeing the photo on Tommy Cattini's desk. Clem didn't only work for Tommy and when news came through that his future was not going to be at Dick Molina's side working for Telemax, Clem had been called upstate for a week to shoot two movies for Falcon, in the hills north of San Francisco.

He returned to the city to the prospect of no work. He drove over to the valley to see what was happening.

He called in to see some friends at Universal but drew a blank. He spent some time talking with the guys as they waited for a lighting change on their soap and then decided to have lunch in the commissary.

Coming out as Clem was going in, he met Brik.

"Hi, Clem! Good to see you," Brik greeted him enthusiastically. "Whaddya working on?"

Clem smiled and stroked his patchy beard as the memory of Brik Peters undressed as a Highway Patrol officer reassembled itself in his mind.

"I'm just hustlin', Brik. What about you?"

"Not hustlin' very well, it seems," Brik joked. "I'm here with Ry. He's working on the new Estevez picture. I gotta day on it in two weeks but . . . Shit! May as well go pump gas full-time in real life as act pumpin' gas into Estevez's tank in a movie."

Clem laughed. He'd instinctively liked Brik when they'd worked together. Nothing had been too much trouble; there had been no tantrums or bad behaviour. Unlike with

Ryder, Clem remembered, who had refused one morning to use a Winnebago which had no curtains. Clem remembered Brik shuffling embarrassed as Ryder had shouted his will. But it had been a will that had won out. Ryder got curtains put up in the Winnebago.

"An' nothin' else?" Clem delved.

"Nope," Brik grinned. "An' if something doesn't come along soon, this boy's gonna be headin' back home."

"Aw, no!" Clem appeared to sympathise. "Don't give up yet. There's plenny ways of turning a buck, Brik."

"Like what?" Brik grinned, acknowledging with that certain smile the fact that both he and the cameraman were gay. "I'm not down to hitchin' rides on Melrose yet, Clem."

"Mebbe I can help?" Clem offered. "I know some people."

"Like to do what?" Brik asked.

"Oh, some shorts . . . educational stuff. Training videos. That kinda thing."

"Gee, Clem. That'd be swell if you would."

"Yeah," Clem concluded, in that strung-out whine which always seemed to convey a secondary meaning, one pregnant with suggestion.

"Catch up with you later," Brik said, excusing himself. "They'll be breaking for lunch soon an' I gotta see Ry."

"'Bye, Brik," Clem drawled. "I'll be in touch."

Clem watched as Brik loped off in the direction of a nearby sound stage. He then went into the commissary and made the call.

"Yeah, hello," Tommy Cattini barked as he picked up on his private line.

"Tommy?" Clem breathed. "It's Clem."

"Nothin' for you, Clem. Sorry. I said I'd be in touch."

"But I *might* have somethin' for *you*," Clem chuckled. "Can I run it by you?"

"I was just leavin', Clem."

"Sit down, Tommy. Just sit down for a moment . . . Are you comfortable? Right. You remember the meat in that photo I saw on your desk . . . The one making like a Highway Patrolman?"

Tommy rifled through the mountains of paper on his wide desk.

"Yeah," he said, removing the cigar from his mouth as his thumb and forefinger withdrew the photo of Brik. "What about him?"

"I think I may have a lead on him."

"So follow it up and come back to me."

"Sorry, Tommy? What did you say? I'm having a little difficulty hearing you. Must be the line."

Tommy stabbed the butt of the cigar out in the overflowing ashtray. "Shit," he whispered.

"What was that?" Clem whined, hardly able to suppress an amusement at the turned tables.

"How much?" Tommy muttered, his lips hardly moving they were viced so tight.

"Ah! That's better," Clem said, raising his voice slightly, "I can hear you better, Tommy. Go on, I'm listening."

"Five," Tommy offered.

"Make it the big one, Tommy," was Clem's ultimatum.

There was a moment's silence before Tommy came back.

"Okay, Clem. But only if we get him. If he bails out, the deal's off."

"Call Buckman Miller. They're the agents," Clem opened up, like a hungry mollusc. "The brand on the meat is Peters, Berrick Peters."

EIGHTEEN

Lindy Green was having a busy day. Everyone seemed to be out at the same time. There were five full-time agents at Buckman Miller but only three had assistants. The two who hadn't, Andy Horowitz and Sally Swzenc (try Schwenck, it's easier), were out out. The others were in meetings and secretaries took longer with clients than their agents. Lindy's job involved playing secretary for Andy and Sally.

The lines lit up again, three calls of which two she could put through. The third call ought to have been for Andy. Berrick Peters was his client.

"Good afternoon, Buckman Miller," she'd intoned as if by rote. "How may I help you?"

As Brik looked to Tommy to be Italian, Tommy Cattini affected what he remembered as the heavy Neapolitan accent of his ancestors.

"I call about Meester Peeders. Berreek. You know heem?"

"Sure we know him," Lindy replied, holding the receiver away from herself and staring at the mouthpiece with disbelief. "Who is calling?"

"Thees heez uncle. Me an' Breek's auntie, we here on vacation from Eetalee an' I loose heez number an' the address. My wife, she say I am a, how you say, seeely jerk, yes? But she remember the name of you. You are the agents, yes?"

Another light flashed up on Lindy's board.

"Yes, we are. But Mr Horowitz is out. He is Brik's agent. I am not supposed to give you his number Mr . . ."

"Cattini. I am Tomaso Cattini. His father's brother."

Another light flashed up on the board.

"Look, I'm sorry . . . Oh . . . Okay. I'll give you his number, Mr Cattini." Lindy didn't often capitulate but it all sounded very plausible. She ran her fingers over the roladex in front of her and repeated Brik and Ryder's number and the address on South Bentley.

"Sankyou, Mees," Tommy acted. "Sankyou vairy much.

You 'ave a nice day, now."

"And you, Mr Cattini," she replied and flipped the line free as she returned to the two waiting calls. "Hope you reach him. I believe he's out at the studios today."

"Sankyou vairy . . ." Tommy said to thin air before he grinned, fairly threw the receiver back into the cradle and rubbed his hands. "Gotcha, wonderboy! Gotcha!"

But Lindy wasn't psychic.

"Buckman Miller, Good afternoon. How may I help you?"

She didn't even write down that Brik's uncle had called. It was only the following day when Andy handed her a ten by eight still of Brik in `Opposite Horizons' to mail that she thought to tell him of the call.

"Italian?" Andy said, puzzled. "I thought his people were Scottish. If there was an uncle visiting from the old country, I wouldda thought he'd'a sounded like Sean Connery."

❊ ❊ ❊ ❊

It wasn't with surprise that Brik read the letter on the Innuendo Productions notepaper he found in the mailbox when he and Ryder got back from the Valley that night. Tommy had decided a 'phone call would have been suspicious. Brik could have easily referred him back to Andy Horowitz. It was Kenneth who suggested writing and mentioning that Clem Barber had had a word.

"Ry! Listen to this!" Brik shouted excitedly and read Ryder the letter. "Gee, thanks Clem. What a great guy. Y'see, Ry! Faggots aren't so bad!"

"Read it again," said Ryder.

"Dear Mr Peters, Clem Barber mentioned to me that you are not working at this time. Before referring this project to your agent, would you call me and make an appointment to come see me. I think I have something you could well be interested in . . . Tommy Cattini."

"Sounds a shyster," Ryder commented, throwing Brik a beer. "But you might as well go see him."

"I'll call him right now," Brik replied, grabbing the 'phone.

Ryder went off to take a shower.

It was Tommy who answered. There was no secretary.

"Hi, this is Brik Peters," Brik began brightly. Before he could go on, Tommy interrupted.

"Brik! Hi! Thanks for returning my call. Do I take it you wanna meet?"

"Is that you, Mr Cattini?"

"Sure. My sec . . . the switchboard closes at five here. We start kinda early."

"Oh, I see. Well . . . Sure. I mean, yeah. When can we meet?"

"Why not right now?" Tommy suggested. "I haven't anything 'til eight. That should give us enough time."

"Fine."

"Don' even shower, Brik. Just come right on over. It's Pico and Cloverfield. Park in back and I'll buzz you in from the lot, okay?"

"Sure, Mr Cattini. I'll be there in twenny minutes. 'Bye."

"'Bye 'bye Brik," Tommy said efficiently, killed the call and dialled Kenneth Morrell.

"That was quick," Kenneth said. He was speaking on the carphone outside the Bel Air Hotel. The valet held the door open, waiting to park the Bentley. "No, I leave that to you, Tommy. I'm sure you can handle it . . . Just don't put the pressure on too soon . . . No, just tell him all the plusses . . . In the meantime, I'll get right on to my dearest and oldest friend . . ." Kenneth giggled. "Yes . . . Won't he be surprised . . . not to say the teensiest bit pissed at me? Good Luck, Tommy, dear . . . Call me, yeah?"

❋ ❋ ❋ ❋

Ryder had immediately offered to come along, but Brik had declined.

In a way, Brik reflected as he drove down Westwood to Pico, this second audition was even more exciting than the first. No strings had been pulled, no favours called in, no ulterior motives were in play. They want to see *me*, he thought. Whatever it is Tommy Cattini wants me for, he wants *me*. I'm going by myself, on my own to see a producer about a job.

The twelve car parking lot was empty save for a rusting Ford whose wheels had long-since disappeared and which lurched crazily to one side, three of the blocks beneath its axles having collapsed. The Innuendo building stood out from its neighbours, like the black tower at Burbank, Brik thought as he parked the Volks and locked it. Innuendo was also painted black, a flat, matt-black against which the several mirror-filmed windows showed up like a blind man's sightless gaze, shielded by reflecting shades. Brik crossed the lot and pressed the buzzer.

The entry phone crackled as Tommy acknowledged his ring and buzzed him in.

"Come straight through and all the way up the stairs opposite," came Tommy's instruction.

The door opened inwards. Brik waited until it had closed and checked it was locked. The tape room was quiet, the slave machines were down and there was no one to watch him, however casually, as he took off his Raybans in the darkened room, lit by only one working bulb. He saw the stairway and crossed the room, his footfalls echoing through the deserted, high-ceilinged space. He mounted the stair, stopping for a moment on the first floor landing. Light came again from a single, naked bulb which illuminated the worn carpeting and the scratched and chipped paint on the matt-black walls. As Brik climbed the second flight, narrower than the first and with no carpeting at all, his soles scratched on bare concrete.

The stairs went no further. To the left he saw an open door, whence light came.

"Through here, Brik!" Tommy called.

Brik took a deep breath just before walking through the door and he walked slowly, almost edging into the frame of the doorway, inch by inch. Tommy sat behind the desk, facing the door and watched with creeping delight as the white of Brik's T-shirt appeared from the gloom, glowing almost unnaturally brightly as though lit by ultra-violet in the backroom of some tacky bar.

"Mister Cattini?"

Tommy half-rose from the chair, pushing himself up. He didn't get up. His chair was too far under the desk and one of the casters had caught in a hole in the threadbare carpeting and he couldn't shift backwards.

The worried look on Brik's face dropped as soon as he saw that he had, after all, come to the right place. The grin broke out and he strode into the room, hand out-stretched.

"Brik. Thanks for coming over," Tommy said, taking Brik's hand. "Please. Sit. Sit down. Can I get you anything? Coffee?"

"I'm fine, thankyou, sir," Brik replied as he sat opposite.

"Yeah," said Tommy, rather lost as to how to begin. This was not a usual interview. Usually they came knowing full well the reason for coming. Yeah, he thought, that was it. They knew they were getting paid to come. It shouldda been Kenny doing this, Tommy reflected. Kenny and his golden tongue.

"So?" Brik started ingenuously. "What's the project, sir?"

"Look," Tommy began. "The `sir' is very nice an' all but it makes me nervous. Tommy, right? I'm Tommy."

"Sure. Tommy. Whatever you say."

Tommy noted the compliance. A real movie producer wouldn't have thought to have looked to pick up on an actor's vulnerability. The moods and temperaments of the big stars were one thing. Most actors just did like they were told. Tommy felt awkward, nailed as he was to the spot. This was a nice guy sitting in his office. Usually they were . . . Fuck it. Tommy had never before given a thought to what his cast were like. What was it Kenny had said about Ron Windel? Worrying symptoms of integrity?

"Good." Tommy coughed, pretending to clear a frog. "Well . . . Brik. You ever done a movie before?"

Brik shook his head.

"Just television, Tommy. But then you know that. What did you think of the show?"

"I . . . yeah. I liked it," Tommy said dismissively for he

hadn't an idea of what Brik was talking about . . . "Not bad. Your first . . . er . . . big part, was it?"

"Yep," Brik replied. He was determined to please.

"That's how I got to know Clem. Clem Barber. He was our cameraman."

"Oh . . . right," Tommy murmured as light dawned. That shit, he thought as Clem's name came up and he worked back over the past six weeks since Clem had first seen Brik's photo. The bastard must have known for six weeks!

"Is there anything wrong, Tommy?" Brik asked, sensing that in Tommy's reflective silence, all was not well. "Is it me?"

Tommy got it together.

"What? Oh . . . nah. Nah. I was thinking, that's all."

"Look," said Brik helpfully, "if I'm not right, please be honest. I know it happens. You see someone's work in one show and when you meet them in the flesh, they're not . . . well, not what you're looking for." Brik relaxed into his chair. He felt easier now that he had voiced his fears. He began to take in the surroundings, the pin-board walls, the fan, the tackiness. What he didn't see on the wall behind him was a photo of Trick Rambler. He could find no clues . . . nothing struck him, except the tackiness.

"Oh, you're right, Brik. You're exactly what we're looking for. You're . . . you're what, six feet?"

"Six-two, hundred-eighty pounds," Brik clarified, guessing Tommy to be about five-nine and nothing less than two-twenty.

"Right. You ever done modelling work, Brik?"

"But . . . I thought this was a movie we were talking about?" Brik replied. "I'm an actor, Tommy . . ."

"Sure . . . We only use actors . . . Acting," he smirked, "is what it's all about, ain't it?" Brik nodded. "So you never done no modelling?" Tommy too was relaxing. He did best when people were needled. If they were needled then Tommy could wheedle and he wheedled good when he knew he had something to gain.

But as Tommy was talking, it clicked in Brik's mind. As though he were making up a recipe, as the ingedients were added one by one, Brik flashed on the finished confection. He suddenly knew what it was all about. And, as if prodded by an unseen goad, he felt as though be were being observed, as if someone was watching him. He turned round.

Trick.

Tommy Cattini.

Innuendo . . . Like the timer pinging to announce the cake was baked, the bell rang in Brik's brain.

Innuendo, he realised, meant porno.

And so, a little late and through no fault of his own, Brik got there.

"This modelling thing is real important, isn't it, Tommy?" Brik enquired, checking the position of his Raybans pushed back into his hair. "It's like . . . How shall I say, an important qualification."

Tommy was a lot of things but he wasn't slow. His nervousness had heightened his prickly and volatile temperament. He sensed a change in Brik's attitude, almost as though he was being played, like a fish.

"So have you or haven't you?" Tommy urged, rather finally.

"No," Brik lied. He stood up and kicked his chair back. Tommy involuntarily pulled back from his hunched position, elbows on his desk. Brik was a big guy, for a fag, Tommy thought and he hadn't reckoned on the scene turning physical. "But if you wanna see what I look like without the clothes," Brik threw out. He started to peel off his T-shirt.

"Hey . . . Quit that!" Tommy barked. "Whaddya think I am? I ain't no fag . . . And . . . You're lyin' to me, Brik."

"I am?" Brik said, insolently. He was no longer buoyed up with excitement; that had been swamped and sunk along with Tommy's integrity. Brik was angry at being toyed with. He disliked Tommy Cattini, had done on sight but way back then, three minutes ago, there was a different job on offer. What Brik faced now was not losing a job, it was a sea change in the basic career.

"Siddown," Tommy murmured icily and at the same

time withdrew the photo from beneath a pile of untidy files. He took it by a corner, hardly touching it between thumb and forefinger, dangled it for a moment and then let it drop to the desk, like it was too dirty to be touched, like he should have been wearing rubber gloves.

Brik looked at himself; at first he didn't recognise who it was, that handsome guy grinning out from beneath the peaked cap, uniform shirt open beneath the holster harness and pulled back to show the naked body, naked from the waist down except for the gun, the gun held against his thigh like a rule. Seen side-by-side, so flagrantly juxtaposed, Brik's hot tumescence and the cold gun created a formidable and unmistakable comparison. Ron Windel may have been an amateur photographer but as a pornographer, his approach was succinctly professional. A photograph can often deceive but there can be no argument about the size of a regular patrolman's gun. "We've been looking for you, *Mister* Peters. I take it you recogise yourself?" Tommy concluded.

Brik's heart leapt as his bravura evaporated. As he picked up the photo, the memory of that afternoon sped back; the room, what the carpet was like, what he'd done that morning, what he was going to do later that night; memories re-discovered like old letters from dead people found at the back of a drawer came alive and fresh and made him remember even how he felt.

"How did you getta hold of this?" he said quietly.

Tommy took out a fresh cigar and leant back in his chair as he lit it.

"Ah ha!" he said with a conniving, complicit grin. He tapped his nose. "Now that *would* be ratting."

"Does Doctor Windel know about . . .?" Brik faltered, unable to believe that Ron had reneged on their deal.

"Whoah, buster. I'm asking the questions here. Like for instance, do your folks know about their faggy lil' boy?" Tommy rejoined. "Where the hell is it you come from? Idaho?"

"Ohio," Brik corrected. He dropped the photo and turned round once again to confront the grinning photo of

Trick Rambler behind him. So was it Trick, he wondered? Brik abandoned the thought immediately. He had already figured why Trick had been so reluctant to talk the other night. Trick was a king and the king was not about to roll over and die to make way for another.

And then he laughed. Suddenly it was all funny, very, very funny. It threw Tommy completely.

"You wanna share the joke? What is this?" Tommy shouted. It made Brik laugh even more; he was almost doubled up with a mirth that needled Tommy to the point of rage. "What is it here that's so *damn* funny!" Tommy bellowed, his face reddening, his neck puffing up over his tight collar. He ripped open his tie and kicked his chair back as he pounded the desk with his fist. "Fer crissake! Shut the fuck *up!*"

Tommy's frustrated scream finally broke Brik's hysteria. Brik bent down, still in a spasm of breathless chuckles, and picked up his Raybans where they'd fallen. He brushed off the dust, wiped the lenses on his jeans and sat down.

"That's better!" Tommy snarled.

"So," Brik began, still smiling. "What's the deal, Tommy? What are we talking here?"

"You have some nerve, buster! Whaddya mean, what's the deal?"

"You want me to do a porno movie, right?" Tommy slowly sat down, frowning. Now, he thought, now what's the guy up to? What did he mean, `want me to'? Tommy had never `wanted' anyone for a movie before. The `want' on his part had never arisen. It was *them* who wanted to; it was the fuckin' *actors* who were supposed to *want*.

"If ya puddit like that," Tommy replied, "yeah."

"And if I *don't* want, you're gonna blackmail me with that photo, right?"

"Well, hell," Tommy blustered. "That's some heavy word, Brik..."

"... but that's what it boils down to, right?" Brik interrupted. As he talked, he thought. *Who* would Tommy show the photo to? His parents? Ron Windel? Who *else* was involved that Brik didn't know about?

"Let's jus' say we thought it might encourage you," Tommy smarmed.

"We?"

"My . . . my associates," Tommy replied glibly, rather pleased with himself for thinking of the word.

"But why didn't you just ask me?" Brik enquired. "Just come right out with it and ask?"

He sounded so reasonable, Tommy became immediately suspicious.

"You mean . . .?" Tommy murmured. "Hey! What *is* this?"

Think, Brik urged himself. Think, Brik. Think.

Suddenly he lunged forward and grabbed the ten by eight and ripped it in two. Then again, into four and kept on ripping it into tiny pieces and threw them like confetti over the desk. It was Tommy's turn to laugh.

"Won't do you any good, Brik," he sing-songed tauntingly. "There's a helluva lot more where that came from."

"I only did it to show you," said Brik, dredging up a defiant grin.

"To show me what!" Tommy spat.

"To show you I'm not afraid of your blackmail. You can't possibly use those shots. Okay, yeah . . . my family, perhaps but there ain't no one else. I'm not working nor ever likely to again's far's I can see. So . . ." Brik sat forward in his chair and fixed Tommy, pinning him to his chair, daring him to blow a hole in his argument. "Like I said, what's the deal?"

Tommy was silent. His eyes blinked as numbers scrambled in his brain. His lips twitched nervously, almost mouthing the figures silently to himself, tasting them before selecting the one he would suggest first.

"Five."

"What. Five what?"

"Hell," Tommy chuckled. "Hundred. Didja think I meant thousand?"

"Try it," Brik said scornfully. "For siiiiize . . ." He extruded the word and made as if to flip the buttons on his fly.

"You crazy?" Tommy yelped. "You *are* crazy, man. I ain't never paid five thousand to anyone."

Brik sat back and looked at his watch. He whistled, a formless tune. He folded his arms and looked around the room.

"I have some time, *Mister* Cattini," he sighed. "But not a lot. You, on the other hand, must be a *very* busy man. I'll be interested . . ."

". . . in what?" snapped Tommy.

"How long it takes us to agree the two thousand dollars you're gonna pay me to make your movie."

"Get the fuck outta here!" Tommy exclaimed.

"Okay," Brik said and got up.

He was halfway down the stairs before Tommy could run out onto the landing and call him back.

"You come back here, buster!"

"Oh," Brik replied, acting as though another thought had struck him, "and then there's the script . . . I don't do crap, Tommy. If it's crap, you won't see me for dust." He continued down the stairs.

"Come back!" Tommy screamed as he followed Brik down the stairs. "No one walks out on Tommy Cattini, you hear?" This he shouted from the mezzanine as Brik reached the first floor. "You'll ruin me! You hear me, Brik?"

"Call me!" Brik shouted as he walked through the empty copying room. His words echoed like racket balls against the bare concrete walls.

The sun had almost gone when he stepped outside the rear entrance and took breath. He folded his Raybans and hooked them over the neck of his T-shirt. As he crossed the lot back to his Volks, a hearse pulled up in back of the funeral parlour. The tailgate swung up, slowly, slowly and came to rest at a crazy angle with an exhausted hydraulic hiss.

NINETEEN

I rather amazed myself at the speed with which I completed my script. Six weeks. It made me immediately doubt the whole project. Surely, people slaved for years, hacking and pasting, slicing and chopping, abandoning the work and starting again. But then, I reminded myself, how long is a short story?

What I hadn't been able to envisage, let alone accomplish, five years earlier had now flowed out of me like water from a faucet. I only knew that I'd finished because the water dried up. Five years on and after countless movies seen and stored, I fancy I'd learned something about the craft. And I must have changed too, as much as had my main character. For a start, he had a face.

As I wrote, I couldn't escape the inevitable image of Brik Peters. Having Brik with me made the script what the book had never been. It seemed real, not *my* reality but the character's. When I'd written the book, I'd been much too young, much too unworldy and inexperienced to realise then that my character *wasn't* and *couldn't* be me. `Parallel' is basically the story of a youngman who leads a double life. It's a theme as old as human imagination but, as Eldon reminded me, without secrecy, love and death, paper would only have been invented to flush down the toilet. It sure as hell would never have had print on it.

Andy was more hard-nosed in his assessment, exhorting me as he had done over the years to `give the people what they want'.

"I think you've finally filled a theater," was how he congratulated me.

We were sitting after lunch one Saturday in Eldon's back yard. I'd swum at least three times in the course of Andy's enforced reading of my script. Eldon and Eugenia, his Mexican housekeeper, had done the dishes and made coffee after which Eldon had made himself scarce. I was determined Andy should read `Parallel' in one sitting and he was an abominably slow reader. It was four in the afternoon before he finished.

"But what do you *think*?" I pressed, being unable, like Andy, to leap over the all-important `x' factor. "Was it any *good*?"

"I have no difficulty with this at all," he replied. "I *love* the guy. Great part for Terri Garr. Streep too if we could get her. It's just the kinda torture she goes for. Hell! I can't wait to get started on this, Jem."

Eldon came out to the garden on his way out to dinner. Andy immediately got up, like it was the Queen or something.

"Andy! Please . . . Sit down. It's lovely to see you again."

"Hello, Eldon," Andy said deferentially and reassumed his seat. Eldon hovered, a hand on my shoulder.

"So what's the professional verdict?" he smiled.

"I think my agent likes it," I replied. "I think he recognises himself."

"Hey, thanks! What's *that* supposed to . . .," Andy began to splutter.

"Oh, shut up," I joked. "And don't worry, I shan't say anything on Johnny Carson."

Eldon patted my shoulder.

"Well, I, for one, feel much vindicated," he said with pride. "I feel like the honorary executive producer."

"But . . .," Andy began, unable to suppress an instant look of terror. "I thought . . ."

Eldon and I laughed which only served to rankle poor Andy even more.

"Don't worry, Andy," Eldon reassured, "I've managed to live over forty years in this town without *ever* having been near a movie studio and I certainly don't intend to start now."

"So, does that mean," Andy said, rather like a small boy asking for candy, "that you wouldn't mind if I . . .?"

". . . was the producer?" I completed his question.

"Sorta."

"Co," I bargained, smiling. "This is a co-production or no deal."

"Co it is," he beamed in agreement. He'd got his candy.

"Marvellous!" Eldon decreed. "Now I really must run. I do hope," he said to Andy, "that this means we'll be seeing more of you now. You've been conspicuous by your abscence, dear boy."

"Oh," said Andy, shuffling in his seat, "thanks, Eldon."

"Must get these things sorted out," Eldon continued. "I sometimes feel like an owl, very old and very wise and rather intimidating but it's just not true. Inside I'm twenty-two, rather silly and I still need young people to play with. Point taken?" He raised an eyebrow as he smiled. Andy grinned.

"Point taken."

"Good. I've always liked you two . . . Perhaps together you were just a mite too much for each other but I've watched you both, how you've grown and you're not half as bad as either would like to make out, you know." He left immediately, scattering his wisdom like carpet tacks, leaving us to find our way, as best as the bare-footed can, to the nearest exit. "Goodnight."

"'Night," I called after him.

We sat for a moment, searching under the table for our shoes . . .

"Well," I sighed, feeling as though I was digesting a very large meal. No. Rather more like I imagine a mother must feel having just given birth. "I've done my bit. It's up to you now." Andy rubbed his hands. "Don't let me down!" I warned, wagging a finger in his direction.

"I . . ."

". . . and *don't* say it!" I jumped in. "Promises are like contracts; they're only ever important if they're broken. When will you learn?"

"Okay already," he mimicked. "No promises. Hey! What d'ya feel like doing?"

I thought for a moment.

"You want to go see the guys?"

"Go over to Ryder's?"

"I mean go over to Brik and Ryder's, Andy. He also serves who sits and waits."

"Oh oh," he replied, heeding my rebuke. "I'm tryin' for him, Jem. Believe me. It'll happen, don't worry about him."

"I *know* it will happen," I replied. "Shall we go? He goes to work around five-thirty, I think."

We went in Andy's Mercedes the four blocks to South Bentley Drive, Andy dreaming big dreams and me clutching my copy of `Parallel' I wanted to give to Brik.

It's hard sometimes not to think that you are what you do. Logically, I knew that I wasn't Jeremy Page because I had suddenly become a writer again. But it was with Brik and Eldon and Andy, and specially Brik, I felt that I was somebody again. Anyway, I was determined that we were all three going to be in this thing together.

❋ ❋ ❋ ❋

Michelle Nersessian had never been particularly thrilled by her name. At first she tried spelling it Meeshelle but her grocer daddy, her millionaire, multi-market, second generation Armenian grocer daddy, had put his foot down. He'd said it made her sound like a Beirut belly dancer and he wasn't about to let his only child make like she was not from the topmost drawer.

But he'd said he'd take Shelley. Taking everything else completely for granted and having achieved one of her major life goals, Shelley Nersessian was now left with just one, to somehow get away from the Nersessian. Temporarily, she had taken to going around calling herself Shelley Ness.

However, in order to achieve a permanent name change and still keep the Jaguar XJS and an allowance that would have halted depopulation on at least three islands of the Phillipine archipelago, she would have to get married in order to do much about the name. She could have become a star but Shelley could neither sing nor act and so that avenue of rebirth was closed.

The grocer's daughter was left with just one option, to become a bride and, at this point in time, Shelley McKigh had rather a pleasant ring to it, thankyou Ryder.

Ryder hadn't even had to buy the ring. Shelley had had no qualms at all about signing Nersessian on her credit card.

After the fortuitous meeting at the beach, Shelley had seen quite a few bright mornings in the bedroom on South Bentley Drive. Now it was Ryder's turn to visit her. Ryder was about to see the sun set for the first time over the horizon west of Malibu where the momma and poppa Nersessian kept house. The Malibu home was only one of a great many Nersessian homes which sparkled on the map of America like Bulgari jewels from Palm Springs CA to Sanibel FLA and north to Park Avenue NYC.

"Oh, man!" Brik exclaimed as Ryder emerged from his two hour toilet in the bathroom in full tuxedo. "You get an Oscar already or what?" Brik was in the kitchen, trying to make a call. He wanted to make sure he'd remembered Ron Windel's number correctly. He let the 'phone cord dribble through his fingers as he appraised Shelley's intended.

Ryder mimed stiff. He inserted a finger beneath the wing-collared starched white shirt and grimaced.

"I look dumb, right?"

"You look great, pal. You look like a fucking star, Ry!"

"Would *you* marry me?" Ryder sighed.

"You never asked me," Brik quipped and pit-pat, up and back went the pretty balloon. "But you're not gonna be standing up all night, Ry. Practice sittin' down so's you don't split your pants."

Ryder lowered himself onto the stool in the kitchen.

"I'll perch. Should I be late, d'ya think? I think it'd look better. 'T'd make me look busy."

"For crissake you're an actor, Ry and it's Sunday afternoon. Everyone has their day of rest including your prospective father-in-law."

"Who're y'calling?" Ryder asked.

"Oh," said Brik. "I was trying Ohio. Line's busy." Brik replaced the receiver on the kitchen wall. He took hold of Ryder's leg and bent it.

"Ouch!" Ryder exclaimed. "I felt that! You just made me

flunk my sperm count."

"She wants your body not your baby, Ry," Brik remarked. "And," he added, "by the look of you, she's been making a little too much with the body."

Ryder was silent for a moment.

"She says she's making a little with my baby too," he revealed, speaking to the floor. He cocked his head on one side and grinned up at Brik.

Brik was shocked. It was a purely conditioned response. Back home, apart from Aids which had started to get talked about, having someone's baby was about the worst thing that could happen to a Scotland teenager.

"Oh, boy!" Brik whistled. "Whatcha gonna do, Ry?"

Ryder laughed.

"Well I'm not having an abortion for starters," he said. "And as she isn't either, I guess I'm gonna be a daddy."

"But why, Ry?" Brik puzzled.

"'Cos there's not a lot I can do about it," he shrugged. "And," he added brightly, "'cos I'm cute and I'm gonna be a *major* star and I talk nice and I'm gonna be jus' the greatest son-in-law poppa and momma Armenia are gonna have and my son or my daughter will be on line for one of the fattest inheritances this state has to offer. I only wish she wanted to change her name from Woolworth. Okay?"

Beneath the fluffy topcoat, Ryder's poodle wore a vest of tungsten steel. Ryder's tail never barked his dog.

"Okay," Brik replied quietly. "Well," he said, lightening up, "guess you'll be needing a matron of honour."

"Guess you'll have to wax your legs," said Ryder, getting up off the stool and adjusting the satin lapels on his tux jacket.

"I'd'a been great in `Some Like It Hot'," Brik sang.

"Would that have been Curtis or Lemmon, man?"

"Me?" Brik preened. "I'd'a been Marilyn, ding-a-ling!"

Ryder looked away . . . It was going too far. Don't, he thought. No, thought Brik. No, they thought together, don't. And nor did they. The balloon floated back up to the ceiling and came to rest, gently.

"So have a good time," Brik called out. "Good luck."

"Yeah," Ryder said, over his shoulder, as he walked out the door. "Take care, now, hey?" The door closed.

"Yeah," said Brik quietly to himself, listening to Ryder whistling as he walked to his car.

Brik went back to the kitchen and took the 'phone again. He pressed out the numbers he wanted and waited. This time, the call went through.

When Ron picked up in Doddsville, Brik's first thought on recognising the voice was, immediately, to hang up.

"Hello." Ron's voice sounded thin and tired.

"Ron?" Brik said uncertainly. "Is that you?"

"This is Ron Windel," Ron replied warily. "Who is this?"

"It's Brik, Ron. Brik Peters."

"Hi, Brik!" Ron perked up instantly. "How's it going, Brik? You know I just come back from LA?"

"Yeah," Brik remarked. "I kinda thought you'd been here."

"Yeah," Ron went on, oblivious of Brik's suspicion. "Stayed with an old med school friend of mine in Bel Air. You seen Bel Air yet, Brik. Gee, now there's *some* property."

Brik listened, his courage building. He hated to broach what had been a mutual confidence but he had to know about the pictures.

"Ron, are you missing any of those photos you took of me?"

"Er . . . I . . . Why, no, Brik. Not that I know of."

"Are you sure, Ron?" Brik asked more firmly. "I have to know, Ron." There was a hopeless silence on the line. "Ron? You still there?"

"I . . . I showed some to my friend. This friend of mine I told you about. Kenny. Kenneth Morrell." Ron paused. "Why, Brik?"

"Oh, nothing," said Brik, acting careless. "Just that they're all over town." He paused. "I thought we had a deal, Ron," Brik said coldly.

Ron was lost for words. Hanging onto the line in his surgery in Ohio, so far away, Ron knew that he had also lost a friend. In fact, he'd lost two friends.

"Brik . . . I'm so sorry. I can't . . . I mean . . . What can I say? I'm sorry. How was I to know that Kenny would..."

"You just trusted him," Brik murmured with accompanying irony.

"What was that, Brik? I know you trusted me, Brik. That's why I feel so bad."

"Whatever," Brik replied, knowing that correcting Ron's mishearing was irrelevant. "Shame you weren't here a little longer, Ron. I coulda given you a lesson in trust. Number one, it doesn't exist out here. Get that wrong just once and you get your ass whipped for free and by as many people as can get a handle on the whip, Ron!" Aw, shit! Brik swore at himself. What was the use, what was the point of getting mad with Ron? He could tell that it was Ron who had been duped, not him. "Sorry, Ron."

"I don't blame you, Brik, believe me. You have every right to be mad at me. Tell me something. Who is it that's got a hold of the shots? How did you get to see 'em?"

"Oh, just some guy," Brik replied. "His name's Cattini. Tommy Cattini. You wouldn't know him."

"But I do, Brik. That's just the point. He makes movies, right?"

"Right," Brik acknowledged in a monotone. "Looks as though he's gonna be making me a major star, Ron." Brik laughed. "That'd be okay except it won't be in the kinda movies I'd had in mind as a career."

Ron groaned. He felt so helpless, so responsible. As usual, what had started as harmless had gotten sinisterly out of hand. The repercussions crackled like the 'phone line. Now Ron got scared. He'd opened himself to the very thing he'd so studiously avoided. And the threat was pointing its finger at him from such an unexpected direction, from so far away where he'd imagined all was safe.

The prospect of being blackmailed by his best friend's business partner hardened into a grim probability.

"Don't do it, Brik. Just say no."

"I've already said yes, Ron."

"Is it money?" Ron asked quickly. "If it is, Brik, I'll mail you some."

"I'm *not* borrowing any more," Brik replied. "I'm doing what I'm doing to repay someone what I already borrowed. And don't pretend to be so damn shocked, Ron."

"But, Brik. I feel it's all my fault."

"Jesus!" Brik exclaimed. "You guys and your guilt. Be responsible for yourself, Ron. Don't paddle your ass yourself, that ain't no fun for you. I *don't* blame you, right? It takes two, remember and I did what I did with you willingly. So did you. It's the same principle, exactly the same. Different circumstances, that's all."

"But you were gonna be an actor, Brik. Don't give up on it."

Brik laughed.

"Oh, I won't, Ron. Believe me, I'm still gonna be an actor but I'm gonna be *my* kinda actor, not their's. That much I've learned already."

"Can I have your number, Brik?"

"Not from me, no, Ron. I'm sure your friends have got it if you ever need to call. 'Bye."

Brik hung up. He'd achieved nothing except satisfaction. He sensed Ron, poor frightened Ron with all that spending money, would never have shit on him and he'd been right. And, he thought, perhaps he'd been just a little too hard on the guy.

Brik had no need that night to pretend to go out to work and Trick had already called to say for him not to come around either. It was almost as though circumstances had conspired to keep Brik at home that night and, although Brik had already determined that whatever he did it was to be an early night, the enforced relaxation could only be for the best. Brik was working the following day, in front of Clem Barber's camera.

Brik picked up Jeremy's script and settled down on the couch with a root beer and a package of Pepperidge Farm lemon cookies.

✻ ✻ ✻ ✻

Ron replaced his 'phone. He sat for a moment behind his desk and then got up. He loosed the blind, the one with the children's pattern of numbers, letters, fluffy ducklings, kittens and puppies. He let go the cord and it coiled up and slapped into its housing with a crack like a silenced pistol shot.

Ron had never hated anyone that he could remember. But, for the first time in his life, Ron knew what it was like to hate. Beneath the cold sweat he mopped away with his handkerchief, he felt such a burning hatred for Kenneth Morrell that had he been in LA, he knew that he could have taken a gun and calculatedly shot his oldest, supposed friend to the heart and not thought twice about the outcome.

Kenneth's betrayal of his trust was such a cold device, as cold as the steel of a blade, cold like the machine-turned precision of a shell case, as cold as the deadly, calculated intent which Kenneth had employed at every fork along the road of his life. If Kenneth had ever had a moment's dilemma as to which of the paths to take at any of these forks, Ron was sure that some diabolic instinct had unerringly pointed him in the direction of personal advantage.

This now, this most recent sleight, was the ultimate and most back-stabbing insult. Placed so quietly and so dextrously on top of the rest of the half-forgotten pile of precariously balanced digs and jibes, put-downs and braggadocio, it broke Ron's patience as surely as the last straw broke the camel's back.

Poor Sherman, Ron thought . . . He smiled, sadly, remembering that summer on the beach in St Thomas. For a time, after Kenneth had effected an introduction, rather foisted himself on the unwitting millionaire, it had not been Kenneth upon whom Sherman had ladled compliments, it had not been Kenneth who had been the recipient of Sherman's initial interest. It was the young, handsome, well-put together, shy, diffident, kind Ronnie Windel.

Ron turned from the window and fingered the gold

chain lying under his shirt. Gold was such a warm metal. The chain had always been warm, for Ron had never taken it off from the moment Sherman had bought it in the ninety degree heat of the St Thomas' jeweller's after their first night together. It was a wonderful three days of stolen moments which had followed, moments stolen from beneath Kenneth's cold and censorious gaze. But the time had come to go home . . . Was it merely, Ron had mulled with aching heart, merely a holiday romance which should end, as these things are often better ended, on the dockside? What was it Kenny had said? `But you have to go back to Ohio, Ron. It's just a holiday romance, don't let your heart rule your head . . . Think of your career. . .'

No sooner had Ron returned to Ohio and joined his father in the practice in Doddsville, no sooner had he filed away the holiday snapshots and got started on what he knew was going to be a lonely life, than Ron heard from Kenny. He heard that Kenny had moved into the Stone Canyon mansion. He heard that Kenny and Sherman would be pleased to see him any time . . . Any time he wanted to visit with them . . . with *them*!

And now Sherman was dead. His heart problems had been carefully mythologised by Kenny, his erratic blood pressure made a shibboleth by the in-house, live-in doctor who always seemed so solicitous . . . "Sherman, honey, don't forget your pills". "Sherman, *don't* do too much . . .". "Sherman, take a nap, dear. You really aren't looking well . . ."

Ron realised now, too late of course, that Sherman Frank had died from an overdose of trust, a lethal cocktail of intrigue and conspiracy which Kenneth had administered as surely as any possible act of euthanasia. No, Ron told himself, not possible, not even probable . . . exit Sherman Frank.

Ron had always liked Sherman; admired him, was prepared to listen to his problems and difficulties. Ron liked Sherman Frank for himself, from the very beginning. Right up to the end. A man, perhaps *the* man in Ron's life, was dead because Ron Windel had taken the wrong fork for the right reasons.

Like Gloria Gaynor once sang: It shouldda been me!

A delicious feeling began to seep through the windows and doors inside Ron's mind, a gentle balm, a healing salve which soothed his hurt like the action of an anaesthetic. He went with the feeling, embracing it, embellishing it into an image of a hypodermic, a blithe yet cold injection, administering a wondrous, easing, cleansing refreshment to his wounded pride and battered regrets. The feeling flowed through him, into every vein and artery, finally consuming him, propagating an addiction so strong, so powerful that at first he could not acknowledge its nature or its source or the course it was bound to take.

Ron looked into the mirror on his surgery wall. The face that met his stare was but a parody of that once young and hopeful man who had, unlike Kenneth, taken the other fork in the path. And as the feeling finally occupied his brain and Ron received it into his soul, he smiled. The face in the mirror smiled in return and it was a sweet smile, encouraging, supportive. Ron felt a release, a rush of relief, freeing him from the pretence and supression of years of playing Mister Nice Guy. Ron found himself finally at peace, basking in the rays of what seemed to be a divine vision.

The time had come for a resolution; the time had come to correct the imbalances of the past which he had borne because... Why? Ron asked. Why, why... *why*?

But the face in the mirror just smiled. The lips whispered just five words: "He's just not worth it".

The feeling, hitherto so alien, so unknown to Ron Windel was revenge.

❊ ❊ ❊ ❊

As Brik wept openly, sobs shuddering through his body, wracking his heart with a sadness so deep, the script of `Parallel' slid to the floor.

Across town, downtown, in a single room on the eighth floor of a mixed-race lodging house, a young Mexican boy smiled into a cracked mirror on the wall and admired his new teeth. They sat painfully in the front of his mouth, six on bottom, four on top - eight straight hours of dental work which had ripped his gums the day before to their raw and bleeding foundations.

But he smiled more expensively than he had been able to before; after all, what was pain and his life savings but investments in a future that was already looking up? Tomorrow would bring another five hundred. He'd talked to Tommy and it was all fixed. He'd have to get up early in the morning to get himself out to Venice. A car took second place to his beautiful new teeth. It would have to be a bus as Clem Barber no longer called him. Clem had moved on but then, Paquito, he reminded himself, so have you.

Soon, he told himself, he wouldn't need to hustle the bars or cruise the intersections, hitching rides. Soon he would be in the big league.

TWENTY

Three days later, I answered the doorbell and it was Brik, returning my script. There was an envelope slipped under the blue card cover. He wouldn't come in when I invited him.

"I think I'll be able to get the rest to you real soon," he said, grinning sheepishly.

"The rest of what?" I said, puzzled. "And come inside for God's sake. I want to talk to you about something important."

"That's important," he said, fingering the envelope. "Go on, open it!"

"Only if you come in."

He looked at his watch. He was faking, I knew it.

"Is Eldon home?"

"No. It's just me."

"Well . . . Okay."

We went into the kitchen and I poured myself coffee. He accepted my gesture, offering him one too and we sat down at the pine table.

I couldn't believe the contents of the envelope. A thousand dollars; in notes. I whistled.

"You must be the best waiter on the coast!" I exclaimed. "I never got tips like that when I was working tables. How much do they pay you?"

He looked fractionally undecided for a moment.

"Let's just say it's above the going rate. And thanks, Jeremy. You got me out of a big hole. I couldn't have survived without you."

"Now don't go over the top," I laughed. "You would have survived, no problem."

"Survived with myself," he corrected. "That's more important than anything as far as I'm concerned."

"Well, whatever," I reflected, looking at the fan of notes. "It's very impressive. So," I changed tack, "what did you think?" I pointed meaningfully at the script on the table between us.

Brik went to stretch out his hand towards the script but he stopped short of picking it up. He just patted it, gently, allowing his hand to rest fondly on the cover, almost caressing it.

"The only time in my life I've ever cried," he said, "really cried, was when I was real small, 'bout ten maybe. I had this rabbit. We both had rabbits." He laughed.

"You and Janna?"

"No," he said, shaking his head. "Me and Ry. This sounds so dumb," he chuckled. "Anyway, I was real fond of this rabbit and Ry was real fond of his rabbit. But one day, Ryder's rabbit died. We had this big funeral, y'know. Full religious rites. And then we went home." He paused. "Next mornin', I went out into the yard to feed my rabbit and it was gone. Door of the run was open and the rabbit had split. I looked and looked for this damn rabbit all over the farm and it had . . . well, it was just nowhere around. I cried so hard, Jem . . ." His voice fell away. "Then Ry came around. `Why y'cryin'?' he says'. `My rabbit's run off,' I says. `No it didn't,' he says, `I let it go'."

"Oh," I said.

Brik thought for a moment.

"It was like if he couldn't have something, no one was going to have it." He sighed. "That's what I thought about your script, Jeremy. It's . . . it's great. Have I made any sense?" He reached out and squeezed my hand.

Now I felt like crying.

"Yeah," I managed to say with some degree of control. "Yes. And," I continued, "talking of your friend, he just called me."

"Ry did?"

"He called to congratulate me. He likes the script."

"Well, I'll be . . ." Brik shook his head. "That guy . . . he's somethin' else."

"Just about half-an-hour ago. I was on the 'phone to Andy and soon as we'd hung up, Ryder called. Should I be honoured? I know he doesn't like me."

"There you go," Brik exclaimed. "You and him both. You both think the other one doesn't like you. You're both

211

wrong . . . It's only that you're both so damn hard to figure. Impossible, y'know? Take my word for it."

"Okay," I replied, hoist by my own petard. "Anyway, what did you think about *him* . . . Christopher?"

Christopher Payton was my hero, my script's hero. I'd transposed the English university at Canterbury into a campus college in middle America. It is Christopher Payton who has the double life.

"I understand him," Brik said. "I don't think I like him but I know who he is . . . Where he's coming from."

"I want you to be my Christopher," I said, with due solemnity, as though I was officiating at some baptism.

Brik looked taken aback, not unpleasantly but as if the thought hadn't crossed his mind at all.

"Me?"

"And only you," I added. "Oh, Brik," I gushed, "this is no pipe-dream, believe me. Y'know I said Andy called?"

"Yeah."

"He's found someone with some development money."

"You mean a studio?"

"No," I said, "an independent. Some guy he knows who has a lot of money to lose and who wants in on a movie at ground level."

"Jeremy! That's *great!*" he cried and reached over and hugged me to him in one of his great arms. "I'm so *happy* for you!"

"I've been pinching myself all morning," I replied for I had. Andy had been so quiet and distinct on the 'phone; there wasn't one mention of ". . . promise", no gushing, no phoney it'll-be-okay-but-it'll-take-time tone in his communication whatsoever. "'Course," I added, calming myself with a dose of cynicism, "I'll believe it when it happens."

"It'll happen," he assured me. "I feel it. Let's hope it's not dirty money."

"What . . . what dirty?" His rhetoric pulled me up short.

"Like drugs . . . You know," he said with a worldly aplomb. Though I dismissed it, Brik had raised a definite point. Andy had said something. What was it? . . . What did our benefactor do? Retail was it? . . . Property?

"I think he's in property," I said uncertainly. "And Andy wouldn't mess with me, Brik."

Brik raised an eyebrow.

"Money's money," he concluded. "And, hey! Sounds as though we're all on our way again!"

"But it all depends on the woman," I added by way of caveat. "Who they can get for Sarah. Andy wants Streep. Whaddya think?"

And so we started to play the movie game.

* * * *

The day after Trick's single scene in the new Innuendo movie was done, he was waiting in the parking lot when Tommy Cattini arrived for work.

Trick had an unbreakable appointment and he needed the money. 'The man' was meeting him at the beach at mid-day and Trick hadn't been out to work in three days. Though usually well-served by 'the man', Trick had screwed-up badly and had been late on his last two payments. The luxury of having his coke messengered over to his apartment had therefore been temporarily withdrawn. Trick was a good customer but not that good.

Tommy nodded in Trick's direction across the lot and both men got out of the cars and hurried in silence to the rear door of Innuendo.

Trick followed Tommy up the stairs and into the office before Tommy spoke.

"Y'know it's only five hundred, don'cha?" he snapped.

"Yeah," Trick replied wearily. "It'll go part way. But I need the rest soon, Tommy. When's the next shoot?"

Tommy unlocked the safe in the wall and withdrew a wad of money which he tossed to Trick who caught it deftly.

"There ain't no next shoot. Not on this one."

"But I only did one scene," Trick protested. "Fifteen minutes. Where's the rest?"

Tommy sighed. The crunch had come. He'd put it off when he called Trick to tell him the location but Tommy knew that to delay any further was impossible.

"There ain't no rest, Trick. Leastways, not for you."

"But . . ." Trick was puzzled. *He* was the Innuendo star. The movies were formula stuff . . . The scripts were still pretty much crap but there was more story line of late and he hadn't even thought to ask about the plot yesterday, so second nature had his performances become. He'd just assumed . . . Just got right on with it. And it had been a good day . . . So what the hell was wrong? He felt he'd breezed through the sequence, breezed high in a cocoon of powdery cloud, wafted along on a current of chemically induced euphoria. He hadn't felt a thing. There was no reason for him to have asked . . .

"Trick . . .," Tommy began gently. "Siddown."

But Trick was way ahead of him and had no intention of sitting down.

"So who else is in this . . . movie?" he demanded threateningly. "You know I don't guest, Tommy. If it's not *my* story, who the fuck's is it?"

"I gotta new guy," Tommy muttered.

"Who!" Trick insisted. "You said it was *my* movie, Tommy." Trick hesitated, his emotions gathering head. "If you're lyin' to me, you're . . . You're snakepiss, Tommy!"

"Hey!" Tommy warned. "Enough with the snakepiss. Who the fuck do you think you're talking to?"

"To one major jerk-off, Tommy! To one rat-bellied slime who's made one helluva lot of money out of me and who doesn't have the *guts* to let me know what's goin' down!"

Tommy snapped.

"That is *it*, Trick! I have *had* it to *here* . . ." Tommy drew his hand through the air over his head, slicing the fetid atmosphere of his office with a vicious finality. "You're *through*, man! Take your fuckin' wad and beat it!"

"Not without knowin'," Trick replied icily. He took one step closer to Tommy. "You gotta tell me, Tommy! Who'd'ya dump me for? Hey! Who the fuck *is* it?" Trick was getting too close. Tommy reached into his drawer and pulled out a thirty-eight and pointed it at Trick. The action produced the desired result. Trick stepped back, immediately deflated. He looked down at the gun as he spoke, now pleading. "You owe me, Tommy."

"I owe you nothing, Trick. You were just a two-bit hustler in the gutter when Clem sent you along. If anyone owes anyone, it's *you* who owes me, Trick. I hiked your rate from fifty to two . . . three hundred? Have I ever asked you for a cut of that?" Trick shook his head. "You've wiped yourself out, Trick. You career's gone up your fuckin' nose. I know it and you know it and it's about time you recogised yourself for what you are. You're on the skids, Trick, on the downhill and y'can't stop. You're late, you're unreliable, you're a pain in the fuckin' ass and I don't *need* you!"

"I just wanna know," Trick replied, almost a whimper. "Please. I *have* to know."

"Okay," Tommy acquiesced. "If it'll make ya feel any better . . ."

Tommy withdrew a casette from the same drawer that the gun had come from, jabbed it into the video and switched on the teevee. Trick raised his eyes and saw the colour emerge from the speckled black-and-white crackle. Tommy stopped the fast forward and hit the play button.

The sequence was uncut, unedited. Paquito was sitting on a bench, across the street from the beach, taking off his rollerskates. The camera was at ground level looking up. There was the sound of another set of wheels approaching and into shot came a black and chrome pair of skates. The camera panned up, picking up the rays of a mid-day sun partially eclipsed by a pair of magnificent calves, then to the knees, then the thighs and the crotch straining against the fabric of black shorts. Up to a white singlet and finally into the face of a dark-haired guy wearing the mirror Raybans.

The camera pulled back; reflected in the shades was Paquito, grinning with his new, white teeth. The guy raised his head, shook out a mane of thick, dark hair and slowly pushed up his shades to rest over the earphones of the

Walkman on top of his head.

"Oh, fuuuuck," Trick whispered slowly. "No . . . no!" He stepped back, stumbling backwards against the wall rubbing his face with his clenched fists, squirming as he came to rest against the poster of him which ripped away from the thumbtacks which held it to the pinboard. "Oh, no!" he roared. "*Nooooo!*"

Trick ran from the room, Tommy heard him almost falling down the stairs. He tossed the gun onto the desk, stabbed at the stop button on the video but missed. He hit the hold. He came out from behind his desk and bent down to pick up the fallen poster. Without a second thought, he screwed it up and tossed it into the trash bin beneath the desk as Brik smiled out from the wavering screen.

TWENTY ONE

Andy and I were sitting on the seventh floor of the Beverly Center eating Chinese food before the movie started. When he could make it, we'd started going to the movies twice a week. If he couldn't make it, I still went, by myself. I thought I had to, that I needed to and of course I was forever making the inevitable comparisons with whatever I watched and what I envisioned `Parallel' was going to be. It seemed such a reality, I had no trouble with my assessments.

I had begun to be obsessed. I tried monitoring my obsession but it was tough. I often thought I bored people, when they asked about it but they never seemed to ask me about anything else.

Andy, of course, talked of nothing else but `Parallel'. I pushed my plate away and mopped my mouth with a paper napkin. I looked at my watch. The horizon seemed to be closing in.

"I don't think she'll take long," Andy said, forking together another mound of noodles. "That's one thing about Streep. If she likes something, she likes it."

"And if not?"

"As I said, I have Terri Garr lined up. Her agent's hot for the idea. And she is very close with Dick Molina."

"I like Dick. I like the fact that he writes as well."

"And he likes you," Andy said reassuringly.

"Which leaves the other girl. The student," I concluded. "I like that actress from *Salem Wharf*."

"Who? Not Audrey?"

"No, not Audrey. Too obvious. No, the girl who played Donna?"

"Oh, yeah. Not bad . . . not bad. I'll run that by Dick tomorrow."

"What does the guy say at Universal? Milose . . . What's his name? Something unpronounceable."

"Milosevic," Andy chimed in. "Teddy."

"Yes, Teddy. How cuddly."

"He's not. But he wants to play."

"But only if we hook a star, right?"

"Right," Andy affirmed. "But it's par . . . Nothing unusual."

"You seem completely unruffled by all this," I observed, interested. "Do you know something that I don't?"

Andy grinned, mischevously.

"Honey bun, *if* I wanted to, I could go ahead and make this picture tomorrow but I want a studio. I want this thing to be totally legit. I want a production office and I want the industry to take us seriously. From day one. And," he added with a sigh and a pretend sob, "I wanna tell Freddie Miller to stuff his job so bad, it hurts!"

"And you're not tempted?" I laughed. "This guy Nersessian would bank-roll you, surely? From what you say, you've got him eating out of your hand."

"Marginal," Andy replied, finally abandoning his noodles. He downed the rest of his root beer. "He's hot, but not that hot."

"This Milo Schmilo or whoever," I asked, "okay, Teddy. Doesn't he want to see Brik?"

"He doesn't wanna see Brik or Ryder yet," Andy replied. He tossed out the remark so lightly that for a second I didn't notice it. It was though I gradually focused on a feather, or a windblown thistledown which had drifted into my line of sight and which floated gently, side to side, down to earth.

"Or Ryder?" I asked with a certain coercion.

"Yeah. It's a good idea to give people a choice. Then they don't feel they're being backed into a corner. It lets them think they're calling the shots. Teddy needs to feel like a big shot. What the fuck am I saying," he added, banging the side of his head with his palm. "He is a fuckin' big shot."

I could not believe what he'd just told me. Brik *or* Ryder?

"You've just broken our agreement," I accused. "I *want* Brik. Christopher is Brik. Brik Peters. *Not* Ryder Mac-fucking-Kigh!"

He patted my arm, almost patronisingly as though I

were joking.

"Don't worry, Jeremy." He leant back on his chair and eyed me, amused at my display of neurotics. "Dick Molina will go nuts with you. Look at you! If you're acting like this now, what the fuck're you gonna be like when the movie's shooting?"

"Andy, I'm very serious. No Brik, no deal."

"Okay," he said, bringing his enthusiasm to heel. "I hear you. Now, can we go see a movie?"

"Right. As long as you understand me, Andy. You should be more careful. Their friendship is at a pretty low ebb and pitting them together like this is a really stupid risk."

"It is *not* a risk," he expostulated. "You might think it's a dangerous game, Jem. But trust me, I promise I know what I'm doing."

"Do you? Dear." I shook my head. "Well. As long as you understand."

"I understand!" he replied, mocking me like a husband plays with a nagging wife. "Now leave it, can't you?"

We piled our trash onto the trays and dumped them.

"Y'know Ryder's getting married, don't you?" he said as we made our way past the unending array of alternative dining, everything from tacos to curry to croissants to French.

"Brik told me. Shelley, I believe. I don't envy her."

Andy laughed and shook his head.

"That guy sure works fast," he said.

"Yes," I said. "Doesn't he just."

"Good luck to him," Andy said.

"He doesn't need it," I opined. "But Brik does."

While Andy bought popcorn, I went to pee. As I stood against the urinal, I saw myself somewhat reflected in the white ceramic tiling I faced. I finished and buttoned-up and went to wash my hands. I suppose I must have been thinking of . . . Why I should have emerged from the restroom with such determination and such clarity of purpose, I don't know.

"Thanks," I said as Andy handed me my bucket of corn.

"I've been thinking."

"D'you think I should go pee?" Andy asked. "I should pee. This movie's three hours," he added as vindication.

"I want to meet Nersessian," I said as he hurried off. "Soon." He stopped; I thought he was about to come back with a reason why not. He didn't look around. I watched him go through the door to the restroom.

While he was away, I tried to think of all those writers I'd known, that long list of screenwriters and all their endless tales of woe of how their work had been bought only then to be changed and re-written and badly acted and wrongly directed to end up as something entirely different on screen. The stories and the victims were legion. "But I am the co-producer, after all," I said as he returned.

Andy must have been thinking too for he was perfectly accomodating.

"Sure." He looked reasonable. "He's been outta town for a coupla days but, yeah. Whenever. How about Thursday?"

"I have classes Thursday."

"Night?"

"Fine," I said, decisively. Then I remembered the party. "Sorry," I corrected. "Can't Thursday. I'm going to a party, some friend of Eldon's. It's a fiftieth and very `A' list by the sound of it. Somewhere in Bel Air."

"Okay. I'll fix up another time with Nersessian. Whose party, by the way?"

We went into the theatre. It was small and we were early so we sat in back, as far away from the screen as possible. The lights were still up.

"Some doctor friend of Eldon's. Kenneth Morrell. D'you know him?"

"Morrell," Andy puzzled. "Kenneth Morrell," he repeated. "Now why should that name ring a bell?"

❋ ❋ ❋ ❋

"Ryder!" Shelley called. "It's for you. It's Andy!" She was about to leave. There were, as she kept on saying, a million things to do about a wedding.

Ryder came into the living room and took the 'phone. "Thanks."

"I have to go, honey," she called from the door. "I'll be about an hour."

"Hurry back," Ryder replied as the door closed. "Hi," he said into the 'phone. "How goes it?"

"Terri Garr *loves* it," Andy began. "And I know I can have George Segal for the father."

"So Streep turned it down," Ryder intuited, piercing Andy's oblique optimism. "Shit."

"No," Andy remarked. "She did not turn it down but do you wanna wait two years, Ryder?"

"Guess I could," Ryder replied laconically, "to do a picture with Streep."

"Guess again, Ryder."

"So what about Teddy? Won't Garr and Segal make his earth move? It'll make Shelley's mom come all over her nice clean kitchen."

"I have a call in to Teddy right now," Andy assured. "In fact . . . Ryder, I'll call you back. Stay by the 'phone."

Andy hung up.

Ryder shook his head and replaced the receiver. He stretched out on the couch with the 'phone on his lap. From the ceiling above hung a two-branch fifties electric light. As Ryder looked up at it, the fitment began to buzz and with a sulky pop one of the lights burned out, blackening the opaque shade.

Ryder heard footsteps coming up the porch's wooden steps and a pounding began on the front door.

"Brik! You in there!" More pounding. "Brik!" Ryder ditched the 'phone and ran to the door. He knew it was Trick.

"Trick!" he said, opening the door. Trick barged past him, one angry man as Ryder could see. "Hey, man! What . . . Brik's out. He's not here."

"So where the fuck is he?" Trick demanded. He stood, legs apart, slightly hunched and tenser than a bowstring, scowling and swallowing his hurt and anger. "You tell me where that motherfucker is, Ryder!" he thundered.

Ryder closed the front door.

"Hey," he started, soothingly. "What's wrong, man? What's happening?"

"Don't gimme that shit, Ryder. You know. What the fuck you guys doin', screwin' me up like this?"

"Like what? I don't know *what* you're talkin' about, man," Ryder said calmly. Trick didn't frighten him though he was bigger and stronger than Ryder. "Look . . . Siddown. Lemme getcha something. Beer?" Trick shook his head. Ryder ignored him and fetched two beers from the kitchen. "Here."

Trick snatched at the can, ripped off the tab and glared at Ryder.

"You still sayin' you don't know?" he accused.

"Trick," Ryder said helplessly. "Why doncha just tell me what's on your mind? Maybe I can help." Ryder sat down. Trick paced the floor a while, snatching swallows from the can.

"I'll kill him," he repeated, muttering. "Fuckin' kill him!"

"Why?" Ryder massaged cautiously. "What could Brik have possibly done that's so wrong?"

"He stole my movie!" Trick blurted out. "The bastard stole my movie!"

"Brik wouldn't steal anything," Ryder assured. "I know him. If it has gone, I'm sure he just borrowed it. Perhaps it's around here someplace if it's that important. Or perhaps you jus' forgot where you put it?"

"Don't get smart with me, Ryder," Trick snarled, pointing a finger threateningly. "I got friends, man. Friends who could take you and your Judas buddy apart . . . like take you *out*, man!"

"Okay . . . okay," Ryder said, calming the situation as best as he could. "But what was so important about this tape, man? I don't understand. Surely you can get a copy?"

"Fer chrissake!" Trick exploded. "I'm talking about a movie, man! Your dear ol' buddy pal got himself hired to do one of *my* movies . . . Unnerstand? Your cute-as-candy buddy . . . your `gee-I'm-jus'-a-dumb-ol'-countryboy' buddy has just featured in the movie that was meant for *me*!"

Ryder gaped. He groaned as the mist of incomprehension cleared.

"Brik has done a porno movie?" he intoned. He spoke like a zombie, as though transfixed. "I don't believe it."

"Believe it!" Trick snapped. "I've just come from the premiere! I *seen* the goddam piece of shit!"

"But . . ." Ryder wondered aloud.

"Aw, come on, Ryder. You're not *that* great an actor . . . Anyway, where else d'ya think he got the money."

"What money?" Ryder enquired.

"The money to pay back his precious teacher. The money he borrowed to keep up. With you," Trick hurled out. "For this!" he added, taking in the room, the house, the car outside with a sweeping gesture.

"But he's been working," Ryder insisted, angry and incredulous.

"Yeah!" Trick agreed. "Screwin' the ass off some lil' wetback shit and makin' like he was *me*! Ha!"

"Why should he?" Ryder countered. "He was makin' good money at the bar."

"Bar!" Trick laughed, mockingly. "He wasn't workin' at no bar! That was for your benefit, Ryder. And for . . . Mister Page." Trick mimicked with apposite sarcasm.

"Oh, shit," Ryder murmured. "Oh, Brik! What have you done?" Trick finished his beer and finally sat down, perched on the edge of the couch, burying his head in his hands, his long hair falling over his tear-stained face.

"How *could* he?" he said, almost wailing with helplessness. "I thought . . . I thought he liked me . . . like we had somethin' . . ."

Ryder sensed the voltage in Trick's anger lessening. Initially, he had been taken so much aback by Trick's revelation that the full implication had not been clear and, for Ryder, there was not merely one implication, but two. The first was that Brik had been somehow duped into doing the movie and that Trick was to blame for it. The second was that, according to Ryder's lights, Brik's had just gone out, although that was business . . . What Ryder faced up to on the first count had nothing to do with business. There was something threatening in what Trick had told him, something which scared him; there was something so enormous and incomprehensible about what Brik had done, without telling, without ever even hinting what he was planning. Ryder felt, once again, very left out . . . Very deceived and very alone.

"You had nothing," Ryder said, as cold as steel. "I know Brik . . . inside and out and I'm telling you that you had *nothing!*"

"Whadda you know about it?" Trick mumbled.

"You used him," Ryder went on. "I don't know what you did to him but you . . . you're a disease, Trick. You've given whatever it is you've got to Brik like you've given him Aids or something. He's gotten caught up in your sick little world like you knew he would and now you decide you don't like it 'cos you can see that he could be better than you. Well, he *is* better than you . . . anyplace, anywhere . . . You don't even hold a candle to him and it's too late. You make me sick, man. Sick."

"It wasn't like that," Trick protested, "you weren't around, Ryder. Remember? He came to *me* because *you* weren't there for him! He couldn't stand bein' around you, man. That's the truth. *That's* the truth, Ryder!"

Ryder got up and went to the door. He opened it and held it open.

"Get out, Trick. Stay away from us. Stay away from Brik. He doesn't need you and you don't deserve him."

Trick was motionless for a while as Ryder coldly passed his sentence. As he stood up, slowly, he said: "So what are *you* gonna do for him, hey? Mister *moovie* star? You gonna *buy* your best buddy like he was a new car? Ya think that'll keep him with ya?"

"Get outta here!"

"Sure, Ryder. It'll be a pleasure." Trick strode over to the door and stood in front of Ryder. "We're not so different you and I . . ."

"Out!" Ryder spat.

Trick laughed.

"In fact, Ry . . . ol' buddy! . . . It was only a matter of time. If I don't deserve him, you certainly don't and you know it." Trick paused, hoping his hometruth had hit home. "You're right about one thing though . . . Brik didn't screw me. He's too nice a guy. Why he did what he did, I don' know. Yet . . ." He paused again. "I know that I," Trick emphasised, "would have done what he did to me and I know that *you* would too . . . You'd'a dumped on him and smelt roses at the same time. Like I know it's only a matter of time before you will dump on him." Trick's quiet scorn infuriated Ryder all the more. "In fact," he concluded, "I'd pretty much guess you're already doin' it, one way or 'nother."

"Goodbye, Trick."

"I'm goin'. If you see Brik, tell him to call me, hey?"

Trick brushed past Ryder and didn't look back as he walked to his car.

Ryder slammed the door behind him.

TWENTY TWO

Nancy Franck Lassman was the name on the passport which lay with other travelling essentials on the empty bed next to the Vuitton suitcase she was filling.

Nancy was due to leave on a cruise. The departure was not for three weeks but Nancy liked to be ready. It was to be her sixth cruise. Not that she had enjoyed the first five that much but cruises were what her friends took and now she was a widow, Nancy had fallen natural prey to the bridge-playing sororities of the Caribbean Adventurer.

That she was only lately widowed was evidenced by the two beds still extant in her bedroom. That it was all a horrible dream, that he'd only just popped out with the glass for the bottle bank, was still a possibility in her numbed perceptions of her husband's passing. But it had been two years now and he hadn't come back. Perhaps, she reflected, it was time to dispose of the empty bed.

Robert, her husband, had died only six months after they had moved from Orlando to the sixth floor of the Fort Lauderdale condo building they had chosen so carefully for what they had imagined would be a decent retirement. Robert Lassman's untimely passing had rocked Nancy's world to its foundations as surely as an earthquake.

But it had been her brother's death, coming only a month afterwards, that had almost destroyed her. Nancy and Sherman Franck were twins. For sixty-five years, they had, as twins are often reputed, felt each other's every tear, thrilled with each other's every happiness . . . well, she'd faked a lot of the thrills, especially as far as Kenneth Morrell had been concerned. Somehow, Nancy could never exactly *thrill* to Kenneth Morrell.

So Sherman had been . . . well . . . Oi vay! So he couldn't help it; so it wasn't his fault. But if there *had* to be someone else, someone other than her, *why* couldn't the person have at least been Jewish! Like that nice Ronnie . . . Ronnie Windel. Now, there was a nice boy and just as much of a doctor as . . . as the other one.

That `the other one' had relinquished Sherman's body for her to inter in the plot next to Robert and next to the one she had bought for herself had at first surprised Nancy and then puzzled her. She was fully expecting to be refused and so her request had not been *that* earnestly submitted; Nancy was not unintelligent; she knew logically that it wouldn't have *really* mattered if Sherman had been cremated like Kenneth wanted. It was just that she remembered when they'd been children; she remembered Sherman saying once that he wanted to be buried, to have a stone and flowers and someone to come visit once in a while and that they'd never be apart. Perhaps it was only a childish whim and Sherman's life had been a succession of whims but when he died, Nancy knew that never being apart was at least one of Sherman's whims that *she* could fulfill.

At first, Kenneth had been adamant until she made it clear that she wanted to bury him in Florida. Kenneth had then acquiesced so easily that it had only made her more convinced that she had been right about her brother's so-called lover. Kenneth Morrell, she knew, would never have visited even once in a while like Sherman would have wanted. Now at least she could visit them both, Robert and Sherman, in a proper Jewish cemetery.

She went from the bedroom, through her living room with its Atlantic view and into her kitchen where she reviewed for the dozenth time that afternoon her arrangements. These included chopped liver, lox, fish the way she'd made it for Robert. She hadn't cooked for a man in . . . it was a long time. Hers had become a world of sad, old women.

Nancy replaced the damp towel covering the various dishes. The entryphone sounded. That would be him, she thought as she looked at her watch. And punctual to the minute. Tony, the doorman, announced Ron Windel and she told him to please let him up. She hurried through to the bedroom, changed her pink maribou house shoes for her second best pair of heels that she'd gotten for the funeral from Lord and Taylor in the mall and, flufling her permanent in the mirror, went and opened her front door.

"Ronnie!" she beamed as the elevator doors opened and Ron Windel stepped out. "How *nice* to see you. And how adorable of you to visit with a poor old lady."

"Hello, Nancy!" Ron smiled warmly as they embraced. Even before she had gotten him into the apartment, Nancy was crying.

He calmed her and made her sit down. He fetched a glass of water from the kitchen where he remarked sadly to himself on her immaculately laid out arrangements.

"I'm so sorry," she sniffed. "So, silly of me."

"Not at all," he assured her. "If you need to, do it. That's what I say."

They talked, small-talked, for quite some while. Ron wasn't absolutely sure as to how he was going to broach the subject he had brought with him on his way to the birthday party in Los Angeles. That she had not been invited was soon established and it did not, he noticed, require a psychic to divine that the vibes Nancy was giving out concerning her opinion of Kenneth Morrell were at best hostile, at worst inimical.

When finally, as though brought to the point by a torture too unimaginable to reveal, by a dilemma as horned as Solomon's when confronted with the disputed baby, Ron confessed the nub of his disquiet concerning Sherman's passing, Nancy was violently shocked. She clasped her hands to her ears as though to hear more would be party to a calumny so evil that she could not bear to even be in the same world as the oracle who spoke of it. Ron felt his phlegmatic conspiracy in danger of collapse.

He thought he heard her right but for a moment doubted his ears.

"Then we must exhume his body!" was what Ron thought he heard.

"But . . .," he said weakly, realising he *had* heard right and that she would finish what he had started, that it was now out of his hands.

"No buts," Nancy said firmly. "If it is humanly possible, I shall make it so . . . After all," she sniffed bravely, "it's my duty."

She leant forward with an expression of such gratitude and clasped his hands in hers, as though he had released her from some terrible darkness. "I've never liked Kenneth and what's more, I want him to know I never liked him. I can think of no better way than this."

Ron was playing a long and difficult shot. The odds were very much against him. If Kenneth had done what Ron suspected him of, there could easily be no traces and no case to answer; if Nancy was unable to arrange for the necessary exhumation order, there would be no case to answer; if traces were found of any alien chemical agent in Sherman's remains, they could be ascribed to any of many quite legitimate clinical reasons.

But for Kenneth to be merely informed, for him to discover . . . Oh, and better, even better . . . For Kenneth to be forced to have to tell Ron of the desperate sickness in the mind of Nancy Franck Lassman which might even possibly lead to an exhumation of Sherman's corpse . . . These possibilities were as appetising to Ron Windel as the delicious second helping of the chopped liver which Nancy served him.

※ ※ ※ ※

When Trick pulled up outside his apartment, he saw the open-topped Volks. He knew he had to play the scene, if only for satisfaction. He slammed his door and saw Brik's dark head emerge over the back of the seat from where he had been lying, shirtless in the sun. Brik turned. He opened his door but did not get out. Trick would have to pass him to reach his door. Trick opened his trunk and removed his bag, slamming the trunk lid loudly and never taking his eyes off Brik's. He sauntered, as nonchalently as he could to his door. But Trick was no actor.

"Hi," Brik said. Trick ignored him. "I said `Hi'," Brik repeated.

How easily did Trick's butch mantle slip from his shoulders to reveal an acid-tongued drag queen.

"Oh! It's you! I didn't see you," he quipped, pushing back his Raybans and squinting in mockery, as though blind, in Brik's general direction.

"Why didn't you return my calls?" Brik demanded. All afternoon, he'd been calling. He'd left messages each time on Trick's service.

"Oh, you called me?" Trick threw out truculently.

Brik jumped out of the car, his shirt in his hand. He slammed the door, bounded up the steps just as Trick was going in. Trick tried to bar the door by standing in Brik's way.

"I said I had to see you, Trick."

"So, I was busy," he snapped, petulently. "Like I'm *busy*, man," he added threateningly, his eyes blazing, his voice quivering with anger. "Permanently busy!"

Brik took no notice, pushed him roughly away from the door which he thrust shut behind them.

"I thought we were friends," Brik said.

"Pardon me while I throw up!" Trick retorted, raising his voice.

"Can we go inside, Trick?"

"Why?" Trick blazed. "I don't want you in my life and I don't want you in my apartment, right?"

"I am in your life and if you opened the goddam door we would be in your apartment instead of bitching in your hallway." Brik pushed Trick bodily towards his first floor door. "Get it the fuck open," he commanded.

Trick opened up, flounced inside and threw his bag heavily at his pursuer.

"So what is this all *about*?" Brik demanded, catching the bag against his chest and throwing it aside.

"You tell me!" Trick screamed. He ran into his kitchen pulled open the refrigerator and snapped open a can of beer. He stabbed at the radio which began to blare out some metal station. Brik thumped the button and the music stopped. Trick turned it on again. Brik took the radio and threw it to the floor.

"So . . . who told you? Cattini?" Brik demanded. The smashing of the radio had broken Trick's fury. He sank to his knees amidst the broken pieces of plastic. "Yeah . . . Tommy Cattini. Whatta shit!"

"Oh, puhleeese! Spare me the righteousness," Trick snapped.

"I was going to tell you, man," Brik pleaded.

"Oh, yeah. Like when?" Trick replied abusively. "Like . . . when they re-po my car? When they throw me out of my apartment? Like when . . . aw, forget it!"

"You mean like when you can't getta hold of any more junk to throw up your nose? Come on, Trick, you don't mean all . . ."

"Fuck you, farmboy! I mean every word! Like you might as well take my car . . . and my apartment. You've taken my goddam job off me! What else have I got that'ya want? Take it!"

Brik went to put his arms round Trick but Trick shrugged clear and pushed Brik away, violently. Brik pinned him against the kitchen wall and forced Trick to accept his embrace.

"So Cattini told you," Brik began as Trick tried to struggle free. "But did he tell you why? Hey?" As much as Trick wriggled, Brik tightened his hold. "Well, good. At least that means I can tell you myself. You remember I told you about that guy Ron? Back home? Ron who took pictures of me?" Trick began to quiet down. "Our friend Cattini gotta hold of some of those pictures from some Doctor friend of his here in LA. He blackmailed me, Trick. He was gonna use those pictures against me."

"Doctor?" Trick muttered. Brik relaxed his grip. He could see Trick was no longer playing, that he was calmer. "Must be Kenny." Brik let go completely and went on.

"And I didn't know it was gonna be your movie, Trick. I swear."

"So how did you . . .?"

Brik sighed.

"Clem Barber," he replied. "Clem was the cameraman on that stupid pilot. It was Clem who told Cattini where I was."

"Oh," said Trick, as the final pieces slotted into place.

Brik folded his arms. Trick turned away and sipped pensively at his beer. "I'm sorry, man," Brik said, reaching out after a while and touching Trick's shoulder.

"So," Trick said, turning to face Brik. "Tommy threatened what? To send the pictures to your mom and dad?"

"Sorta," Brik replied. "But I didn't do the movie 'cos of the blackmail."

"So why d'ya do it?"

"I wanted to," Brik replied. "In the end, I just wanted to."

Trick shook his head. He looked at Brik as though he were insane.

"But... Why?"

"What is this?" Brik asked. "Don't tell me you're shocked? *You* do them for God's sake?"

"Yeah," Trick replied. "Sure I do 'em," he went on, like he was explaining basic math to a nuclear scientist. "I do 'em 'cos I know I ain't gonna get nowheres else doin' anything legit."

"But you told me lots'actors did 'em," Brik said, puzzled.

"Actors!" Trick spluttered. "That's what *they* call themselves, man. No one else would."

"Well, I'm not ashamed," Brik said defensively.

"No one expects you to be ashamed, Big Boy," Trick said gently. "But you really don't know what you've done, do you?" he added, confirming his suspicions that Brik had not been in a proper state of command of the perspectives.

"Sure I do."

"The fuck you do," Trick replied. He opened the refrigerator and took out two more beers. He peeled the tabs off and handed one to Brik. "Come here, dingaling," he said and pulled Brik through to the living room. "Siddown." Brik sat. "Don't you realise," Trick began, "that if anyone in this town sees that movie, word'll get around like a brushfire? You won't just need to change your name. You'll need surgery on your face before anyone'll take you serious again."

Brik was quiet for a moment. At first it seemed that Trick was right, that he had done the dumbest thing anyone could have done.

"But there were still the pictures, Trick," Brik justified. "Cattini had them all. I ripped the one up he showed me but he just laughed. Said he had 'em all. Ron confirmed that. Cattini would have waited 'til . . . well, they'd've always been hanging over me. So, I thought, what the hell? Go for it. Do the movie, take the two grand and . . ."

". . . the *how much?*" Trick exclaimed.

"Two thousand dollars," Brik repeated, bracing himself for what seemed like another outburst from Trick.

Instead of exploding with anger, Trick broke out laughing.

"Two . . . thousand . . . dollars!" he roared, doubled up. "Oh, god! Oh man! *That's* funny!"

"I should have gotten more, I know," Brik observed with a great helping of self-reproach.

"More!" Trick exclaimed. "You're joking, man? Y'know the most I ever got?"

"Tell me," Brik sighed.

"A grand," Trick announced. "One measly fuckin' single one."

"So," Brik said rather uncertainly, "I did good, yeah?"

Trick moved his seat and sat next to Brik, sliding over the arm of the chair and landing almost in Brik's lap. He kissed Brik, on the cheek.

"Yeah. You did good, Big Boy."

Brik grinned.

"Does that mean I'm forgiven?" he said hopefully.

"Ain't nothin' to forgive, I s'pose," Trick replied, nestling against Brik's still shirtless torso.

"Good," Brik replied. "Like I said, I don't want us to have secrets, Trick. I want us to be friends. Jeremy told me that staying friends is what counts."

"Sure," Trick agreed, lazily. "Hey! You haven't told him, have you?" he said suddenly, whipping around in the chair.

"Who? What?"

"Your teacher. You haven't told him about doin' the movie, have you?"

"Hell, no!" Brik exclaimed. "That dumb I'm not. I wanna be in his movie, man."

Mention of the movie, Jeremy's movie, made Trick realise what he'd done. He remembered only too well but he discounted the memory. He had done the unforgivable, telling Ryder. But given that Ryder had been so loyal, given that Ryder hadn't even believed him . . . No, Trick discounted, Ryder wouldn't even ask Brik. Like the rest of that part of their lives, Ryder would act like it simply wasn't there.

"Hey," Trick said, having settled himself once again. "You wanna make some money with me?"

Brik turfed Trick off his lap, laughing.

"No, man. I am not doin' twosomes with you. No way!" he said, laughing but nonetheless definite. He stretched out his hand and helped Trick up off the floor.

"Honey, there ain't no one I know could afford us together. Ain't no one that rich in this whole world," Trick joked.

"But . . .," Brik said, raising an eyebrow. "You *do* have something in mind, don't you?"

"Uh huh," Trick smiled. "It's a split fee. Just an appearance."

"So . . . Where?" Brik asked. "And how much?" he added. "I'm not saying I will, mind."

"Don't tell me you'd turn down a hundred bucks and as much champagne as you can drink for jus' jumpin' out of a li'l ol' cardboard birthday cake?" Trick offered.

"A hundred . . . are you telling me you get two hundred bucks for jumpin' outta birthday cakes?" Brik whistled in disbelief.

"Are you with me?" Trick pursued.

"Do we do this thing naked?" Brik enquired further.

"No way, man!" Trick retorted. "Naked's a lot extra."

"And you're *sure* that there's no . . ."

". . . not unless you want to," Trick assured. Brik looked almost convinced. "Whaddya say? Yeah?"

"Oh . . . okay," Brik agreed.

"Great!" Trick said.

"You bein' straight with me?" Brik urged insistently. "Something tells me you got reasons for all this."

"Perhaps," Trick agreed mysteriously. "But it has nothing to do with you. I just need to see the look on someone's face . . ."

TWENTY THREE

I am not, have never been and will never be a party person. Party people are not afraid to trumpet themselves, their jobs, their status, their interests, their likes, their dislikes at the drop of a party hat. Party people never ask questions, real questions of any depth or personal import. Party people have no interest in finding out about people in the way that non-party people want to find out. Party people don't wait to be approached. Party people work parties like high-rolling gamblers shoot craps, loudly, obviously, intently and professionally. And party people never listen to anything with which they cannot immediately identify as acceptable, desirable or developable into social or financial profit.

I am not a party person because I feel there is nothing of any particular interest about my life, character or work to trumpet about and therefore I am reduced to asking the questions which cue the well-rehearsed lines that the party people are waiting to speak. I am a feed man, the straight man to the starring comic and, thus cast, I am reduced to listening. Eldon has just assured me that for every party person there has to be a non-party person to make a successful party; one to talk, another to listen. I do not agree with his thesis nor do I even acknowledge the logic. How, I have always thought, could I ever be of any possible use or advantage to a party person when I have nothing they could possibly want and when I want absolutely nothing from them that I cannot get from yellow pages or accidents of fate?

Perhaps, one day, I will understand parties better. But, perhaps, I won't.

Finally, given that I have been inveigled into going with Eldon to this particular party, I have to admit from my feeble experience, that American parties are easier to handle than English ones. I cannot speak for parties taking place in any other national culture as I have no knowledge of them. At least the Americans have the good grace to come clean with their trumpeting and trumpet all the required information as a necessary foreplay to the real action. 'Hi! I am this that and the other' - name, job, residence - to which protocol dictates that I am supposed reply with equivalent information. The length of the ensuing party intercourse will depend on names - do we know anyone in common and, especially in Los Angeles, do I have better names to drop than you - on jobs - what do I do that you might need and pay me for in goods, services, introductions, favours - on residence - if I live in as desirable an area as you live, we can talk; if I live in a noticeably less or markedly more desirable area, the intercourse will have limited value.

If all that sounds cynical, it's not. It merely serves as a cloak for my chronic shyness, anal retentiveness and an upbringing which omitted any basic party training on an adult level.

"It'll be fun," Eldon said as we waited at the light on Hilgard and Sunset. Vague, hazy yet horribly real memories of being taken to piano lessons by my mother returned to me and I wished she'd substituted party lessons instead.

"No it won't," I replied, sulkily.

"Alright. It won't."

"Thankyou."

"It certainly won't be fun if you arrive telling yourself it won't be fun. Can't you look on it as an experience?"

The lights changed and we pulled onto Sunset, turning almost immediately into the lower Bel Air Estate. It wasn't a sunny evening. It was grey and there was a fall atmosphere, peaky and a little damp.

"Why should I?"

"Because you're a writer. It's all good copy, Jeremy."

"But I'd never dream of writing party scenes," I retorted. "And if I had to I'd make them up. Party scenes are always embarrassing. They're staged, just like parties. There," I said with a hint of triumph. "QED."

"Perhaps they're intended to promise a little embarrassment," Eldon contended. "Like danger. What's life without a little danger?"

"Easier," I replied. I sighed. "And it's all very well for you. Everyone knows who you are."

"How can they?" he grinned, "when I don't even know myself. Anyway, I'm older. It's the one and, I assure you, only good thing about being older. You have the dubious privilege of people being more likely to be polite to you."

"But that's exactly what I mean," I replied. I looked at my watch. "In less than fifteen minutes, I shall already have given two different answers to the same question..."

"...`And what do you do, Mr Page?'," Eldon said, for me.

"Exactly. If I say teacher that usually produces about as much reaction as if I'd said clerk."

"So try writer," Eldon suggested.

"Which opens an entirely different can of worms. One novel and one as yet unproduced screenplay hardly makes me Danielle Steel, does it?"

"You have better legs, dear," Eldon quipped.

"Thanks," I said, looking at the alien tuxedo pants which disguised my two and only social assets. "Well, at least I might get a decent doctor after tonight. You did say this Kenneth was a doctor?"

"I have it on good authority he once graduated from med school if that's what a doctor is," Eldon replied disdainfully as we passed the Bel Air Hotel.

"I take it you don't rate him," I observed.

"I wouldn't take a chilled gerbil to him," Eldon replied rather acidly and unusually. Usually, Eldon never said an unkind word about anyone.

"Oh," I said. "So why did you accept the invitation if you dislike him so?"

"His lover was a very, very dear friend of mine."

"Was?"

"Ummm," Eldon replied thoughtfully. "I accepted because I thought Sherman would have wanted me to. And," he added, "because there's usually some titillating little `angle' to Kenneth's parties."

"Like...?"

"Like unusually handsome and often quite intelligent waiters," Eldon replied statistically, "who have been known to be rather interested in what old and quite ungentlemanly scholars have to impart."

"Oh," I said. "I see."

"No you don't, dear boy. When you get to my age, titillation is all that's left you. Ah. Here we are."

Eldon pulled his Cadillac into the driveway. There seemed to be few guests as yet as the car was easily parked by the uniformed valets, hired for the night from the Bel Air at double rate. Eldon retrieved his birthday gift from the trunk before the car was whisked away, back down the drive. So *that's* how it's done, I thought, immediately noticing the windows of the front rooms of the house thronged with guests.

"Some property," I remarked, straightening my bow tie.

"A veritable Pandora's Box," Eldon replied as Kenneth Morrell appeared at the double front doors.

"Eldon! How good of you to have come."

"Kenneth, my dear. Happy birthday," Eldon replied, handing Kenneth the store-giftwrapped package. Kisses were exchanged, party kisses, polite, meaningless kisses.

"Oh, how *dear*," Kenneth gushed. "Do I open it now?"

"It'll keep overnight," Eldon said. His smile was so impenetrably warm, so succinctly plausible. But Kenneth couldn't wait. He withdrew the bottle green, roll-neck cashmere with suitable oohs and aahs and, "Perfect. Thankyou".

"And this must be our writer-in-residence," Kenneth said, extending his hand. "Welcome. I *adored* your book, by the way."

Well, of course, other things being equal, from that moment on Kenneth could have been my friend for life. I glanced at Eldon who betrayed not even a wink of having pre-primed Kenneth as to my party person status. And I cared not a whit, for in the few comments he made, it was obvious that Kenneth Morrell *had* read my book.

"Thankyou," I replied, awkwardly re-arranging the plaudits which hung after fifteen seconds of Kenneth's acquaintance like layers of floral garlands round my neck.

"Now, come along inside," Kenneth ushered, "and meet some people. Jeremy - what a *darling* name that is - I promise you absolutely no competition. Not another writer in sight and everyone's just *dying* to hear about your movie. So exciting for you, dear."

In the hallway, some musical Salvadorean friends of Julio and Dolores had been press-ganged into an impromptu mock-mariachi band at the lure of Kenneth's shilling and were playing Tijuana-type music to infuse the atmosphere with the required degree of carnival jollity.

As we passed through the hallway, it seemed that already several guests were giving themselves a tour of the property, encouraged by Kenneth. He called to one pair of handsome yuppies: "And don't forget the backroom, dears. I have a brand-new movie showing there for your pleasure." He accented the word pleasure with a wink and the two handsome yuppies giggled like schoolgirls.

"And dirty movies to boot," I muttered aside to Eldon."

Yes. And *so* therapeutic, don't you find?" he muttered through a wide smile as he advanced on a group of fiftysomethings whom he recognised.

The drawing room was filled with guests, mostly men but the odd sprinkling of female pulchritude on the arms of those who either swung a little in both directions or who never came to tux parties without a token piece of haute couture to add that dash of propriety to their proclivity. What a heady cocktail! The hum of conversation was punctuated with frequent high-pitched squeals, shrieks and hoots of social delight. I plunged in, was thrown in, at the deepest end of the pool.

Eldon and I were soon separated. I talked for a while to a tall, grey, elegant woman who designed things. I think it was carpets we were talking about. She seemed to be of the impression that the whole of the south of England was littered with palladian mansions through whose gracious rooms one padded on massed Persian rugs. Why disabuse her? I was moved on to chat to a rather opulent looking grey-haired musical gentleman of the movies and his young, classically trained accompanist who lived with their *adorable* European Schnautzers next door to Dorothy Lamour - *dear* Dorothy. They made me positively guilty that I had never gotten to know Schnautzers, let alone Dorothy Lamour.

Of course, it wasn't my movie that interested those people to whom I was introduced and with whom I chatted. The mooted stars of the movie were, however, of satisfactory interest and in themselves vindicated my name, job and status sufficiently to captivate my fellow conversationalists for a decent length of time.

As I moved on, I noticed Eldon being refilled most attentively by a stocky young blond waiter. As my ears wagged, I overheard the name `Kyle' being mentioned in almost the same breath as `Shakespeare'. Eldon caught my eye over Kyle's shoulder, fluttered his eyes for the briefest moment before returning to his glittering literary prize.

I almost collided with the two handsome yuppies, cloned precisely in their fashionable tuxes, so fashionable as to cause me to wonder whether or not they were rented. The tuxes, of course.

"Good movie?" I enquired good-naturedly.

They looked at each other and shared a sufficiently libidinous acknowledgement.

"I've seen some movies in my time," said the one.

"But that is some hunka fun," declared the other.

"So you'd recommend it," I said, for want of furthering an obviously limited conversation.

"Sure put a smile on his face," betrayed the first.

"Go check it out," advised the second. "Gee, Kenny sure knows how to pick 'em, doesn't he?"

The question was addressed to me. Ha, ha, ha . . . I laughed, gaily, faking it like I'd seen others doing all night long.

"Oh doesn't he just?" was my rhetorical response. "I'm Jeremy . . ." But I never finished. They'd seen someone else, over my shoulder. I moved on, emerging from the crush at the perimeter of the room where a tallish, sadly overweight man waited with an empty glass. I smiled.

"Great party," I said. "Hi, I'm Jeremy Page."

"Yes," he replied, jerking out of what seemed a reverie. "Yes. Hi. I'm Ron. Ron Windel."

"Good to meet you," I affirmed. "Are you . . . are you from LA."

"Er . . . no, No, I'm not. You're British, right?"

"Indeed I am," I said. "Though I've often been mistaken for an Australian. It seems that most Americans find it hard to tell the difference." I could have bitten my tongue as soon as I heard the words slither out. But Ron laughed.

"Most Americans have a hard time with most things outside the fifty states," he observed. Rather an educated man, I thought. Diffident too, not the usual brash, you're-my-new-best-friend American. "Have you known Kenny long?"

"Oh, I don't know him at all," I replied. "I'm almost a gate-crasher. I came with Eldon Stuart."

"Ah, Eldon," beamed my new best friend. "Wonderful man. Sherman was very fond of Eldon."

"So I gather," I replied.

There was an awkward moment's silence after which Ron said: "Hey, don't let me keep you. Weren't you just off someplace?"

"Me? Oh, no. I was thinking about . . . well, I heard there was a movie in back."

"Yes," he replied, curtly. "So I heard too."

"You . . . er. . . you're not fond of . . . movies," I fumbled.

"Not that one," Ron said. He sighed and looked for a moment rather embarrassed. Trust me, I thought, fancying that I'd just asked the only straight man at the party to come check out a gay porno movie. "Let's just say I have a personal disinterest in it. But don't let me put you off. Anyway, I've seen it already."

"Oh," I said, now hovering rather than concentrating my attention. "Well, nice talking to you, Ron. I'll . . . catch up with you later?"

"Sure," he replied. He half-smiled, looked at his watch and put his glass down on a sidetable before edging around the melee and out into the hallway.

I looked for Eldon but couldn't see him and instead of foisting myself on more unsuspecting guests, decided on the alternative, vicarious pleasure of taking myself to see the fabled movie.

I followed a fellow non-party person whom I'd noticed getting drunker by the sip as he lurched across the hallway and down a corridor. The two young and handsomes caught my eye and waved. I crossed over to them.

"Is that the way to the movie?" I asked, pointing in the direction of the swaying drunk.

"First on your left," they chorused.

"Kenny has one of those *huge* screens," the first intimated with lascivious double entendre. "In the games room. Have fun!"

I waved my thanks and, carried aloft on a cloud of what was a very good champagne, went on my way.

As I rounded the right-angle in the corridor, I saw that there was a cluster of guests around the door in question. The cluster was in general taller than me but I saw it begin to part, allowing someone through. Bracing myself to take my place in the huddle, the emergent movie fan turned out to be Eldon. He saw me and seemed to shudder.

"Naughty, naughty," I teased. "So what's it like?"

"Ah . . . Jeremy." He seemed quite distrait.

"Well . . . It must be good to have affected you like that, Eldon." I laughed. He took my arm.

"It's time for the cake," he said, falteringly. "We can't miss that. Kenny has such wonderful birthday cakes."

"I'll join you in a moment," I assured him. "I have to see this movie. I seem to be about the only person who hasn't seen it."

"No," he said quickly. "I mean, later. We have to see the cake cutting."

He propelled me back down the corridor and back into the drawing room. I thought it odd behaviour but . . . champagne is such a buffer, I thought no more about it as he introduced me to a retired executive from Columbia who'd come up from Laguna Beach for the party.

The lights of the drawing room chandelier suddenly

flashed on and off and were then dimmed, only a spotlight illuminated the crush. The conversation dimmed too and in the doorway, two waiters now wearing tall chef's caps and aprons appeared and the crowd parted before them. They were pushing a trolley on which was a perfectly decorated and enormous birthday cake sporting if not fifty, then certainly twenty-five large candles.

Following the procession was a self-appointed toastmaster, the musical Schnautzer-loving friend of Dorothy's, and Kenneth Morrell, the host himself. The guests were pressed around the perimeter of the room as the toastmaster cleared a space around the trolley.

"If you please, ladies and gentlemen . . . Pray silence, if you please . . ." The conversation reduced to a murmur. Kenneth stood with his hands folded in front of him as the toastmaster began the anniversary eulogy, droning on about the specialness of the anniversary and the specialness of Kenneth. "And so," he concluded, "please raise your glasses . . . ladies and gentlemen, and drink a health to our generous host and loving friend, Kenneth . . ." The room's glasses were raised and everyone sang "For He's a Jolly Good Fellow" followed by "Happy Birthday To You, Happy Birthday To You . . ."

Then everyone clapped. No one called for a speech as Kenneth obviously didn't intend to make one. Instead he bent low and blew out the candles. All credit to him, he did it in one long, controlled breath. All out. Yet more applause.

Then, with ear-splitting volume, the music speakers situated in all four corners of the room blasted forth with a current dance record and the innocuous birthday cake split open like an exploding paper bomb and two men leapt forth, kicking through the ribbons and the bunting, kicking away the wheeled and now redundant trolley and began dancing madly to the violent dance hit.

What had been a single spotlight turned into a strobe, pulsating and flashing via some electrical connection to the music. Some people covered their eyes with a spare hand as they guided each other away from the throng and out into the hallway. The majority remained and served to tighten the perimeter of the arena where the two young men danced, forming a tuxedo wall of hand-clapping, ecstatic faces. The dancing boys wheeled and turned, rather expertly. I confess I was by this time so drunk that I was standing on a chair, a rather flimsy empire-style side chair covered with an expensive silk damask. Once again, I seemed to have lost Eldon.

I saw Kenneth Morrell being dragged rather than persuaded into the midst of the frenzied dance. He seemed completely phased at the public exposure and merely stared, as though entranced, at each of the boys in turn. His limbs hung, like those of a rag doll as they turned him and wheeled him before finally releasing him. He stumbled, dazed back into the crowd of guests.

The music segued into a different title, similar beat and the lights pulsated a little less heavily. The boys seemed to be working in unison, dancing not only to their happy thronged audience but also to themselves, even hugging each other as though exhibiting their private selves to their public following. The crowd loved this display of intimacy and cheered and whistled as though encouraging the performers to even greater feats of exhibitionism.

The boys worked slowly around the perimeter, allowing the clapping hands to come just so close and then to withdraw. Everyone seemed to be enjoying it hugely as was I, swaying and clapping along with everyone else, however precariously I balanced on my expensive perch. It was all such wild abandon, such joyous celebration, so blissfully innocent . . .

Until the boys reached my side of the floor.

It wasn't Trick I recognised so instantly. It was Brik. Perhaps it was his hair that had previously disguised him. He looked so different with it gelled back and gathered under the pirate headband. But I knew him, with a certainty that thudded and echoed in my guts so hard I could feel myself squirming, as though alive with snakes gnawing at my insides. I froze. I tried getting off the chair but the guests had crowded so close against me that I couldn't find the floor with my foot. I knew he would see me. I watched as his eyes, enjoying each moment of this glorious exhibition, flirted with every guest as he involved them in turn in his performance, male and female alike.

He and Trick were dressed identically in white Converse baseball boots, thick white socks slipped down to their ankles and white, thigh-hugging knee-length sport pants. Their bodies were oiled and they seemed to sparkle like acres of jewels as flashes of strobe lighting reflected off the beads of oil and sweat adorning their writhing, rhythmic contortions.

It had to come my turn. When Brik's eyes found me, I feigned non-recognition. I think I just stared, blankly but I knew he recognised me. Only for a moment did a very professional smile leave his face but he didn't break his dance, nor his concentration but purposely paid no further attention to me.

The audience's enthusiasm became wilder and wilder; lethal overdoses of adrenalin were willingly exchanged between the watchers and the watched. I could feel it flowing into Brik like love and I could see him reacting to it, hooked on the ecstacy he had brought them to and, instead of stopping, taking them even higher. The music track came to an end. Instead of a smooth segue, there was a gap in the music.

Someone shouted: "Loved your movie, man!" Another called: "Are you really Brik Peters?"

Brik turned to both sources and raised a clenched fist in the air and waved. Trick then took his hand and together they raised their held hands in mutual salute. The crowd roared. The music started again and the boys each grabbed a partner from the throng and pulled them into the dance. The assembly broke ranks and everyone started dancing.

It let me off my rock and from it I stepped into the hard place. I found Eldon and steered him out into the hallway.

"Did you know about this?" I asked.

"No," he replied. "No, Jeremy, I didn't."

"What has he gotten himself into?" I wondered aloud. "That was Trick Rambler, wasn't it?"

"Yes," Eldon replied mutedly.

The two gay yuppies passed by, arms entwined.

"Hey," said one to me, "didn' I tell ya that he was one hunka fun!"

"Who?" I replied, rather bemused.

"The new guy," his friend expanded. "The one dancing with Trick Rambler in there."

"I'm sorry," I said, "I don't quite understand."

"Didn'cha see the movie yet?" the first boy enquired. "He's the guy I was tellin' y'about. What's his name, honey," he said, turning to his friend.

"Brik . . . I think," drawled the friend and ran his tongue suggestively over his lips. "Couldn'cha just *eat* him up!"

I felt the pressure of Eldon's hand on my arm, trying to edge me away.

"He was too much for that li'l Mexican kid back there," swooned the first. "I wish I had money," he continued. "I'd blow a week's rent for a night with Brrrik!" He pronounced the name of my Brik, *my* Brik, with a down and dirty growl.

"Jeremy, I think we should go," Eldon said firmly.

"Wait!" I said. It had taken it's time but the truth of all I'd been piecing together was dawning. "Are you telling me," I asked, almost accusingly of the two youngmen, "that Brik Peters was in the . . . the porno movie here?"

They seemed amused. One of them even giggled and the other nodded in a direction over my shoulder.

"Why don'cha ask him y'self, honey?" he giggled. "And y' know what they say . . . The camera never lies!"

I turned round and saw Brik and Trick emerging from the drawing room each holding flutes of champagne, their arms round each other's shoulders. They were drenched in sweat. It coursed in rivulets from their pectorals, down and over their perfect washboard bellies and soaked into the thin layer of cotton from which their shorts were made, turning the garments into virtually transparent veils, clinging to every contour of their loins. As they walked into and through the hallway, guests male and guests female hailed them like victorious gladiators; groping hands brushed against muscled arms, teasing fingers touched flesh, patted sculptured shoulders; lecherous faces raked the youngmen with laser eyes. The boys graciously and politely acknowledged the admiration.

I was standing with Eldon right in their path. I had to face them. It was like a dream, everything slowed, surreally decelerated.

"Hi," Brik said as our eyes met. He grinned, somewhat abashed, I felt. He put out his hand and touched mine. "Trick," he said, gaining his companion's attention, "I'd like you to meet Jeremy Page. Jeremy this is Trick Rambler."

I swallowed. I couldn't speak. Trick offered his hand. He smiled with such friendliness it made me want to disappear, to crave the floor to open and for me to fall through to hell.

"Ya kidding!" Trick grinned. "Hey, Jeremy. It's *so* good to meet you. You can't begin to know how much my buddy here talks about you. In fact it's great to meet you. Any friend of Big Boy here's a friend of mine."

"Thankyou," I managed to mumble, my throat dry and constricted. Trick's term of endearment was not lost on me.

Behind us, at the foot of the curving staircase, the mariachi strollers had re-assembled and began tootling up a version of `South American Way'. Eye yai, eye yai, there is melody in the music . . .

"So what are you doing here?" Brik asked me.

"I'm . . . I'm just here," I replied. What *am* I doing here, I found myself thinking but I couldn't react, I couldn't unscramble my confusion. I wished he'd just go away. I didn't know what to say, how to act . . . I was a shuffling wreck.

"Hi," said Trick to Eldon and extending his hand. "I'm Trick Rambler."

"Eldon Stuart," replied my mentor. "A very energetic performance, may I say."

"Thanks," Trick said. "We bin practising. Haven't we, Big Boy?"

"Night and day," Brik replied, flashing a wide smile.

"Well, boys," Eldon said, assuming a maternal command. "You're going to catch your deaths if you don't get dressed. Be off with you. I'm sure," he added, glancing askance at me, "we'll do all our catching up later."

"Yes," I mumbled, forcing the weakest of smiles.

"Right," Brik said. "So, see you . . . tomorrow?" he suggested.

I nodded. He touched my arm again and then, with Trick, hurried down the corridor to where they had changed their clothes.

"Come on," Eldon said. "We're off."

We waited on the steps as the party noises continued behind us, waiting for the valet to bring around Eldon's car. It was only nine o'clock. The party had a long way to go even for early-to-bed LA.

"You saw it," I said quietly, after a long sigh. "You saw him in that . . . that piece of trash, didn't you?" I remarked bitterly.

"Yes. I did," Eldon admitted.

"And that's why you made me watch the cake thing."

"Yes. I honestly had no idea, Jeremy." He too sighed. "I don't know which would have been worse for you."

"Would you have told me?" I asked.

The cream Cadillac's tyres screeched on the brick drive as the valet sped it to a halt in front of us.

"I don't know, Jeremy," Eldon said simply. "I honestly, right now, don't know."

❉ ❉ ❉ ❉

Apart from the surprise double whammy in the birthday cake, Kenneth Morrell had another good reason for remembering his fiftieth birthday.

He hadn't taken taken the call himself. Julio had written down the message, as best as his spelling allowed. He searched the rooms of the house for his employer whom he finally located; Kenneth was giggling drunkenly with three of his guests to whom he was showing off his collection of Brik's photographs in the locked privacy of his study.

Julio knocked.

"Who is it?" Kenneth called. He gathered all the ten-by-eights together and replaced them in the file, fearing the knocker could be Ron Windel.

"Julio, sir."

"I don't want to be disturbed, Julio," Kenneth barked.

"Okay, okay . . . yessir," Julio replied, hardly hearing over the music and laughter. He slipped the message under the study door.

"Sorry," Kenneth apologised to the group of older guests. "I suppose I have to see what the idiot wants." He crossed the room, picked up the note and unfolded it.

`ORTORRITEES CONSIDRIN ORTOPSEE ON SHURMUNS BODDI. APPEE BURTAY NANCY FRANK LASSMAN'

Kenneth felt the prescence of a cold hand, a searingly ice-cold hand, very close to his heart.

TWENTY FOUR

Eldon, like a kindly teacher, excused me from classes the following day. I didn't have to call Brik, he called me and twenty minutes later I was pouring coffee for him.

Initial shock had turned to a smouldering, righteous anger which, like magma pressured deep in the earth, was pressing at every point of contact with the outside, waiting only to hit upon the weakest point before effecting the inevitable eruption.

"I really didn't know he'd be showing the movie last night," Brik began. "And nor did Trick."

"Was it a sneak preview?" I enquired unkindly, "or is it already on general release?"

"I figure you must be pretty mad," he said, ignoring my initial question.

"And why should you think that?" I replied coldly.

He shrugged.

"You weren't exactly overjoyed to see me last night," he observed.

I cracked. I didn't know my skin was so thin. I banged the cafetiere down so hard, I frightened us both. Hot coffee spurted through the loose lid and sprayed my shirt, my hands and the table top.

"Dammit!" I felt myself shaking with rage. "Dammit!" I shouted. Brik blinked and looked down at the table.

"Dammit what?" he asked quietly.

"Damn . . . everything!" I ranted. "Damn you, Brik. Damn me and . . . and damn this whole lousy town. Look! Look at what it's done to you . . . You've only been here a couple of months!"

"But what *has* it done to me?" he said reasonably. "Tell me. Look at me. I'm still me. I haven't grown two heads."

"Oh, Brik!" I exclaimed, retreating into scorn. "I obviously overestimated you. If you can't see . . ." I hesitated. His eyes challenged me to continue. "Jumping out of birthday cakes, half-naked . . . Making porno movies, for God's sake . . . What would . . . What would your parents say? Don't you *see*?"

"Okay," he replied. "I'll tell you what I see. Jumping out of birthday cakes whole or half-naked is hardly a criminal offence. I'd have done it for you . . . for Andy . . . anyone. And it earned me a hundred bucks, half Trick's fee. Porno movies . . . okay. Maybe, but . . ." He faltered. "But as far as my folks go, they ain't likely ever gonna find out. Not that it's their business. And *not* that it's any business of yours, Jeremy."

I wheeled round and tore the chair from beneath the table and sat down. I banged my fist on the table as I lashed out.

"Wrong! You don't know how *wrong* you are. It is my business, Brik. More than you think. Firstly there's *my* movie . . . You might not think it's so important but it's my whole life up to now and maybe the key to the future, not just my future but hopefully *yours* too. Can you imagine what Andy would say if he knew about this . . . this stupid porno thing? Can you imagine what Teddy Milosofuckingvic would say at Universal? You'd be out, Brik. Out on your ear and you'd deserve it. Your thoughtlessness could maybe blow our whole deal. And it'd make me look . . . look a complete and utter *fool*!"

"Ah," he said, knowingly, nodding his head with a look of mock wisdom. I was incensed.

"And what does `ah' mean?" I spat out.

"Skip it," he said flatly.

"No!" I cried, now in a frenzy of frustrated temper. "No, I will *not* skip it. It's not just my movie, I'm concerned for you, you little idiot! You might as well know that when we left Scotland to come out to this asshole place, your father asked me that I should keep an eye on you out here. Do you know what that meant for him to have to ask that? He's a strong and stubborn man, Brik, but he bent, like an ash tree in a gale, low enough to have to ask me, a stranger to look out for his son. I'm under oath, Brik. What do you think about that?"

He sighed. He looked up and pondered my expression as though trying out the keys on a ring of possibilities ascertaining which was the right one to unlock the door he had to open.

"Jeremy," he said thoughtfully, "I know that you think that in some way LA has done something terrible to me. But y'know what I worry about?" He started to get up. He was half way up; then he was standing up. His movements, obviously prefacing a departure, obstructed my momentum. I remembered back to the Sunday confrontation on Indian Road; I remembered how hard I worked at preventing a walk-out by Brik's father.

"What?" I said limply. "What are you worried about?"

"You," he said. "Don't worry about me. LA hasn't done anything to me that I didn't want to happen. Think about yourself."

He started for the door.

"Don't go," I said. "Please."

"Do you care for me?" Brik asked.

I just looked at him, looked and thought, Oh, dear Lord ... I think I must have prayed, prayed for a gift of tongues, other men's tongues which could say for me what I found so ridiculously impossible to say myself.

"Of course ... Of course I care," I managed to say.

He slowly came back to the table and resumed his seat.

"Care?" he urged gently. "What's this care? I love you, Jeremy. Don't you see that?" I shook my head. "I know what you feel for me," he continued. "I know that you have a hard time with it. I'm *not* a little idiot, you know. I may be young, but I'm not blind. I know what you're afraid of ... You need to *know* first, don't you? You want some kinda guarantee?"

I nodded, impaled on a pang of guilt, flailing like a snake, its neck trapped under a forked stick.

"Oh, Brik ... I'm so sorry."

"Don't be," he insisted. "It's your way. It's not unlike my way. We're not so different, Jeremy. But it's not right for us, yet, for either of us. I also need to know. It takes two, y'know."

"But ..." I began. "What about Trick?"

"I don't know," he replied with a shrug. "Ask Trick. I

only know about me."

"So you're not . . .?"

"Jeremy," he said, reassuringly, "we all need to grow up. You did some of yours with Andy, right?" I nodded. "I'm doing mine with Trick. He . . . Well, I think Trick kinda needs me and I *know* I need *him* right now. But," he added, touching my hand across the table, "we have to keep friends, Jeremy. I wanna keep friends with everyone and it's tough. Take Ry. I don't know what's happening there and I know he doesn't. But I know I don't want to lose him. Friends, remember? That's the most important thing. Just like you said. Throw that away and there'll be nothing to come, no future at all. Yeah?"

"Yes," I agreed meekly. I took my courage in my teeth and held both his hands in mine. He didn't withdraw. He returned my grasp and massaged my pathetic little hands in his, kneading my fingers and the joints of my palm with tenderness. I knew he was doing it but strangely, I couldn't appreciate it. "But *why* the movie, Brik. I have to know about the movie."

"Sure," he said. "I can understand that."

"Well?"

"You remember that guy I told you about. In Doddsville. The one who took pictures of me?"

"I remember you telling me, sure."

"Well, Ron gave a whole bunch of 'em to a friend of his here, in LA. This guy," Brik laughed at the thought, "who's party you went to last night, by the way, handed one on to a guy called Cattini, Tommy Cattini. That fancy doctor and Cattini have a business together for porno stuff and one of their cameramen who saw the picture of me was the guy who shot our teevee pilot." Brik spread his hands. "Simple."

"So they blackmailed you?" I asked in conclusion, in horror, hypnotised by what I perceived to be such evil manipulation of an unprotected innocent.

"I can't blame anyone," he said. "It was all circumstances. I was in debt, no prospect of working . . ."

"Oh, no," I groaned. "So *that's* where you got the money

you gave me." He nodded. "Oh, Brik, why? You must have been so unhappy. Why didn't you tell me?"

He raised his eyebrows and shrugged away what I took to be regret.

"I really didn't know what to do for the best so I just decided to do what was inevitable as best I could. Course," he laughed wrily, "at first I wanted to go kick the shit out of Ron Windel but . . ."

". . . who?" I interrupted.

"Ron Windel. The guy in Doddsville."

"But I met him," I blurted out. "He was at the party last night. He seemed so . . . so *nice*!"

"He is nice," Brik assured me. "I told you. I liked him a lot. Still do. In fact I'm seeing him later today. He's as pissed at Morrell as I was. Ron didn't know what Kenneth was going to do."

"Jesus!" I cursed. "If I was you, I'd want to murder them both."

"For what? You have to understand, Jeremy. I didn't mind making that movie. I didn't *mind* having Ron shoot pictures of me. I enjoyed it." He paused. "You have to know that about me, accept it. It's me. And . . ." He was about to add something but didn't finish.

By this time I was reeling. I didn't know how much more I could assimilate. I'd reached the point where what I was hearing was no longer sinking in. My mind was racing off on a hundred tangents. I could think of nothing more focused than a chain which began with Andy, linked on to Teddy Milosovic at Universal and ended up with `Parallel'. Brik was my Christopher. Brik was also mine and I was losing him. I had to hang on and the only handle I knew of on which we had a mutual grip was `Parallel'. He *had* to get the part. Had to.

"I don't know what it's going to take, Brik," I said grimly, "but somehow, I'm going to get hold of that movie. If necessary I'll buy it back from them. Everything's for sale in this damn town and I'll pay whatever it is they ask."

"Save your money," he said quietly. "For all I know it's out already. Whaddya gonna do? Run round the whole damn country knockin' on folks' doors offering them money for their bona fide tapes?"

"But I have to try," I pressed. "Can't you see? Now you have to understand, Brik. If Andy and the studio find out about that movie . . . I mean, if we ignore it and go ahead with `Parallel', if it should ever come out that I'd known about your movie all along and hadn't said anything . . . I'd feel terrible, Brik. I'd feel I'd let everyone down."

The ramifications suddenly assumed a dynamic all their own, for me, for Brik, Andy, Brik's parents . . . the list ran on endlessly.

"Oh," he said. "Oh, shit. I see what you mean."

"Yes," I said. "It's not pretty, is it?"

✻ ✻ ✻ ✻

As soon as Brik left, I rifled through Eldon's 'phone book. Nothing under Morrell. But there wouldn't have been. The listing would have been under the lover's name. Sherman . . . what, I puzzled, dredging through names, was his damn surname? It came to me and I looked under `F'. There it was Franck. Sherman Franck. It was crossed through and Kenneth's name pencilled in above.

I dialled the number.

Whoever it was that answered wasn't Morrell or Windel.

"May I speak with Mr Windel," I asked. "Ron Windel?"

"Jussa minute," came the reply and I heard the telephone being laid down on a hard surface. I waited maybe a minute before Windel picked up.

"Who is this?" he said.

"Mr Windel?" I said. "This is Jeremy Page. We met last night although you probably don't remember."

I heard the other telephone being replaced in its cradle.

"Oh, yes. Mr Page. I don't remember us talking for long but, of course, I remember you. How can I help you?"

"It's not me who needs your help, Mr Windel. Look, do you think we could meet," I requested. "It's about Brik. Brik Peters?"

Oh, that sharp intake of breath. Why is it always such a

giveaway?

"Please don't be alarmed," I continued hastily. "Please don't hang up. I mean you no harm, Mr Windel, I assure you. I know all about the pictures and it's not about them . . . well, not directly."

"Go on," he said. I could smell his fear. "As I said, it's about Brik. He's got himself into a terrible mess."

"Yes," Ron agreed. "I know."

"We have to help, Mr Windel. I know you don't have to and I suppose I wouldn't blame you if you backed down, but we have to help."

"Yes," he said. "Yes. You're right. Should we meet?"

"Oh, yes!" I exclaimed. "Yes, please."

TWENTY FIVE

In the picture business, things take their own time. Pressure betrays need which displays weaknesses which get taken advantage of which makes losers. It's a fine balance. Too much pressure and the lid blows; too little and the pot never boils. When things go slow, they go so, so slow; when things go quick, they happen faster than expected and often take a person off-guard.

Lindy buzzed Andy in his office as soon as Teddy Milosovic's assistant put his boss's call through to Buckman Miller.

"Teddy! Hi!" gushed a jaunty Andy Horowitz. "I just got the contracts back from my writer. He's signed, sealed and delivered. We're all set at this end."

"That's good," came the voice from Universal Studios, "'cos I'm gonna drop you in it, Andy. We've had a picture cancelled today and I can show you a green light *right* now if you can promise to roll in three weeks."

Andy was taken off-guard. He leant so far forward on that executive high-back swivel chair, the spring action nearly shot him forward into his open desk drawer.

"What?"

"Three weeks. I take it there's a problem."

"Er . . . Problem?" Andy said, quickly recovering. "No way, Teddy. No problem at all." Andy covered the mouthpiece and yelled through to Lindy. "Get me Terri Garr's agent *now*!" he barked. Returning to Teddy, he was all calm, cool and collected. "Course I have to check with the agents but I'm pretty sure that date'll fit. Terri's in Mexico but she's so hot for this, she'd fly back from the moon to do it."

"Great. And George?"

"He's cool. Gee, this is good news, Teddy."

"Yeah. For us too. Now, about the kid. My people here prefer the bigger guy . . . what's his name? Baywick?"

"Er . . . Berrick, Teddy. We call him Brik."

"Yeah. Him. We're going for him as of today. I saw Dick

at lunch and it's cool by him. Your other client's made runner-up. It was touch and go, y'know but, hell. Can't all be winners. I know they look kinda similar it's just that the other guy, who is it . . . ?"

". . . Ryder. Ryder McKigh."

"Yeah. Him. My people think he's a little too . . . bright? Know what I mean? Could take away from the girls."

Oh, Shit. Andy had been dropped in it but not like Teddy Milosovic had thought.

"Fine," Andy lied. "Listen. I'll get back to you just as soon as I've done the rounds of the agents, okay?"

"Sure."

"And the production office, Teddy?"

"Take the one the cancelled picture's moving out of," said Teddy. "They're vacating now. 'Bye."

"'Bye, Teddy." Andy hung up. "Shit!" he swore, wondering how the hell he was going to get around not only Ryder but Ryder's heavyweight father-in-law-to-be and his new partner.

Think, Andy, he urged himself. Think, man. Think.

But there was no other way around. Whatever was to happen was Ryder's business anyway. Bring Ryder in, Andy's instinct told him. Let Ryder sort out his own breaks.

"Lindy!" he called, reflecting that hopefully this was the last day he'd have to demean himself by shouting through a door to a shared secretary.

"Yes, Andy?"

"Get me Ryder McKigh at his home, yeah? If he's not there, try . . ." and Andy repeated a car 'phone number which belonged to Shelley's XJS.

"Sure, Andy."

"Oh, and Lindy?"

"Yes, Andy?"

"When I've spoken with him, would you step in here for a moment. I have . . . never mind. I'll tell you in private."

Lindy appeared in the doorway.

"You have what?" she asked.

"I have a proposition," he whispered.

Lindy giggled.

"Oh, Andy!" she vamped. "I didn't know you cared."

❋ ❋ ❋ ❋

"Hi, Shelley," Brik said. He was watching a movie at South Bentley Drive. "Where's Ry?"

Shelley Nersessian, or Shelley Ness as she had insisted on being called, came in and shut the front door. Never knowingly under-dressed, she looked this afternoon not unlike a walking warehouse for unrolled tobacco leaves. Tans, taupes and muted gingers were currently favoured fashion colours and Shelley was wearing all of them, in layers. She had that semitic, Middle Eastern limpidity which often made her look vacuous although inside she was A1, guaranteed, all-American princess. Though she wouldn't have liked to admit to it, there was more of grocer Poppa Nersessian's street trader's traits in her than her gentle brown eyes belied.

"Hi, Brik," she smiled. "All alone?"

"As usual," Brik said, flicking down the teevee volume on the remote.

"Ryder's collecting some messages," she said. "Mind if I join you?"

"Not at all," Brik said. As she edged in beside him on the couch, wafting her chosen day's perfume in his direction as she slumped down in her layers of Melrose couture, Brik fancied she looked worried. "Are you okay, Shelley?"

"Me? Oh, fine. Just fine."

"Ryder still treating you okay?" Brik enquired. "'Cos if he's not, just say the word!" he joked, "an' I'll see to it."

"My knight in shining armour," she said although she looked away as she smiled. "Do you mind if I talk to you about something?"

"Talk away," Brik said. "I kinda sense something's not right. Can I help?"

"Well . . . yeah. In fact," she added, "you're the only one who can help."

"Shoot. Go ahead," Brik said and flicked the teevee off

altogether.

"It's this movie," she began. "Y'know. Your teacher's movie?"

"What about it?"

"Gee," she sighed and looked as though she was about to abandon her question altogether. "Maybe I shouldn't?"

"Shouldn't what?" Brik asked with increasing concern. "What's happened?"

"Well . . . nothing. At least, not for Ryder."

"Shelley . . . just say it. What am I gonna do? Chew your head off? It's me, Brik . . ."

"I want you to step aside," she said quickly. "Not only for Ryder but for you, too."

"Excuse me?" Brik enquired, thinking he had surely misheard her.

"I want you to step aside," she repeated. "Let Ryder take the part."

"For what?" Brik exclaimed, horrified. "Why?"

"For the fifty thousand bucks I'm gonna give you. I checked already. That's what they were gonna offer you."

Brik blinked. He ran his hand through his hair and shook his head slowly, side to side, in utter disbelief.

"Do you know what you've just said, Shelley?"

"Sure I do. I wouldn't ask you to do this for nothing, Brik. You won't lose money."

"Shelley," Brik found himself explaining. "It's not a matter of money. You don't understand. It's Jeremy . . . it's his picture. He wants me for the role."

"No," she said quickly, "it's you who doesn't understand, Brik. Believe me."

"Then explain," he urged, rather crossly.

"I can't," she said, shaking her head vehemently. "And I don't have that much time. Ryder'll be here soon. You *have* to accept. You'll see. I'm doing it for you, Brik."

"No, Shelley. I can't," Brik said firmly. "I can't and I won't. End of story. This conversation did *not* take place, right? I like you and I wanna go on liking you. Let's just forget this ever happened."

Shelley stood up and took her bag.

"Okay," she acquiesced. "But you'll see."

She turned quickly on her booted heel and marched out, click-clacking across the polished wooden floor as she went. Brik got up and went to go after her but the door was already shut. He watched her hurrying down the path to her car as Ryder pulled up in his Bronco. They seemed to exchange a few words before she got in her Jaguar and drove away. Ryder got out of his car and walked quickly and purposefully up to the front door. Brik opened it.

"Hi," he said.

"Close the door, Brik," Ryder said curtly. "And siddown. I have something to say."

"Oh boy!" Brik exclaimed, almost in despair. "What is this with you and your girlfriend?"

"She is *not* my girlfriend," Ryder snapped. "She is my fiancee, geddit? There's a major difference, *not* that you would appreciate."

"Now wait a minute," Brik launched defensively, "why doesn't everyone calm down here? What is wrong, Ryder?"

"I knew it," Ryder pronounced quickly, "I knew it all along." He was pacing the length of the house, from the kitchen door through into the living room and back. Brik remained in the middle of this trajectory. "You weren't taking me seriously. I just knew you weren't." He paused a moment in front of Brik to make a point. "I am going to marry her, Brik and there ain't nothing you or anyone else is gonna do to stop me."

Brik was nonplussed. Ryder was making no sense.

"So who's stopping you, Ry?" Brik waited, hoping for a response but Ryder continued to march around the house. "I'm certainly not. If it's what you want, marry her. Sure I take you seriously. I just wish I could believe you loved her."

"I do love her, scuzzbut!"

"It's nice to hear you say it, Ry. I'm . . . I'm pleased for you."

From the other side of the room, Ryder shouted.

"Well you don't seem particularly *happy* about bein' so pleased for me!"

"I am happy, Ry. You tell me that's what you want, then that's it. That's fine by me and I'm happy for you." Brik shrugged. But he spoke rather flatly. There truly was no enthusiasm.

"No," Ryder said quickly. "That's not good enough. You're . . . not . . . *happy*!" Almost manically, Ryder put his fingers next to his eyes and into the sides of his mouth and pulled the flesh back in a crazy mockery of a smile. It made Brik laugh.

"Watch it," he advised. "No one'd marry you looking like that, certainly not Shelley."

Ryder abandoned the ugly face and became immediately cold and hard, apparently rational.

"Exactly," he said, almost in a hiss. "Not only do I have to stay beautiful," he emphasised, "but I have to be super beautiful. An' y'know what that mean's Brik?"

"It means . . . gee, Ry. How the fuck should I know? I don't even know whatcha talking about!"

"I'm talking rich beautiful . . . I'm talking *munnee* beautiful!"

"You're crazy," Brik dismissed.

"No!" Ryder screamed. "I am not crazy!"

Brik began to get angry. Ryder was definitely acting like a crazy person. It was a Ryder Brik had never seen before, like a man possessed.

"I think we should talk, Ryder," Brik said firmly. "I mean really talk. Or you should go see a doctor," he added.

"Ha! You'll be the one going to see doctors!" Ryder huffed. "Doesn't it ever even cross your mind who you're daisy-chaining with?"

"Meaning?"

"Meaning Trick. Who else?"

"You leave Trick outta this. Or I'll start in on Shelley. You see who you see, I see who I see. Leave it alone, Ryder. It's none of your business."

"Wrong," Ryder sang out. "It is my business and at the moment, farmboy, you are messin'in *my* business. And you know just what I mean."

"You're making as much sense as smoke signals in a

hurricane, Ry."

"Okay," Ryder said conclusively. "As you didn't take up Shelley's very generous offer, I guess it's spelling-out time. 'Member spelling class?"

"Yeah," Brik said pointedly. "I was better than you."

"Why did'ja do it Brik?" Ryder suddenly asked. "Dammit, *why*?"

"Do what?"

"The movie . . ." Ryder's voice trailed away as though he couldn't bear to recognise Brik's stupidity. "That *dumb* porno movie?" He raised his head and fixed Brik with the finality of the done deed.

Brik wondered only for a moment, after which he immediately eschewed the avenue of denial.

"So who told you?"

"Your . . . friend? Is that the right speak? I'm not familiar with your sorta terminology," Ryder patronised.

"Not Jeremy?" Brik replied, surprised and hurt.

"Him!" Ryder sneered. "Don't tell me *he* knows all about it too?"

Brik nodded. "He knows. But who told you?"

"Trick did."

"Liar!" Brik retorted.

"Ask him . . . oh, he was so mad with you at the time, mad as hell." Ryder paused. "Made it up now, have we?" he teased. "Li'l kissy kissy and all's forgiven?"

And there, pop! Ryder burst the pretty balloon. No longer would they bat it back and forth, one to the other, playing with it and wondering for how much longer they could keep it up. Pop! Bang! The loud noise turned the little children's smiles of wonder and delight into tears. The noise frightened them.

"Ryder!" Brik warned, "shut up. Just listen for *one* moment. Lemme tell you . . ."

"No!" Ryder hollered. "No, you listen to *me*. Your friend Trick has got you into a whole lotta shit that I don't wanna know about. It's another you, Brik. I don't know this . . . this new guy an' I don't care to." Ryder's tone of derision diverted for a moment into a little oasis of amusement. "In fact," he laughed. "It kinda makes it easier." He reassumed his martial attitude, strutting about and sounding more like a pettyfogging general exacting punitive tribute from a defeated renegade. "You say Jeremy knows about this movie of your's?" Brik nodded. "I'm sure he has his . . . reasons?" Brik didn't bristle as anticipated so Ryder went on. "Well, Andy doesn't know . . . Nor does Teddy Milosovic and nor do the money guys at Universal. Nor does Andy's backer. I'm tellin' you, Brik, Jeremy might wanna keep schtum for *his* reasons but they're not very clever reasons and they're certainly not very commercial."

"So whaddya gonna do 'bout it?" Brik sighed.

"Me?" Ryder laughed. "Me, I'm gonna do zip about it, Brik. Zilch, zero, nada, niente. You're gonna do something about it. You wanna hear the good news?"

"Oh, Ry," Brik said sadly, almost wearily.

"The good news is that *you're* number one for Christopher. Unanimous choice . . . over at Univeral, at least."

"Great. I know," Brik acknowledged in a tired, you're-boring-me tone of voice.

"But do you know the *bad* news?" Ryder sing-songed but from a vantage point made safer by the presence of the couch between them.

"Hit me," Brik replied.

"You're gonna step . . . Aside," Ryder said with slow and deliberate intent.

Brik laughed.

"I'm *what*?" He paused and shook his head, like he was shaking water out of his ears after swimming. "You and Shelley both? What is it with you?"

"Listen!" Ryder hissed. "I am playing that part. D'you hear? Me. *Me*. If you don't step down by tomorrow morning, I am gonna tell Andy, Teddy . . . like everyone about that porno stunt of yours and they'll drop you like one hot son-of-a-bitch that no one will ever wanna touch again with rubber gloves!" Ryder spoke his ultimatum with dreadful precision. "Tomorrow morning, right?"

Brik's face started by being blank. He swayed slightly, as

though he were dazed. Slowly, he smiled, the smile spreading so gradually, as though by the millimetre. He began to laugh, at first just the occasional chuckle and then more frequently and from deeper within him.

Ryder looked puzzled. Brik's anger was usually so volcanic, so predictable.

"I gather I really don't need to have you repeat what you just said?" Brik asked, through what seemed a completely well-motivated grin. "Do I?"

"You heard me right," Ryder replied gruffly. He held his ground as Brik advanced across the room. But Ryder was frozen rather than fearless.

"You know something, Ry?" Brik said as he quickened his approach towards his lifetime's friend. "I been meanin' to give you this for some time . . . trouble was . . . I mean, why you didn't get it before was that I figured it was gonna cost me too much . . . Not money, mind. Least, not then. But I was dealin' in something more precious. Something you can't git at the counter." Brik seemed lost in the current of his flow of words, as though he were allowing himself to be taken whither it led. "'Cept the bank ran dry of that particular currency an' so I guess I'll just have to use the other money . . . just like the rest of you." Brik was still smiling, chuckling here and there.

But it was at this point that Ryder realised that the situation he had propagated was reverberating; he could feel the ripples of the shockwaves rebounding. He felt the earth shivering beneath his feet. Suddenly, Brik was within reach, just an arm's length away. Instinctively Ryder shielded his face and at the same time made to run for the door.

Brik pulled his arm back, clenching his fist as he did so and let fly, with all his anger and strength. The punch landed on the side of Ryder's head. As he pulled his arm back for another one, Brik said, rather quietly, as though administering punishment to a recidivist child: "That punch cost me twenty-five thousand dollars . . . This one comes out a little less . . . after all, we can't forget our agent's commission . . . Can we!" He hit Ryder again but the blow deflected as Ryder raised his arm and ducked the punch.

Brik didn't pursue Ryder. In fact, Ryder saw his friend walk in the opposite direction, away from him and into the bedroom he occupied. Apart from a closet opening and a few rustling sounds, there was silence from the room.

At first, Ryder thought it best to leave, to just open the front door and split. But there was curiousity left. He hadn't been hurt. As he was edging in the direction of Brik's door, Brik appeared with a zipper bag, overflowing with socks, T-shirts, all stuffed in the bag's open maw; his prized leather jacket lay between the handles.

The boys looked at each other. There were questions on Ryder's face; there was also concern and there was fear.

"Goin' someplace?" Ryder said. From somewhere, he managed to dredge the temerity to grin as he pointed as Brik's bag.

Brik merely looked. Though his eyes were dry, there was a loss deeper than a sea of tears in his throat. He snatched his keys from the hallway table, opened the door and left.

"You can't run away from this one, Brik," Ryder called after him. "Tomorrow mornin', right! Y'got 'til then!"

✲ ✲ ✲ ✲

Twice in as many days.

Brik was becoming a regular visitor to Eldon's house. We were sitting in the living room after dinner and heard the Volks pull up.

"Well," Eldon observed as I went to the door, "he might not love you yet but I'd say he has a hard time living without you."

"I wonder what's the matter now?" I queried aloud, partly in response to Eldon and partly from what I fancied were the two virtually sleepless nights I'd just passed. I opened the door.

"Hi," Brik said briefly. "You have a problem, Jeremy."

"Come in," I said, ushering him into the living room. "Problems, problems. Always problems. Can I get you anything before we solve this latest one?"

"No. Thankyou," he said. "Hi, Eldon." Brik turned and frowned. Obviously what was to be said he wanted to be private. But I didn't want to be private. I'd come to and passed that point where I wanted the drama and intrigue to involve me any further. What was to be said could now just as easily be said in front of witnesses. Eldon had hardly been reluctant to hear news of my plans when I told him the outcome of my very pleasant and constructive lunch with Ron Windel.

"Eldon and I have no secrets from each other," I said, rather firmly. "Sit down, Brik."

Eldon beamed across his coffee table. It was a sort of benign pleasure which shone from his face, but spiced with a degree of inner knowledge, the hint of which made him speculate.

"Ryder knows about the movie, Jeremy," he said. "As everyone does by now, I suppose? Right, Eldon?" He fixed the older man with a wry, quizzical frown.

"You mean the..."

"I mean the fuck film, Eldon. Let's not pussyfoot. There's no need." He snapped a little brusquely.

"Brik!" I remonstrated.

He got up. "Oh, I'm sorry. I . . . Eldon, please forgive me."

"Nothing to forgive, dear boy," said Eldon, calming the ruffled air with soothing hands.

"Ryder . . . My . . . my friend . . ." The words seem to catch in Brik's craw. "Ry's just told me he's gonna tell Andy and all the other guys about the porno movie if I don't let him have the part in 'Parallel'. I got 'til tomorrow morning.

"So, there it was. Out of the closet and naked as dawn. Simple. Plain language, no messing about.

The words hung there in Eldon's drawing room like corpses swinging from a row of public gibbets. I was horrified.

"But he can't . . . He has no . . . Brik? He's crazy."

"He is crazy," Brik admitted. "He's so determined to

marry Shelley and he figures her folks think there ain't gonna be no weddin' 'cept he can prove he has a future."

"And to do that he's prepared to trample all over yours . . . let alone mine. I mean, where do I come into this thing? It's my goddam movie! I told Andy he had no business suggesting Ryder for the part."

"He what?" Brik queried in astonishment.

"Just what I said," I replied and picked up the 'phone. "But now it's my turn to interfere."

"Oh," said Eldon, a little too wisely. "Brik, are you sure you wouldn't like a drink? I have a feeling we shall all be needing one by the end of the evening."

Eldon was already out of the room when Andy picked up.

"Ye'slo . . ."

"Andy? It's me. Are you alone?"

"Yeah. What's up?"

And as I was about to launch into my I'm-disgusted, I'm-insulted, how-could-you-do-this-to-me, or-to-yourself-for-that-matter routine, I realised I couldn't. I would be giving Andy the rope to hang Brik with. If I told Andy what Ryder had done, I'd be telling Andy that I hadn't been straight with him either. There was only one chance for Brik . . . only one chance for me if `Parallel' as conceived was to go ahead. That chance lay in the outcome of Ron Windel's activities that afternoon and the telephone had been ominously silent.

"Er . . . Oh . . . Nothing. Now I think about it, absolutely nothing. Sorry. Hope I didn't wake you?"

"No," he replied. "Are you sure you're okay?"

"Sure I'm sure. 'Night."

"'Night."

I slammed the phone back.

"I can't . . . I just realised. I can't tell him. Not now. Not yet, anyway."

Think, Jeremy, I urged myself. Think, man. Think.

The key to it all was Ryder. If I could only get to Ryder.

"Why not?" Brik said. "Why can't you tell him?" He was echoed by Eldon who came through with more ice.

"Because . . ." I faltered.

"Oh," said Eldon for he was party to more lies than Brik. "Yes. Of course."

"Would you mind letting me know what's going on?" Brik asked impatiently. "You never said anything about Ryder being involved in this movie!"

"Andy said he had it under control," I replied.

"What else has been going on behind my back?" Brik demanded.

"Ron Windel . . ." I began.

"What about him?" Brik urged.

"I had lunch with him yesterday. We're . . . well, he's gonna try and buy your movie back from Cattini, Brik."

"But I told you, it's a waste of time."

"Maybe . . . Maybe not. Ron's pretty determined. Maybe by tomorrow morning, there won't be a movie for Ryder to tell about. Then . . ." I clapped my hands together, gleefully, like some spiteful child. "He'll learn . . ." I pronounced. "People like Ryder always trip up sooner or later."

I had worked myself up into some state of righteous wrath. I must have sounded so pompous, so insensitive. After I finished ranting, I heard the silence. I turned my attention back to the room. Eldon was looking at the floor; Brik looked as though he was about to weep.

"You . . . can't," Brik said mournfully. "Why d'you want to hurt him like this? If you're doing it for me, don't. I don't want this. It's tough enough anyway with all this . . . this revenge making it even more complicated. We'll never work it out this way."

I was unsympathetic. I couldn't have felt less sympathy had I been deaf and not even heard Brik.

"Of course I'm doing this for you," I countered, "He's hurt you once too often. I've always thought he was a pushy little bastard and he's about to get his comeuppance."

"Don't call him a bastard," Brik commanded. "He's not a bastard, d'you hear!"

"Oh, yeah! Really?" I spat "He . . ." I stopped myself,

just in time. I wanted to wound, to hurt someone really badly in an aimless and wildly random defence of what had turned into a fight for my corner.

"Jeremy," Eldon murmured, reproachfully. He knew I was overstepping the bounds of decent behaviour, that what I was pronouncing was unworthy. That I was being judge and jury as well as executioner at that moment, I was simply unaware. Even if he'd tried to tell me, I wouldn't have even heard. Brik's news had triggered a syndrome where I had become immune to myself; pride and a wild, territorial atavism were fuelling passions which I would have to spend before they subsided. "Are you sure that all that's really up to you?" he queried.

"I'm absolutely sure. I'm the one who's being manipulated here. I stipulated Brik for this part for very important reasons. It's *my* movie and no one is going to screw it up for their own selfish advantage."

"I don't need this," Brik announced. "Let him have the part if it means that much to him. Jesus! If he's prepared to go this far, let him have the goddam thing. He obviously needs it a helluva lot more'n I do!"

"It's not yours to throw away!" I exclaimed. "You talk as if it's some wrapper . . . some unimportant play-pretty . . . a worthless geegaw! It's *my* movie."

Brik stood up, squarely. I must have appeared like one of the screaming harpies and he, the intrepid Jason. He stood his ground.

"You're right," he agreed. "At least, to a point. It was your movie."

"It's is not was," I hissed. "That movie *is* going to be made."

"Then get real, Jeremy," he warned. "We're not talking about a book you've written . . . This isn't about a one-to-one, not anymore. What was your baby is now a teenager. You can't necessarily control it. It's out, in the world. . . it's making its own way. How it'll turn out isn't down to you one bit."

"Oh, isn't it?" I retorted haughtily. "Well, you'll see. I'll show you how much control I have. If you pull out, Brik, I will simply pull the plug on the whole deal if necessary. I'll take my script back, tear it up and no one will get to play the part. Least of all that little shit you persist in protecting!"

Oh, dear Lord. When I'm reminded of this little scene, I shudder at the viperish, maddened termagant from whom my friends cringed that night. What must I have put them through, frothing like some rabid dog, lunging first at this one, then at the other with foam-flecked snapping jaws, so frightening and yet so sick with blind ambition?

"Jeremy, you must listen to Brik," Eldon interjected.

"Why?" I spun round. "Are you against me too? Why are you all against me? Why are you giving in? You're capitulating to Ryder's threats like he was some latterday Goliath!"

"And you?" Eldon interjected, "are David?"

"Tomorrow morning," Brik said carefully, "I am going to call Andy and tell him I can't do `Parallel'. It's as simple as that, Jeremy, and there's nothing you can do about it. It's not me you're thinking of now, it's you . . . Face it. Deal with it and until you have, leave me out of it."

"And," Eldon said, with stern gravitas, "I rather think you can't pull the plug as you say. You've signed contracts, haven't you? You're in the system now, Jeremy. I'm not sure how you stand legally but I have a feeling you can't just decide to pull out. Too many other people's livings are riding on your property for you to still have such total control. I may be wrong, but . . ." He shook his head. "I don't think I am."

"I'd just hand back the money," I countered.

"An' you think they'd just give you back your script?" Brik remarked.

"They would," I insisted. "Andy wouldn't go against me. I am the co-producer, after all."

"You putta lotta faith in Andy," observed Brik.

"And," Eldon added, "co-producers co-produce, they don't suddenly turn into fifth columnists."

"Like I said, Jeremy. Get real. This is Hollywood. You think you're the only one with a conscience. Perhaps you are. But I'd advise you to ditch it like immediately if you plan on stayin' around."

He strode towards the door. I was speechless.

"Brik!" Eldon called. "Where are you going?"

"Trick's," he replied.

"You don't have to," Eldon offered. "I mean, if you'd prefer to be alone, you can always stay here. Have some time to think."

Brik grinned, not with gratitude but with a certain venal amusement.

"I don't think that's such a very good idea, do you, Eldon? I don't want to be that alone."

I didn't allow Eldon any chance to reply.

"What if I went to see Ryder?" I called out to Brik's back. "Got him to change his mind?"

Brik turned. The look on his face was wearied; patient, accomodating but finally tired.

"Do what you like, Jeremy. It's your life, your movie. Like I said, leave me out of it."

"But I'm only doing it for you!" I sobbed.

He shook his head.

"No you're not," he said. "Like I said, worry about what LA is doing to *you*, Jeremy. Worry about yourself for a while. I do."

He left. Neither Eldon nor I saw him out.

"Oh, dear," said Eldon.

I think I was already running to my room for a jacket and my car keys. Wherever Ryder was I'd find him.

TWENTY SIX

Ron did it on his way to the airport.

He'd decided against going to see Tommy Cattini as he'd first indicated to Jeremy. Since they had parted in the restaurant parking lot after lunch, Ron had decided to remain invisible. He also decided that to have anymore truck with Jeremy Page would render him vulnerable. This part of his revenge, he wanted for himself.

Confronting Tommy with reason and requests was not the answer. Nor was offering money which Tommy would take only then to demand more. Furthermore, Ron had realised since talking to Jeremy that as their first plan's only secret weapon was integrity, using it to try and crack Cattini was bound to prove a reverse analogy; who'd ever heard of an ice pick smashing an iceberg?

No, he thought, discarding his original intention as a tide of fervour swept him almost fearlessly along. I'll torch the place. Burn it.

Like burglarise, Ron decided arsonise had a nice ring to it. Goodbye, Innuendo Productions. But not before he'd made an astute and carefully rehearsed telephone call.

Kenny wasn't even home when it came time for Ron to leave for the airport. Six o'clock struck from the chimes of the longcase clock in the hall and its echoes died away.

Ron decided to wait no longer and didn't care that Kenny had forgotten the leave-taking. The last time he'd seen Kenny would be just that - the last time.

Having bid his goodbyes to Julio and Dolores and tipped them handsomely, Ron drove to Pico and Cloverfield and parked within sight of the rear lot of the black Innuendo building.

He watched as the rear door opened and closed several times over the period of half-an-hour. Various personnel got into their cars and drove away.

It was almost dark. It was difficult to see properly but it seemed sensible to assume that the building was empty, as soon as Ron saw the unmistakable figure of Tommy Cattini emerge and lock the premises, twice; yes, Ron thought to himself as Tommy even tried the handle of the door, ensuring it was properly shut. Yes, they're all out.

He watched as Tommy drove out of the lot and away, staying on Pico.

Ron reversed his hire car against the rear door of Innuendo. He opened the trunk and removed the first of three refill gas cans, screwed the spout nozzle to the first and emptied it against the rear door and through the wide mail box flap. Then he stuffed all the cotton clothing he wasn't wearing through the mail box flap. It caught in the wire basket behind the door and onto this wick, Ron poured the contents of the second gas can.

He reparked his car and walked across Pico to a 'phone point and called the LAPD. He spoke to a telephonist, briefly. He only gave the name of the company. He didn't want the emergency services to arrive too quickly. He mentioned specifically Tommy Cattini and Doctor Kenneth Morrell and stated that the arson was for insurance money. Ron also added that if the LAPD would care to check with the authorities in Fort Lauderdale, Mr Morrell's name was linked to the exhumation order on the remains of the late Sherman Franck, recently requested by his sister Nancy Franck Lassman.

He hung up, returned to the parking lot, repeated the reversing procedure and emptied the final can of gas into the mail box. He shut the trunk and reviewed his preparations. He knew full well that the fire might not take, that it would be spotted and the fire department called. But it was a helluva sweet thing to try, he reminded himself and nonchalantly flicked a zippo, tossing it in through the mail box.

He got in his car, drove away. An hour later he was on the Cleveland plane.

The fire lapped only lazily at first. Had Ron been peering through the mailflap, he would have been an anxious man. But in forcing the nozzle of the refill cans through into the stuffed mail basket, Ron had loosened it from its fixing onto the door. As the fire took hold of his gas-soaked shorts, socks and undershirts, the basket fell from the door and rolled over once before coming to rest against the side of the first of ten pallets loaded with blank video cassettes delivered that afternoon. It was the load meant for Brik Peters' debut movie.

Obviously, one of the hotter movies, it burned beautifully.

The occupants of the first black-and-white on the scene knew the neighbourhood. It seemed that Innuendo was not unknown to the police department.

"Let the fucker burn," said Officer Joanne Bly to her partner. "Let it burn a while. Then they can come put it out. If they really have to..."

✳ ✳ ✳ ✳

As Innuendo burned, Trick was driving back from a double date - on the first, he earned, on the second, he spent. A regular client called him from one of the LAX hotels and Trick came out an hour later five hundred bucks better off. He made a call and drove to Venice and spent four hundred, two hundred to reduce his debt, two hundred for immediate consumption.

There are fires all the time in LA but unlike every other major city, because LA is so dense and low-built, the plume of smoke from even the smallest blaze stands out like an oil fire in a desert. Trouble is, it happens so often that folks take about as much notice of a fire as they do the searchlights that rake the sky almost every night in some or other part of town. In the old days the lights were turned on for movie premieres; lately it's just for a new supermarket or mall, even a wedding or gallery opening. It's a shame that the only person who thinks it's special is the guy paying the bill.

It takes a lot to make a Los Angeleno get out of his car. Trick drove by the fire, one block west and didn't even notice.

He got home and even before showering, tried out a couple of lines of his afternoon's purchase. He slotted a

Whitney Houston CD into the player and assembled his equipment.

Yeah. He sniffed again. He cleared the remaining dust from the mirror and rubbed the powder onto his gums. Yeah. Not bad . . . Not bad.

It wasn't bad.

It was worse than bad.

Five minutes later, Trick collapsed in the shower.

It was poison; the coke had been cut with a deadly toxic. Trick wasn't the only one that day.

Whitney sang on.

By the time Brik came by, the album was through. Brik rang the entryphone bell. There was no answer from Trick's apartment.

A neighbour, the guy who lived above Trick, came out of the building and recognised Brik.

"Forgotten your key?" he drawled as he held the door open for Brik to come into the hallway.

"Yeah," Brik smiled, "I'm always doin' it."

"Well, ring on *my* bell anytime . . ." came the riposte.

Brik smiled his thanks but made it clear there was no more conversation to be had. The neighbour smiled, resigned and went on his way.

Brik put his ear to the apartment door. He could hear nothing except the shower running. He stood outside, banging on the door calling Trick's name. He knew Trick was inside. His car was parked out front and the engine was warm. The noise of the shower ran on; Brick knew Trick never spent more than two minutes under the shower.

Brik stepped back and hurled himself against the apartment door. It wasn't strong. Brik felt it give in the frame. Trick hadn't double locked or chained the door - it was caught only on the flimsiest bolt. Brik took a longer run, as long as he could in the confines of the small hallway. The door caved in, splintering the frame at the point of contact.

Brik ran in, straight to the bathroom.

Trick was lying slumped against the tiled wall, the water

streaming over the back of his head which was tipped forward onto his chest. His hair was plastered to his scalp and carrying the water away. Foam gel or shampoo had spilled from its plastic bottle in the shower and the bubbly lather had spread like a living mutant dry-ice over the edge of the shower pan and all over the bathroom floor. Brik ripped aside the plastic shower curtain which tore through its fixings. He threw it aside and turned off the shower and bent to listen for breath and pulse. Water dripped from the showerhead onto his back as he gathered Trick's inert body to him.

Trick was alive. There was a pulse and faint breathing.

Doctor . . . Doctor. Brik gathered all the towels he could and wrapped them round Trick whom he propped upright in a sitting position on the bathroom floor, against the toilet bowl. Keep him upright, Brik remembered from somewhere. Vomiting can cause choking.

911 . . . 911. Brik lost no time in attempting further first aid. He ran into the living room, always a mess. He couldn't find the 'phone at first. He followed the cord, finally threw aside Trick's shirt and grabbed the 'phone.

Before 911 answered, Brik slammed the 'phone down. He'd seen a 911 before. At the house next door on South Bentley a coupla weeks earlier. First the fire department, then the paramedics. A reporter turned up, even a television crew. No. He desperately racked through his reactions checking for alternatives.

Morrell. Doctor Morrell.

The name and the face leapt into Brik's mind. What was his number? Where did the guy work? Wasn't his office in Westwood? Or had he said Brentwood? Trick's workbag was where he'd left it, by the couch. Brik pulled it open and rummaged through the paraphernalia of Trick's profession - leather shorts, athletic wear, rubbers, a leather jacket. Then he found Trick's filofax. He flipped to M and there it was. Kenneth Morrell. Brik dialled.

Julio did get one night a week off. That night, Kenneth was answering his own calls. He was not best pleased, the previous call having been from the Fire Department, enquiring as to his status vis-a-vis a company called Innuendo Productions whose premises had just been razed to the ground. Kenneth was desperately trying to get a call through to Tommy Cattini when Brik's call came through.

"Yes."

"Doctor Morrell?"

"Who wants him?"

"Please! This is real urgent. Tell him it's Brik Peters calling. Tell him Brik!"

"Well, this is Kenneth, Brik. What's wrong? I'm afraid I have no time to socialise right now. I have an immediate, personal emergency to deal with."

"So do I," Brik panted. "It's Trick. He's OD'd on something. Coke I think. He's hardly breathing."

"Then call 911."

"But I can't! What if he gets recognised!"

"Jesus, Brik. It's not Myrna Loy we have here."

"Think of the *papers*, Morrell. What if he *was* recognised? Pretty big story - just as seedy as they come. PORN STAR OD's. Like it? I wonder which company he filmed for? Oh, yes ... Innuendo Productions ..."

"You *have* to call 911, Brik. Unless you can drive him to the hospital yourself."

"But can't you call the paramedics? Use your influence?"

"No!"

"Whaddya mean, no?" Brik shouted angrily. "He may be dying!"

"Listen, Brik. I am not getting involved. Understand?"

"No!" Brik yelled. "I do not understand. I'm telling *you*. Get the paramedics over here right now or I'll blow your whole operation, Morrell. I'll personally blow your dirty cover. Not only will I do that but I will *personally* rip you apart. Now ... Now do *you* understand?"

"Are you threatening me?" Kenneth barked.

"Yes!" Brik screamed. "Yes I'm threatening you!!"

"Right," Kenneth replied, coldly. "Stay there. I'll be right over. Keep him warm and try and wake him. If you wake him, keep him awake."

❋ ❋ ❋ ❋

I had thought to find Ryder alone if I found him at home at all. I hadn't counted on Shelley.

Ryder opened the door and seemed unsurprised to see me.

"Hi, coach," he welcomed. "Come on in. Brik's not here."

"I know," I said. "It's you I've come to see."

And then I saw Shelley.

"Well," he beamed at me. "You have perfect timing, coach. We just this second got through finally fixing the date for our wedding, haven't we, honey?"

"And you're the first to be invited," she cooed.

"'Course, you'll getcha embossed formal invitation through the mail."

"Well," I said, the rug surely pulled from under me, my ire temporarily suspended. "Congratulations . . . to you both." It would have been churlish of me . . .

For once, I caught the self-reproach in time, quelled it and backed off from further fears of seeming impolite, rude. `Be it', my Hollywood conscience whispered in my ear. . . `Go on, if you feel it, Be it. Be churlish. You owe it to yourself to express what you feel'.

"Thanks," they chorused.

"Mr and Mrs Ryder McKigh," Shelley mused to me. "Doncha think that's a wonderful sounding name?"

Ryder grinned, preening.

"It has a certain . . . ring?" I volunteered. "But, aren't you going to do that American thing and call yourselves by both your names?"

Shelley laughed. Ryder laughed, at first. His expression froze as he realised what his bride-to-be was saying.

"I don't think Shelley Nersessian McKigh does too much for me?" she joked. "Do you?"

She turned from me to seek vindication from her fiance. His show of immodest pride had turned to a horrified, wide-eyed alarm.

"That certainly is a mouthful," I remarked, drily.

"Nersessian? That would be an Armenian name, right?"

"Something like that," Ryder butted in. "Now, how about a li'l celebration drink, coach. Lemme see what we have in?"

"I'm not thirsty," I snapped. "Sorry, Shelley. I'm afraid I need a few words with Ryder. Alone."

The betrothed sought each other's approval. Ryder took Shelley's hand.

"We come as a team, coach," Ryder announced. "So, what's on your mind?"

"Interesting name," I said. "Nersessian. Not one I'd forget if I'd heard it before."

"It's . . . a very interesting name," Ryder replied defensively. Then, with a grin accompanied by a kiss moued at his intended, he said to Shelley, unctuously: "After all, it's the name of my bride."

They kissed. Longingly. Excruciating script, I thought. I suddenly saw them very objectively.

"And also the name of the father of the bride," I added, unimpressed by the pre-marital display of affection. "Your father, Shelley, has very wide business interests, I understand. Everything from greengrocery to film production, it seems?"

"Excuse me?" Ryder said, speaking for them both.

"Save it, Ryder," I snapped. "You're very good, better than I first saw when you were only an amateur but even you need better lines than that to wriggle out of this one. Brik's told me what you've both been up to. Shelley," I absolved, "I like to think you weren't acting badly. I choose to think you were trying to save Ryder having to destroy his best friend." She looked away. "But you, Ryder," I said, tensing even the muscles in my fingers, so much did I want to leap on him and strangle him, "for you there can be no excuse. You've cajoled, connived, lied, cheated and deceived. It looks as though it's got you where you want to be but I tell you, Ryder . . . You'll do my picture over my dead body." I took breath. "That's a promise," I threatened, with a serpentine hiss.

Ryder, faced with the listing of his recent credits seemed

somewhat shamed. At first he didn't answer. He looked abashed. He and Shelley stood even closer together, their arms round each other's waists. Finally, they looked searchingly at each other before she broke away from him, sat down and lit a cigarette.

"There's other ways of seein' it," Shelley observed. "Think about it from Brik's point of view."

"I am," I snapped. "Sorry," I added, "I seem to be the only one who is."

"Wait a second," Ryder interrupted. "Just run this one, *Mister* Page . . . So Brik does your movie and say it's a smash. D'you think the guy who made the porno feature is just gonna stay quiet and say nothing? He's got one piece of merchandise that he could treble, quadruple, I don' know, hundred-ple his take on jus' by lettin' it out to the press that the latest name in town, Brik Peters can be seen au naturel in a *gay* porno movie for the price of a coupla hamburgers." Ryder paused.

"It'd be kinda cruel," Shelley remarked. "To get to be so famous only to have it pulled from under you. He made a mistake, Mister Page. A straight porno movie . . . Well . . . Maybe he'd get away with it. But a *gay* one? His mistake and it's up to him to pay for it."

"A very convenient morality," I said, "but not one that I embrace. And, as a matter of fact . . ."

"No! You're wrong!" Shelley exclaimed. She stubbed her cigarette out angrily. "Left like this, the porno movie might be forgotten. People will forget and in enough time, they might, just might, not associate Brik with it in future. But if Brik makes your movie, Mister Page, he sets himself up front as a target for anyone, fair game for any mudslinger around. If you can't see that, you're not only blind, you're *not* a friend of Brik's. It's not a pretty sight, seeing someone destroyed in public. Systematically destroyed."

I struggled for a reply. Of course, there was logic in what they said. Horrible but irrefutable logic.

"I don't think that's how Brik sees it," I said. "And I don't blame him. It's not unlike betrayal. Of his life as well as of him."

"Hey!" Ryder warned. "That's enough! You think what you damn well please, man, and you all can live just how you wanna live but think about this . . . What the hell use would it have been for me to have just said nothing and let Brik go ahead and make a fool of himself? Wouldda done him no good and me no good neither. We came out here together and I figured if one of us couldn't do the part, the other one should. Least one of us'd be earning decent money and wouldn't have to go doin' dumb porno movies to pay back loans!"

My temper rose. Having heard Brik's version not an hour before, I wanted to throttle Ryder, I wanted to hit him so hard, beat on him so badly . . .

The telephone rang. It prevented me from saying more than I could handle. It at least allowed me to think that there we stood, adversarially, slanging each other rather than attending to Brik, blaming each other for a situation which Brik, I realised, had under control. But it was Brik's control; it wasn't mine and it wasn't Ryder's and *that* was our problem.

As all these thoughts rattled through my mind, Ryder waited while the 'phone rang, obviously prepared to let it keep ringing. At last, I gestured that he should answer it. Shelley was closest and picked up.

"Hello . . . Yes, Brik . . . Hi . . . Sure . . . He's right here." She handed the 'phone to Ryder. "It's Brik," she announced.

"Yeah . . . Hi," Ryder said and listened. "Yeah . . . Right . . . Sure . . . We'll be right over . . . Sure."

He replaced the 'phone.

"What . . .?" Shelley began.

"Grab your things," he said and pulled her up from the couch by the hand. "It's Trick. He's OD'd. Brik wants us at the hospital."

Shelley hauled ass with the best. She and Ryder were outta the door before I could fully respond. I ran after them and slammed the door behind me.

"Can I come?" I called after them.

"Sure," Ryder yelled.

"Follow us," Shelley shouted.

Their Jaguar and my Jeep raced away in a convoy of burning rubber and squealing tyres.

Just like the movies...

※ ※ ※ ※

The poisoning wasn't as bad as it had first seemed to Brik. Kenneth and he had gotten Trick stumbling down the steps of the apartment building and into Brik's car. They drove to Cedars Sinai and within minutes Trick was being pumped, cleaned out, connected to drips and tubes and was showing signs of coming round.

Brik had been right. Kenneth's presence had been more than a help. It had probably been invaluable. But, however priceless the help, Brik had been soured by the grudging, sulky way in which the help had been given. The help had been extracted, dragged from Kenneth Morrell like a penny being prised from a wealthy miser. Brik was angry and disgusted.

Kenneth only stayed long enough at Cedars to make sure from the hospital doctor that Trick was going to pull through.

As soon as the busy doctor had delivered his prognosis, Kenneth made to leave. He and Brik had been sitting, silent, in the waiting area at the end of the seventh floor corridor.

"Aren't you coming in to see him?" Brik asked. "The doctor said we could."

Kenneth made it very obvious that he would regard such an act with abject disdain.

"No," was all he said. "It might interest you to know, Brik, that I predicted this. I've seen it all before... so many times. So many pretty faces." Kenneth gripped the handle of his black bag tightly and seemed to Brik a little too satisfied with the quasi-obituary. He straightened himself but added, as a parting shot, "Let's hope it doesn't happen to you, Brik."

Kenneth retreated, quite as effectively as Joan Crawford,

with a flippant toss of his head. Brik ran after him. He spun the older man round, one big hand on his shoulder. Kenneth tried to duck and lurch away but Brik grabbed his left wrist.

"Not only are you partly responsible for Trick," Brik accused, "but you're certainly answerable to me for what you did with Ron's pictures. You're gonna pay for that, Morrell. I swear. I didn't believe Ron when he said how heartless you were. I couldn't believe anyone alive could be that heartless but . . . Ron was right." A nurse passed by and Brik threw his arm round Kenneth's shoulder, like he was comforting a friend. The nurse lowered her eyes as she walked by. "Me?" Brik breathed, a vicious smile on his lips, "I could lay you out flat right now, Doctor. But it wouldn't hurt you enough." Brik laughed. "Ha! Who knows? You'd maybe even like it. But one day, Morrell, one day someone'll hit you where it really hurts . . . in your wallet."

"Let go of me or I shall scream," Kenneth said wetly. Brik relinquished the wrist. "Perhaps you have already," Kenneth said meaningfully. "Hit me . . . As you so . . . so crudely put it." Kenneth hesitated before levelling the accusation. "Have you? Was it you? Tonight?"

"Excuse me?" Brik replied tartly.

"It was, wasn't it?" Kenneth shimmered, furious both at what he was suddenly thinking and also that he had had to think it in the public corridor of a hospital.

"What are you talking about, Morrell?"

"*You* burned my goddam building, didn't you? It was *you* who torched Innuendo. You or Trick. Or both!"

"Torched . . . What . . . ?"

"My building . . . It burned tonight. To the ground. Everything burned . . . Including your movie, *Mister* Peters. You are dead . . . Dead! It won't be me who'll get you but it'll happen. Believe me. You are about to disappear, Brik Peters," Kenneth hissed, ". . . like you never even existed! I hope your mom and dad have some pictures to remember you by because if they don't, you'll simply vanish from the face of the earth!"

"Just like your lover . . ."

"What did you say?" Kenneth enquired grimly.

"I said," Brik replied, raising his voice, "just like your..."

"Shuddup!" Kenneth squeaked.

"Goodbye, Doctor. I look forward to your account in the mail."

Kenneth scurried away. Brik watched him get into the elevator at the end of the corridor.

The arriving elevator bore Ryder, Jeremy and Shelley. The descending elevator bore Kenneth Morrell down to the lobby where two uniformed officers of the LAPD awaited him. It's one of the tiresome problems which result from professional people who rely so heavily on message services - they can give too much away at entirely inopportune moments. Poor Kenneth. Both Tommy Cattini and the LAPD knew he was at Cedars Sinai and would be until he checked in once more with the service. Poor Kenneth. The LAPD got to him first.

"Hey!" Brik said, smiling slowly, "thanks, guys. Thanks for coming."

"Sure," Ryder said.

"How is he, Brik?" Shelley asked.

"Good... well, not *good* but not... bad. He's gonna be okay."

"That's... good," Ryder said, betraying nothing except embarrassment, displaying nothing of the intense and immediate concern which had prompted him to rush to Brik's side as soon as the call had come.

"I see you found him," Brik said to me, indicating Ryder standing somewhat apart from where we hovered outside Trick's room.

"Yes," I admitted. "As you can see."

"Is Trick awake?" Shelley urged. "I'd like to just... y'know. Tell him to hang in there."

"Sure," Brik said. "Go right in."

"You coming, Ryder?" Shelley said.

Ryder nodded and she took his hand. He seemed reluctant to go inside.

"What's wrong, honey?" Shelley muttered. "It's okay." She sounded encouraging, like a mother allaying the fears of a little child.

"Ry's not too fond of hospitals," Brik butted in, on his friend's side. The remark jerked Ryder to attention. He seemed set to remonstrate but merely nodded his head in silent agreement. "We've had a little too much hospital, one thing and another, right, man?" Brik finished off, clapping Ryder lightly on the shoulder. Ryder nodded again.

They went inside Trick's room. Brik led me aside, to the empty waiting area and we sat, next to the coffee machine and opposite the rubber plant.

"Did Ron manage to buy my movie back?" Brik asked under his breath.

"I don't know, Brik," I replied apologetically. "I haven't heard from him."

"Well, I hope he didn't," Brik enlarged. "Morrell just told me that the place got torched tonight. Burned to the ground. Everything. Including my movie and all the stock."

"What?" I replied in open-mouthed amazement. Then I laughed. The thought of that nice but rather ineffectual Ohio practitioner planning and completing an arson attack was suddenly very funny. And then the other thing dawned; Brik was off the hook. Rather, *was* Brik off the hook? He must have been reading my thoughts.

"No," he said simply. He merely touched my arm and left me. I didn't follow. I didn't want to see him at Trick's bedside. "Ryder does the part."

"But . . . You're free. You can do it now. Don't you want to?"

He looked at me for a moment as though he was rethinking his decision. But he wasn't. Something told me he was only weighing up whether the final refusal he was about to voice was going to put a period to a friendship.

"I want," he said slowly, "I want Ryder to do it." He turned and went into Trick's sick room.

Ryder and Shelley came out almost immediately. Shelley had to go make a 'phone call and Ryder sat down. He didn't sit next to me; he made that very plain.

"I don't understand you, Ryder," I said. He looked away, at first. Perhaps he was right to do so; there was nothing more we had to say to each other that night. I felt humiliated and drained. The natural welcome I had given to Brik's news of the burning of Innuendo had had to give way to the fatalistic acceptance that he'd just said no . . . Turned me down. If 'Parallel' was to go ahead, it would be with Ryder. All I had to console myself with was that the film would go ahead because of Brik, although without him, for it all now seemed like some eerie piece of deja vu, a pre-navigated destiny.

But as far as Ryder and I were concerned, it was like we were both members of the same board, yet politically entrenched on opposing sides, implacably dug-in yet each knowing that we had to face each other again the following morning, or the next week or certainly at some future meeting of the same board. "I just don't understand," I repeated.

"No," Ryder said, "I don't suppose you do."

I decided to take the plunge, the final plunge. I had teetered at the brink so many times, for what seemed like so long, the suddenness of wanting to rid myself of the dizzying responsibility of the secret was ultimately lost on me.

I'd dressed it up all ways but, now, that dilemma of whether to tell or hold my peace was naked and mewling and needed immediate attention. I suppose it wasn't like an ordinary secret and it certainly didn't lie peacefully, not on my chest at least. I needed to offload it. My keeping Brik's father's confidence and respecting Mrs MacSween's integrity weren't doing me or anyone else any good. Maybe . . . Just maybe if I brought it all out into the open, faced Ryder with the truth about him and Brik, just maybe he wouldn't behave so crassly and cruelly to someone who was in reality his brother in flesh as well as spirit, de facto as well as de jure . . .

"I know all about you," I said, certainly. "Mrs MacSween told me."

"Mrs Doc MacSween?" Ryder asked.

"Uh, huh," I nodded. "Not that she told me . . . She didn't exactly *tell* me," I said hesitantly, "but I couldn't help putting it all together."

"This is some jigsaw," Ryder chided gently. He wasn't being antagonistic, I knew, but his remark goaded me further.

"Your . . . your father . . ." I faltered.

"Yeah. Go on," Ryder said, flatly.

"Your father and Brik's father," I began, "after they came back from the Vietnam . . ."

". . . I don't know how long it took," Ryder continued for me. He spoke as though from the inside of some impenetrable, invisible cocoon, "or how they all ever got it to work but . . .," he sighed, ". . . well, they did it. Folks knew my daddy'd been shot up pretty bad. I don't know how many really knew just *how* bad . . . But, he came back from that war with no balls and only a li'l bitty piece of his dick left. Came back home to loving, faithful, patient Dory . . . but he came back all shot up while his best buddy just down the road a piece came back to his ever-lovin' Mitzi with all his right parts still in all the right places." Ryder turned to me. "How'd you feel, coach? With no dick to beat on, huh? Pretty weird feelin', hey?"

"You . . . you knew all the time?" I said incredulously.

"What Brik's daddy did for his best buddy?"

"I suppose," I replied. Ryder cowed me, humbled me, flayed the skin off my back with a whip of softest, gentlest intimacy.

"My daddy couldn't bear it," Ryder went on, "when Mitzi started with Brik. He couldn't bear that my mom would never be able to have a baby of her own, that the farm'd never get passed on, not even to a daughter. So, he asked Don . . . Jesus!" Ryder's eyes filled with tears. "What a thing to ask your best friend to do . . . My . . . daddy had to ask his best buddy to screw my momma just to get me!" Ryder was choking on his sobs. I went to put my arm round him but he moved away. "No!" he exclaimed. Spurning my concern seemed to help him pull himself together.

"How long have you known, Ryder?" I persisted.

"That Brik and I are half-brothers?" he asked, wiping tears from his cheek with the back of his hand. "Coupla years . . . My daddy told me . . . Almost the last thing he said. In that . . . that hospital room in Doddsville . . . He'd been there so long, momma just couldn't go any more, she cried so . . . Left it to me . . . Most days . . ." He put a brake on a torrent of emotions. He swallowed, twice, allowing himself time to stop the tears. "S'like Brik said . . . I'm not too fond of hospitals."

"Does Brik know what you know?"

"Perhaps . . . perhaps not," Ryder replied.

"And . . ."

"And no," he said. "I *don't* want him to know."

"But doesn't it make any difference?" I pushed.

"To what? To what *you* think I've done to Brik?"

"Yes," I admitted.

"Makes no damn difference at all," he replied conclusively.

"Ummm," I breathed. "Yes. It obviously doesn't."

"We're brothers," he said. "Isn't that enough?"

"I thought it would entail more than just . . . enough?"

"Now don't go telling him," Ryder said. He sighed. "Oh, I know I can't *stop* you telling him and making with the honesty an' all but it wouldn't do no good. It'd take all the mystery away . . . A guy can have so much honesty . . . Brik and me . . ." Ryder shrugged. "We need as much mystery as we can get, right now 'cos we've still got a long ways to go."

"I see," I said.

"No you don't," Ryder advised, quite correctly. "At least, not at this moment, you don't. You might. One day."

"How?" I pressed. "It's not too easy, this one."

"Try writing it down, coach," Ryder said, standing up. Shelley was returning down the corridor. "It'd make a pretty good movie, huh? Somethin' for my buddy and me to fight about *next* year?" He turned his attention from me to Shelley. "Everything okay, hon?"

"Sure. Can we go now?"

"Yeah." Ryder conceded. "'Night, coach. See you on set."

"Goodnight, Mister Page," Shelley added. "Nice to have met you."

"Likewise." I said. "Good luck."

Arms entwined they walked in the direction of the elevators and left me sitting alone.

I sat for about five minutes until Brik came out of Trick's room. I heard him saying he'd be back later with some things. He saw me, slumped in the chair.

"You still here?" he said. "Drive you home?"

"I have my Jeep," I said. "Thanks all the same." I felt as though this should have been a momentous fork in the road . . . one of those farewells that was a casual 'catch-ya-later' on one level yet an adieu-adieu on another. "What will you do?" I asked rather emptily.

"I gotta go back and get some things for Trick and then mend the apartment door . . . I had to break it down to get to him," Brik explained.

I smiled. How wonderful it must be to be able to attend not only to the love of someone but also the edifice that houses that love. At that moment, the edifice seemed almost more important than the love. Would God, I wondered, have survived so long without a church to live in?

"I meant for work," I said.

"Oh . . . I have some plans."

"So have I . . . I have this idea for a movie . . ."

Brik held up his hand.

"So do I," he said quickly.

"But mine is . . ." I started to gush.

". . . and so is mine," he interrupted.

We laughed.

"One thing's certain," he said, taking my arm in his. We walked together, arm in arm, down the corridor to the elevator. I felt very grown up.

"What?" I said.

"Mine will *not* be featuring Ryder McKigh." He pressed the `down' button.

"Yes," I said, watching the light flashing as the elevator

descended, through the successive floors. "But, you know, I have an equally certain and horrible feeling that mine will..."

Also Available

Packing It In
David Rees

This collection of essays, written and arranged to form a year long diary, opens with an all too brief visit to Australia, continues with a tour of New Zealand and a final visit to a much loved San Francisco, before returning to familiar Europe (Barcelona, Belgium Rome) and new perspectives on the recently liberated Eastern Bloc countries (highly individual observations of Moscow, St Petersburg, Odessa and Kiev). Written from the distinctive and idiosyncratic point of view of a singular gay man, this is a book filled with acute and sometimes acerbic views, written with a style that is at once easily conversational and utterly compelling.

'Rees achieves what should be the first aim of any travel writer, to make you regret you haven't seen what he has seen . . .'
Gay Times

ISBN 1-873741-07-3
£6.99

Vale of Tears: A problem shared
Peter Burton & Richard Smith

Culled from ten years of *Gay Times's* popular Vale of Tears problem page, this book, arranged problem-by-problem in an alphabetical sequence, is written in question and answer format and covers a wide range of subjects.

Problems with a lover? Who does the dishes? Interested in infantilism? Why is his sex drive lower than yours? Aids fears? Meeting the family? How to survive Christmas? Suffering from body odours? Piles? Crabs? Penis too small? Foreskin too tight? Trying to get rid of a lover?

Vale of Tears has some of the answers – and many more. Although highly entertaining and sometimes downright humorous, this compilation is very much a practical handbook which should find a place on the shelves of all gay men.

'*An indispensable guide to life's problems big or small . . .*'
Capital Gay

ISBN 1-873741-05-7
£6.99

The Learning of Paul O'Neill
Graeme Woolaston

The Learning of Paul O'Neill follows the eponymous hero over nearly thirty years – from adolescence in Scotland in the mid-sixties to life in a South Coast seaside resort in the seventies and eighties and a return to a vibrant Glasgow in the early nineties. As the novel begins, fifteen-year-old Paul is learning fast about sexuality as his Scottish village childhood disintegrates around him. After many years in England, he returns to Scotland trying to come to terms with the sudden death of his lover. His return brings him face-to-face with the continuing effects of adolescent experiences he thought he had put behind him. And his involvement with an ambiguous, handsome married but bisexual man raises new questions about the shape of Paul's life as he arrives at the threshold of middle-age. This is an adult novel about gay experience and aspects of sexuality which some may find shocking but which are written about with an honesty that is as refreshing as it is frank.

ISBN 1-873741-12-X
£7.50

On the Edge
Sebastian Beaumont

An auspicious debut novel which combines elements of a thriller and passionate ambisextrous romance and provides an immensely readable narrative about late adolescence, sexuality and creativity.

'Mr Beaumont writes with assurance and perception...'   Tom Wakefield, Gay Times

ISBN 1-873741-00-6
£6.99

Heroes Are Hard to Find
Sebastian Beaumont

A compelling, sometimes comic, sometimes almost unbearably moving novel about sexual infatuation, infidelity and deceit. It is also about disability, death and the joy of living.

'Highly recommended...' *Brighton Evening Argus*

'I cheered, felt proud and cried aloud (yes, real tears not stifled sobs) as the plot and the people became real to me ...'
All Points North

ISBN 1-873741-08-1
£7.50

Millivres Books can be ordered from any bookshop in the UK and from specialist bookshops overseas. If you prefer to order by mail, please send the full retail price and 80p (UK) or £2 (overseas) per title for postage and packing to:

Dept MBKS
Millivres Ltd
Ground Floor
Worldwide House
116-134 Bayham Street
London NW1 0BA

A comprehensive catalogue is available on request.